SHE SHIFTED TOWARD HIM, LIFTING HER FACE TO HIS. . . .

His lips brushed her cheek again, even as caution pealed sharply through him.

Honor—

She turned her face to his and her lips found his unerringly. . . .

No, his mind warned even as his mouth opened over hers. He gripped her jaw, angling her head so he could reach her fully. She rolled up on tiptoe, meeting him, and the feel of her sweet, hot mouth kicked through him like straight whiskey.

Desperate, hungry, searching, their mouths fused, easing a tightness in his chest. At the same time, his body hardened in a surge of power, of want.

She lied about Onash. You have to ask her.

With shaking hands he gripped her arms and put her away from him.

"No," she moaned, reaching for him.

"Elise," he rasped, barely able to draw in a breath. His body shook with reaction and sweat slicked his palms.

He'd never lost control like that. Never.

IF ONLY

Debra Cowan

A Dell Book

For Roy,
who makes every difference in my life

Published by
Dell Publishing
a division of
Bantam Doubleday Dell Publishing Group, Inc.
1540 Broadway
New York, New York 10036

ISBN: 0-440-22196-X

Printed in the United States of America

Published simultaneously in Canada

September 1997

10 9 8 7 6 5 4 3 2 1

OPM

Regret plays a haunting refrain

If Only . . .

Honor and truth and trust pass away

If Only . . .

The heart cries for redemption

If Only . . .

dsc

PROLOGUE

June sunshine glanced off the peaks of the Blue Ridge Mountains and skimmed like water across the valley toward Elise Worthen's home. Pure midday light revealed in grisly detail what she'd done.

Her shoulders ached. Her arms throbbed. Still she dug, her ungloved hands scraped raw from the shovel's rough handle. Blood from her blisters mingled with the sweat on her palms, stinging, urging her to drop the shovel, but she couldn't.

Guilt gnawed at her, but she squashed it. She refused to think or to feel. She was doing what she had to, just as she'd done for four long years.

She pushed herself, digging faster. Black Virginia dirt flew around the frayed hem of her dress; still the hole was so shallow, *too* shallow.

Cannon fire no longer boomed over the rolling hills

of her home. The feet of countless soldiers no longer marched in tedious, frightening rhythm past Fair-brooke. The War Between the States had ended almost three months earlier. But not the horror. Not *this* horror. It persisted, acute and stark and desperate.

This year, no telling breath of spring hung in the air, no teasing scent of morning glories or roses or wood violets. All trampled under the feet of soldiers, North and South. Instead the air was laced with the sharp sting of regret, of death, of loss.

The hole grew deeper, larger, blacker. Deep enough to cover her sins, to hide them, to save her life.

Finally, when the hole was deep enough, she dropped the shovel and turned, wrestling an ungainly burden from the back of the wagon. They couldn't hurt her now. Tears stung her eyes. They could never hurt her again. As long as no one found them.

She rolled the heavy burden into the shallow pit. Refusing to look, stanching the scream of horror and fear and regret that welled in her throat, she lifted the shovel and began turning dirt back into the hole.

CHAPTER ONE

The old-iron smell of blood and gunsmoke burned the air. Her screams echoed through the cool stone of the house, the gentle summer breeze. Blood, blood everywhere.

"No." Her harsh voice shattered the quiet reverence of the day.

Elise Worthen stood in the family cemetery at Fairbrooke, assaulted once again by the agony of uncertainty, an overwhelming sense of aloneness. Was Logan dead? Lost in the war like so many others?

The early morning fog had lifted, wreathing the crest of the Blue Ridge Mountains to the west. Even the glorious sight of the sun streaming through the clouds did little to comfort her.

Four months since the end of the war. Two months since she'd—

Elise stanched the thought, though she could still feel the blood on her hands. Desperate to erase the memory of what she'd done, she wiped them down her skirts, over and over.

She couldn't eat, couldn't sleep, and sometimes she

was certain she was coming unhinged. She'd lost the glove—one of a pair Mama had divided between her and Logan—and so every day she came here, to her parents' graves, and it gave her some measure of comfort.

The old families of Franklin County had supported her through the burial of her parents. Elise was sure she would have gone stark raving mad if she'd had to say good-bye to them alone.

Coralee Bronson, Mr. Bailey, and Justine Delavant had all been a tremendous support, but none more than Gramps. He wasn't her grandfather, not by blood anyway, but Thomas Kensington had become her family during the long, aching months of the war and the lonely hours since she'd lost her parents and Rithy.

Chaos, collapse, and destruction had taken the place of order in her world, yet she had managed to handle them. Until the murder of her parents and Rithy.

Until Cal had broken their betrothal. And now Elise feared she must face the loss of her brother. There had been no word from Logan for almost a year.

Toward the end of the war, no one here had received letters from the boys, but news of battles and defeats and finally surrender had reached them. Since then, nothing.

Nearly everyone from Moss Springs, Mount Royal, and Mount Pleasant had returned or was accounted for. Except Logan. At least Gramps knew his grandson, Jared, was coming home. She was glad and deep down hoped that he might be able to tell her some news of Logan. They'd both served as scouts for John Singleton Mosby's Rangers.

Standing beneath the spreading dogwood branches that shaded her parents' resting place steadied Elise's doubts.

Papa's Colt revolver, now hers, lay on the ground, loaded and ready as it always was these days. Lawlessness and greed had replaced barbecues and parties in Moss Springs, as it had in every southern town. Since war's end, Virginia, like every other southern state, was considered an outlaw and had been placed under military patrol.

The milling influx of people seemed to echo in the raucous chirping of whippoorwills and swallows. Leaves and broken twigs swirled in sporadic devil winds. Even the air vibrated with uncertainty.

She stroked the coarse granite of her mother's simple marker, wishing again for the glove Mama had left her, but her frequent searches had yielded nothing. Since her parents' deaths, Elise had often wished for something tangible to hold, to remember them by.

She didn't want to dwell on the losses—her parents, Rithy, Cal.

Her heart twinged as she thought of her fiancé and lifelong friend. Cal Drayton had returned from the war, slight and bitter, his blond hair shot through with gray. He had broken their betrothal because he couldn't provide for her. Despite her arguments that they could muddle through, he wouldn't be swayed. He and his sister, Lindy, had packed their meager belongings and left a month after Appomattox.

A slight breeze stirred the midday heat and the

scent of wisteria and dirt and clean air wafted to her.
Today there was no burnt smell of gunpowder in the
air, no odor of blood, though in her dreams she knew
she would always smell those things.

She missed the delicate fragrance of wood violets
and wondered if they would come up on Fairbrooke
next spring. The Yanks had trampled to death everything this close to the house. Still, the stubborn morning glories and quaker-ladies splashed defiant bursts
of scarlet, pink, pale blue, and purple over the hills
and around her parents' resting place.

The ground vibrated and she became aware of
thundering hoofbeats. Fear, her merciless companion
for the last two months, shot through her as she
scooped up her revolver and turned. A lone rider
veered off the drive leading to the house and pounded
toward the family cemetery. Panic stretched tight
across her chest.

She prayed the rider was only passing by, looking
for a piece of bread to tide him over, though lately
she'd gone days without seeing a soldier passing
through on his way home. Stepping outside the gate,
she eased up to the trunk of the dogwood, shielding
her eyes from the sun's glare.

A man reined up several yards away and dismounted slowly, as if it hurt him to move.

"Stop, sir!" she called to him, cocking her revolver.
"Don't come any closer."

Blinding sunlight prevented her from seeing his
face, though she had a vague impression of broad
shoulders and a slouch hat. Her grip tightened on the
gun. Had she been discovered?

Despite the heat of the day the man slipped on a Confederate-gray uniform jacket over his dingy undershirt, then walked toward her. The sight of Southern gray did not reassure her. Men stole all manner of articles from soldiers. Nor was she intimidated by the double lieutenant's bars on the collar. She fired, nicking a corner of his hat.

"Elise!" He snapped to a halt.

Now she saw his face and she dropped the gun as relief swept over her. "As I live and breathe! Jared Kensington!" She rushed around the tree. "It is you! Oh, my! Oh, goodness!"

"Elise." He removed his hat and eyed the missing corner in surprise before pressing the hat to his chest.

She wanted to touch someone she knew, someone who knew Logan almost as well as she did, someone from the old days. Jared and Logan were nine years older than she, so Elise hadn't known Jared well, but before she thought, she had launched herself at him, locking her arms around his lean middle and hugging him hard.

Jared stiffened, then one arm, muscular and big, came around her back and he hugged her in return. He was thin, this side of gaunt, but still sturdy. His chest, always broad, was somewhat sunken from what she remembered in the years before the war. The top of her head didn't quite reach his chin, and she could feel the steady thud of his heart beneath her cheek.

He held her for a few seconds, not tightly, but firmly. His voice rasped out, rueful with a tug of sadness. "It's quite a change to find someone who doesn't care about the dirt of war."

Pain tinged his words and sudden tears stung her eyes. Overjoyed that he'd made it home alive, hoping he had news of Logan, she looked up at him. "Yours is noble dirt, Jared."

His intense green gaze probed hers, full of pain and loss, then his eyes shuttered against her.

She realized then that she was pressed full against him, and her breasts tingled at his heat. She gently disengaged herself, a flush warming her skin. "How are you?"

"About the same as you, I reckon." His voice was deeper than she remembered, coarse with memories she could only guess at.

He'd lost weight, but his features were browned and rough-hewn, as unyielding as the Blue Ridge Mountains. His strong chin, deeply dimpled in the center, spoke of a solid determination. Pride rimmed his stance, and she was secretly thrilled that he stood so tall and straight. She'd seen too many men stooped with age and war.

But it was his eyes that pierced something deep inside her. The dark green of wet leaves, they were shadowed with unspoken horrors. His wavy dark hair hung over the collar of his uniform jacket and a slight growth of beard stubbled his jaw.

She realized she was staring, hungry for the sight and sound of someone familiar. "Your grandfather must be overjoyed."

"I haven't seen him yet, but I'm looking forward to it." He flashed her a half-smile, shifting from one foot to the other.

"You just rode in?"

"Yes." He fiddled with his hat.

He'd come here first? Sudden dread flicked at her. "Have you . . . news? Of Logan?"

Pain tightened his features and he looked down, pulling something from the pocket of his jacket. He held it out to her and Elise took it with trembling fingers.

Short and lacy, it was the mate to her glove. It was the one Mama had given Logan before the war.

"No," she whispered, her breath a sharp pain in her chest. "Not Logan, too. Not after everything else."

Her legs gave, but Jared caught her before she folded to the ground. Dropping his hat, he pulled her tight against his chest. "Elise, it's not the worst."

His heart beat strongly beneath her cheek, and for just a breath she let herself lean into his strength, his power. Surrounded by the mingling scents of dirt and man, she felt safe for the first time in months. Bracing herself, she said, "Tell me."

He hesitated, glancing toward the house. "Where are your parents?"

She gripped his arms, desperation threading her words. "Tell me first."

"He's alive, but—"

"Where is he?"

"He was taken prisoner back in November."

"Prisoner?" Dread clutched at her. "He's been in a Yank prison?"

"He's been on Johnson's Island in Lake Erie."

She shook her head, unfamiliar with the place.

"It's a couple of miles offshore from Sandusky, Ohio."

"I thought all the prisoners were released after Appomattox!"

"I was told he was, but it's going to take him some time to get home."

"It's been four months." Restless impatience churned and she paced in front of him, clutching the newly returned glove to her lips and trying to breathe in some scent of Logan. "Something's happened. What if he's—"

"Please, none of that." He touched her arm then, steadying her riotous thoughts.

"Yes, you're right." She studied the glove, smiling wistfully. "These have been in my family for four generations. My great-grandmother Worthen made them."

"Beautiful," he said huskily.

She looked up and caught her breath, suddenly aware that he was staring intently at her. She felt flattered and cornered at the same time.

Truth be told, Jared had always intimidated her somewhat. Of all Logan's friends, Jared was the quietest, the most self-contained. She had always felt a sense of uncertainty around him, as if she never knew where she stood in his opinion. "And you? How are you?"

"I'm fine." His gaze roved over her in frank appraisal, his eyes heating. "You're a sight for sore eyes. You surely are."

A thrill shot through her and she put a hand to her hair, wishing she could smooth the tangled curls. "I'm sorry I acted like a ninny earlier. I thought you were going to say Logan was—well, you know."

"I would've heard by now if he hadn't made it," Jared said firmly. "It's gonna take a while for news to get through. You can't give up hope."

"I won't." She exhaled a deep breath. "It helps to know that you've seen him. I apologize for going to pieces like that."

"No apology necessary. I wish I could tell you exactly where he is."

"Will you come up to the house for some water? Or some bread? I'm afraid that's all I have to offer at the moment. Besides sweet potato pie."

He hesitated, his gaze shifting to the house. "I'd be beholden."

As they walked up the rise toward the house, her skirts brushed his leg. Shaken by the flex of lean muscle against her thigh, she stepped away from him. Behind them, his horse snorted and blew, following at a leisurely pace.

"When did you last see Logan?"

He hesitated, his voice tight. "Before he was taken."

"What did he look like?"

"He was fine." He glanced at her, but his eyes were inscrutable. "He'd lost a little weight, like the rest of us."

"He was all right, wasn't he? You'd tell me?"

"Yes, I would tell you." Shadows darkened his eyes and he glanced away. His voice rumbled out, bitter and sharp. "We were on a scout for Mosby, Elise. And we were separated. I'm sorry."

It was difficult for him, she realized. Surely he didn't blame himself? They walked between two of the abandoned slave cabins and stepped onto the dirt drive. "Thank you for what you did tell me."

His gaze met hers then shifted away. As they reached the porch he lifted his hat, pointing it toward the cemetery. Quietly he said, "I noticed the markers. Your folks?"

"Yes." She swallowed and looked down. She would be mortified if anyone, especially a friend of Logan's, ever learned what she'd done. "Rithy, too."

He was silent for a long moment then compassion softened his voice. "I'm sorry."

"Thank you." She knew he felt the loss too. Jared and Logan had trailed after Rithy, first as young boys then as young men seeking his advice. The free Negro could've left Fairbrooke anytime during his life, but he'd chosen to stay with Curtis Worthen, whom he considered a brother.

Jared lightly touched her elbow, guiding her up the porch steps. A note of wistfulness crept into his voice. "Everything's changed, hasn't it?"

"Yes, *everything*."

"What happened? To your folks and Rithy?"

Her heart kicked into a wild rhythm. She turned away, unable to look at him. "They died together. They were—"

The thunder of horses' hooves cut off her words. She and Jared turned together toward the sound. Two men pulled rein at the bottom of the porch.

She recognized Sheriff Restin, his bald head gleaming in the sun, his cheek protruding from a wad of snuff, a permanent line of tobacco juice staining one side of his mouth.

But she didn't know the other man. He stood about six feet tall, his thick dark hair slicked back. He wore a store-bought suit, brown with small white checks, and a felt bowler. His thin face was unlined, so it was difficult to guess at his age. His light brown gaze darted about nervously, taking stock of Elise and Jared as well as the front of the house.

Panic crawled over her. Why was the sheriff here and who was this man?

With great effort, she kept her voice from cracking. "Sheriff, what brings you out this way?"

Jared slid a sideways glance at her and she cautioned herself to remain calm.

They'd found her out. She couldn't halt the thought and hoped her face didn't betray her anxiety.

Toby Restin hooked his thumbs in his belt and puffed out his chest, eyeing Jared curiously. "You from around here?"

"Yes." Jared leveled a flat stare at the man.

"This is Jared Kensington, a family friend," Elise said.

Jared edged closer, his stance clearly protective, his gaze never wavering from Restin.

Recognition sparked the man's eyes. "You'd be kin to Thomas Kensington?"

"His grandson," Jared said curtly.

Restin nodded, jerking his head toward his companion. "This here's Mr. Anthony."

"Hello." Elise forced herself to speak evenly, but her stomach churned. Was Mr. Anthony some other Federal agent come to tear up what was left of her world?

Sheriff Restin moved his ever-present toothpick from one side of his mouth to the other. "Mr. Anthony's now headin' up the bank."

Elise frowned, the tightness in her chest easing. What did that have to do with her? "How . . . nice."

The banker's cold gaze raked over her and chills slid under Elise's skin. Jared's warmth wrapped around her, reassuring and constant, but Elise still felt as if she were about to shatter. She gripped the glove Jared had given to her.

"Is there some business you have here?" Jared's deep voice clipped the words.

Mr. Anthony flashed a brittle smile. "I'm sure you can understand that the bank is getting things in order, trying to restore some direction.

She frowned. *What* was he talking about?

"I mustn't put off the bad news," Anthony said with a patently false smile. "I've come to collect on the lien, Miss Worthen."

For a second, Elise comprehended only that the two men hadn't come for another reason. Relief rushed through her and she exhaled a shaky breath, her legs wobbly. She was vaguely aware that Jared was pressing a steadying hand to the small of her back.

At last Mr. Anthony's words penetrated and she repeated dazedly, "A lien?"

Jared extended his hand. "She'd like to see it."

A lien? For what? Trying to think through her panic, she nodded. "Yes, I'd like to see it."

Mr. Anthony smirked, pulling a piece of paper from his pocket and unfolding it for her to read. "Your father took it out several months ago."

"No. He wouldn't do that." She glanced from Mr. Anthony to the sheriff, annoyed by their smug attitude. As she scanned the piece of paper, Elise's breath caught and shock slammed into her. There, on the bottom of the mortgage, was Curtis Worthen's bold scrawl. *Oh, Papa, what did you do?*

She'd thought he had provided so well for her and Mama because of shrewd management and the war bonds he'd invested in. But now the war bonds weren't worth the paper on which they were printed.

He'd mortgaged Fairbrooke. That was how he'd managed to buy food and supplies in the wake of ever-increasing prices.

Still half in shock, she shook her head. "I don't know anything about this."

"Mr. Onash was supposed to talk to you."

"Who?" Startled at hearing Onash's name, she jerked. Beside her, Jared stilled. Onash had said nothing about any lien, only about wanting Fairbrooke. And her.

Anthony and Restin frowned at each other. She could feel Jared's gaze, sharp and intense, boring into her. Though Jared still watched the two men on the steps, Elise could feel his attention centered solely on her.

Restin squinted at her. "Mr. Claude Onash? He's an agent with the Treasury Department. I believe he came out here to talk to you about the place."

"Nobody ever talked to me about a lien on Fairbrooke." *That* was true. Onash hadn't said anything about a lien—only that he would have Fairbrooke.

Restin eyed her dubiously. "Ya know, I haven't seen Claude in about a month. Or two."

Panic edged through her. Had Onash told the sheriff of his plans to obtain Fairbrooke? Elise knew the two men often worked in tandem. Both Restin and Anthony stared expectantly at her and she asked quickly, "How much is the lien?"

"The remainder is four hundred and twenty dollars."

"Four hundred—" For just an instant, anxiety pressed in on her, wiping out her relief that they hadn't come about the murders.

"Hell!" Jared exploded. "She can't pay that kind of money and you damn well know it. At least not right now."

"If you can't pay," Mr. Anthony addressed Elise, "we'll have to ask you to vacate the premises. It *is* the law."

"Fairbrooke is my home," she snapped.

"Actually, it belongs to the bank." Restin spat a thick line of juice off the porch.

Elise curled her lip in distaste. "*If* I can't pay."

Jared leaned down, speaking in a low voice, "I have some money, Elise, but nothing close to that."

She was touched and surprised at his offer. "Thank you, but that won't be—"

"Miz Worthen, it's no secret how hard the war's been on everybody." Sheriff Restin glanced pointedly at the peeling paint on the outside of the house. "But the bank cain't give charity."

She wanted to scream at them to get out. She briefly considered running them off with her revolver.

She'd lost her parents. And Cal. She couldn't lose Fairbrooke, too. But how could she pay—

"If you'll wait right here . . ." She turned and hurried inside the house, catching the look of astonishment on Jared's face.

She raced up the stairs, her heart pounding as she skirted scars in the wood floor and the ragged threads of old carpet.

Restin's voice followed her upstairs as he spoke to the banker. "This is gonna be some place when Mr. DeWitt gets it fixed up."

"That staircase needs to be repaired."

Anger burned through her. Mr. DeWitt, whoever he was, would never have Fairbrooke. She hurried to her wardrobe and pawed through her old tattered petticoats until she reached the one on the bottom, still toting two rows of ribbon that she hadn't used to tie bandages for some passing soldier.

The money formed a lump under the thin cotton, and she pulled it from the hidden pocket. Carefully counting out the required four hundred and twenty dollars, she was pleased to see that fifty-five remained.

Holding the money tightly, she hurried back down the stairs.

"Elise?" Jared met her at the door.

She flashed him a halfhearted smile and stepped around him. Barely keeping the triumph from her voice, she held out the money to Mr. Anthony. "There you are."

The banker plucked it from her hand, rapidly thumbing through the stack. "I'm sorry. I can't take

Confederate scrip—" His head snapped up. "This is Federal money."

"Yes." Elise met his gaze, hoping he couldn't see the panic in her eyes.

The banker's jaw dropped and he looked dazedly at Restin. Jared said nothing, but she felt his gaze on her, as astonished and curious as the others.

The sheriff snatched the money from the banker, looking from the paper in his hand to Elise and back again. "How can that be?"

All three men looked at her expectantly and Elise swallowed. "My father had some money set aside."

"Federal money?" Anthony sneered.

"Yes." She lifted her chin, refusing to give in to the doubt circling through her.

Jared rubbed his neck, but said nothing.

Restin muttered to Anthony, "Mr. DeWitt ain't gonna like this."

Elise was getting tired of hearing about this Mr. DeWitt. "I'd like the lien now. And a receipt."

Mr. Anthony gazed at her and seemed about to refuse.

"It's the law, after all," Jared drawled, his hand going to the gun at his hip.

"Mr. DeWitt's the new owner of the bank. And the property that borders yours."

"Delavant Hall?" Jared turned to her, sadness clouding his green eyes.

Elise nodded in confirmation, then held out her hand to Mr. Anthony expectantly. "I'm paid in full, as you and the sheriff will both attest."

The banker hesitated, then thrust the lien at her. "I'm afraid I wasn't prepared to write a receipt."

"I wasn't prepared to turn over my money, either." He patted his pocket.

Elise controlled her temper with an effort. "If you don't have a pen, I have one. I'd like a receipt."

Anthony glanced at Restin, who shrugged, his face still slack with disbelief.

Jared stepped up and the banker quickly reached into his pocket. He pulled out a small inkwell and a gold pen, items Elise hadn't seen since the first year of the war. He quickly scribbled the amount she had given him then added *Paid in full.*

"If that's all?" Her mother had taught her better manners than to run off any visitor to their home, but Mama had never met Sheriff Restin or this new banker. And Elise wasn't sure how much longer she could keep from screaming. She felt trapped from three sides. Jared's green gaze saw entirely too much.

Anthony and Restin stared at each other for a long moment, then Anthony's gaze shifted to her, a hard smile twisting his lips.

"Good day," she said pointedly, moving to the top of the steps in a blatant gesture for them to leave. Reaction set in and she trembled from head to foot, her stomach clenching with unease. Perhaps she shouldn't have given them that money, but what choice did she have?

The men walked down the steps and mounted their horses. As they disappeared at the end of the oak-lined drive, Elise bit out, "Fairbrooke belongs to my family and it always will."

"They're gone." Jared touched her arm. "They can't bother you anymore."

"I hope you're right." She wrapped her arms around herself, feeling a chill despite the late summer heat.

Relief swept over her, nearly buckling her knees. They hadn't come for her. They hadn't discovered her secret.

Yet.

"Are you all right?" Jared moved in front of her, his intense gaze peeling through every layer of her defenses.

Trying to keep from breaking down and telling him the horrid things she'd done, Elise gave a tremulous smile. "Yes. I'm glad you were here and I didn't have to face them alone."

He studied her for a moment, mild speculation in his eyes. "It's a good thing your father had that money."

"Yes." She turned away from his too sharp gaze.

"What happened to the Delavants?"

"Mark and Bradley were killed at Chickamauga."

Jared cursed. "A damn bloodbath."

Elise nodded. "When Justine learned of it, she and Francie went to her people in Missouri."

"So did this Onash fellow confiscate their property?" Jared's gaze narrowed.

She shrugged. "I don't know. He must have."

"And sold it to DeWitt?"

"I suppose so, yes." Elise didn't want to talk about Claude Onash, especially with Jared. "May I get you a drink of water now?"

"I should be getting on home."

"Your grandfather will be thrilled to see you." She walked him to the bottom of the steps. "I appreciate your stopping to tell me about Logan."

"You're welcome. And don't worry, Elise. He'll make it home."

"I'll keep believing that."

"Good." His gaze settled on her face. "You sure you're going to be all right?"

"Yes, I'm fine. Don't spare another thought. Just get on home to your grandfather. Tell him I'll be by tomorrow, as normal."

"He's still got a way with women, I see." Jared grinned and her knees went suddenly weak at the transformation. The haggard lines on his face eased away and his eyes sparkled with a mischief Elise had never noticed.

She smiled. "That bout with pneumonia only slowed him down for a while."

Jared nodded and settled his hat on his head. "You've got your gun. That's good. You should keep it close."

"I intend to." She glanced around, surprised that she had forgotten it in her excitement at seeing a familiar face. She'd left it down at the cemetery.

"I'll look in on you tomorrow."

"There's no need." She didn't want to run into that probing gaze every time she turned around. "I'll be fine."

"I promised Logan."

Which meant he would live here, if he had to, until

Logan returned. If she argued, Jared would wonder why. "Very well, I'll see you tomorrow."

He touched the brim of his hat and mounted his horse. She smiled and waved as he rode off, but apprehension stroked up her spine.

She should've been relieved that someone familiar was home, but Jared's sharp gaze seemed to pierce through all her lies straight to her soul.

Clutching her mother's glove, Elise wondered what Jared would think if he knew she'd gotten the money to pay her lien from the very same Claude Onash the sheriff had asked about.

The very same Claude Onash she had killed.

CHAPTER TWO

Startled at hearing about the death of Elise's parents, Jared was hesitant to leave her alone, but the unexpected awareness that had erupted between them unsettled him and he rode on to Briar Rose.

His entire visit to Fairbrooke had been curious. Jared wasn't sure what surprised him more—that Claude Onash's name had been mentioned or that Logan's little sister had grown up.

Jared had known Elise all of her life, but he had never noticed the deep indigo of her eyes or the smattering of freckles across her straight, finely boned nose. Or the way her breasts would fill his hands. Mentally he calculated the difference in their ages, determining that she would now be twenty-one. A woman indeed.

As he rode away, awareness hummed through him. He was unshaven, still wearing his uniform pants and only his long-sleeved undershirt. His suspenders dangled at his sides; his boots were caked with mud. Having Elise so close to his filth embarrassed him, but she'd smelled so good, so clean, like rain and sultry summer flowers.

And he liked the way she said his name. *Jah-red*, slow and sweet, as if she savored the way it tasted on her tongue.

Hell, that was fanciful! He told himself his interest was strictly due to the responsibility he owed Logan, but it wasn't true. When she'd hugged him, he'd been too surprised to move at first. Then he hadn't wanted to. The feel of her against his body stirred his blood in a way it had never been stirred.

Oh, there had been women. Jared appreciated beauty and softness and sly wit delivered with a velvet tongue, but no woman had long held his attention. Certainly no woman had ever gained his trust. Not after his mother had abandoned him.

The entire incident that had occurred at Fairbrooke among Elise and the banker and the sheriff nagged at Jared. It was too much a coincidence that Jared had come home seeking the one man whose name had been mentioned on Elise's porch. And she claimed not to know Claude Onash.

She had been shaken when Mr. Anthony presented the lien, but she'd managed to hold it together. She appeared to have no idea that her father had taken out a mortgage on Fairbrooke. And Jared knew enough about Curtis Worthen to know he would have kept such information from his wife and daughter, unwilling to worry them with financial matters, war or no war.

If Elise had told the truth about Curtis setting aside

the money she'd used to pay the lien, then where had he gotten it?

Federal money.

Claude Onash.

It was too much a coincidence, and Jared didn't believe in coincidences. But how could Elise be involved with Onash?

He found it hard to imagine that her beautiful trusting eyes could conceal any secrets, but he'd learned young and well at his mother's knee that beauty often hid the most treacherous heart. And he'd sworn never to be taken in by a woman's wiles the way his father had been.

Still, his head protested Elise's involvement. She was his best friend's sister! Jared knew Logan as well as he knew himself. And he recalled with a stab to his heart the stark terror in Elise's eyes when she'd thought her brother was dead.

He wished he had more definite news for her, but Campbell McMillan, Jared and Logan's longtime friend from West Point, had learned about Logan what he could. As a new appointee to the Treasury Department, Cam had access to information that Jared did not. Now Jared must learn what he could about Onash, the Treasury agent who'd absconded with government money. A man without honor who'd proven again the corrupt reputation Treasury agents were reaping down South.

Jared wished he could allow the relief, the sense of homecoming, to wash over him, but he was here because of his vow to find the stolen money. He had a job to do.

As he covered the three miles to Briar Rose, he tried to keep his mind on the case, but his thoughts drifted to the woman he'd just left.

Lord, she'd felt good pressed against him, making him long for the naked flesh of a woman. He could still feel the imprint of her body on his and relived the confusing sense of protectiveness that had swelled through him. She wasn't his responsibility, at least not for long.

He rounded the last curve in the road and glimpsed the two-story house where he'd grown up, surrounded by a thick stand of walnut and cypress and oak trees. Elise might not be his responsibility, but Gramps was.

Briar Rose, named for the wild roses his grandmother had planted all along the surrounding split-rail fence, still stood. The surrounding land was blackened, scarred, yet the house was defiantly intact. He touched a heel to Trick's flank and the horse galloped through the open gate.

Jared peered through the trees, many of them stripped bare from frequent summer storms and from lighting fires for Yankee patrols. His heartbeat kicked up in anticipation. The grass was trampled in spots, high in others, but there were no gaping holes at his home.

The dark redbrick of the house and the kitchen behind looked intact. The stables were standing, but as he neared he could see the white trim of the eaves and doors were pocked with bullet holes.

Anger flared anew, though he realized how lucky they were. The house could have been torched like so many he'd seen. As long as Gramps was all right, they could start over. The reward Cam had promised him in exchange for finding the money Onash had stolen would go a long way toward rebuilding Briar Rose.

As he rode up to the front of the house, his heart swelled. The simple structure was relatively unscathed. The wide flat steps leading to the porch were scarred with boot prints and mud, but the stair rails were intact. Eight square colums were evenly spaced across the front of the house and connected by a lattice rail. Peeling, chipped white paint was visible only when one neared.

Four windows, two on either side of the wide front door, were open. Two of them were broken. Gramps had patched them with scraps of wood. The windows of the three bedrooms upstairs looked intact, as did the knee-high balcony railing that ran the length of the second story.

Briar Rose wasn't as large as Fairbrooke, which was part of its charm for Jared. He and Gramps had managed just fine.

The yard was empty. The several sharecroppers, black and white, who'd worked the land had gone west just before the war began. Jared dismounted, exhaling in a sudden surge of pride and relief. He was home. Finally home.

The door opened and Gramps stepped outside, his green eyes widening. "Jared, my boy! It *is* you!"

He moved slowly down the stairs, reminding Jared painfully how they'd both aged in the last four years. Jared himself felt sixty instead of thirty.

He took the shallow steps two at a time, grabbing his grandfather in a bear hug. "Gramps, how are you?"

"Just fine, my boy. Just fine." Gramps hugged him tight, his slight body belying the strength in his wiry arms. "You made it. You made it. Thank you, Lord."

Gramps' voice cracked and for a long minute, neither spoke. They simply held on. Since Jared's mother had left him at the age of six, the two men had only had each other. Two lone bachelors, Gramps had always called them.

Jared's eyes burned. He couldn't believe he was finally home. For the first time in his life Gramps looked every bit of his seventy years, and he was thinner than Jared had ever seen him.

The older man coughed and drew back to measure Jared with his sharp green gaze. "You need some fattenin' up."

"That would be fine by me." He clapped his grandfather on the shoulder. "How are you? How's that cough?"

"Fine, fine." Gramps waved away his concern. "It's a blasted pneumonia. Just hangs on and on, like tar."

Jared glanced around the porch. "The house seems to have survived."

"We did all right. Better than a lot of our neighbors."

Jared nodded. "I stopped by to see the Worthens on the way. I had news of Logan."

"You heard about Curtis and Charlotte?"

Jared nodded, heaviness pulling at him.

Gramps clucked in sympathy and shook his head, concern clouding his eyes. "And Logan?"

Jared hastened to assure him. "The last I heard he was on his way home. He was held up in Ohio."

"Prisoner of war?"

Jared nodded somberly.

"Damnation," Gramps said softly. "How'd Elise take it?"

"All right, I guess."

"That poor girl, she's had a rough time. One thing after another. Cal Drayton broke off their engagement, then her parents—"

"Elise was engaged?" This, too, startled Jared, though he knew it shouldn't have.

"Yessir. Then her parents were murdered and now she has no assurance that Logan will even make it home."

"Her parents were *murdered*?" Shock rocked through him. "She didn't tell me that."

"It's no wonder. She never talks about it." Gramps guided Jared into the house. "She came home and found them one day."

Jared's heart ached for her. There had been so much death on the battlefields. Why did it have to spread over to farms and homes and towns? "You've grown close to her?"

Gramps' eyes softened. "We've been taking care of each other."

Jared squeezed Gramps' shoulder. "I'll have to thank her for that."

He followed Gramps into the house, pleased to see that it didn't appear the Federals had set up in here. "Who murdered the Worthens?"

"Nobody knows. And that fool of a sheriff hasn't done anything about it."

"That would be Sheriff Restin?"

Gramps nodded, walking into the small sitting room to the right of the front door. "Their funeral was one of the biggest I've ever seen. Reverend Lyle managed to scrape together enough for two headstones."

"Good." Jared's joy at being reunited with Gramps dimmed in the realization that Elise was totally alone—at least until Logan returned. He was swept with a sudden urge to go to her, comfort her, but he pushed it aside. "I met the sheriff while I was at Fairbrooke."

Gramps turned from the window. "What was he doing there?"

Jared walked to the faded green-and-gold-striped wing chair and ran his hands over the brocaded fabric, a sense of peace seeping through him. "He was with the new bank manager, Mr. Anthony."

"Hmmm, don't know any Mr. Anthony."

"How about Claude Onash? Do you know him?"

Gramps frowned. "Yes, I've heard of him. I think he's a Treasury agent."

"Yes." Again Jared hoped that hearing Onash's name at Fairbrooke had been merely a coincidence. Tomorrow he would go into Moss Springs and ask questions about Claude Onash as well as Curtis Worthen's finances. If Curtis had really had the money, as Elise said, then why hadn't he, instead of Elise, paid the lien?

Gramps turned to him, his eyes filling with tears. "I'm glad you're home, boy. So many didn't make it."

"I know, Gramps." Jared squeezed the other man's shoulder.

His grandfather reached up and clutched Jared's

wrist. "Mark and Bradley Delavant, the Haley boys, Jeff Scott. They're all dead."

"Elise told me Justine Delavant went to Missouri."

Gramps nodded. "We're lucky we sold those horses to the army at the beginning of the war or we might not have a place to call home."

"I've got a little money, my army stipend. But I'm on a job now and we'll have enough money to rebuild Briar Rose, buy a couple of studs if we want to."

"You're on a job? What kind of job?"

"Doing a mutual favor for Cam. He agreed to look for Logan, and in exchange I took an assignment with the government."

"I'm glad to hear Cam made it through the war, but the government?" Surprise sharpened Gramps' words. "Army?"

"No. As a Treasury agent."

At his grandfather's arched brow, Jared explained. "Two days before Appomattox, a shipment of cotton was seized in Richmond. The money from the sale was to be used for the currency-for-gold exchange, but it was stolen. By Onash. I know he had a partner, but that's all I know."

Admiration gleamed in Gramps' eyes. "And you've already managed to track him down."

"I'd like you to keep all this in confidence, Gramps. Things are pretty shaky right now and though I've got a couple of leads, I don't want to go stirring up anything too soon."

Gramps nodded. "All right."

"So you don't know anything about Anthony, this new banker?"

"Nope." Gramps walked over to the fireplace, running his hand along the dusty wood front. "Never had nothing to put in the bank so didn't have cause to go there."

Jared nodded. "I hope to get some answers tomorrow."

Conflicting emotions churned inside Jared. He was thrilled to be home, but apprehension snaked up his spine. He didn't know what to make of Elise's pulling out that stack of Federal money. And her nervous defiance in paying the lien put him on edge.

He'd come home following a lead on Onash and Jared didn't like that his first hint of the man had surfaced at Fairbrooke. He didn't like it one bit.

"She what!" Tullar DeWitt slammed a fist atop his polished pecan desk. He looked at the two men who stood in the small office, located upstairs in the First Bank of Moss Springs, which he now owned. "How could Elise Worthen pay off the lien?"

Restin and Anthony looked at each other, then Anthony blinked nervously. Clutching the curved back of a leather chair, he held out the bills to Tullar. "She paid us with Federal money. We can't figure it."

DeWitt grabbed the money out of Anthony's hand and cursed violently. He'd been counting on foreclosure so he could have Fairbrooke for himself.

Elise Worthen had paid off the mortgage to Fairbrooke. Now Tullar would have to think of another way to get the land that adjoined Delavant Hall, his most recent purchase.

"Mr. DeWitt, I should probably put that money in the bank," Anthony ventured timidly.

Tullar considered the bills in his hand. They were an annoying reminder of the money he still hadn't found. He wanted Claude's fifteen thousand. He *needed* it if he was to be accepted as a member of elite society, which he had every intention of doing. No more white-trash labels for him.

"Here." He thrust the bills back at Anthony. When Claude had disappeared about two months ago, Tullar became suspicious that his partner had packed up and left Moss Springs.

He had returned only yesterday from Lynchburg, looking for Onash in the place where they'd originally divided the money, but he hadn't found the man.

"I can't imagine where she would get that money." Hershel Anthony glanced at Restin. "If her father had such a nest egg, then why would he need to take out a mortgage?"

Precisely, Tullar thought. Where *had* a daughter of the South gotten a wad of Federal currency? Unless she'd been performing favors for the Union soldiers? Not possible. DeWitt would certainly have heard about *that*.

"Maybe Claude gave it to her," Restin wheezed. "He was always trying to cozy up to her folks, had that fool idea about her marrying his boy."

"Why would Claude give it to her?" Tullar moved to the window and stared across at Bailey's Dry Goods.

"I don't know." Anthony frowned, staring at the money in his hand as he muttered, "But Miss

Worthen sashayed upstairs and tripped right back down with this, pretty as you please."

DeWitt spun, staring at Restin. Had the idiot unwittingly hit on the truth? Maybe Claude *had* given her the money.

Restin stared at DeWitt, then glanced at Anthony. "I don't know if he gave her no money, but I do know he was going out there to talk to her. He told me so on his way out of town."

"When was this?" Tullar's gaze narrowed. Had Onash been thinking of double-crossing *him?* Tullar knew of Claude's obsession with Fairbrooke. He and his son Pervis had been secretly living on the edge of the property for weeks, making noise about having the eight hundred acres. And the girl.

Restin frowned, fingering the gold filigree inkwell stand on Tullar's desk. "About two months ago, I guess."

"The last time any of us saw him." Tullar's voice crackled with impatience. Despite the sheriff's willing cooperation when Tullar wished it, the man irritated the hell out of him. "He told you he was going to the Worthen place?"

"Yep, he did."

"And have you asked Miss Worthen if she knows where Claude might be?" Tullar's voice was deceptively soft.

Restin's face was blank as a new slate. "She says she don't know him."

"That's right, she did," Anthony put in, watching Tullar carefully.

Telling himself to calm down, Tullar neatly folded

his handkerchief and slid it into his breast pocket. "Haven't either of you wondered where Claude has been? Or what might have happened to him?"

Restin scratched his bald head and belched. "I just reckoned he was out of town."

Anthony shuffled the money into a neat stack, looking bored. "You think something happened to him?"

"Don't you think it's a little strange that he headed out to Fairbrooke and never turned up again?"

Restin's face puckered in concentration. "I guess."

DeWitt cursed under his breath at the sheriff's slow wit.

Anthony frowned. "So, you do think something happened to him."

"I don't know." Tullar saw no reason to tell Anthony and Restin anything *he* knew.

"Want me to go back out there and ask some questions?" Restin offered, staring at the ornate clock on Tullar's wall.

"Not yet."

"I had to sign off on the mortgage and leave it with her," Anthony said.

"Fine." Tullar's mind raced. Somehow Elise Worthen had gotten the money to pay off her father's mortgage. How? Claude had gone out there and no one had seen him since. There was a connection. Tullar knew it.

Restin picked up a crystal paperweight from Tullar's desk and tossed it from one hand to the other. "Thomas Kensington's grandson was there with her. Anthony didn't have much choice about leaving the mortgage without a fight."

"It's no problem." Tullar snatched the glass weight from the man's hand and returned it carefully to his desk with a glacial stare. He wasn't worried about the four hundred and twenty dollars. It was going in the bank, which he owned. "Well, gentlemen, I've got work to do. And so do you."

Restin squinted at him. "I guess you'll let me know if you need anything."

"Yes." Tullar eased down into his new leather chair. If Elise Worthen had gotten that money from Claude, where was Claude? And where was Claude's share of the money? "Good day, gentlemen."

"I'll make a note of the Worthen payment in the ledger," Anthony said from the doorway.

"You do that."

Anthony and Restin let themselves out and Tullar swiveled in his chair, steepling his hands together beneath his chin as he stared thoughtfully out the window.

Elise Worthen was the first link to Onash that Tullar had found. One way or another he intended to have Claude's half of the money, just as he had planned since he and Claude had hatched their little scheme.

Claude's job as an agent for the Treasury had provided the perfect opportunity for him and Tullar to steal the money gained from the sale of southern cotton. Instead of the twenty-five percent that Claude and his partner, as agents of the Treasury, were allowed to take from the sale, Tullar and Claude had killed Claude's partner and taken the whole thirty thousand dollars.

After Tullar and Claude had split the money, they

had gone their separate ways. But Tullar had kept his eye on Claude. He intended to have all that money, one way or another. He followed Claude and his wife to Moss Springs, where they took advantage of war's end and Claude's government job to pluck up some of Virginia's choicest land, which had been confiscated by the new government or abandoned.

Tullar had obtained Delavant Hall through Claude. He knew that Onash's lust for the Worthen property stemmed not only from his desire to keep Tullar from owning the adjoining land, but from some misguided notion that he could convince Elise Worthen to marry his spineless puppy of a son, Pervis, who didn't have the brains to wipe Tullar's boots without assistance.

Tullar *would* have that money. He was on his way to being respectable, even if it was among Yankees. Unlike most Southerners, he didn't care who'd won the war. He intended to prosper, to have what he'd never had in South Carolina.

He wasn't burdened by foolish pride or patriotism; he was practical and patient and cunning. A combination that had enabled him to land on his feet more than once.

Until today, Tullar had had no clues about the money. Now, he knew that Elise Worthen had paid her mortgage with Federal money that no one could explain.

Claude had gone to Fairbrooke and somehow the Worthen gal had gotten her hands on Claude's money. Tullar doubted Claude would have willingly parted with that money, which meant she'd taken it.

It was time to pay a little visit to Miss Worthen. Tonight.

Shadows and mist surrounded her, pulled her deeper into sleep, deeper into the dream. She and Jared were dancing in the dining room. She knew it was a dream because they'd never danced before. They floated in a waltz and he gazed down at her with tender green eyes.

Then a hideous picture of the Onashes flashed in front of her. Fear pounded through her, then eased. She and Jared were alone again. He leaned down and kissed her. He'd certainly never kissed her before, but his lips on hers felt familiar.

Suddenly his kiss turned brutal, his hands bruising on her waist, and she struggled to get away from him.

His eyes blackened with fury and he gripped her wrists, shoving her arms behind her back. "Liar!" he yelled. "Murderer! Liar! Murderer!"

"No, no." She woke, panting. Her body was slick with sweat and she shook with a bone-deep chill. "No. No."

She rubbed at her eyes, trying to banish the image of Jared's face, hard and savage with rage, his green eyes brittle. Her dream lingered like a fog, and she imagined she saw a man sitting on the edge of her bed.

His face was in shadow and the sweet scent of sandalwood nearly overpowered her. All she could see was a shock of salt-white hair. She blinked, feeling sluggish and weary, trembling from the dream.

Pushed herself back against the massive headboard, she opened her eyes. And screamed.

There *was* a man—right on the edge of her bed!

Elise scrambled off the opposite side, grabbing her gun from beneath the pillow. "Who are you? What are you doing in here?"

She leveled the gun at him, her hands shaking so badly that she knew if she fired, she would blow a hole through the wall and miss him completely. Moonlight rippled through the bare windows and shadows undulated on the walls, the floor, the ceiling, making the room shift and swell.

The man sat quietly, his face shrouded in shadow. Cold, unblinking eyes studied her.

"Get out," she shrieked, trying to steady the gun. She still shook so badly, she couldn't sight him.

"My dear, before you do something rash, you should know that several people are aware that I'm here. Including Sheriff Restin." His drawl was soft and cool, definitely southern and his voice seemed disembodied in the twisting shadows of the bedroom. "He'd know to look here first if something . . . unfortunate happened to me."

"Who are you?" Nervous, she stroked the hammer, still struggling to get him in her sights. Why did the gun seem so heavy, so awkward in her hand? Thoughts crowded through her mind. How could she get rid of him? She didn't want to kill anyone else. He wasn't a Yank. "What do you want?"

"I'm a friend of Claude's."

"Claude?" Her breath froze in her chest.

"Don't play games, my dear." He nodded toward the gun. "Is that what you did to Claude? Shot him?"

"I don't know what you're talking about." Her teeth chattered on the lie and nausea rolled through her, making the floor dip beneath her feet. Who was this man? How did he know about Claude? How did he know about *her*?

The man clucked his tongue and pulled something from his pocket. Moonlight glinted off the blade of a small, lethal curved knife and Elise stiffened. He scraped at one fingernail, glancing at her as casually as if he were at a social. "I know Claude came out here to talk to you about your beautiful home—"

"No."

Quick as a flash, he aimed the blade point at her, unfurling his length from the bed. "Let me do the talking."

Shoot him, her mind urged. But her conscience wouldn't allow her finger to squeeze the trigger. She couldn't spend the rest of her life killing people to protect her secret.

"I know you paid your daddy's mortgage today. With Federal money that didn't belong to you."

She opened her mouth to speak, but he shook his head and walked around the end of the bed. She backed up until her legs hit the heavy wood of the bedside table.

The man stopped a few feet away. She couldn't tell much about his features. His eyes were dark and hard in the shadows, his build slender and tall. His hair gleamed like quicksilver.

Her breath knotted painfully in her chest and she tightened her grip on the gun.

"Four hundred and twenty Federal dollars is a highly unusual possession for a southern gal, wouldn't you say?"

"Who are you?"

"I told you, a friend of Claude's. And that wasn't his money you took to pay your daddy's mortgage. It was mine. I want it back."

"That was my father's money." Defiantly, she repeated what she'd told Sheriff Restin and Anthony earlier in the day.

"Can you prove that?" His voice lashed her like a whip.

She stiffened, refusing to let him see that she was ready to swallow her tongue from sheer terror. "Can you prove it wasn't?"

"Obviously not." He eased closer.

She thumbed down the hammer on the gun and he grinned so broadly, she could see the flash of his teeth in the darkness. "The money you took from Claude is mine. I want it and I want it now."

"I don't know anything about any money!"

He leaned into her face, his voice low and calculating. "I can outlast you, my dear. I'm a patient man and I'm sure I can convince you to return it."

She turned her head away, desperate to escape him, fear crawling over her skin.

"If I don't get my money, the sheriff will start asking questions about Claude." His breath burned her face. "You can take my word on that."

"I don't—"

He placed a finger over her lips and she recoiled in terror. Her gun drilled into his chest. All she had to do was pull the trigger, but her entire body was frozen.

His voice slid over her. "You can't run from me. I'll be everywhere you look. *Everywhere*. Even in your dreams." He laughed, his finger painfully grinding the soft flesh of her lips into her teeth. "Remember that."

She opened her mouth to refuse, to protest, but he disappeared. As soundlessly, as suddenly as he'd come.

She blinked, searching the play of shadow and moonlight. Shaken, she managed to release the hammer on the gun before it thudded to the floor. She sank down onto the bed, trembling so hard her muscles ached. What was she going to do? How was she supposed to find money she knew nothing about?

Obviously the man was after more than the fifty-five dollars hidden in her petticoats. A noise creaked through the house and she snatched up the gun, scooting against the headboard and curling into herself.

That man had walked into her bedroom as bold as Sherman going into Atlanta, and she'd been at his mercy. Was she going to pay the rest of her life for shooting that no-account Claude Onash and his son?

Hot tears chapped her cheeks and she buried her face in her arms, crying for the first time since she'd laid her parents to rest. She wished for Logan, for her parents, for someone to lean on, but there was no one.

CHAPTER THREE

I'll be your shadow everywhere you go. Everywhere.

The intruder's words taunted her. Elise was shaken and angry. Tension stretched across her shoulders and her head pounded from straining to see into the trees at the edge of Fairbrooke. Was he there?

There was no movement beyond her own and that of a few chickens strutting about the yard. She'd washed her sheets at dawn, desperate to erase his sweet sandalwood scent from her room.

All morning she'd jumped at every creaking twig, every squawking bird. She'd hoped that staying busy this morning would convince her she was being foolish, but her unease had only increased. What was she supposed to do? She didn't know about any money besides what remained in her petticoat.

She didn't want to focus on that. Reaching inside her skirt pocket, she brought out her mother's glove. Since Jared had given it to her, she kept it close at hand, drawing reassurance from it. Jared had also

brought good news. Logan was coming home. Hope
and anticipation swelled inside her.

Midmorning sun beat down on her as she stood at
the pump, her arm throbbing with the effort to coax
water with the rusty handle. The brook behind the
house, for which her great-grandmother Worthen had
named Fairbrooke, was only several yards away down
a small hill, but Elise didn't want to stray from the
house, in case that man returned.

She shivered, despite the perspiration sheening her
skin, and shifted her thoughts to her brother. Would
Logan's eyes be hard with pain and loss, as were
Jared's?

She recalled the dream then. In her dream, Jared's
eyes had been tender, hot with desire for her. And
while it had made sense last night, today it seemed
pure nonsense. She smiled a little. Imagine Jared
looking at her that way.

You're a sight for sore eyes. His voice played through
her mind, causing a flutter of sensation in her belly.

Strange how she'd never noticed the way his eyes
lit from within when he smiled, how the rough features of his face turned devastatingly handsome.

She tried to recall if she'd ever felt that little flutter
around Cal. She'd even allowed him to kiss her boldly
with his tongue when he left for the war, but she
couldn't recall this shivery nervousness. Of course,
she was no longer that girl. In fact, the memory made
her feel old and tired and detached.

As Jared was leaving yesterday he had looked at her
hungrily, as if she wasn't quite what he'd expected, as
if she'd surprised him. At the memory, anticipation

shivered through her and she brushed it away. No doubt Jared's interest in her was strictly driven by his promise to Logan. Or the fact that she'd paid off Papa's mortgage.

The lien. The money. *What* was she going to do?

"Elise?"

At Jared's unexpected voice behind her, she squealed and dropped her bucket of water. The chickens screeched and scurried off. All the tension crowding through her splintered.

"Oh, blast! Look what you made me do," she snapped, righting the bucket and staring at the water it had taken her grueling minutes to coax out of the rusty pump.

"I'm sorry." He bent and lifted the bucket. "I thought you heard me ride up."

"No." She realized how cross she sounded. "I'm sorry. I didn't mean to snap at you. It's this blasted pump. The handle's rusted and—"

"I'll take a look."

"Oh, that's not necessary."

He positioned the bucket beneath the spout. "Here, I'll refill it for you."

Having him here instead of in her thoughts rattled her. "I'm sure you have things you need to do."

"I'm doing what I need to." He smiled, the gesture lighting his eyes to a startling green.

Her stomach clenched and she moved away from him, too aware of his clean masculine scent.

He took off his hat and held it out to her. "Do you mind?"

"No." She took the hat, still warm from his head, and her fingers clutched its worn softness.

He rolled up the sleeves on his white cotton shirt, exposing strong forearms dusted with dark hair. She stared at his broad square hands, tanned to a dark leather. They were competent, strong hands. Hands that could soothe or command. Or protect.

Since that man's visit last night, she'd been a hairbreadth from blurting out to someone she could trust the horrible truth of what she'd done. But who— Gramps? Jared? No. She couldn't involve anyone else in the crime she'd committed.

Oh, where was Logan? Apprehension crawled over her and her skin prickled. She tightened her grip on Jared's hat, watching the play of muscle under his shirt, mesmerized by the width of his back, the solid profile. Even though he'd lost weight, he was still a big man.

As Jared's strong arms worked the pump handle, the grating screech of the rusted implement was drowned out by the fear in her thoughts. She cast frequent surreptitious glances over her shoulder and into the trees that bordered the back side of Fairbrooke.

That man last night had said he'd be her shadow until she found his money. Was he even now hiding in the trees, watching her?

"There we go. Where do you want it?"

She stared blankly at Jared for a minute, then realized he was talking about the water he'd pumped. "Oh, in the garden."

His gaze weighed her for a second, then he walked

toward the back of the house. She followed, her stomach fluttering nervously.

He held the creaking gate open for her and she walked inside to the garden, turning to take the water from him. "Thank you."

He handed her the bucket, his gaze steady on her face. Nervous already, she turned quickly away, sloshing water on her arm. The cool liquid felt nice on her heated skin, and she poured out the remainder into the waiting earth.

There were only a few rows to tend now—carrots, new potatoes, sweet potatoes. Her mother's huge garden was only a fraction of its former size, but there was no need for more. There was only her now. And Logan, once he returned.

"Something else I can do while I'm here?"

Tell me everything's going to be all right. But instead she said, "Tell me Logan's really coming home."

"He is. I believe that, Elise."

She nodded and gave him a small smile, her attention divided between her brother's handsome friend and the midnight visit she'd received last night. Where could she look for the man's money? How was she supposed to know anything of Claude Onash, except that he and his son had killed her parents and tried to rape her?

She realized Jared was looking at her expectantly. "I'm sorry. You said something?"

He nodded, compassion deepening his voice. "Gramps told me about your parents. I'm sorry."

"Thank you." She pushed away the memories that crowded through her.

"You found them, didn't you?"

She nodded, resisting the urge to wipe her palms down her skirts.

"It must've been hard."

"Yes."

"Were they cut down in surprise?"

"I'm sure they tried to fight—" Though still preoccupied with thoughts of locating the money, she realized something strangely intense in Jared's question. She gazed at him full on. "I don't really like to talk about it."

He looked as if he would ask more, but then he nodded, his gaze softening. "Do you need anything while I'm in town?"

"No, but thank you." Maybe there was something at the old abandoned sharecropper's house where Papa had found Claude living with his son.

"Gramps is looking forward to your visit today."

"Visit?" Yes, she would look at the cabin.

Jared frowned. "You sure you're all right? I must've spooked you more than I thought."

"Oh, I'm fine." She swallowed, trying to get a grip on her wayward thoughts. "Yes, I'm taking Gramps into town to see the doctor."

"I told him I could take him, but he insisted on waiting for you."

She smiled and walked through the gate, anxious to get Jared on his way so she could check out the sharecropper's cabin before she went to Briar Rose for Gramps.

"I can see why he would prefer the company of a beautiful woman over mine, but I am his grandson."

"Oh, nonsense!" She handed him his hat, hoping he couldn't hear the nervous tremor in her voice.

"Is there something going on with the two of you that I should know about?" His eyes warmed and Elise felt suddenly trapped in a silken web.

Had she ever noticed how charmingly he smiled? It took the starch right out of her legs. She gave a delighted laugh. "How indiscreet, Jared!"

"Yes, isn't it?" He grinned, and for the second time she found herself wanting to confide in him, wanting to walk into his arms and let him soothe away her fears.

But she couldn't. She wouldn't. "Thanks for your help with the water. And I'm sorry for snapping at you earlier."

"You looked as if you were deep in thought. I should've announced myself."

"I'll forgive you if you'll forgive me," she said lightly.

His gaze roamed her face and lingered on her lips. "Done."

Her stomach gave a funny flip and she resisted the urge to lick her suddenly dry lips.

After a moment his gaze returned to hers. "Things sure do change, don't they?"

"They certainly do." She automatically thought of the horror, the constant guard she had kept up since the murders, but she knew Jared was talking about something else.

As he rode off down the driveway Elise recalled the deliberation in his eyes when he'd asked about her parents' murders. She'd been preoccupied, but his questions appeared more than concerned. They had been . . . purposeful.

Suddenly he seemed every bit as dangerous and threatening as the man in her bedroom had last night. Jared's eyes, deep and intense, could see straight through to her soul, to the horrible thing she'd done.

Somehow she was going to have to avoid him. If only Logan would come home, then Jared wouldn't come around so much. Though she felt a stab of disappointment at that, she knew it was for the best.

She waited until his dust had cleared before going to the barn and saddling Majesty. She had a couple of hours before taking Gramps to the doctor. Just enough time to search the sharecropper's cabin to see if Onash had left anything there. And make sure the bodies hadn't been disturbed.

Elise reined up in the clearing at the bottom of the hill. The cabin, small but sturdy, sat between two towering walnut trees. Stands of walnut and oak, dotted with wisteria and mountain laurel, surrounded the small clearing. Bright fingers of sunlight wove through the leafy branches. The occasional trill of a whippoorwill sounded softly through the quiet air.

Elise gripped the pommel of her saddle, wishing she could turn and race out of here. But the white-haired man's threats pounded through her mind.

If I don't get my money, the sheriff will start asking questions about Claude. You can take my word on that.

She glanced around, squinting into the shadows, but she saw no sign of his white hair, heard no movement. She deliberately kept her gaze from the thorny bush across from the barn.

Her throat tightened and panic swelled inside her. Taking a deep breath, she dismounted and shook out her skirts. She pulled her gun from her pocket and walked into the house.

A pair of pants hung over the back of a wooden chair next to the fireplace. Brown woolen slippers rested next to the chair. An empty black kettle hung in the fireplace. A few dirty dishes, cloaked with spider webs, plainly attested that no one had lived in the house since Claude and Pervis.

There was one bedroom, the sheets grimy with dust and stale with the odor of sweat. She wrinkled her nose and looked under the mattress, then the bed. Nothing.

She walked outside. A mouse scurried across the porch and darted around a chipped crock. An ax lay next to a small store of wood beside the door. She gingerly checked the outhouse and found nothing. A plow, two bridles, and a shovel were all she found in the small barn.

With her shoe, she moved the hay and dirt clumped on the barn floor, searching for a hole or someplace that could be used to hide money, but there was none.

A crudely made ladder leaned against one wall, and she propped it against the loft floor then climbed up. There were only a few discarded bolls from a crop of cotton.

Unease thudded through her and her nerves stretched taut. She climbed down, walking outside to scan the trees and bushes that circled the house. She saw no path, no freshly mounded dirt to indicate a secret hiding place of any kind.

I'll be everywhere you look. Everywhere.

Her spine prickled as though she was being watched. Though she strained to catch a sign of that white hair, she saw no one.

She circled in front of the house and barn one last time, but she kept her distance from the thorn bush next to the barn. She knew what was under that bush. Or rather *who*. And she wasn't going near the Onashes again.

Nothing appeared to have been disturbed. She'd found no money, no papers, no sign of anything except proof that *someone* had been living here, as Papa had said. The knot in her stomach tightened.

Now what was she going to do?

Jared could still smell the soft lilac scent of her. He didn't see how Elise could smell so good when she'd been working in the garden and at the end of summer, but she did.

As he rode into town, he tried to figure out why Elise intrigued him so. Those indigo eyes could entice a man to do just about anything, including one who knew better than to trust a woman's eyes. He couldn't figure it.

He'd always regarded her as Logan's little sister, as a *girl*, but she was a woman full grown. Her eyes were matured by pain and loss and uncertainty, just as most were after the war.

There was an understanding of the world's ways, yet they still retained a warmth. When she smiled, he felt the kick all the way to his toes. He'd never been affected like that by a woman, certainly never by Elise.

Why the hell hadn't he noticed her before? It didn't matter. She deserved more than the fleeting attention he bestowed on women. His idea of a courtship was asking a woman to dance twice.

That guileless no-nonsense way she had of looking at him reminded him of Logan. And she didn't stand on ceremony. She'd welcomed him as warmly as Gramps had, as if she was truly glad to see him, and not just to get news of Logan.

But he'd sure spooked her this morning. She'd looked tired and those sapphire eyes were haunted. He'd never seen her angry, and her nervousness reminded him of the way she'd been the other day in front of Anthony and Restin. Had they been bothering her again?

Her slender body had vibrated with unease. Was it because of him or something else entirely? He knew that haunted look because he felt it himself. Seeing that same lost emptiness in her eyes made him want to hold her, reassure her, and he resented that. His father's life had meant nothing to him after his mother left, and Jared had sworn never to be led around by a woman.

He didn't want to feel responsible for anyone but himself and Gramps. And getting back the money he'd sworn to find.

He reined up at the south end of town. Scores of people, clustered like pesky mosquitoes, teemed across the street, up and down the planked boardwalk that connected a strip of businesses now shiny with the sheen of virgin pine. The rain-soaked hills that rolled beyond the town presented a poor contrast to the bustling activity around him.

At least Moss Springs hadn't been burnt to the ground, but the brown earth was scarred from cannon and artillery fire, marching soldiers, trampling horses. Here and there a burst of defiant green assured that the land would recover from its brutal treatment, but just now everything looked stymied, depressed, burdened.

And yet the town breathed, moving with new life. Hammers rang out, their sharp clanging somehow making the sun's glare seem even hotter, steamier. Interspersed with old businesses and new, several tents flapped in the breeze.

A new plankboard walk connected the new hotel and the bank and the sheriff's office. Moss Springs seemed to be recovering from the effects of the war, aided by the clumps of blue uniforms roving the streets and the Federals' money, no doubt.

Jared fought back a swell of bitterness. He himself was working in an official capacity for the new government, and he wasn't proud of it.

He hitched Trick in front of the saloon, gratified to see that even this early in the morning, Slim was open. Judging from the muffled rise and fall of voices inside, he already had customers, too.

Jared knew from the excessive drinking he'd witnessed throughout the war that many men would find it difficult to give up once back home. Somehow the end of the war either made people want to drown their losses or celebrate what they'd pirated.

Jared had no intention of advertising that he was working a case for the Treasury Department—not after evidence had surfaced about the many agents who had stolen and killed and caused so much pain to Southerners.

Yet here Jared could ask questions of Slim without raising suspicions. He still knew some people in town and hoped he could learn what he needed to about Claude Onash and even Curtis Worthen without having to inquire in an official capacity.

He stepped inside the saloon, surprised to see that Slim had a new floor. The round mirror behind the bar was gone and in its place was a long rectangular painting of a naked blond woman reclining on a horse, her breasts coyly covered by her long, flowing hair. Jared arched his eyebrows.

Slim called out to him. "Jared Kensington! Good to have you home. Logan with you?"

"No." Jared strode into the saloon, taking off his gloves and tucking them in his waistband. He reached Slim and shook his hand. "He should be home soon, I hope."

The stocky bald man clucked his tongue. "I'm glad to hear he's coming home. Too many of ours didn't. Guess you heard about the Delavants and the Haleys?"

Jared nodded, wondering if this sick feeling would ever go away, this emptiness inside that had shadowed his heart since the war.

"What'll you have? It's on the house." Slim moved

behind the bar, puffing as he wedged his large girth through the slender opening space.

"Thanks. A whiskey." Though the place was still mostly empty, a card game had started in the corner. He recognized Lowell Sanders and raised his glass in greeting to the old man.

Sanders had lost an eye at Fort Sumter and been sent home only to go straight back with a unit passing through from Mississippi. Jared had run into him at Sharpsburg and was glad the man had made it home. Only a few days after Sharpsburg, he and Logan had been called up from their cavalry unit to Mosby's 43rd Battalion.

"So how's your Gramps these days? That cough gettin' him down?"

"He seems to be doing all right."

"How long you been back?"

"Since yesterday."

A tall red-haired man pushed through the doors and walked over to the card table.

Slim snorted. "Damn Yanks. Act like they own the place."

"It's going to take some getting used to," Jared said mildly, not wanting to get off the track of learning what he could about Onash. "There sure are a bunch of new people in town."

"Ain't that the truth." Slim rested his elbows on the bar and jerked his thumb toward the cardplayers. "All them, except Lowell, got here after the war."

Jared nodded. "I heard the bank's been sold."

"Yeah. Tullar DeWitt's his name."

"Where's he from?"

"Hell, who knows? Nobody knows anything about him, except he seems to be rich. Cain't figure how most decent folk are dirt poor and these people come swooping in here, throwing money around and pushing their way in."

"I'd heard tell he bought Delavant Hall."

"Stole it, more like."

Jared raised an eyebrow. "Stole?"

"One of them Treasury agents, Claude Onash, came down through here, confiscating property right and left, got ahold of Delavant Hall after Justine and Frannie left. This DeWitt says he bought it from the government. If you ask me, it weren't the government's to sell."

"I agree."

Slim excused himself and moved down to the end of the bar, asking if anyone at the card table wanted a drink. After they had hollered out their orders, Slim came back and commenced pouring liquor.

He edged down to Jared, eyeing the table of men he'd just left. "They're all talking about how Elise Worthen paid her daddy's mortgage."

Jared glanced over at Slim's customers, smoke spiraling up in the air.

"I'm just glad that damn banker didn't get Fairbrooke," Lowell Sanders spat out. "DeWitt already owns Delavant Hall and the bank."

The red-haired man muttered something and dealt another card.

"They're all wondering how she got that money," Slim said with a sharp glance at Jared. "I'm wondering that myself. Heard you wuz out there when the banker showed up."

"Maybe Curtis had some saved up," Jared offered, sipping at his drink.

"Well, if that's true, then why did he have to take out a loan by putting up his house?"

Jared shrugged. He'd asked himself the same question and didn't like the suspicions snaking through his mind.

Slim carried a tray of drinks over to the table, then returned to the bar. Jared declined a second whiskey and Slim eyed him, frowning.

"I'm wondering if maybe Elise got that money from Onash. He had some, you know."

"Onash?" Jared's senses prickled. "How would she do that?"

Slim hesitated, then leaned closer, his voice low. "Onash has been going all over town, saying as how he's going to own Fairbrooke and get Elise for his boy."

"What do you mean? Marry her?"

Slim nodded. "Maybe she agreed and he gave her the money 'cause of that."

"She didn't say anything to me about getting married, except to Cal Drayton," Jared said dryly.

"Well, that's over," Slim said dismissively. "He and his sister just up and left."

"What else do you know about Onash?"

"Nothing really. He rented a place from John Fiedler on the edge of town. His wife died soon after he got here and he visits her grave every Sunday, fresh flowers and all that."

"Nothing else?" Jared prompted, anticipation pumping through him.

Slim shifted as if uneasy. "Just what I said about Elise. Called her a firebrand and such. Said he'd get her for Pervis then he'd have Fairbrooke."

"Did Onash ever approach her about it?"

"Not that I know of. I do know he went out there a couple of times and talked to her daddy. He kept bragging about how he could force Curtis to turn that property over to him because there was no way Curtis could repay the mortgage at the bank, but as far as I know, he didn't ever call Curtis on it."

"When was the last time you saw Onash?"

"He hasn't been in here for a while. Over a month. Kinda strange, that. He and his boy used to play poker on Tuesday nights, never missed a game. Hmmm, come to think of it, I haven't seen his boy either."

Jared leveled another gaze at the table full of card-players. He didn't ask for a physical description. Thanks to a sketch provided by Cam, Jared knew what Claude Onash looked like, right down to the two missing fingers on his left hand.

So, where were Claude Onash and his son? How was it possible for Curtis Worthen to have a "nest egg," as Elise had said, if he hadn't been able to make his last loan payment?

"You know anything about the Worthen murders?"

"My understandin' was that Elise'd been to town and found her folks when she got home." Slim clucked sympathetically. "Can you imagine that?"

"Did you see her in town that day?"

"Nope, but that don't mean nothin'. She don't make a habit of comin' in here."

Jared's chest grew tight. "But you might've seen her around town."

"I might've, but I didn't." The barkeep eyed Jared curiously.

"I imagine the funeral was hard on her. Did everyone attend?"

"All of us what knew 'em."

"Even Onash?"

"Nope. He wasn't there." Slim paused, considering. "Funny thing. As bad as he wanted that land, you'd think he'd be circling around like the vulture he is."

"Maybe he'd already left town," Jared suggested, though his gut didn't agree.

Slim pursed his fleshy lips. "Reckon so."

Jared had more questions now than when he'd started. Maybe a few more inquiries would clear some things up. He left the saloon and worked his way around town, keeping his questions discreet, speaking only to people he knew.

But two hours later, Jared's gut knotted with the suspicion that Elise knew something about Claude Onash.

Hugh Bronson's wife, Coralee, ran the livery now and knew Onash had gone out to Fairbrooke at least twice, because the man stabled his horse at the livery. Coralee thought she'd seen Elise in town earlier that day, before Elise had returned with Gramps and the bodies of her parents.

Mr. Fiedler, who had rented Onash his house on

the edge of town, said Onash had given him notice that he'd be moving out. Both repeated that Onash had at least once referred to the hope that Elise would marry his son, and both confirmed what Slim had said about Onash's visiting his wife's grave every Sunday.

People might not have known Claude Onash well, but they all knew that each Sunday he visited his wife's grave—without fail.

But no one had seen the man for at least two months. The last time Coralee had seen him, he'd been headed to Fairbrooke, just before the Worthens were found murdered.

Was there a connection between Onash's disappearance and the deaths of Elise's parents? If Onash had killed Curtis and Charlotte, that was a powerful reason to leave town.

A sick feeling crawled over Jared. He didn't like Elise being linked, even casually, to Claude Onash and that stolen money, but he could hardly ignore what he'd heard.

Onash had talked about Elise and Fairbrooke.

He had told several people that he'd been to Fairbrooke on at least two occasions.

He'd planned to go out to Fairbrooke and hadn't been seen since that day.

Jared stood on the north end of town, outside of the New American hotel, and his gut snarled in knots. There couldn't be a link between Elise and Onash. There couldn't.

But everywhere he turned, there was.

He recalled her nervousness when Anthony and Restin had asked whether Onash had been out to see her. He replayed the quick explanation she'd made about having that god-awful amount of money. He remembered the haunted look on her face this morning.

Jared didn't like where his mind was taking him. No sir, he didn't like it one bit. He stared down the main street, crowded with wagons and children and hurrying people. Elise would be coming into town soon with Gramps.

He still had a few questions to ask, and reluctance burned through him as he crossed the street and stepped inside Bailey's Dry Goods. Once inside the cool, dim interior, Jared removed his hat, looking around for David Bailey.

"Jared Kensington?" Mr. Bailey rushed out from behind the counter and grabbed Jared's hand, pumping heartily. "Oh, it's good to have you home. You're looking fit."

"Thank you."

Mr. Bailey asked after Gramps and Logan, and Jared explained that his friend was on his way home. At the news of Logan's capture and imprisonment, Mr. Bailey's eyes clouded with sympathy. "I hate to hear it."

"You know what a tough old boot he is." Jared clapped him on the shoulder. "I'm looking for him any day."

"That's good." Mr. Bailey rubbed his papery forehead. "That's real good for Miz Elise, poor thing."

"Yes. I know she's had a rough time of it."

"Not that she would complain, mind you, but how

much can a body stand? She's lost her parents and Rithy."

"Yes, I heard. She found them at the house, didn't she?"

"I believe so."

"Did you see her in town that day?"

The other man paused in the doorway leading to the back room. "No. Not before she came in with your grandpa. That's when we heard what had happened at Fairbrooke."

Apprehension bloomed, but Jared tamped it down. She could've gone any number of places besides Bailey's.

He picked up a sack of flour, then asked for some sugar, molasses, and a pouch of ground coffee.

Mr. Bailey wrote down Jared's purchases on a small tablet, offering with a halfhearted smile, "I can put this on credit for you, if you'd like?"

Jared imagined it would be a hardship for the man. He smiled and shook his head, pulling a ten-dollar note from his pocket. "I have some money."

"I don't mind. I did it for everybody during the war."

"Think you're going to get your money back?"

"From most people. They pay when they can. Like Curtis. He paid his account clean off, but it's up again."

"He paid up? How did he do that?"

"Well, he got a loan from the bank. But I guess when it was gone, he was back in a bad way again." Setting a can of molasses on the counter, Mr. Bailey went in the back for Jared's coffee. "Miz Elise don't come into town much. She's got about twelve dollars on her account right now, but I don't mind. She'll pay me when she can. She doesn't like to be beholden to anybody."

Dread kicked at Jared. If Elise had money from her father's nest egg, why hadn't she paid off her account at Bailey's? Like Mr. Bailey said, she was prompt about repaying debt. On the rare occasion they'd had to incur debt, the whole family had been prompt about repayment.

After a few more minutes, Jared gathered up his purchases and retrieved Trick from the livery. Instead of heading straight out of town, he rode behind the businesses and row of houses on the fringe of town to the cemetery spread on a rise within view.

Mr. Bailey, too, had mentioned Claude Onash's weekly trips to his wife's grave. Without much trouble, Jared found Myra Onash's headstone, noting how expensive it looked in comparison to the simple markers that surrounded it.

Made of granite, hers was a large rectangular headstone supported by two flat arms extending slightly out from the base. Myra's dates of birth and death were engraved beneath her name.

It was a little more ornate than most, but Jared saw nothing extraordinary about it. A cluster of withered morning glories lay at its base, reinforcing the information that Claude hadn't been around for a while.

"Where's your husband, Myra?" Jared muttered. "Where's that damn money?"

He shaded his eyes and looked out over the cemetery. Its size had tripled since before the war, full now of boys from home. Foreboding clicked through him. What were the chances that Claude Onash just talked big and had never approached Elise about Fairbrooke or marrying his son?

Jared had no hard evidence, just suspicions that sawed at him like a dull blade.

She'd told Gramps she had returned from town and found her parents and Rithy, but no one could say for certain that they'd seen her in town. Why would she lie? *Unless*—

Jared froze. What if she'd been there when her parents were murdered? What if Claude Onash had killed her parents and Elise had retaliated in kind? *That* would explain Onash's disappearance.

Denial roared through Jared and he shook his head. He had nothing to support such wild thoughts—no bodies, no account at all of Elise's whereabouts. All he had was a connection between Elise and Onash. A connection he had to follow, despite the cold dread clawing through his chest.

He had promised Logan to look after Elise until he returned, and Jared meant to follow through. But he couldn't ignore what he'd learned today.

He remembered the calluses on her delicate hands and how she'd held everything together, waiting for Logan to return.

He felt again the warmth that had spread through his chest when she'd hugged him yesterday, her eyes bright with genuine joy that he'd made it home.

He recalled the stark horror in her eyes when she'd thought Logan was dead and how she completely believed Jared's assurances that Logan would return.

Jared hated like hell to ask her about Onash. His heart urged him to let it be, but his head clamored something entirely different.

She'd lied about knowing Onash and Jared had to find out why.

CHAPTER FOUR

An hour later as she and Gramps rode into town, Elise tried to convince herself that a strange man hadn't stealthily invaded her bedroom last night. She'd found no money, but neither had she seen that man again.

Not this morning at the house, nor at the sharecropper's cabin. Perhaps he was bluffing. Or perhaps he'd found what he sought and left town. The tension across her shoulders lessened.

"It's hard to believe Drucilla Hawthorne is a doctor. She's quite a stunner."

Gramps' comment snagged Elise's attention. "Thomas Kensington, surely you're not suggesting she's not smart enough to be a doctor simply because she's pretty?"

"Well, if she can doctor as good as she looks . . ."

"Oh, you!" She swatted at him, letting the mellow day lull her into a tentative calm.

He chuckled and patted her knee. "You know better than that. I just like to see you get riled up."

She smiled, keeping a cautious eye on the twisting, curving road behind them and the tree-clumped hills alongside. "You're feeling full of yourself today."

"It's not every day a man is tended by two beautiful women."

"Even if one of them is a Yank?" Elise drawled, watching a hawk spiral into the sky.

Gramps chuckled. "Even if." He sobered, looking out over the landscape, still gouged and brown and barren. "The time for hurt is past. We've got to move on. All of us."

Elise nodded, knowing he was right. Even Robert E. Lee shared Gramps' philosophy, but few Virginians were willing to follow Lee's example of forgiveness. And in truth, any problems Elise might have with Yankees didn't lie with Dr. Drucilla Hawthorne. Elise had met the woman on a previous trip to town and had found the doctor charming. Dr. Hawthorne seemed genuinely interested in helping people, northern or southern.

No, Elise's problems stemmed from Claude Onash and her resulting mistrust of *any* government official. Admittedly the gouges in the earth were healing over. Sprigs of green grass fought their way up through the burnt-out layers. But the people, all of them, carried scars that wouldn't be so easily healed.

As they drove into Moss Springs, there was no sign of the white-haired man, and the pressure across her chest eased. The town was bustling. From the livery on the south end of town, past the jail, the hat shop, Bailey's Dry Goods, and the bank, the dark blue of Yankee uniforms still clotted the view. She watched the milling uniforms, the people without names and faces who passed by, and felt almost a stranger herself.

Gramps patted her hand. "It's going to take some getting used to, that's for sure."

She nodded, smiling as she drove into the livery.

Gramps stepped down from the wagon and extended a hand to Elise. "Jared said the sheriff paid you a visit yesterday."

Her gaze snapped to the older man. She should've guessed Jared would tell Gramps she'd paid the lien. "Yes," she said cautiously.

"If they bother you again, I want to know."

"Oh, Gramps." Elise smiled and squeezed his hand, hoping he couldn't hear the relief in her voice. "What would I do without you?"

"You'd pine away, I expect." His green eyes twinkled and he tucked her hand in the crook of his arm, telling Coralee they would return for the wagon. Once outside, he said, "Jared can help you, too."

Her heart kicked into double rhythm and she gave a small laugh, focusing her attention on the busy street. "I don't need any help."

"He was concerned when he learned about your parents," Gramps said soberly.

Elise recalled the way Jared's gaze had traced over her this morning—slowly, thoroughly, as if mapping a route—and her stomach dipped. She didn't want to talk about him, but she was touched by the concern in Gramps' face. "He stopped by this morning."

"Is that so?" Gramps slid a mischievous smile at her.

"Oh, you!" She flushed and quickened her steps.

"Stop teasing me. We're going to be late for your appointment with Dr. Hawthorne."

The doctor's office was on the opposite side of the street, next to the telegraph office. Still holding Gramps' arm, Elise wove her way across the street, amid people and wagons and horses.

Four boys jostled and pushed between her and two women on her left. Gramps shooed them away with his hat. "Watch out, you young pups!"

He gallantly bowed to the other two women, a statuesque redhead and a softly rounded blonde.

Gramps smiled blindingly at the blonde. "Good day, Matilda. You're looking quite splendid today."

The woman blushed and lowered her eyes demurely. "Good day, Mr. Kensington."

Elise grinned.

"Hattie, you're looking . . . vibrant," Gramps said cheekily to the redhead.

She rolled her eyes. "You're an incorrigible flirt, Thomas Kensington. Good day to you."

She took the other woman's arm and swept around them. Gramps watched them go, his eyes sparkling as he watched the sway of their skirts.

Elise pulled him along. "You'd best behave yourself or I'll tell Jared."

"Elise, have pity on an old man." He settled his hat back on his head, looking wounded. "My pleasures in life are few. . . ."

"That doesn't work on me, Gramps, and you know it."

"You're a hard-hearted woman," he grumbled, not masking the twinkle in his eyes.

She replied in mock sternness, "Someone must take you in hand."

"And what beautiful hands you have, my dear."

"Oh, you! Hush."

They neared the doctor's office and Elise picked up her skirts to walk up the two short steps. Keeping a firm grip on Gramps' arm, she steadied him on the bottom step.

From the corner of her eye, she spied a brilliantly shined pair of boots and glanced up as the door of the doctor's office swung open.

"Watch yourself."

"Thank you—" The words jammed in Elise's throat.

Watch yourself. She knew that voice.

The man removed his hat and white hair shone like cotton. His eyes were brown, cold and hard like a frozen, bottomless river. Recognition slammed into her. Even though she had never clearly seen his features or his eyes, she knew him. The man who'd come into her bedroom!

Horror burst inside her and her muscles tightened. *Watch yourself.* Had that been an admonition to her? A threat? She balked, prepared to bolt.

Gramps clamped a hand over hers and shot a puzzled look at her as he stepped inside. "Thank you, sir."

"My pleasure." The voice was silky smooth, his thick drawl sending a shaft of ice through her.

Her throat ached with the urge to scream and her heart thundered savagely against her ribs.

Gramps gently pulled her along. "Come, my dear."

Where had that man come from? Where had he
been? Had he followed them into town? Had he been
waiting for them? Her chest closed up in panic as she
followed Gramps through the door.

"Good day, Doctor."

Elise was vaguely aware that Dr. Hawthorne answered from her desk, where she sat writing in a large
book. Elise felt the man's gaze skimming up her back-
side and goose bumps prickled her flesh. She wanted
to slam the door.

She was sure Gramps could see the horror on her
face, hear the pounding of her heart, but he swept off
his hat and smoothed back his thick silver-streaked
hair, seemingly unaware of her distress.

As the door closed Dr. Hawthorne wiped her hands
on her spotless white apron and walked toward them.
"Thomas! How nice to see you. Hello, Elise."

Elise nodded dumbly. She couldn't catch her
breath and the floor wobbled beneath her. But it
wouldn't do for Dr. Hawthorne or Gramps to think
something was wrong.

Woodenly she helped him over to the exam table
that Dr. Hawthorne indicated in the middle of the
clinic. She and the doctor each held his arm as
Gramps eased onto its edge.

Gramps chuckled. "Seems like there are more new
faces everytime we come to town."

"Yes." Elise managed to keep her voice steady.
"Dr. Hawthorne, do you know who held the door for
us?"

"Elise, you must call me Dru." She smiled and

when Elise nodded, she continued, "That was Tullar DeWitt. He owns the bank."

"And Delavant Hall," Gramps grumped.

Dr. Hawthorne wrinkled her nose. "He reminds me of a snake oil salesman."

"He does!" Elise laughed weakly at the comparison and the distasteful expression on the other woman's face.

Staring out the window, she tried to calm her racing heart. She'd so hoped that she had escaped him, but she hadn't. Where would he turn up next? Her nerves stretched to ragged edge.

Watch yourself. Yes, the words were subtle, easily misinterpreted, but she knew they had been a threat. She knew now he would never leave her alone until she found that blasted money.

Besides the sharecropper's cabin, where else could she look for it? Thank goodness Jared hadn't come into town with her and Gramps. One look at her with those intense green eyes and he would know she was hiding something desperate.

Dr. Hawthorne said something else about DeWitt and Elise pulled her attention back to the other woman. Quick-witted and kind, Dr. Hawthorne was only a few years older than Elise. And the Bostonian was petite, with lustrous dark honey-blond hair and gray eyes.

Elise had never seen such a combination before. Dru's features were wide-spaced and well defined, her skin a creamy pale gold. Elise thought the woman striking in a unique way.

"Ever since DeWitt bought the bank, many are

having to come up with money they don't have to pay off their loans. He doesn't seem to have much mercy. In a way, it may have been better for Mrs. Delavant to leave before she saw what happened to her property."

"Could be." Gramps nodded thoughtfully.

"He's getting as much of a reputation as Mr. Onash."

Elise's heartbeat faltered and her gaze swerved to Dr. Hawthorne. "Mr. Onash?"

"You know, Elise, that Treasury agent." Gramps shifted on the exam table. "He's the one confiscated Justine's property, then sold it off to this new bank owner."

Elise nodded, her heart thudding with dread.

"They seem to be in competition to control the whole town." Dru undraped her stethoscope from around her neck and placed one end over Gramps' heart. She bent, listening intently for a moment, then moved to another spot under his ribs. "Or at least they did."

"Did?" Elise's throat ached.

"Well, no one has seen Mr. Onash in several weeks."

"Hmmmph," Gramps grunted. "Sounds like good riddance to me."

Dru smiled, straightening. "That seems to be the opinion of most people."

Elise's heart thudded and she turned back to the window.

Dr. Hawthorne stepped around to Gramps' back, placing the stethoscope on his ribs. "I heard your grandson has returned."

"Yes, he certainly has." Gramps' voice softened and Elise felt an unanticipated kick in her blood.

"I'm so glad."

"I'll bring him in to meet you sometime. He's probably never met a woman doctor before."

"I'd like that."

"So would he. Wouldn't he, Elise?"

"I'm sorry, what?" Elise moved away from the window, wondering what people were saying about Onash's disappearance.

"I said Jared would like meeting Dr. Dru, wouldn't he? A woman doctor and all."

"Oh, yes." She smiled and crossed her arms over her breasts, feeling suddenly very vulnerable. "I'm sure he would."

"The word is that your brother is coming home, too, Elise." Dru looked up, compassion stamping her features.

She nodded, trying to shove DeWitt out of her thoughts. "Yes, he is. Hopefully soon."

"Good. I'm glad." Dru's gray eyes darkened with sympathy and understanding. "One of my brothers didn't make it."

"I'm sorry." Elise could see in the doctor's eyes the same hurt she'd suffered and felt a sudden connection with this woman from a place she'd so recently considered an enemy. She touched Dru's arm.

The doctor smiled and stuffed the stethoscope in her apron pocket. "My other two did, though. I'm very thankful for that."

"Yes. That's wonderful." Elise really meant it and

offered a fervent prayer that Logan would soon be back at Fairbrooke.

Dru walked over to a small table crowded with bottles and bandages. "Thomas, your lungs sound good. I won't send any medicine with you this time, but I do want you to take care and watch what you do."

"I'd rather one of you ladies watched me."

Elise shook her head and shared a fond look with Dru.

The doctor grinned. "If I thought you were serious half the time, I'd really worry."

Gramps slid down off the table and lifted Dr. Hawthorne's hand, kissing it gallantly. "If I were younger, both you ladies would need to watch me very closely."

"I can't keep up with you now," Elise teased.

"Maybe Jared's more your pace."

Elise's gaze shot to Gramps, but he was grinning at Dru. He didn't mean anything by it, not really, but her heart gave a funny flip anyway.

Dr. Hawthorne walked them to the door and bade them farewell. She wanted to see Gramps in another week, to check his progress.

As Elise and Gramps walked back to the livery, tension lashed Elise's shoulders. Was DeWitt watching her again? Where was he? A sense of helplessness rolled over her and she bit back a groan of frustration. It wouldn't do to alarm Gramps, but she wondered how long she could tolerate this insidious sense of being watched, being manipulated.

Dread lodged in her throat, and despite telling herself that DeWitt had made his point and wasn't likely to come around again today, she fought the urge to look constantly over her shoulder.

"Elise, are you all right?"

The concern in Gramps' voice penetrated her fear and she gave him a brilliant smile. "Of course. Just thinking that I'd better watch you around Dr. Hawthorne."

"She seems a genuine person."

"Yes. She does." For the first time in years, Elise felt kinship with a woman over something besides the wait and worry of the next death list. It was a nice feeling.

And it was totally obliterated by the memory of Tullar DeWitt's brown eyes staring coldly, menacingly into hers.

Tullar DeWitt—she hated his name—wasn't going to leave her be until he got that money. He'd made that eloquently clear simply by his presence at Dr. Hawthorne's office.

Even an hour later, apprehension slid up Elise's spine. She stood in the barn doorway, her dress hiked up between her legs, as she worked over Majesty's right rear hoof.

Every whisper of the wind taunted her with DeWitt's words. Every creaking board made her shoulders tighten. Usually the sweet scent of hay and fallow earth reassured her, familiar scents, things that hadn't changed despite the war.

But today she couldn't rid herself of the memory of DeWitt's cold brown eyes, the fact that he'd been only inches from her in town. It seemed he would, indeed, follow her *everywhere*.

Dread lodged in her throat like a cold stone. She felt as if she were sliding into a dark void where she had no control. Despite the heat of the day, a chill snaked down her spine. She was going to pay the rest of her life for defending herself against Claude Onash. Even so, she knew she would do the same thing again.

Tears of frustration burned her eyes and she blinked them back. What would DeWitt do if she couldn't find the money? He seemed certain that she had it or knew where it was. How was she to convince him that she knew nothing about it? Perhaps she could talk to him.

Resistance rose at the thought, but she didn't totally dismiss it. She had to do something.

She removed Majesty's old shoe and dropped it to the ground, picking up the one she'd purchased from Coralee today. The chickens strutted around in the barn, squawking and gurgling. Majesty shifted and snorted, her tail flicking against Elise's back.

"I'm sorry, girl. I'm hurrying."

Elise stared down at the horse's hoof, seeing in her mind the cruel eyes of Tullar DeWitt, the sick triumph of knowing he had her at a disadvantage. Anger and fear slashed at her. She took a small nail and placed it in one hole of the horseshoe.

Her hands shook and she couldn't get a grip on Majesty's hoof. Sweat slicked her palms, causing the small hammer to slip, and Elise hit the side of the shoe rather than the nail.

The nail flew into the air and Elise drew in a quavery breath. "Blast!"

She had to get ahold of herself, but she was at her wits' end. Where was the money, if not at the sharecropper's cabin? She had no idea where else to look. And no one to turn to for help. She believed DeWitt's threat to send the sheriff after her. She couldn't involve anyone else, no matter how much she might want to confess. Helplessness slid through Elise and she bit her lip.

She redoubled her efforts to concentrate on Majesty's hoof and managed to drive in one tack. Majesty swished her tail, flicking Elise in the face with the coarse hair. She pushed both Majesty's tail and her own tangled curls out of her face.

Sweat dampened the fabric of her worn blue calico under her armpits and down the curve of her spine. The backs of her legs ached from bending. She'd already shod the other hoof, and it had taken nearly as long as this one.

Majesty stomped, causing Elise to scramble for balance. She drove in another tack, her mind racing to think of another place she could look, something she could do.

She had thought the nightmare of war was the worst she would ever have to endure, but Elise was afraid Tullar DeWitt had introduced her to a new kind of torture—sly, unpredictable, increasingly ominous— one that might never end.

She positioned another tack on Majesty's shoe and brought the hammer down. She missed completely, slamming her thumb with sharp, brutal precision. Crying out in frustration and pain, she threw the hammer as hard as she could. It somersaulted through the air and hit the ground, bouncing into the grass.

She dropped Majesty's hoof and stumbled blindly toward the hammer. There had to be something she could do. If she didn't find that money, what would Tullar DeWitt do to her?

She'd lied to him. Why? Jared stood several yards away from the barn, watching her. Even from here he could feel her frustration and that shimmering awareness he'd experienced before.

She had pulled her dress up between her legs, exposing trim calves, the curve of slender thighs. Heat streaked through him and he wondered how her eyes would look in passion—cloudy and soft as the sky at dusk? Or sharp and clear like the first brush of a storm?

As she worked over the horse his gut pulled one way, his heart another. He had questions to ask her, but instead he was concerned with the way her smooth brow furrowed in worry, the way her dress hung on her slight frame.

They'd all been through hell the last four years, he reminded himself, and Elise was strong. He'd seen glimpses of a velvet-gloved strength when she'd faced Anthony and Restin. The war had to have wrought changes in her, as it had in him. But how desperate were those changes? What did he really know of her as she was now, except that she was Logan's sister?

She'd lied about Onash, for certain. What else?

Reluctance crept through him. He didn't want to

ask her, but he had to. He couldn't let the tie of friendship or the new tenuous connection he'd felt with her this morning sway him from his job. He'd given his word to find the money and he would. Honor was all that was left to him now.

She drew back with the hammer, then cursed, yanking her hand quickly away from the horse's hoof. Jared winced as she threw the tool and dropped Majesty's leg.

She stumbled out of the barn and into the grass. She reached down to pick up the hammer, but instead of straightening, she sank to the ground. Jared took a step toward her and heard a choked sob.

She'd hurt herself. His gut clenched and he bolted toward her.

He skidded to a stop just behind her. "Elise?"

She gasped and twisted toward him, her skirts tangling around her ankles. She pushed herself up from the ground, surreptitiously wiping at the tears on her cheeks. "Oh, I didn't hear you ride up," she said brightly.

He frowned. "Are you all right?"

"Yes, of course." She straightened her shoulders, but they seemed so thin and fragile beneath the worn fabric of her dress. She wiped again at her cheeks, her eyes glimmering.

Her skin was pale and deep purple shadows rimmed her eyes. Despite the wavering smile on her pretty face she looked lost, and his heart turned over in his chest. "Are you sure?"

"I hit myself with the hammer," she said in disgust. "You'd think I'd never shod a horse before."

A sudden anger rose up in him that she even had to shoe her own horse. Just as quickly, he wondered why he should care. When the hell would Logan return? He, not Jared, should be looking out for her. But Jared had promised.

"Let me see."

"No, I'm fine."

She stepped around him, but he gently grasped her wrist, turning her hand up toward him. Her thumb was red and already swelling. He grimaced. "Ouch."

"Don't." Her voice shook.

He glanced up, shocked to see fresh tears roll down her cheeks. Loss and desperation darkened her eyes and the sight grabbed at something deep inside him, some primal protective instinct he'd never suffered concerning women. He knew damn well they could all take care of themselves, knew damn well that most used tears to their advantage.

He dropped her wrist, preparing to step away, and she sagged against him, sobbing.

Hell! His eyes widened. What was he supposed to do now? He'd never soothed a crying woman, couldn't abide them. His instincts screamed for him to go, but the misery in her sobs kept him locked in place.

Feeling completely inept, he muttered, "It's all right."

He wasn't sure she heard him. Her slender arms locked around his waist; her face burrowed into his neck. And his world crashed to a stop.

He didn't want this—to be clutched as if she depended on him, as if he could make a difference to her troubles—but he couldn't pull away.

Honor, his mind screamed at him. Honor demanded that he release her, separate himself from the sweet feel of her body, which was already affecting him. Yet the other side of that honorable sword demanded that he be the gentleman and comfort her.

His mind ordered him to step back, but his arms tightened around her. In some deep, hard place inside him, he needed to feel her warmth, her touch, as much as she seemed to need his. But the crying . . .

Lord! Sobs tore out of her, and the desperate way she turned to him made him feel he should know how to help. He didn't. Instinctively he knew she was crying over more than a smashed thumb, but he felt as useless as a gelding covering a mare. Helpless and incompetent.

He knew no soothing words to say, but his hands moved over her reflexively, stroking her shoulders, her back.

Breasts to his chest, her thighs teasing his, she draped down his body like a silk veil. He tried to close his mind to her, but his body responded swiftly, savagely, and opened into a long, pulsing ache.

Honor, his mind screamed again. He wouldn't touch her, except for this small bit of comfort.

She hiccuped against his chest and moved her head, her hair brushing his jaw. Reflexively he bent toward her, inhaling her sweet scent, her musky warmth. Desire tapped through him in a low, throbbing rhythm.

Honor. He pulled her tighter into him, burying his head in her hair. The soft lilac scent of her drowned his conscience. He stroked the thick curls that tumbled down her back, her hair sliding under his hands like silk. Sunlight threaded through the whiskey-brown strands until they shimmered with golden fire.

Her sobs had changed to soft ragged sounds against his shirt. A distant voice urged him to step away. But her arms were latched tight around his middle, her breasts teasing him with each breath she took. She snuggled closer, like a kitten seeking warmth, and their cheeks brushed. Lord, she was so soft.

He cradled her to him, grazing her cheek with his lips. They felt dry and rough against the smoothness of her skin. She shifted toward him, lifting her face to his, and his lips brushed her cheek again, even as caution peeled sharply through him.

Honor . . .

She turned her face to his and her lips found his unerringly. A sob shuddered out of her.

No, his mind warned even as his mouth opened over hers. He gripped her jaw, angling her head so he could reach her fully. She rolled up on tiptoe, meeting him, and the feel of her sweet hot mouth kicked through him like straight whiskey.

Desperate, hungry, searching, their mouths fused, easing a tightness in his chest. At the same time his body hardened in a surge of power, of want.

She lied about Onash. You have to ask her.

He wanted to back her up against the tree, raise her skirts, and pump into her with all the vicious energy churning in his body. Control finally penetrated the raging sweep of lust that had ruled him. With shaking hands, he gripped her arms and put her away from him.

"No," she moaned, reaching for him.

"Elise," he rasped, barely able to draw in a breath. His body shook with reaction and sweat slicked his palms. Lord. Oh, Lord.

She opened her eyes then and stared dazedly at him. Her mouth was swollen and red from his, her eyes sharp blue with desire. Then she flushed. "Oh . . . my stars."

"Forgive me." Heat shuddered through his body and a savage curse rose up in him. He'd never lost control like that. Never.

He cleared his throat, glancing at her though she kept her gaze averted. "I shouldn't have taken advantage of you like that. I'm truly sorry."

"No, Jared." She looked at him then, embarrassment flushing her cheeks. "You didn't take advantage. I did. You were only being kind and I threw myself at you like a ninny."

"It won't happen again," they said in unison.

His eyebrows arched.

A smile tugged at her lips.

Jared said stiffly, "I will never speak of it."

"I know," she said, sobering.

They stared at each other for a long moment, the silence growing awkward and stilted. Finally Jared pulled his gaze away and stepped around her, trying to tamp down the desire clawing through him, the memory of her ragged moan. "Is . . . everything all right, Elise? You're not in some kind of trouble?"

"Trouble!" She laughed shortly. "What kind of trouble would I be in?"

"You just . . . Something seemed to be bothering you when I rode up."

"Oh. Well, I'm fine now." She cleared her throat, glancing away. "Thanks to you."

He turned, studying her, wondering if this was her sly way of calling him to task for a kiss she had initiated. He frowned, able to discern only sincerity in her face. Perhaps he should press her about what was obviously bothering her, but instead he said, "Let me finish shoeing the horse for you."

"I'm sure you've plenty to do at Briar Rose. I'd hate to impose."

"You're not." He walked into the barn and lifted Majesty's foot. With three well-placed blows, he had the shoe in place.

Elise followed him to the door. "Thank you."

"You're welcome." He placed the hammer on a short workbench next to the wall and walked outside. How was he supposed to question her about Onash now, after that kiss? What the hell had come over him?

That kiss had addled his brain something fierce, had completely taken his mind off the reason he'd come here in the first place. "I brought you something."

"You did?" Her face was still faintly flushed and her eyes smoky with passion.

With effort, Jared forced his gaze away from her and strode over to Trick, unwrapping the bundle behind his saddle.

"A pump handle!" Elise moved up beside him, her arm brushing his. "Jared, thank you!"

Guilt twinged at her obvious pleasure. He wasn't using the gift as a bribe, not exactly. She did need the handle. And he needed to ask her some questions. "I could put it on for you."

"I'm afraid you'll have to. I have no experience with pump handles." She laughed in delight and ran her hands over the shiny new piece, as if he'd presented her with a new dress or a bonnet instead of a chunk of iron. She smiled up at him, her eyes glowing with pleasure. "You're doing far too much for me."

His body tightened at the way her hands stroked the length of the piece. He wanted to feel her hand on him. . . . Damn, if he followed these thoughts, he'd never find out why she'd lied about Claude Onash. Dryly, he said, "It's only a pump handle, Elise."

"I know." She grinned. "Isn't it wonderful?"

He chuckled as they walked over to the pump. Jared rolled up his sleeves and tossed his hat on the ground. Elise brought her father's wooden toolbox from the barn and set it next to Jared, then moved to sit on the edge of the porch.

"The town's changed quite a bit." He pried off the old pump handle. "There sure were a lot of unfamiliar faces today."

"I hate it that people come here to profit off the war," she said vehemently. "Some of them aren't so bad"—*like Dru*, she thought—"but others . . ."

He glanced at her, intrigued by the force behind her words. "At least Slim and his saloon are still around."

"Ah, so you were at Slim's." She grinned, a teasing lilt to her voice. "Gramps said you were going into town for business, not drinking."

She swung her legs and though each gentle billow

of her skirts revealed only the tops of her dainty black boots, he was reminded of the trim calves he'd glimpsed earlier. And the kiss they'd shared.

A soft heat spread through him and he deliberately kept his gaze focused on the pump rather than on her. "Funny thing, but you were the main topic of conversation."

"In the saloon! I don't think I like that. Why?"

"Word's out that you paid off your mortgage."

Her laugh seemed forced. "That's hardly news."

He leveled a gaze on her. "It is, if no one else can pay theirs."

CHAPTER FIVE

*H*is pointed observation stripped past the languorous desire still ebbing through her body. The same unswerving attention he'd devoted to that kiss was now turned on her in suspicion. Or was it merely curiosity?

Jared gazed unblinkingly at her, waiting, and Elise fought the urge to blurt out exactly where she'd gotten the money to pay the lien.

Sweat slicked her palms and she could feel the blood drain from her face. *Don't be intimidated*, she ordered. *It's only Jared. He means nothing by it.*

She couldn't let guilt prod her into saying something that might make him suspicious. *More suspicious*, she amended, chafing under his steady regard.

"Well, I suppose that would be worthy of gossip." She smiled, and forced herself to remain seated on the porch.

Frantically she tried to gather her wits, tried to dismiss the burn of Jared's lips on hers. He didn't know anything. He couldn't. He'd only brought up the

money because he'd heard talk about her in town today.

He pulled his gaze from her and looked down at the
pump handle. "Yeah, I suppose so."

She swallowed, her hands gripping the stone edge
of the porch.

"Slim said something funny about you, too."

"I can't believe no one had anything more interesting than me to talk about." She wanted Jared to leave,
pump handle or no.

His eyes narrowed to slits against the setting sun.
"He said Claude Onash used to talk about you quite a
bit, but I told him you didn't know the man."

"You did?" Apprehension snaked up her spine and
her bruised thumb throbbed. Jared's green gaze
seemed to pierce right through her soul. Certain he
could hear the thunder of her heart, she added teasingly, "Since when did you start listening to gossip?"

"Seems he had this notion of you marrying his
son." His gaze slid to hers and held.

Her mouth went suddenly dry and her throat ached.
What was she supposed to do? Confess that Claude
Onash had said exactly that just before she'd killed
him? She gave a small laugh. "Slim doesn't even have
a son!"

"Not Slim," Jared said flatly. "Onash."

"Oh." She licked her lips, tension knotting her
shoulders. "Well, if I didn't know the man, how would
I know that?"

Jared kept working, but Elise sensed that he had
stilled, like an animal sensing a snare. "I heard today
that no one has seen Onash for about two months."

"Yes, I heard that too."

He arched an eyebrow, his gaze measuring.

She had the startling sense that he was feeding out information like bait leading to a trap, but why? Unable to sit still any longer, she levered herself off the porch. "From Dr. Hawthorne," she said coolly, struggling to keep her voice even.

"Dr. Hawthorne?" Jared shook his head, frowning.

"She's your grandfather's doctor. She's new in town." Hoping to shift his attention, Elise plowed on. "She said Gramps seems completely healed, but she wants to see him next week. You can take him if you'd like. I think he wants you to meet her."

"A woman doctor, huh?" Jared eased off the rusted handle.

Elise laughed, refusing to wipe her clammy palms down her skirt. "That's exactly what Gramps said when he met her."

Jared's gaze lifted to hers, steady, strong, stirring. Her heart knocked against her ribs, and for a moment she feared he would pursue his curiosity about Onash.

"I appreciate your taking care of Gramps while I was gone."

Relief swept over her at his words. "I was happy to do it. Both of us were—"

"Alone." Jared stared at her strangely.

"Yes. And I've always been fond of him."

He grinned, shaking his head. "Most women are."

She smiled, the tightness in her chest easing. Perhaps Jared *had* only been curious about what he'd heard in town.

He tested the pump handle, then adjusted a part

near the spout, allowing her to shift the subject from Onash and her father's mortgage. And she had no doubt that he allowed it.

Despite the ease with which he'd slid into the subject, she had the very strong sense that he was suspicious about the money she'd used to pay the lien.

He finished quickly and rode out, but unease needled at her. Though Jared hadn't pressed her about Onash, she knew his pointed observations wouldn't be the end of it. Just as that kiss had sparked something impossible to ignore, so had their conversation.

And there wasn't a blessed thing she could do about it.

If she refused to answer his seemingly innocent questions, he would definitely pursue the subject. And she couldn't tell the truth. Perdition!

Her secret was safe, but she felt no relief. Instead she felt the dark, heavy pull of foreboding.

Sweet velvet surrender. Jared could still feel the heated glide of her lips against his, the teasing play of her tongue inside his mouth. Desire hammered through him.

He hadn't learned a damn thing except that he wanted her like hell afire.

He'd wanted her to dispel the suspicions gnawing at him. Instead they'd only sharpened, edging through him now in the wake of unease and dread. Why did he suddenly feel as if he were trapped in a slowly closing net?

Not only had he failed to corner her on everything that Slim had told him, but he'd kissed her. Since his

return home, he'd tiptoed around a growing awareness
of her and that first touch of her lips against his had hit
him with the force of a cannon blast.

Responsibility. Fascination. Want. They all layered
upon each other until he could scarcely tell the difference. Such different emotions, all for the same
woman.

Seething beneath it all was suspicion. She hadn't
avoided his thinly veiled questions, but she had sidestepped like a spooked filly.

Tangled with his suspicion and want was the abso-
lute certainty that she needed him. And the amazing
realization that he gave a damn. She had seemed genuinely troubled today and he wanted to comfort her.
He, who hadn't the slightest notion about such things.

Yet he couldn't ignore his suspicions. In fact, he
feared she was more involved than he had imagined.
For every leading observation he'd made, she had
danced away. He'd never played such a game with a
woman before, and while it frustrated him, he also
found it challenging.

He had allowed himself to be swayed by her obvious distress, but no more. One way or another he
would get his answers.

Long after he arrived home, thoughts of her
haunted him. The taste of her clung to him, soft and
sweet like a teasing bit of honey nectar. Annoyed, he
pushed thoughts of her away. As the sun dipped behind the mountains, he and Gramps made their way to
the creek behind the house.

Clear and cool, the water flowed over dark rock and
earth. Oak and poplar lined the bank, their green

leaves clicking in a sporadic breeze. Scents of grass and dirt and fresh air floated through the night. The dark red rays of fading sunlight skated across the glassy surface of the water like fire.

In the summer, he and Gramps bathed here every night. The thought of the creek had sustained him when he'd been stuck in sweltering mosquito-infested heat or slimed in mud up to his neck or fighting to escape the suffocating stench of blood.

He sank into the waist-deep water with a sigh, hoping to ease the ache in his body and stem thoughts of Elise. But the cool slide of water over his body reminded him of the velvet stroke of her tongue against his. His chest still burned from the weight of her breasts. He grew hard at the memory and looked down at his growing erection, cursing.

He didn't want or need complications like this. He had promised Logan to watch out for her until he returned, and Jared felt fairly certain that didn't include wanting her so badly he ached down to his core. Nor did it mean he could ignore the suspicions that had only intensified in the last few hours.

He glanced over at Gramps, who floated on his back in a spot just beneath a gnarled oak tree. Perhaps his grandfather could shed some light.

"I stopped by to see Elise today. Took her a new pump handle."

"Mighty fine," Gramps murmured drowsily.

Jared grinned, rolling onto his back to follow his grandfather's lead. "She was upset."

"Upset!" Gramps scrambled and splashed to a sitting position, finally righting himself. "Why? What happened?"

"Whoa!" Jared shielded his eyes against the late-day rays of the sun, looking at his grandfather. "She's all right. She wouldn't say what upset her, but I did ask."

Gramps ran a hand down his whisker-stubbled face. "She was acting a little strange in town today, too."

"Strange how?" Jared stood, steadying himself on a rocky shelf beneath the water.

Gramps shook his head. "I don't know. Restless. Preoccupied."

Jared was damn sure restless, though he doubted it was for the same reason. Savage want still coursed through his body and he couldn't rid his mind of the feel of her, the scent of her.

Gramps grabbed his razor and shave soap from a nearby rock on the bank. "You should ask her. She'll tell you."

"Somehow I don't think she would," Jared muttered.

With the straight-edge poised at his jaw, Gramps gazed sharply at Jared. "Elise isn't like other women. She's straightforward, dead-on honest."

"Nobody's honest all the time, Gramps," he said lightly.

"Elise is." Gramps threw the soap at him, then scraped at the whiskers on his jaw and chin.

Jared quickly washed his hair and face. Something about her put him on alert. While she had welcomed him, he had felt that she was anxious for him to leave, anticipating something. "You've become very fond of her."

"Every woman's not like your ma, Jared."

"I know that," he retorted, tossing the soap back to Gramps. But most were. He'd had enough experience with virgins and widows and whores. At least whores were usually honest in what they wanted from men.

At one time or another he suspected the motives of all women, and yet somehow other women seemed easier to read than Elise. Flirts or shy virtues, they wanted marriage or money or simply the use of a man's body. Elise seemed to want none of those things, at least not from him.

Gramps climbed out of the water, toweling off briskly. "Mark my words, boy. You give her a chance and you won't be sorry."

"A chance for what?" Jared said with a laugh as he climbed onto the bank.

Gramps eyed him speculatively. "I can tell interest when I see it."

Jared shifted uncomfortably. "It's nothing like that."

"Of course not." Gramps glanced at Jared's still evident erection and chuckled into his towel. "Of course not."

Hell! Jared snatched his own towel and vigorously scrubbed at his wet hair. He wished his interest in her were only physical. Wished he could pursue this burgeoning heat that spread through him every time he was near her. But the truth was at stake here.

Who was the real Elise? Warm and open on the one hand; guarded and reserved on the other. A woman had never so fascinated him. How could he be drawn to a woman he suspected of lying?

He'd wanted her to convince him that she hadn't lied about knowing Onash, but she hadn't. Now restlessness and misgiving gathered inside him like a stirring storm. He didn't know how or to what extent, but he knew Elise was somehow involved with Claude Onash.

Seeing her today, kissing her, had only whetted Jared's appetite for more. A deeply buried part of him longed to get to know her, to be near her, but he knew better than to be deceived by the urges of his body.

His job was to find her connection to Onash, and yet he couldn't ignore his promise to Logan. He was honor-bound to protect her. For that reason, he couldn't dismiss her obvious upset today. An hour later he found himself back at Fairbrooke.

His lips moved over hers with ruthless gentleness, coaxing, demanding a surrender she'd never given before.

She wanted Jared, with a fierce, deep longing that burrowed into her blood and lingered. She'd never wanted a man that way, certainly not Cal.

Elise lay in her bed, staring at the play of moonlight on the ceiling, trying to ignore the heaviness in her breasts, the ache between her legs. The house was quiet tonight, the silence cloying. She hadn't dreamed of the murders. She simply couldn't stop thinking of Jared.

She didn't want to be drawn to him. She was.

She hadn't meant to unravel like old yarn when he'd kissed her. She had.

She didn't want to think about him incessantly. She did.

Frustration boiled inside her and she surged out of bed, walking to the window. Midnight pressed across the land like a giant wave. Moonlight slanted over the familiar angles of the barn, slipped between the branches of the oak outside her window, but still she couldn't escape the feel of Jared's lips, the sense of security she'd felt in his arms.

Though she didn't want to replay that kiss over and over, neither did she want to allow the other thoughts that niggled. Thoughts of Tullar DeWitt.

She had turned to Jared out of desperation, out of the need for comfort, and he had given her that. But something unexpected, something . . . exhilarating had sparked between them. Even now her blood hummed at the thought. She recalled with aching clarity the feel of his back beneath her hands and the fierce possession of his kiss.

She knew he hadn't been unaffected. His arousal had pressed hard against her lower abdomen. At the memory, heat fluttered between her legs and she flushed in the darkness. *Wanton,* her conscience scolded, but her heart refused to heed.

For that brief instant of glory, she'd forgotten everything except Jared. And she had felt safe.

Then he'd apologized and said it wouldn't happen again. Disappointment stabbed at that, but she knew it was for the best.

Fear and arousal mingled. She couldn't stop thinking about Jared's kiss, but neither could she dismiss DeWitt's threat. After seeing him in town today, she had no doubt he would go to the sheriff as he'd threatened. Perhaps he already had.

No, she reassured herself. If he had, Restin already would have been to Fairbrooke. Still, a need grew to make certain that Claude and Pervis hadn't been disturbed, to check the sharecropper's cabin once more for the money.

She tried to squash the urge, but finally admitted she wouldn't be able to sleep until she'd gone there.

She shimmied out of her nightgown and pulled on her chemise and dress. With the weight she'd lost, she didn't need her corset. She hadn't worn it in months anyway and was glad to be rid of the infernal thing. She stuffed her feet into her sturdy everyday boots and crept downstairs. Even knowing she was alone in the house didn't prevent a chill from scuttling across her shoulders.

In the darkness, everything loomed dark and heavy. Shadows draped the corners, the edge of the stairs. In the foyer, moonlight sketched the wood floor, dimly highlighting the doorway to the sitting room, the dark shape of the table within. Moonlight filtered through a hole in the roof, playing crescent-shaped patterns on the floor.

Cool night air puckered her flesh and she hugged herself. Reaching the front door, she pulled it open and stepped onto the porch, staring out across the sooty night-blackened land as she moved toward the steps.

She would see for herself that Claude and Pervis were where she had left them, and perhaps she would find some clue about the money this time.

She drew even with the porch columns and a man stepped out of the shadows.

Startled, she stifled a scream, reaching into her skirt pocket for her revolver. "Who's there?"

"It's me, Elise." A masculine voice rumbled out of the darkness.

"Jared!" She exhaled loudly and lowered her gun, her heart kicking painfully against her ribs. "You scared me to death!"

"Didn't mean to."

"What are you doing here?" Her voice was sharp as she squinted into the darkness, now able to make out his broad shoulders and dark hair. He blended into the night, flowing shadow against the cool white of the porch column.

He turned toward her, and as her eyes adjusted to the dim light, she made out his carved features, tight with concern. Her heart still raced and awareness sizzled through her.

"I'm staying the night."

"You're staying— Whatever for!" Her gaze shifted to his lips, then away.

"It was obvious you were upset earlier." His voice dropped, husky and low. "I thought it a good idea that you weren't alone."

"So you decided to stay the night on my porch?" How was she supposed to go to the cabin now? His nearness unsettled her, made her want to smell the rich dark scent of him, touch him.

"Yes." He shrugged, reaching into his pocket. "Were you going somewhere?"

"Oh. No. Of course not." Certainly not now. "I . . . couldn't sleep."

He nodded and she heard the scrape of a match against his boot, then a flame flared. In the brief flicker of light his gaze measured her, speculative and steady. She shivered as he lit a cheroot and shook out the match. Silver smoke spiraled into the night.

She couldn't afford to raise his suspicions, not after his questions today. There would be no trip to the cabin tonight. Drawing in a deep breath of night air, she moved to the opposite pillar and leaned against it, fighting to appear relaxed. "It helps if I come outside."

"Elise, if you're in trouble, I'd like to help."

She stiffened, crossing her arms beneath her breasts, keeping her voice light. "I've already told you, I'm in no trouble."

He shifted toward her and the sweet scent of tobacco drifted across the porch. "Maybe you'd like to tell me."

His voice was soothing, seductive, not the least bit intimidating. Yet her skin prickled as if he'd issued a threat every bit as menacing as DeWitt's. Which was ridiculous. Jared had nothing to do with Claude Onash or the money. "There's nothing to tell."

"You can't sleep," he pointed out.

"Oh, that happens a lot," she dismissed airily.

"I might be able to help." His hand settled on her shoulder and she started, unaware that he had moved so close.

His heat flowed into her. She could feel the power of his body, coaxing her to yield her secrets. Moonlight played over his features, softening the hard line of his jaw, the sharp glint in his eye.

For an instant she wanted to go to him and let him hold her the way he had a few hours ago. "Don't be silly. I'm fine. You needn't stay."

"I've already decided." He removed his hand but stayed behind her.

She looked over her shoulder at him. "I've been here alone for some time now."

"Well, now *I'm* here."

The smug tone caused her to purse her lips. "Well, I can't invite you in."

"There's no need."

"You can't sleep on the porch!"

"Don't sleep much anyway."

"Why not?" She didn't want him to ask questions in return, but her query was out before she could stop it.

In a flash his features hardened and something tugged at her heart. Intrigued, she inched closer to him. "Jared?"

"Just can't sleep in a bed, that's all." He took a deep drag on his cheroot, tension vibrating from his body.

It was the first hint he'd given that he suffered aftereffects of the war. "Things were really bad, weren't they? No one will discuss it, but I know they were."

"It was bad for everyone." His flat tone revealed none of the restless energy swirling around him.

"But some suffered more than others—" Her voice broke as she thought about Logan, locked away in a blasted Yankee prison camp.

"Elise, don't do this to yourself." Jared shifted toward her, his eyes gleaming black in the shadows. "I swear on my honor that Logan will be fine."

"I know." She edged closer to him, wanting to soothe that restlessness, wanting to offer the same comfort he'd offered her earlier. Wanting to kiss him again. "I want to know about you. Will you be fine, Jared?"

His face shuttered against her, turned hard in the moonlight. "Of course."

She knew she should go inside, escape the seductive pull of his deep voice, the mystery lurking beneath his words that hinted at an unshared pain. She found herself wanting to know about him, what he'd suffered, what he dreamed. "I'm sorry you suffered—"

"Dammit, I didn't!" Defiance and anger crested on his features.

She stared at him in surprise. "You had to. Things were too awful—"

"No."

The single word lashed her and she drew back. Rage pulsed from him, a throbbing vital presence in the darkness.

"It wasn't me. It was . . . your brother. Old men, boys . . ." His voice cracked and he turned away. "Taken off to God knows where. Made to suffer unspeakable acts. All because I—" He broke off, agony raw in his voice.

Elise drew in a choked breath. There was something he hadn't told her about Logan. She knew it, felt it in the sudden burn in her chest. She gripped his forearm, pulling him back to her. "What happened to Logan? What are you keeping from me?"

"Elise . . ." Reluctantly, his gaze met hers. "I told you everything I know."

"But you said horrible things had happened to him. Because of you. How can that be? He was captured by Yanks. You said so."

He sighed heavily and his gaze dropped.

"Jared?" Panic nudged at her. "What is it? Is he—"

"Damn, I'm sorry. I shouldn't have started this."

"Well, you did! So finish it."

Indecision shadowed his features, then his shoulders sagged. He seemed to age right before her and his eyes darkened with unspoken horrors.

"Jared?" Her voice ached.

"We were on a night raid. It was my watch." The words exploded from him as if he couldn't suppress them any longer. As if he couldn't bear to hear himself say them. "We were behind enemy lines. I went over the ridge to check and they followed me back. The damn Yanks were right behind me and I never knew it."

"But—"

"Why didn't they take me? Why?"

His voice throbbed with agony, and Elise hugged herself, wishing away the pain that lanced her.

"What happened?" she whispered.

"They knocked me out and took him," he said hoarsely. "I looked everywhere for him, but there was no sign."

"Then how do you know he's coming home?" Desperation sharpened her words and her nails dug into his arm. "How do you know? Do you even know where he is? Or have you been telling me he's all right so I wouldn't worry?"

"No." His gaze, still tortured, met hers. "A friend in Washington has definitely found him. It's as I said. He will be home."

She studied his eyes, trying to discern if he was only attempting to ease her mind, but she could find only sincerity in the green depths. At last she sighed in relief. "Thank you. I know you did everything you could—"

"Did I?" His lips thinned and his eyes were ravaged by guilt, by uncertainty. "Why didn't I hear them?"

"That's not your fault."

"I could've stopped them."

"How? You were hurt as well."

"I—"

"You're blaming yourself and you mustn't. Logan knew the risks, just as you did. He wouldn't blame you. I don't, either."

"You should. I'm here. He's not."

"He'll be back." Only slight doubt quavered in her voice. "You said so."

"Yeah, I said so," Jared said with a self-deprecating twist of his lips. "At least I've kept my promise."

She stilled inside. "What promise?"

"I swore to look after his family."

"And he promised you the same thing." Such a thing was typical of Jared and Logan's friendship. So why did she feel disappointed?

Jared frowned. "Yes."

"So that's why you've been so concerned with my welfare."

Uncertainty clouded his eyes. "I don't—"

"That's why you're helping me, isn't it?" It stung to realize that his interest in her hadn't changed, the way hers in him had, and she challenged him quietly. "And what about that kiss?"

"I wouldn't say that helped either of us," he retorted, his eyes unreadable.

"Of course. You're right." She stepped around him, moving toward the front door, trying to dismiss the hurt his words had caused. "You're sure you don't need anything to make you more comfortable?"

He paused so long that she glanced over her shoulder.

"I'm sure," he finally said, his eyes glittering in the darkness.

"Very well. Good night." She walked inside and closed the door, her chest tight.

Loneliness, need, and frustration crowded in on her as she moved up the stairs and into her bedroom. She stared out the window all night, alternating between thoughts of the Onashes and of the man downstairs who had somehow become more than her brother's friend.

CHAPTER SIX

How did she always manage to get to the heart of him? What in hell had possessed him to blurt out his guilt about Logan's capture?

He knew why he'd done it. He wanted to erase that trust in her eyes. He felt suffocated by that trust. He didn't deserve it, not when he was trying to get her to admit a connection with Onash that she obviously wanted to hide.

Early the next morning, Jared leaned against the cool cypress column of the porch and smoked the last of his cheroot. The rich scent of tobacco wafted into the morning air. Sunlight, pale and butter-yellow, climbed over the hill and slowly peeled away the shadows of the night. He wished he could dispel his shadows as easily. Namely, Elise.

She was the one woman who could make him forswear every vow he'd made to himself after Mother. Elise could make him forget how he'd been abandoned and betrayed, how his father had given his heart to Jared's mother only to have her callously disregard his feelings.

After Jared's mother left, his father had gone after her. Charles Kensington had returned to Briar Rose a year later in a pine box, shot in a duel defending Cecily's honor. Jared's mother hadn't been heard from since.

Cecily was probably dead, and Jared didn't care one way or another. Because of Gran and Gramps, Jared had seen the truth and peace that a husband and wife could share. He knew it existed, but not for him. After what had happened to his father, Jared had vowed never to be vulnerable to a woman.

Elise was getting too close and so he'd withdrawn from her. Cursing, he took a long draw from his cheroot. He could still see the hurt in her eyes when he'd pretended that kiss was a mistake.

Temptation grasped him with an iron fist, tugging one way then the other. Her blue eyes had glowed with innocent passion, an eagerness to learn the mysteries between a man and a woman. He could have her, but at what price?

He knew her family, knew her brother, and couldn't imagine that she would blatantly lie and steal. But she was hiding *something*.

He'd definitely surprised her in the midst of leaving last night. If she were only restless, as she'd claimed, then why had she been fully dressed? Where was she going?

How was it that every time he got within five feet of her, his thoughts scrambled and he forgot he had a job to do? Well, he wouldn't forget again. He wouldn't be distracted again by the sweet lilac of her scent, the welcome heat of her touch.

He ground out his smoke and began to carefully search every inch of the area around the house, starting at the pump. Deliberately closing his mind to further thoughts of her, Jared searched meticulously through the grass, the barn, the outbuildings that housed the dairy and the kitchen, and came up with nothing.

He walked to the front of the house, intent on having a look around before Elise came outside. There seemed to be nothing out of place in front of the rambling stone dwelling or on the verandah that wrapped around the entire house.

The remains of his cheroot lay on the ground. He moved to the opposite side of the steps, cocking his head for a different angle. Sunlight slanted over the porch and he spied a spot in the stone that looked shades darker than the rest. His initial thought was that it was only shadow, but as he moved up the steps he saw the landing was stained.

Perhaps with age or dye. Circling the spot, which spread to the porch's edge, Jared spied a similar stain on the top step, but not on the others. The darker hue probably came from the natural cast of the stone, deepening as it aged.

Moving into the barn, he checked on Majesty and Trick. On seeing Jared, the stallion tossed his head and wickered. After a quick pat on the horse's neck, Jared brought in a bucket of fresh water for both horses. His search through the other stalls turned up nothing except bits of straw, old horseshoe nails, and a wooden bucket.

He tossed a fresh pitchfork full of hay in to each horse. Majesty snorted and stomped in appreciation. Trick poked his head over the wooden wall that separated them, sniffing her as she whinnied softly at Jared.

"You leave her be, Trick," Jared warned with a grin. "She's old enough to be your grandmama."

He whistled softly as he worked, the shadows of the night fading in the face of familiar activity. Just as he did every morning, Jared ran a careful hand over his stallion and checked the horse's feet for pebbles or loose shoes. He did the same to Majesty, smiling when the mare arched her head into his caressing hand.

Once finished with the horses, he poked through a stack of rusting and unused farm implements—hoes, shovels, scythes, but he found nothing suspicious. He glanced briefly at an old plow, then climbed into the loft.

Light streamed through the slatted wood, gilding the few pieces of straw scattered about. He wished he could forget how the moonlight had played over Elise's features, caressing her skin the way his hands itched to do.

Ever since he'd felt her body against his, he hadn't been able to stanch the image of her breasts, full and pale in his hands. The feel of her taut belly pressed to his. He wanted to peel her clothes from her body and run his hands over every inch of ivory skin. Even up here in the middle of dust and hay and dirt, he could smell the sweet woman scent of her, wanted to lay her down and explore her with his lips, his tongue, his teeth.

He heaved out a sigh and pinched the bridge of his nose. The sooner Logan returned, the better.

A sharp clang ripped through the air. Startled, he froze, his muscles tightening, alarm flaring inside him. Pealing and steady, the noise ricocheted inside the barn, stabbing straight through his skull.

Bang. Bang. Bang. Just like the pop of a gun. Or artillery fire.

Over and over, sound crashed through the stillness of the morning, ambushing him. He made his way carefully to the wall, peering out between the slatted wood. Unceasing. Clanging. The noise pounded through him.

He saw nothing, could only hear the incessant pounding, and up in the loft, the sound mushroomed. Louder, more shrill, deafening. The noise clawed through his skull, unlocking the images he hadn't allowed himself to remember.

Men screaming. Blood so deep it covered the sole of his boots. Smoke. Flames. Chaos. Guns and cannon firing and firing and firing.

Pictures merged. He and Logan fighting in hand-to-hand. Both of them falling. Horses screaming and flailing, going down. Blood covered the ground, the sky, burned the air. He couldn't stop the pictures. Or the noise.

Bang. Bang. Bang.

The images fused, gathering in a frenzy to roll through him like a runaway locomotive. Pain, guilt, shame. Jared winced and scrambled for the ladder, desperate to stop the noise.

The pounding ceased for a moment, and he hauled in a deep breath. Poised halfway down the ladder, he hung his head between his arms. His whole body shook and cold sweat slicked him from his nape to behind his knees. His chest heaved as if he'd run through enemy lines.

Then the noise started again. *Bang, bang, bang.* Over and over and over. His body jerked at each sharp sound and he stumbled blindly down the ladder.

He reached the door, realizing at last that it was only the clang of a hammer. He knew it had nothing to do with the war or Logan, but he had to make it stop. Intent only on that, he sprinted for the house.

Elise wielded the hammer as though it were a conductor's baton. Last night as she'd tossed restlessly in bed, she'd spied another hole in the ceiling, going clear through to the roof.

Thank goodness Jared was already gone. Though relieved, she was a tad disappointed too. She had lain awake all night, thinking of him, haunted by a sense of sadness. There was nothing she could do to alleviate his sense of guilt over Logan's capture.

Desperate to ignore the fact that she was on top of the roof—the *very* top—she focused instead on the steady rhythm of her pounding. And try as she might, she couldn't erase thoughts of Jared.

Despite the kiss, despite the sense that she had glimpsed a deeply buried part of him last night, Elise still recalled that intensely curious look in his eyes when he'd casually mentioned Claude Onash. She might not know Jared as well as Logan did, but she knew Jared Kensington didn't do anything casually.

Restless anticipation churned through her. He was definitely interested in Claude, but why?

She worked carefully, using the scraps of wood she'd gleaned from behind the house and around the cellar. She had precious few nails and used what she could from the old pieces before borrowing from Papa's nail supply, dwindled to nearly nothing in the war.

The steady lift and fall of the hammer should've kept her attention. Lord knew, she should focus on her task so she didn't slam another finger as she had yesterday. But she kept seeing Jared's eyes as they had been last night, tortured and deep and . . . needing.

She kept feeling his lips on hers, the warmth of his body wrapped around her, the comfort he'd offered. She had been able to give him none of that.

And she should be glad. There was something about him that warned her off, cautioned her to be more guarded. Just like finding him on her porch last night.

He had slipped out of the darkness like a night wraith and her breath had jammed in her chest in the moment before she'd recognized him, fearing that he might have been DeWitt. Or Restin.

Had Jared really been concerned about her welfare, as he'd said? Or was he watching her? She couldn't dismiss the possibility, especially after his pointed observations about Claude Onash.

There was no way he could know what she'd done to Claude and Pervis Onash. Jared hadn't even known them. But still, apprehension inched over her and her nerves pulled taut.

Slam! Slam! She would hammer Jared Kensington right out of her mind. The early-morning sun gained strength, creeping up into the sky and blazing onto the roof. Several swallows dove through the air and perched on top of the roof, twittering.

The small scraps of wood she used formed a lop-sided square over the hole, but at least they would keep out the rain. Her swollen thumb was a lovely purple-green color and she carefully kept it tucked into her palm. She stretched out on her stomach, using the lip of the roof for a foothold as she reached up to hammer on another piece of wood.

"Elise!"

Jared's voice boomed in the sudden quiet. She jerked, dropping the hammer. It skittered down the roof and she slid toward the edge. Shrieking, she grappled for a hold.

She bumped to the edge and one leg went over. Jared grasped at her skirts as she dangled precariously over the edge.

"Oh!" She squeezed her eyes shut, her nails digging into the roof. "Jared!"

"I've got you." One big hand wrapped around her upper thigh, completely exposed now due to her sliding descent. He braced his body against the ladder and the house, and hefted her to a more secure position.

With her face crushed against his chest, she reflex-

ively slammed her thighs together, imprisoning
Jared's hand between them. Her heartbeat wild and
flittery and she glanced down, mesmerized by the
darkness of his hand against the pale cotton of her
stockings.

"You all right?" His breath misted her face.

She made the mistake of looking down. The
ground spun and dizziness swept over her. Dragging
her gaze back to him, she swallowed. "Yes."

"Good." He smiled.

She became suddenly aware of their intimate position. Reaching over his arm, she shoved down her
skirts as best she could, her blood sizzling with a startling wildness. Her heartbeat wild and fluttery in a
frightening blend of exhilaration and danger.

It was confusing. It was exciting. It scared the wits
out of her.

His green eyes were sharp with a mix of hunger and
resentment. She recognized that, though she didn't
understand. She knew she should move, but was reluctant to leave his solid strength. "Forevermore!
Why were you yelling at me like that?"

"That infernal hammering," he growled.

"Well, you nearly scared me into falling!"

"You nearly split open my skull with that noise."
Tight lines bracketed his mouth.

She could still feel the heat of his hand on her
thigh, and she flushed. Flustered by his smoky masculine scent, she asked crossly, "What are you doing
here? I thought you were gone."

He levered himself onto the roof beside her. "I was
in the barn, looking after the horses."

"Oh."

They were both breathing hard, and Elise noted the rapid tap of his pulse in the hollow of his throat.

The tension eased from his features and he grinned, thumbing back his hat. "You're pretty jumpy."

"Well, you would be, too, if someone was sneaking around scaring the wits out of you!"

"I didn't exactly *sneak*."

"You came up behind me like a snake in the chicken house!"

He laughed, a rich, full-throated sound that made her want to smile. "A snake! Now hold on!"

"And last night, you scared the life out of me. Hiding like that on the porch." She tugged at her skirts again, feeling the need to cover herself as much as possible. "I do not like being surprised, sir."

"All right. I *have* surprised you twice, but I wasn't sneaking."

"Sneaking," she said firmly.

His lips twitched. "I apologize."

"You're not the least bit contrite." She pursed her lips to keep from smiling. "But I suppose I must thank you for rescuing me."

"I suppose. Are you sure you're all right?"

His voice drifted over her and she looked up to find his gaze fastened on her lips. Again that secret heat fluttered inside her.

His eyes darkened. "Perhaps I should beg your forgiveness."

For what? She couldn't remember. All she could focus on was this raw need flaring to life inside her, the way her skin tingled, and the spot on her leg that still burned from his touch.

"For scaring you," he quietly reminded, as if he knew exactly where her mind had wandered.

"Yes," she said hoarsely, leaning slightly toward him. "I think you should beg. Forgiveness."

Tension arced between them, and Elise ached deep in her soul.

"I think," he said in a low voice, "I should help you with the roof."

The roof? She blinked. "Oh, yes."

"You shouldn't be up here doing this yourself."

"And who else is going to do it?" Disappointment nipped at her, but he had been right not to kiss her. "I'm perfectly fit. And despite what you saw yesterday, I can wield a hammer."

"I won't feel that you've forgiven me unless you allow me to finish for you."

"Very well. I'll help you and we'll finish that much faster. I'm sure Gramps is wondering where you are."

"He knows."

"He does?"

"Of course." Jared moved past her on his hands and knees, picking up the hammer and another scrap of wood to continue the job.

"He doesn't mind you going off at all hours of the night?"

"He wants to know you're safe."

Perhaps Jared *had* only come last night out of concern, but she couldn't ignore the sense that there was another reason.

He arranged two scraps of wood in such a way that

they overlapped and formed a shingle. Impressed, Elise handed him a nail and Jared hammered it into place with a single careful blow. They found a rhythm of sorts and for a short time worked in relative silence. She noticed that he used the hammer far less than she had, although his work seemed to be more sturdy.

Unable to forget that jolting moment between them a few minutes ago, she found his presence at once reassuring and unsettling.

"I expected you to be married by now."

"What!" Elise's jaw dropped.

He plucked a piece of wood from her hand. "To Cal."

"Oh." Though she imagined Jared had known of her betrothal, she certainly had not expected him to take an interest.

"I know he returned from the war. Gramps told me."

"Yes." She hesitated, wondering if he would pursue this issue as single-mindedly as he pursued that of Onash. "You know, Jared, you don't have to do this. I can do it."

"Elise, don't misunderstand," he said quietly. "I'm not asking because I think you should have a man looking after you."

"What is it you're not asking?"

"Why you and Cal aren't getting married."

"Is this something else you learned in town?" She couldn't keep the sharpness from her tone.

"No. Gramps told me." Jared glanced at her. "You don't have to say. I'm simply . . . curious."

Jared Kensington wasn't *simply* anything, but Elise

didn't say it. While she wasn't embarrassed by Cal's breaking their engagement, neither was she overly anxious to discuss it. But Jared *had* asked. "He couldn't provide for me or a family and felt that we shouldn't marry."

"I'm sorry."

His sincerity prompted her to venture further. "It was a shock and I was hurt at first. But I'm fine."

"No, you don't appear to be pining away." He eyed her speculatively. "Weren't you in love with him?"

"I liked him and we got along famously, but we were friends. Only friends," she added reflectively.

"He didn't make you swoon?"

Elise studied his rugged profile, wondering at the abrupt harshness in his voice. "No. Not really."

"So a man must make you swoon to be considered suitable for marriage?"

"I didn't say that." She frowned at the sharpness in his gravel voice. "I only said Cal didn't affect me that way. I take it you think I'm silly."

"Naive," he said baldly. "Lust plays havoc with your body and your mind. You shouldn't trust it. You certainly shouldn't base the decision of your future on it."

Had he always been so cynical? "I'm not basing any decisions on *lust*. I want to marry for love, and while I loved Cal like a brother, I wasn't *in love* with him. I mean, I thought I was, but . . . And what about you?" she challenged.

His head swerved toward her. "What about *me*?"

"Haven't you ever wanted to marry?"

"No."

His flat, unemotional tone intrigued her. She could remember Jared with lots of girls, but no special one. "Why not? Your grandparents were married for a long time."

"My Gran was very special. Too bad there aren't more women like her."

"I agree." Jared's grandmother had died when he was fifteen. Elise had often thought that Mavis Kensington had weathered away with love and gentle guidance the bad memories of a mother who had abandoned Jared, but what had happened to his father? "You judge all women by your mother?"

"Try not to judge them at all." He drove home a nail with particular force, his blunt tone causing her to feel a prick of disappointment.

So, he tarred all women with the same brush. "What about your father? What happened to him?"

"He was a fool." Jared leveled a steely gaze on her, declaring the subject off-limits. "What about you? Do you want a family?"

"Yes, someday."

"Any new prospects for a husband?" His tone changed again, now light and casual.

Not if I'm in prison for murder. Elise handed him another scrap of wood and spoke over the slam of the hammer. "If you haven't noticed, not too many boys returned from the war."

He stiffened as if he'd been cornered with a bayonet, and Elise wished she could take it back. Had the sad truth of her statement reminded him of Logan?

"I'm sorry," she said.

He spoke in a flat monotone, as if he hadn't heard her. "You could've married Claude Onash's son."

"I wouldn't marry that miserable—" Caught off guard at his words, she barely collected herself. "I couldn't marry someone I didn't know."

"Ah, yes. That's right." He eyed her thoughtfully.

Elise had the sinking suspicion that she'd just failed a test. "Yes. And I wouldn't marry anyone who worked for the Treasury Department. Corrupt no-accounts, all of them."

His lips twitched. "Surely there are some honest ones lost among the bad?"

"I doubt it."

"Why?"

How could she tell him without revealing that she knew Claude Onash, that she had killed the man and his son? "As a whole, the men who work for the Treasury have the reputation of brigands and liars. I've seen what they've done down here, how they've taken advantage."

"True enough." Jared moved to another hole they'd discovered above the one he'd patched. "It's funny you didn't know Onash, Elise. He sure talked about *you* a lot."

"What do you mean? Why would he?" She sounded unnerved, even to her own ears.

Jared gave her nothing more than a glance, yet she felt as if his regard never wavered. "Seems he wanted Fairbrooke."

"What!" How had Jared learned that?

"He told Slim he'd been out here a couple of times, that he'd spoken to you about buying it."

Apprehension knocked against her ribs. Why wouldn't Jared leave this alone? "Nobody ever spoke to me about buying Fairbrooke."

"Coralee Bronson said that the last time Onash was seen, he was on his way out here."

"Coralee!" Elise straightened so abruptly, she nearly toppled backward off the roof. She steadied herself with a shaking hand. "You saw Coralee at Slim's?"

"No."

"Why do you keep bringing up Onash?" Her voice thinned as she struggled to maintain her composure. "I told you I didn't know him."

Jared laid down the hammer and turned to her, his green gaze piercing. "Look, Elise, I heard some things in town the other day. And if I heard them, the sheriff's bound to hear them, too."

"What kind of things?" Her throat went as dry as stale flour and her nerves stretched taut.

Jared drew up one knee and rested an elbow on it. "That Onash had been out here. Remember, the sheriff asked and you said he hadn't?"

"I said no one ever spoke to me about buying Fairbrooke. No one ever did." His steady regard made Elise feel every bit as vulnerable as when she'd been dangling from the edge of the roof minutes ago.

Jared's voice was quiet, but deliberate. "And what about what Coralee said?"

"Someone came out here asking about Delavant Hall. That's probably what Coralee is thinking about. I don't know if it was Onash. The man didn't give his name."

"Right."

His gaze seared into her soul and pressure squeezed her ribs. Jared's probing questions made her feel as though she were being woven into a snare. She was tempted to scream out the truth, but she couldn't.

"Onash told several people he intended to have Fairbrooke. Yet you told Sheriff Restin that Onash didn't speak to you about buying it."

"I believe I said Mr. Onash never spoke to me about the lien." Elise's mind raced. *Exactly* what had she said to Sheriff Restin and Mr. Anthony that day when she'd paid off the mortgage?

"Did you ever speak to Onash?"

Panic sheared through her and she inched toward the ladder. "What is this, Jared? Why are you so curious?" She gave a nervous laugh. "I feel as though I'm being interrogated."

He sighed and rubbed the back of his neck. "If I find it hard to believe that you didn't know the man, so will the sheriff. If you're hiding something, he'll find out."

"Just like you think you did?" she snapped.

His gaze pierced her, peeling away every layer until she felt he could see her black soul. "The sheriff will ask you these same questions, Elise. If you know something, tell me."

"But I don't." It was so tempting, the thought of confessing everything and hoping that Jared would understand, stand beside her if it became necessary.

He eased closer to her and she gripped the ladder.

"I can help you, Elise."

He couldn't. If she were discovered, no one could.

And how could she involve him? He was the only person Gramps had left. They'd survived the war together and she simply couldn't risk involving Jared in this.

She managed a shaky laugh. "Go on with you! There's nothing to tell, but thanks for your concern."

She expected him to press further, but when she glanced at him, his attention was focused on a point beyond her.

"Someone's coming."

She turned, squinting down the long tree-lined drive and into the sun. "It's a man, I think."

He moved to the ladder. "I'll take care of it."

"I have my gun."

He put one foot on the top rung. "Maybe it won't be necessary."

Elise watched the person walking down the drive. Yes, it was a man. Nearly as tall as Jared. And limping. She followed Jared down the ladder, stepping quickly away when he lifted her down.

Together they walked to the edge of the circular drive and Elise shielded her eyes against the sun.

The man drew closer and hope flared. *Please tell me something about Logan*, she pleaded silently as the stranger drew nearer. His gait, though uneven, struck a chord within her and her breath caught in her throat. "Logan!"

"Elise, wait!"

Jared reached for her, but she was already moving. She snatched up her skirts and flew down the drive, oblivious to the pebbles pricking her soles through her worn shoes. Logan was home. At last.

"Logan!"

Her brother picked up his pace, stumping unevenly toward her. Relief and joy swelled in her chest. He was home! Just as Jared had promised.

She could feel Jared at her shoulder, but her attention focused on Logan as she ran into her brother's outstretched arms. He dropped a crude stick and crushed her to him, lifting her clear off the ground.

Elise hugged him and kissed him and clasped his beloved face between her hands, feeling his whisker-rough skin. Wiry strands of silver shone in his dark hair, and tiny new lines fanned out from his blue-gray eyes. His face was worn and tired, but still handsome.

"Oh, Logan!" she sobbed, squeezing him tight. "How are you? Are you all right?"

"I'm home, little one. I'm home." His voice sounded rough as sand, and he clasped her tight. She felt him shift, then move one hand, extending it to Jared. "Kensington. What a relief."

"I'm glad to see your ugly face." Jared's voice was rough with emotion, causing Elise's eyes to burn. "Welcome home."

"Thanks for finding me," Logan said quietly.

The men clasped hands behind her and she squeezed her eyes shut, soaking in the security of the tight circle they made. Logan was home. Everything would be all right.

CHAPTER SEVEN

*F*or the moment, she pushed Jared's warnings about the sheriff to the back of her mind. Now that her brother was here, Jared wouldn't be spending so much time at Fairbrooke.

Her relief was pierced by a sharp stab of disappointment, but she quickly turned her attention to Logan. She could tell him about Onash! He would know what to do.

But as she took in her brother's appearance, uncertainty niggled at her. His once broad shoulders were stooped and frail. Though it was late summer, he wore his full uniform, which hung as though two sizes too big, yet his skin felt clammy to the touch. His collarbone jutted out sharply; his eyes were sunken in a pinched face. His skin, though burned by the sun and wind, was tinged with a gray pall. But the look in his eyes gave her the most pause—they were hot and bitter and hard.

"Let me look at you." Logan's blue-gray gaze studied her, reflecting a sad pride. "You're beautiful, Elise.

I guess I hadn't expected you to grow up while I was away."

"I still have these." She grimaced, indicating the sprinkle of freckles across her nose.

He laughed and hugged her. "Yes."

"I knew you would come back," she said happily. "Jared gave me the glove."

Logan nodded, shadows crossing his face.

"Jared said you were in Ohio. Was it terrible?" She released him, shocked at the feel of his ribs beneath her hands. "Are you sure you're all right?"

"I'm fine." He coughed, a sharp hack that made Elise wince. "Where are Mama and Papa? Rithy?"

"Logan . . ." She glanced at Jared.

Her brother caught the look and said sharply, "What is it?"

Jared reached out, but Logan batted his friend's arm away. "Tell me, dammit! What's happened?"

"They're . . . they were . . ." Elise's eyes burned, but she wouldn't cry. It would only upset Logan further. Pain and anger merged. Why did she have to greet him with this kind of news?

Logan's fingers bit into her shoulder. "Elise?"

"They were killed." She could barely get the words past her tight throat. "Murdered."

Shock flashed through his eyes and he grasped her shoulders. "What! Both of them?"

"Yes."

Jared stood quietly, his features pained.

Logan shuddered and her heart clenched. He'd been through so much already, and now this. "Logan, I—"

He crushed her hand in a bruising grip. "Who? Looting Federals? Bloody bastards! I'll kill them!"

"No, Logan!" Startled, Elise grabbed his arm, absently noting the stiff feel of dirt embedded in his gray coat. Glancing at Jared, she tried to calm her brother. She'd never seen him like this. "No, not Yankees."

"Who then?"

She realized her mistake too late. She couldn't very well tell the truth with Jared standing nearby. "No one knows. I found them on the porch."

"Rithy, too?"

"Yes."

"No one saw anything?"

She wanted desperately to blurt out everything, but now was not the time. She forced herself to shake her head. "No. Nothing."

"Isn't the sheriff working on it? Doesn't he have any leads? How can three people be murdered and no one have a clue?"

She wanted to tell him that she'd snatched a small inkling of justice, but she could only stand and watch her brother's anger and suffering. "The sheriff says there's nothing to go on."

"By damn! I'll kill whoever did this—" He broke off, choking and coughing with such force that his chest seemed to rattle.

Elise reached for him. "Please, Logan. You'll hurt yourself."

"She's right," Jared put in.

Rage flushed Logan's face and his eyes glittered with such hatred that Elise drew back.

"Logan—"

"I can check into it for you."

Jared's quiet offer had Elise jerking toward him. "What?"

He shrugged, looking at Logan. "I can talk to the sheriff, if you like. I've got business in town tomorrow."

"Yes. Do."

No! Elise wanted to scream. Don't give Sheriff Restin a reason to come out here. But she could say nothing.

Logan turned toward the cemetery. "Are they there?"

"Yes."

"How could Papa let this happen? Why didn't he do something?"

"I'm sure he did the best he could, Logan." She shivered, not wanting to recall that bloody day. Nor did she want to step around the truth as she needed to do. "He was discharged because of injuries. He'd lost one eye and an arm."

"Dear Lord." Logan's voice cracked and he bowed his head. "I had no idea."

She hated this, hated telling her brother that their parents were dead, hated telling him that she didn't know who was responsible. She tugged on his arm. "Come up to the house. I can get you some water or make you some tea."

"Got any whiskey?" he asked Jared.

Jared shook his head, grinning. "Not with me."

"Get me some."

At Logan's demanding tone, Elise exchanged a look

with Jared. He shrugged and fell into step beside them.

"Are you hungry?" Elise hugged his arm, thrilled to have him home. "There's not much, but—"

"Don't baby me," he growled. "I'm not a baby."

Elise blinked. "Of course you're not. I just thought . . ."

"I'm sorry, little one." He squeezed her hand. "I'm not used to the attention. I'm sorry."

"It's all right." But Elise couldn't ignore the hurt at her brother's brusque treatment. *He's been through a lot,* she told herself. *It will take time, for all of us.*

Elise slowed her steps to match her brother's, and Jared trailed behind. Logan stumped unevenly up the porch steps, leaning heavily on the stick and on her.

He halted on the landing, looking around. "The place looks good."

"She's done it by herself." Jared moved up beside Logan and smiled.

Her brother stared out over the grass and trees, to the cemetery beyond. Fatigue deepened the lines fanning out from his eyes, the creases around his mouth. He seemed so frail.

She hugged him gently, carefully, frightened at the unsteadiness of his body. *Oh, Logan, what did they do to you?*

He turned to Jared. "Kensington, I appreciate everything you did."

"Wasn't much."

"Nonsense," declared Elise. "He helped a great deal. We were patching the roof when we saw you coming up the drive."

Logan eyed Elise. "*You* were on the roof?"

"Well, that hole wasn't going to fix itself."

At Jared's curious look, Logan explained. "One time we climbed up there and I jumped down on the other side and took away the ladder. She was scared witless. Wouldn't jump down so I left her up there and went fishing. She stayed up there until Rithy climbed up to get her."

"I've never forgiven you for that," she glared playfully.

He sobered instantly. "I'm sorry you had to go up there."

"Nonsense!" Shocked at the guilt lining his face, she hurried to reassure him. "I was fine. Besides, Jared came up to help."

"I imagine Cal's been helping as well."

Not this, too. When she didn't answer, Logan turned to her, his eyes narrowing.

"*Has* Cal been helping you, Elise?"

"Not exactly." Leery of her brother's abrupt moods, she hesitated.

Pain darkened Logan's eyes and he asked hoarsely, "Was he lost?"

"No." Elise touched his arm. "He made it home just fine."

"Then what?"

She glanced at Jared. "Do we have to discuss this now?"

"Don't worry about Kensington. He's as good as family."

She sighed. "We are no longer betrothed."

"Why not?" he barked.

"Cal felt he couldn't provide for me and he didn't want to take a wife that way."

"If you want him, I can change that, Elise."

"If I want him?" She shook her head, pleased that some facets of her brother remained unchanged. "Logan, he's not a fish we threw back or a bonnet I've had my eye on. Don't be silly."

"I don't want you dishonored." He scowled.

"Forevermore! You know Cal better than that. He was a perfect gentleman and I know he felt just awful about breaking the engagement. It was humiliating enough for him to admit it to me." She looped her arm through his. "Besides, he and Lindy are gone anyway. They moved just after the war."

"Like so many others," he said tiredly.

"Yes."

As they walked toward the house Elise sneaked a glance at him. His appearance was familiar, reassuring, yet she felt she barely knew the man beside her. She had so anticipated his arrival, eager to share jokes with him and to experience the overprotectiveness she'd so often complained of in the past. But this new Logan was a stranger.

Nonsense. He simply needed time to get back to his old self. Elise smiled. "I've been saving up for your return. I'll cook a chicken for supper tonight. And some sweet potatoes."

"Sweet potatoes." Logan closed his eyes, a rapturous look stealing across his face. "I haven't had sweet potatoes in years."

"You'll have them tonight."

"Kensington, you and your grandfather come for dinner."

Uneasy with the prospect of facing more of Jared's scrutiny, Elise's gaze shot to him.

He eyed her speculatively, as if he knew she didn't want him to stay. "We wouldn't want to intrude on your first evening home."

Elise breathed a sigh of relief.

But Logan insisted. "Do we have plenty of food, Elise?"

She hesitated an instant too long. "For four, yes, I suppose."

Logan shot her a sharp look. "I want you to come, Kensington."

"We'll bring something, too. Greens and preserved pears—"

"And whiskey," Logan put in.

"And whiskey." Jared grinned, shaking the hand his friend had extended. He halted at the bottom of the porch steps. "I'd better be going."

"We'll see you around seven," Logan called, walking inside the house.

"All right."

Elise started to follow Logan, but was halted by Jared's hand on her elbow.

"I apologize again for scaring you, up on the roof. I had no idea . . ."

"I'm fine." She turned to him with a soft laugh. "No harm done."

She didn't want to recall the gentle strength that had prevented her fall or the touch that even now burned her thigh.

Jared's gaze measured her, then moved thought-fully to the door behind her. "He'll be fine, Elise. He just needs to rest up."

"I'm sure you're right." She smiled, relieved and at the same time disappointed that Logan's return meant the end of Jared's frequent visits. "Thank you for helping me. And for finding Logan."

"My pleasure." He tipped his hat, then walked the length of the house and crossed to the barn.

She waited on the porch, suddenly aching with a sense of loss. As Jared rode out of the barn she lifted a hand in farewell.

He reined up in front of her. "Remember what I said. I might be able to help you if you're in some kind of trouble."

"Jared—"

"Just remember." With that, he kneed Trick and set off at a canter down the drive.

She was tempted to call him back, confess every-thing, especially after the shock of seeing that her brother wasn't as she remembered. But she didn't. Jared couldn't help anyway.

She went inside and closed the door, walking si-lently to the doorway of the parlor. Logan stood with his back to her, staring at something on the rose silk-covered wall in front of him.

Despite her relief and joy, she approached him cau-tiously, telling herself that Jared was right. After a lit-tle time, Logan would be healed. But the reassurance didn't stop the sinking of her heart. She couldn't tell him about the Onashes. Not yet.

Jared's warnings crowded back. As relentless as his

questions had been, she knew the sheriff would be merciless. She had to go to the sharecropper's cabin and make certain all was undisturbed. Tonight, after Logan was asleep.

Jared rode for home, his thoughts seesawing between Logan and Elise. Jared's pleasure at his friend's return was underscored by disquiet. Logan looked like hell and his ebullient spirit had withered into a bitter, dark one. He hardly seemed strong enough to take care of himself, let alone Elise.

You shouldn't care, reminded a pragmatic voice in Jared's head. *Your role as protector is over.*

With Logan home, Jared intended to discard this protectiveness that seemed to rule him with regard to Elise. Resentment surged through him. He was *not* her keeper.

He had a job to do and would have to flat ignore the want, which even now knotted his gut, engendered by their encounter on the roof. The heat of her leg had burned his palm, and when her thigh had tensed beneath his touch, he'd been assaulted by the mental image of those legs wrapping around his hips, drawing him into her sweet warmth.

This damn awareness seemed to increase threefold every time she was near. Despite his knowing that she was somehow mixed up with Claude Onash and his son. And he knew she was, as sure as he knew his own name.

He had expected her to jump out of her skin when he'd told her what he'd learned in town, yet she hadn't panicked. She had an answer for everything.

Her answers had been specific, and at the same time, misleading.

I said no one ever spoke to me about buying Fairbrooke.

I said Mr. Onash never spoke to me about the lien.

Strangely, Jared believed both those things to be true, but her answer implied that Onash had never visited Fairbrooke. Jared never took anything on implication.

Onash had told too many people that he intended to have the place for Jared to believe the man hadn't approached Elise, or at least her parents, about the plantation.

She had also referred to Onash's son in the past tense, not the present, which Jared found powerful curious.

He shook his head, a reluctant grin edging his lips. She was shrewd, he admitted. And cagey as a wildcat. He admired the way she managed a tightrope dance of words, but he also had to get to the truth.

She was hiding something with a desperation that surrounded her like that soft lilac scent she wore. At just the mention of Onash's name, her eyes had fringed with near panic.

He hoped Elise heeded his warning, such as it was. If he was questioning her about Claude Onash, it wouldn't be long before Sheriff Restin did the same.

He'd tried dancing around the subject and gotten nowhere. Every time he tried to corner her, he came away with nothing. He'd never been so distracted from a single purpose, not even with bullets coming at him or when he had stared down the length of a bayonet.

The time had come for plain speaking. And he intended to start tonight at supper.

"My dear, you positively put the moon to shame."

"Gramps, you're an incorrigible flirt!" Elise smiled as he kissed her hand. "I'm so glad you came. We can celebrate Jared and Logan's return. And your bill of good health from Dr. Hawthorne."

Gramps' eyes twinkled and he glanced at Jared. "I was beginning to think you preferred my grandson's company to mine."

Jared shot Gramps a dark look.

"Nonsense," Elise said, feeling a little flutter in her stomach. "You're welcome anytime."

Jared doffed his hat, his gaze tracking over her with unsettling thoroughness, from the hem of her turquoise silk to the stray curls that framed her face. She fought against the flush that heated her blood.

"You look lovely, Elise." His quiet voice stroked over her and she nodded, her smile faltering slightly.

Though her scooped neckline was modest, cut only to the beginning swell of her breasts, she wondered if she should have lined her cleavage with a handkerchief. When she donned the turquoise dress, she'd thought only of welcoming Logan home in her best remaining gown. But perhaps this had been a mistake.

Jared stared at her hungrily—as if he'd like to touch her—and she wondered fleetingly, shockingly, what it would feel like.

Sensation fluttered again in her belly and she pulled her gaze from his, taking his hat. "Please come into the dining room. Logan's waiting for us there."

With an apologetic look, Jared held up a half-full
bottle of whiskey. "You might want to put this away
until after supper."

"Yes—"

"Ah, good. You're here." Logan stumped into the
doorway just as Jared was handing the bottle to Elise.
"I'll take that, sweet sister."

He plucked the bottle out of her hand and swept
his arm out in an expansive gesture. "Gentlemen,
come into our home and feast your eyes on the lovely
remains."

Gramps' eyes widened and Jared frowned.

"Logan!" Appalled, Elise cast a quick glance at
Jared and hurried to her brother, intent on smoothing
over the awkward moment. "Please, come in. Supper's ready and we can sit right down."

She saw no reason to point out that only four of her
mother's twelve chairs remained to march along the
walnut dining table, or that places in the rose silk wall
covering had worn away or that the sheer lace curtains
had wilted at the windows.

Logan shrugged and eased himself into the closest
chair at the end of the table near the door. Jared and
Gramps pulled out the chair next to Logan's and
waited as Elise sank down. Both took seats across
from her.

She had set the table with her mother's pale, fine
bone china, which had remained safely hidden in the
cellar throughout the war. The table looked pitifully
bare when compared to the large spread of meats,
breads, sweets, and vegetables they'd enjoyed in the

past, but as long as they were together with enough food for everyone, Elise was well satisfied.

She noted uncomfortably that Logan uncapped the whiskey and poured a healthy amount into a crystal goblet, not even waiting until after dinner.

Disquiet inched through her. She'd considered again telling Logan about the Onashes as soon as Jared had left, but her brother had disappeared and she hadn't seen him until minutes ago.

"It looks delicious, my dear." Gramps beamed.

Logan swallowed a good portion of his liquor, then straightened in his chair. "Yes, Elise. You've done a fine job."

No one seemed to mind that the chicken was old and a bit overdone. She had also managed four nice-sized sweet potatoes from the garden and cooked them with the remaining brown sugar, hoping Logan wouldn't mind the missing butter.

Gramps and Jared had brought green beans, which were still warm from the cooking Gramps had given them. Elise put the pears for dessert in a bowl and placed them at the end of the table.

Throughout dinner, Elise glanced frequently at Logan, glad to have him home, yet concerned at the amount of liquor he consumed.

She would have preferred to concentrate solely on him, but she couldn't ignore Jared's intense regard. Since the time he and Gramps had arrived, he'd barely taken his gaze from her.

Though some part of her found his attention stirring, she was nervous about the way his gaze stripped right past her defenses. It burned like a torch over her neck and lingered on the swell of her breasts. Her heartbeat throbbed low and steady, like the call of a gathering rain, and she couldn't bring herself to look at him.

She'd worn no hoops so that her skirts would cover her old scuffed kid slippers, and the dress slid against her body like a caress. Jared's steady regard made her feel as if he could see right through her two muslin petticoats, chemise, and drawers.

Logan ate quickly, hunched over his food protectively, as though he feared someone would take it away. He seemed oblivious to both her and their company, and Elise shifted uncomfortably in her chair. Gramps caught her eye and winked reassuringly, easing some of her anxiety.

Logan pushed his plate away and sank down in his chair, cradling his goblet between his rough, grimy hands. "That was superb, Elise. Especially given that you had next to nothing to work with. Don't you agree, Kensington?"

"It's delicious." Jared gazed steadily at Logan.

Her brother sipped at his whiskey, one hand fingering the label on the bottle. "You know, they had an abundance of food in Ohio. Of course, we didn't get any of it. Part of their torture was to eat in front of us then scatter the scraps around to see who would scramble for it."

"More pears?" she offered, holding out the chipped china bowl. Inside she cringed at the cruel picture her brother painted.

Gramps took one then passed them to Jared. Logan

slumped farther into his chair and sipped at his whiskey.

Elise swallowed, hating to hear even a hint of her brother's suffering. She was surprised that he had even mentioned the prison camp. He'd always been stubbornly overprotective, believing that women should be sheltered from such grim realities. Though she had often begged him to tell her his secrets, this was one time she was happy not to know.

"I thought we could plant more pecan trees next year." She looked expectantly at Logan. "Perhaps sell the nuts in town?"

He waved a hand dismissively. "Whatever you want is fine."

"That's a dandy idea," Gramps said. "Have you thought further about planting more cotton or tobacco?"

"The land seems too tired for tobacco. Maybe corn." Elise glanced at her brother, wanting to draw him into the conversation, erase the sullen stare. "I thought Logan would know better than I what would be best."

"Do whatever you want." He scowled. "Did you know we could barely get water? Stuck out there on a lake and we had to wait for the floodgate from the kitchen to be raised. All manner of filth came through that water."

He knew better than to act so churlish in front of company. Elise fought her rising irritation and embarrassment. Despite the families' close ties, Jared and Gramps were still guests at Fairbrooke.

Twisting her hands in her lap, she said, "We've a

new doctor in town, Logan. You should have her take
a look at your leg."

"A woman doctor?" he snorted, pouring another
glass of whiskey.

She looked at the glass he'd refilled four times.
"Gramps likes her. He says she's good at her job."

"And she's pretty, in a different sort of way,"
Thomas Kensington confirmed with a wink. "A
Northern girl."

"A damn Yank?" Logan sneered. "No, thanks.
Rather have my leg rot off than another Yank touch
me. Especially another butcher. Besides, no doctor
can help me now."

Elise looked down at her plate, uneasy. She knew
Logan had suffered, but did he have to talk about it in
front of their guests? Perhaps she could convince him
later to see Dru.

Jared spoke, his voice calm. "The Delavants moved
on. Went out to Missouri to be with Justine's people."

Elise shot him a warning glance and Jared nodded
slightly. She hoped he believed she didn't want Logan upset, which was partly true, but neither did she
want the conversation to veer toward Tullar DeWitt,
who now owned Delavant Hall. She relaxed somewhat, seeing that Jared was trying to divert Logan's
attention.

"Hell." Logan stared into his glass, swirling the amber liquid absently. "You know, those Yanks broke my
leg. I didn't fall. They beat me with an iron bar.
That's how it was broken. Then they wouldn't let me
see a doctor."

Oh, Logan. Elise covered her mouth, horrified.

"We lived worse than pigs up there. Penned together like animals, starved, covered in bugs. Any food we were given was scraps—"

"Worthen." Jared's voice sliced through the room like a blade. "Why don't we talk about something else?"

Elise's gaze moved to him. His dark features were rigid, flushed with anger, and his body was tight with the effort to control himself.

"What for, dammit! This is what we have. Memories, nightmares, the legacy of the Union army."

"Logan, please." Elise leaned toward him, moving the bottle of whiskey out of his reach. "Don't upset yourself."

He bolted upright. "Give me that bottle."

"No." She stiffened in her chair, meeting his fevered gaze with her own. "You've had quite enough."

"Elise, hand it over." A vein bulged in his temple and his eyes were frantic.

"No," she said more softly.

"Haven't they taken enough from me? Must you torture me, too?"

"Logan!" she cried, surging out of her chair. "I would never hurt you. Never. I only want you to be well, to be the way you were."

"I'll never be well, Elise," he spat. "Don't you see what they've done? Don't you see I'm not whole anymore? Things will never be all right again. Stop pretending that they will."

"Worthen!" Jared pushed away from the table, his chair legs scraping across the floor.

Elise barely registered Jared's fierce anger. She

stared at Logan, her mind blank with shock. What had happened to the brother who'd always joked and made her feel better? Who'd always found the bright side of a problem? Who'd refused to ever let her quit?

Tears burned her eyes and she shook her head. "You're home, Logan. We have each other and that's more than a lot of families have. I believe that means things *will* be all right."

"You're wrong, Elise. They left me nothing. Nothing, do you hear?" he shouted, slamming his fist against the table. "Look around you! Look at this house! Look at the land—scourged, bled, battered and wasted."

Her lips trembled and she pressed her knuckles against them as pain jagged through her.

"A hollow, empty shell. Just like me," he whispered hoarsely, sinking down into his chair. Tears streamed down his face. "Just like me."

"Excuse me." She barely got out the words before she bolted for the door and ran. She had never seen her brother cry. Never. And his tears were her undoing. She couldn't bear to see him so defeated, so bitter, so *different*.

For the first time in their lives, Elise was his protector. And she didn't know if she was up to the challenge. Lord help her, she didn't know if she wanted to try.

"You damn fool." Jared was stunned at the savage protectiveness that rose in him as he glared at Logan. "Why did you upset her that way?"

Gramps glanced between the two of them speculatively.

Logan shoved an unsteady hand through his hair, eyeing Jared balefully. "Since when have you become my sister's champion?"

His words echoed the ones Gramps had said to Jared only yesterday, and resentment flared. He checked the urge to haul Logan out of his chair and dunk his head in the horse trough.

Fighting the rage boiling up inside him, Jared measured his words. "Perhaps you've forgotten common courtesy around women. You would certainly be excused if that were the case."

His friend had the grace to flush. "No. No, I haven't, but Elise is strong—"

"She's your sister. You should be more careful of her."

Jared threw down his napkin and walked out, cursing under his breath. He strode through the foyer into the small library, wishing he could dismiss the pain he'd seen in her face, but her blue eyes haunted him. She was upset and she shouldn't be alone. She'd been alone far too long as it was.

He caught himself listening for her, trying to find her, and he redirected his steps. She wasn't his responsibility. Already Logan probably felt remorse and was looking for her. Jared had no obligation to check on her, to protect her. He did, however, have an obligation to Cam and the United States Treasury Department.

He needed distance from her. Gramps and Logan would make certain she was all right. Intent on getting some air, he walked back to the library and across the room, stepping through the open doors leading to the verandah. He froze.

Etched in shadow and moonlight, Elise stood at the railing and stared out into the darkness, her pale slender arms wrapped around her waist. His chest tightened and a slow burn inched under his skin. Aching, he recalled the soft velvet of her skin, the feel of her lips opening under his.

The single pearl clip she'd used to pull back her hair gleamed in the dusky light. Her thick curls, darkened to mahogany in the night, rippled to the middle of her back. Several stray tendrils fell over her shoulder to trace the hollow of her delicate collarbone. She appeared fragile, though he knew she wasn't.

Leave, he ordered himself. *She's not your responsibility.*

But even from here, he could feel her sadness and his purpose wavered. Again.

CHAPTER EIGHT

Jared walked soundlessly across the verandah, intending to ask her some blunt questions about Onash, but as he saw her shoulders sag, reason battled with compassion.

He reminded himself how she'd lied about Onash, but he knew as soon as he halted behind her that he was in trouble. Her soft scent floated around him, beckoning, tempting. The turquoise silk flowed over her slender body like color from an artist's brush, painting to perfection her proud shoulders, the trim nip of her waist, the flare of her hips.

Hell and damnation. He clenched his fists against the urge to slide his arms around her, to turn her face to his and kiss away the pain he'd seen moments ago. He wanted to comfort her, not catch her in a lie.

Her skin gleamed like polished alabaster against the vibrant gem-colored fabric. The bodice edged the swell of her breasts and he wanted to trail his lips over her skin, feel the weight of her in his hand.

She looked over her shoulder, the moonlight cresting on her high cheekbones and illuminating the pure blue of her eyes. Her smile was wobbly. "I'm sorry."

His heart turned over in his chest. He could see no trace of tears, but knew she'd been crying. "I—we were worried when you didn't return."

"I . . . just needed a breath of air. I'm fine."

"Clearly, you aren't," he said quietly.

Agony pinched her features. "It was awful for him, wasn't it?"

She stared up at him with trusting blue eyes, and he couldn't bring himself to lie to her. She was strong, he'd seen that, but how much could one person endure? Though Logan was alive, the person he'd been before the war appeared to be very much dead. "Yes, I think so."

She nodded, swallowing hard and looking out into the night. "I shouldn't have lost my temper."

"Perhaps you should've lost it sooner." Jared decided he should've pounded Logan after all.

That coaxed a fleeting smile from her. "We'll never know how he suffered. How could they have done those things to him? How could anyone—"

"Elise, don't." His voice was rusty, choked. His palms itched to touch her, just once, for an instant. And he realized his hand was on her shoulder. "Don't do this to yourself."

"You're right. He'll be fine." She took a deep breath, her breasts swelling. "*We'll* be fine. We will."

He couldn't decide if her words were scored by determination or desperation. Fascinated by the slide of moonlight on her creamy skin, he skimmed one finger along her collarbone. Her skin was warm and smooth beneath the calluses of his finger; her skin ivory next to the copper of his.

She edged closer to him, though he wondered if she was even aware of it. "Just as you said earlier, Logan needs time. It takes time to recover from the effects of war. Time for all of us."

Jared studied her, fighting the urge to stroke the swell of her breasts, to dip his finger into the shadowed valley between. There was another time she'd said something so cryptic. She'd spoken with bleak certainty about doing whatever was necessary to survive. *What had she found it necessary to do? Did it involve Onash?*

With a start, he realized he was caressing her, stroking the beginning swell of her breast with his knuckle. Blood throbbed low in his belly and he cursed silently.

Slowly he removed his hand and jammed it in his trousers pocket. "I was in town today. I spoke to the sheriff."

"Oh?" She stilled, her fingers curling over the stone of the railing. "About Mama and Papa?"

"No. Onash." He clenched his fist, still safely in his pocket, but his shoulder brushed hers. "He's finally investigating the man's disappearance."

"Onash." Her voice was clipped, hard. "What about my parents? Do you think he'll even try to find their murderer?"

Jared realized the frustration she must feel that nothing had been done. "He said he was looking into it, though he's turned up nothing yet."

She glanced quickly at him, and he thought he read relief in her eyes.

Surely he was mistaken. Elise could have no reason for not wanting an investigation. Could she?

With a jolt of irritation, Jared wished he weren't so suspicious, wished he could turn his back on his job, but he could more easily quit breathing. He shifted, leaning one hip against the railing as he watched her. "Sheriff Restin has started asking questions about Onash all over town."

She gave a sharp nod, clasping her hands behind her back and moving in measured steps across the verandah. Flashing him a saucy smile, she said, "Now that Logan's home, you needn't bother with me anymore."

"Are you trying to get rid of me?"

"Gracious, no!"

She was, however, trying to change the subject. He took his hands from his pockets and moved toward her. "I figure it won't be long before the sheriff is out here asking you about Onash."

"Why would he ask me anything?" She paced in front of him, her fingers tangled in her skirts. Though her question was breezy, he noted she wouldn't meet his gaze.

It seemed nothing would do but plainspeaking. He rubbed the suddenly tight muscles across his neck. "Because you're hiding something. You know something about Onash."

She froze, naked panic flashing through her eyes, then she swept past him. "Ridiculous! I already told you—"

He grabbed her wrist, pulling her flush against him.

"Elise, you won't be able to charm your way past Restin. If you know something—"

"I don't." She tugged against his hold. "Jared, let go."

"You're damn poor at lying." His thumb stroked the soft inner skin of her wrist, and he wanted to trail his hand up the inside of her arm, skim the curve of her breast. Desire curled through him, fluttering, burgeoning, growing like a wild thing. "Unusual for a woman, to be sure."

"I don't know what you mean." Her chin lifted and she stared unflinchingly into his eyes. "No gentleman would call a lady a liar."

"You're right." Her pulse thumped frantically in her throat. He wanted to push her into the shadows and peel away that turquoise silk, taste every inch of her satiny flesh. "I hope you know what you're doing with this cat-and-mouse game. The sheriff won't be satisfied until he has answers. Real answers."

She turned her face away, her cheek brushing his. "Why do you care?"

Her soft scent and the tease of her body against his sent want lancing through him. He could have said it was because of Logan, but that was no longer true. He could have told her it was because of his obligation to Cam, but he wasn't ready to relinquish that information just yet.

"Damned if I know." He didn't understand this hollow piercing in his soul, this need to claim her.

She trembled, but when she lifted her gaze to his, he saw defiance, not fear. Though he admired her spirit and wanted her like hell afire, he meant to get a straight answer from her, for once. "Did you know Onash?"

"I told you he'd never been here."

Jared lowered his voice, his breath stirring the hair at her temple. "I didn't ask if he'd been here. I asked if you knew him. Yes or no?"

She angled her chin, irritation sparking in her blue eyes. "You've an uncommon interest in the man."

Still grasping her wrist, he measured her with a granite-hard stare. "Some."

"Why?"

"We're not talking about me. We're talking about you. Did you know him, yes or no?"

He kept his voice low, striving to maintain some semblance of calm. He wanted to rail at the little idiot, bully out of her what she knew. Yet his determination was jumbled with the damnable ache between his legs that prodded him to forget his suspicions, to kiss her again.

"I know who he is."

Her scant admission only fueled his frustration.

"Was he involved in your parents' deaths, Elise?"

Panic flickered in her eyes even as she said coolly, "If he was, that would explain his absence, wouldn't it?"

"Oh?" Jared's breath jammed in his chest. Did she mean that Onash was dead? Did she *know*?

She countered pointedly, "If you killed someone, would *you* stay around?"

"Suppose not." How could she seemingly answer his questions yet tell him nothing? His grip tightened on her wrist. "Did he speak to you or your father about the lien? The property? The house? Did he ever speak to you or your father about purchasing Fairbrooke?"

"No."

The mutinous set of her jaw whipped his irritation to a higher level. "He never spoke to either of you about it at all?"

Her gaze met his, challenging yet hinting at fear. She wrenched from his hold and moved quickly away. "You forget yourself, sir. You're in my home. I won't be interrogated like a common thief!"

Common thief? Interesting choice of words.

She faced him, chest heaving, her eyes shooting blue fire. His blood stirred at the sight of her and he tamped down the lust that surged to unrestrained life inside him.

Three strides brought him in front of her. "The sheriff won't be so gentle with you."

"Gentle! I've seen lust-crazed stallions tread with more care."

He heard the murmur of voices coming toward them and lowered his own. "Don't fight me, Elise. It could be your undoing."

"Meaning what?" she demanded sharply.

He couldn't believe he'd hinted at his job. The last thing he needed was for Elise suddenly to be suspicious of his motives. He'd certainly never get anything out of her then.

"What did you mean?" she pressed, her eyes narrowing.

At that moment, Gramps and Logan walked through the door. Though it saved Jared from answering, it also stalled any further attempts to question her.

He gave her one last hard stare before turning toward the two men. "Be warned."

So much for plainspeaking. She'd gotten him so riled, he had completely forgone any finesse. He should have handled her delicately, patiently, as he would a spooked filly.

". . . should've known to look here first," Logan groused, his gaze moving curiously from Jared to Elise.

Jared stepped away from her, still taunted by her lilac scent, the velvet of her skin. Their gazes met briefly, then she looked away.

"Ah, Jared's with her." Gramps moved onto the verandah with Logan.

Jared attempted to allay the curiosity burning in Logan's eyes. "I spoke to Sheriff Restin today."

"What did he say?" Logan limped up, halting between Jared and Elise.

"Nothing much." From the corner of his eye, Jared saw Elise start. "He has been asking a few questions though."

"About the murders?"

"Yes, of course," Elise put in quickly.

"Did you learn anything?" Logan asked Jared. "You asked around, didn't you?"

He nodded, feeling Elise tense beside him. "I didn't learn much. Not yet anyway." *About the Worthens or the Onashes.* Given Logan's ambivalence, Jared didn't think it wise to relay his suspicions concerning Elise.

Gramps touched her arm. "Are you all right, my dear?"

"Yes." She smiled gratefully at him, but when she looked at Jared, defiance darkened her eyes.

He cursed silently. He hated lying to his friend, but for the first time in their friendship he was uncertain of Logan's reaction. He could respond in his usual calm fashion or he could explode. "I told Elise the sheriff had already spoken to some people in town and I'll try to follow up, see if I can learn anything else."

She seemed to pale in the dusky light and moved closer to Gramps.

"Is that all the sheriff is doing? Asking questions?" Logan snapped. "I'll pay him a visit tomorrow. Surely there's something more he can do."

Elise looked as if she would protest, but instead turned to Gramps. "Your pears were delicious. Thanks so much for bringing them."

Logan continued, "We'll see how he likes it if I put my weight behind yours."

Jared elbowed him in the ribs, indicating Elise with a tilt of his head.

Logan glanced at his sister then nodded, chagrined. "I'm sorry, Elise. I don't mean to upset you. And about earlier—well, I was a horse's ass and—"

"Logan, please!" Elise held up a constraining hand, though she was grinning. "I suppose I'll just have to forgive you since you're going to be around for a while."

"Yes, a long while." He tugged on a stray strand of hair at her shoulder and grinned.

Relief and hope spread across Elise's features, and

Jared couldn't stem the stab of jealousy that Logan, not he, had coaxed such a look from her.

But that was as it should be. He had a job to do and finally had gotten her to admit that she knew who Onash was. It wasn't much, but it confirmed Jared's hunch of a connection between her and the Treasury agent.

He should've been pleased. But all the way home, he couldn't escape the haunting, inexplicable sense that he was going to regret what he'd learned tonight.

She gazed around the sharecropper's cabin, trying to ignore the want that shimmered through her, the desire still tugging low in her belly. She was restless, edgy, and tried to keep her thoughts strictly focused on her search, but Jared invaded them at every turn.

She wished he had kissed her again. She wondered what his hands would feel like on her body—coaxing like the first touch of sunlight on a flower, or sure and demanding?

She recalled the compassion in his eyes tonight as he'd reassured her about Logan. And then that fierce determination concerning Onash. She never should have admitted anything to him. Though she hadn't confessed to knowing Onash, she knew Jared's suspicions had been whetted.

He said he was only curious, but she no longer believed that. His questions were too intense, too pointed.

With rising alarm, she felt as if she were being backed into the closing jaws of a trap, DeWitt on one side, Jared on the other. If Jared was right, she could soon expect Sheriff Restin as well. That apprehension should have quelled this shivery heat inside her, but it hadn't.

Despite her body's treacherous response to Jared, her brain, at least, was still engaged. Jared's suspicions had driven her back to the sharecropper's cabin. She had to make certain he indeed knew nothing.

Logic said he couldn't know that Claude and Pervis had inhabited this cabin. If he knew, he would've asked her about that, too.

After another thorough look, Elise finally exhaled, but her relief was mixed with frustration. Everything appeared undisturbed, yet there were no further clues about the money.

As she mounted Majesty and turned for home, Elise wished fervently that Jared had no interest in Onash, only in her. Did he feel this wild yearning, this reckless urge to surrender to the passion that hummed between them?

She knew he'd wanted her tonight. She had wanted him, too. Until he'd started pressing her about Onash. No, this desire wasn't one-sided, but she knew Jared wouldn't act on it.

Perhaps because of the honor he wore like a shield. Or the promise he'd made to Logan. Longing swept through her, and she ached to shatter the restraint he employed with an iron will.

Which was insane and dangerous. He was already asking too many questions, prying at the raw secret she carried.

She should be glad of his distance. His uncommon curiosity about Onash set her on edge. She'd glimpsed a ruthless side to him tonight. Beneath the gentleman, the protector, lay a man with the attack instincts of a cornered wildcat.

Those green eyes had pinned her with a combination of fascination and suspicion, a dangerous darkness she hadn't noticed before. Energy seethed beneath the polite surface, threatening to erupt at any moment.

It made her nerves tingle, her blood heat. And boded ill for her. If he ever learned what she had done, that intensity would turn savage with condemnation.

Somehow she had to find the strength to put aside this growing wish that there could be more between them.

She arrived home and slowed Majesty to a walk so as not to wake Logan. He had helped her clean the supper dishes, then disappeared. To his room, she supposed. She had slipped out about an hour later.

She walked Majesty into the barn and dismounted, her thoughts turning to DeWitt. Though she hadn't seen the man today, she knew he was probably watching. Waiting. A chill scuttled across her shoulders. She wished she could confide in Logan, ask for his help, but he wasn't ready to deal with anything yet. She had realized that at supper tonight.

She uncinched Majesty's saddle and reached to pull it off.

"It's a little late for a ride, isn't it?"

DeWitt! The saddle thudded onto the mare and Elise whirled, reaching into her pocket for her revolver.

"Now, now." He moved in a blur, and before she could pull away, he grabbed her arm. Long fingers bit into her flesh like cold steel as he plucked the gun from her. "I thought you might have some news for me."

"I don't." Elise stood motionless, fear knotting her stomach.

He leaned closer, his breath hot in her face. "Nothing?"

"No," she gritted out, fighting the urge to grab for her gun. Even in the shadows she could see the hatred in his eyes, completely belying his soft tone.

"What a pity." He clucked. "I guess it's time for that visit to Sheriff Restin."

"How do you expect me to find anything if you bring the sheriff into this?" She struggled against his hold, but his grip tightened until her fingers ached.

"I feel you're not living up to your part of our, uh, bargain." His voice slid over her like groping fingers, and she felt something touch her face.

Her gun! He brushed the tip of the barrel along her jaw and Elise froze, terror clutching at her.

"I'm losing my patience. I don't think you're trying your best to find my money."

"I already told you I don't have it and I don't know where to look."

He pressed the barrel of the gun under her chin and tilted her face toward him. In the musty heat of the barn, the scent of sandalwood was suffocatingly sweet, tinged with cruelty, and her nostrils flared.

His gaze bored into her, as dead and cold as old

ashes. "I notice your brother is home from the war. How sweet."

She swallowed, panic thumping at her.

DeWitt moved the gun, teasing the curls that brushed her temple, drawing the cool steel down her cheek. Her legs trembled so badly, she thought they would give out.

"It would be a shame for something to happen to him, don't you think?"

"You leave him alone!" She jerked instinctively, then froze as DeWitt drilled the gun into a spot just above her ear. Cold sweat slicked her body and she could barely hear over the rush of her heart. "He has nothing to do with this."

"Maybe not yet, but if you don't hand over my money, he will." DeWitt moved behind her, his chest brushing her back, his thighs pressing against hers. "Wouldn't that be a terrible irony? For him to survive the horrors of war only to succumb to an unfortunate tragedy?"

She recoiled, her skin crawling. Desperate fear pumped through her. "Leave him out of this. Please."

He reached over her shoulder and stroked her cheek with one finger, as cool and severe as the gun barrel. "That will be up to you, my dear. Remember that."

She nodded, her fists clenched to fight him off if he touched her again. After a few seconds she realized he was no longer touching her back or her shoulders.

She turned her head slightly, then spun around. He was gone.

Rushing to the door, she stared out into the night.

Empty, black, desolate. Trees stirred and locusts groaned, but she saw no sign of DeWitt, heard no sounds of a retreating horse. From the corner of her eye she caught a glint in the moonlight, and looked down.

Her gun lay there, discarded like a toy, a clear symbol that DeWitt found her completely unthreatening. Fear sliced through her, buffered by determination.

She would tell Logan. Together they would find a way to deal with DeWitt. As she picked up her gun she recalled her brother's earlier behavior, and doubts wormed in. Logan wasn't physically or mentally prepared to fight another enemy so soon, but she needed him.

She stuffed the revolver into her skirt pocket, hurrying toward the house. He wouldn't let her down.

Fifteen minutes later, dread raked over her with a cold heaviness. Logan was nowhere to be found. Not in the house, or the barn, or the abandoned slave quarters. Nowhere.

It would be a shame for something to happen to him, don't you think? What if he were to succumb to an unfortunate tragedy?

Fear choked her. What if DeWitt had already made good on his threat? What if even now Logan were lying somewhere injured or—

Don't borrow trouble, Elise warned herself. *Think.* She searched the house one more time, then every stall inside the barn, but there was no sign of him. He wasn't at the cemetery. He was nowhere near the house.

Panic shot through her like a stray bullet and she rushed to the barn, saddling Majesty again, this time using her brother's old saddle. She tried to stay calm, to think. Perhaps he'd gone to town or . . . to Jared's.

Yes, maybe he'd gone looking for his friend. Probably for more whiskey. He was with Jared. He had to be.

Jared climbed out of the creek and toweled off. Fifteen minutes of hard swimming had done nothing to erase the feel of Elise next to him. Even now, breathing hard and dripping wet, he could think only of having her naked in the water with him, of skimming his hands over sleek wet skin, cupping those full breasts.

Damn! He'd need another dunking if he didn't stop this. A raw, aching hunger flared deep in his belly. He wanted her and he was damn tired of fighting it.

But he had to. Elise wasn't a woman to be dallied with. Not only because she was Logan's sister and a lady, but also because she was hiding something about Onash and possibly about the money, too.

Tonight hadn't gone exactly as he'd planned, but he'd managed, by her admission, to tie her to the corrupt Treasury agent. Which was more than Sheriff Restin had done.

Jared would lay money that Elise had more than one thin tie to Onash and was managing quite well to keep the truth to herself. Was there a way he could slip past her guard, convince her to confide in him, or even wear her down until she told him what he wanted to know?

It was damn hard to summon any enthusiasm or even anger at her lies when he couldn't erase her gentle scent, which still clung to him despite his late-night bath. Nor could he ignore the way her eyes had clouded with desire before they flared with anger.

Being so close to her tonight had released something inside him, fast and deep and primal. He'd wanted to haul her up to him, strip those clothes off her body and thrust into her with reckless abandon. But he would never allow himself to lose control like that.

Even telling himself that didn't ease the brutal pounding of his blood, the want that flicked away at his restraint like the burning kiss of a whip.

He tugged on his army pants then his boots. Draping the towel across one shoulder, he headed for the house. As he tromped through trees and tangled underbrush, he fought against the frustration edging through him.

How had he ever gotten so involved with her? It had started out because of his promise to Logan, but the promise had quickly dimmed. She was spirited and brave and strong. She had a way of doing what she had to without hesitation or skittishness.

Like shoeing the horse, when she'd been raised with others doing it for her. Or fixing the roof when she hated being up so far. Yes, he liked her determination and the way she hadn't allowed herself to be cornered by his leading questions.

It amazed him that he could like anything about her when he knew she'd lied, knew she was hiding something still.

He sighed and massaged the muscles in his neck, cording with tension again.

As he moved through the clearing and around to the front of the house, the thunder of hooves penetrated his thoughts. Who could be riding hell-bent at this hour? He jogged around to the front porch in time to see the shadowy form of horse and rider emerge out of the darkness. They blended into the night, screened until they reached a crest of moonlight.

Elise! Concern steepled his heartbeat. He tossed the towel onto the porch and walked out to meet her.

She pushed Majesty as hard as she could and skidded to a stop in front of him. Gravel and dirt sprayed his boots. She rode astride and scrambled off the saddle in a flurry of skirts and petticoats, completely ignoring, or oblivious to, his outstretched hand.

"Elise, are you all right?"

She rushed past him and up the bottom two steps. "Is he here?"

"Who? Logan?" Jared's gaze tracked over her, making certain she was uninjured. "What's happened?"

She turned back to him, alarm stark on her features. "Please tell me he's here."

"I'm sorry." Jared shook his head, unsettled by her frantic tone. "He's not. What's wrong?"

"He's gone. I can't find him anywhere!" Her voice rose, fringed with desperation. "I'm afraid something has happened."

"Slow down. Tell me everything." Concerned now, he walked up the steps and took her elbow, ushering her inside the house. Releasing her, he turned up the kerosene lamp on the hall table.

In the soft amber light, her eyes were wild. Her chest heaved as if she'd run from Fairbrooke instead of ridden. For a moment her gaze locked on his bare chest, but there was no desire in her eyes, simply blank despair.

He cupped her shoulder. "Elise . . ."

"I have to find him, to tell him—" She licked her lips and gripped his arm. "I've looked everywhere— the house, the barn. I was so hoping he would be here."

Jared shook his head, taking in her pinched features, the fear dilating her eyes. "Let me get a shirt and I'll help you look."

"Thank you." She clasped and unclasped her hands nervously.

"Are you all right?"

"Yes. Hurry. Please."

He squeezed her shoulders, trying to reassure her, then took the stairs two at a time, his boots crashing against the wood. He nearly collided with Gramps, who stepped out into the hallway tying his robe.

"What's all the ruckus?"

Jared walked into the room next to his grandfather's explaining as he jerked a shirt from his wardrobe and shrugged into it. Grabbing his Colt, he shoved on his hat and went downstairs.

Gramps followed him and greeted Elise, a worried look on his face.

"Maybe this wasn't a good idea." Her voice was low with uncertainty. "I didn't know where else to look. I thought he might have come here. I didn't mean to disturb you."

"Shhh, it's perfectly fine," Gramps said, concern clouding his features as he glanced at Jared. "I'll get dressed and come too."

"Why don't you stay here?" Jared suggested. "In case Logan does show up. Both of you should stay."

"No." Elise pulled away from Gramps, her eyes worried. "I'm coming with you. If something's happened—"

"We don't know that." Jared caught her gaze, willing her to calm down, to trust him. He didn't want her to come, but he could see she was past reason. "We'll find him. He'll be fine."

She kept her gaze on his, nodding. Fear and desperation clouded her eyes. "I hope it's not too late."

Jared and Gramps exchanged frowns. *Be careful*, his grandfather's gaze warned.

Jared nodded then took Elise's elbow, steering her out the door. "Where do you think we should start?"

"He can't have gone far. He doesn't have a horse."

"The woods around Fairbrooke?"

"Yes." She hesitated. "Yes, I suppose."

"Elise, don't worry," Gramps said. "Jared will find him. You know he was the best scout in the army."

She nodded, though Jared could tell she had no idea what Gramps had just said.

His grandfather followed them to the door, patting her arm. "I'm sure Logan's fine."

She wrapped her arms tight around herself. "I hope so."

She was more than worried; she was on the verge of panic. She seemed convinced that some harm had befallen her brother. Why? Jared wondered.

She paced the porch as he saddled Trick and led the stallion from the barn.

"Did something happen?" he asked, giving her a hand up on Majesty. "Did you two have words again?"

"No, nothing like that." She tucked her skirts around her, absently covering her ankles. "I left—I mean, I went outside for a while, thinking he had already gone to bed. I wanted to talk to him, but when I went to his room, he wasn't there. I looked in the dining room, thinking he might be drinking, but he wasn't there either." Her words spilled out, tinged with returning panic. "I looked everywhere."

"He can't have gone far," Jared soothed.

She nodded, alarm making her features appear pinched and sharp in the moonlight.

He touched her hand, startled at how cold it was. "He'll be all right, Elise."

"I hope so," she whispered, wrapping her hand around his as if he were pumping life into her. "Thank you."

"Ready?" Surprised at the tightness of her grip, he returned the pressure of her hand.

After a few seconds, she released him and kicked Majesty into a canter. They rode into the night, and Jared couldn't help thinking this was the damnedest case he'd ever worked. Here he was, helping his only suspected link to a thief.

CHAPTER NINE

$\mathcal{F}$ear still whispered through her, but having Jared helped calm her. They reached Fairbrooke and as he readied each of them a lantern in the barn, Elise made one last search of the abandoned slave cabins.

"He's not there." She stepped into the barn, taking one of the lanterns from Jared. "What if—"

"Let's take this one move at a time."

She knew he was right and nodded, fending off the panic that reached for her.

Outside, Jared quickly scanned the grounds and inclined his head to the east. "Let's start there and work our way around the house and up the brook."

"All right."

"Stay close. Do you have your gun?"

"Yes."

"If we become separated, fire two shots in quick succession."

She nodded and they set out across the yard. Jared shortened his long stride to better match hers and they moved briskly through the oaks that bordered

the drive. Elise pressed close to him, her gaze squinting beyond the small arcs of light provided by the
bobbing lanterns.

Please, please. Let Logan be all right. If DeWitt had
done something to him—

Stop. Concentrate on finding him.

They moved through a field once ripe with corn,
now fallow. Elise faltered on a clump of dirt and Jared
steadied her with a hand on her elbow. His touch
burned through her but, strangely, calmed her panic.

As the trees thickened, she and Jared drifted apart
until several yards separated them.

"Logan!" she called. "Logan!"

Jared's voice echoed behind hers, strong and reso-
nant on the crisp midnight air.

Dirt gave way to a mossy carpet. Oak and walnut
and pine clumped tightly, flanked by bushes and
vines and an occasional rock. Owls hooted in a sing-
song pattern. Elise kept her mind clear, refusing to
consider that Logan could even now be floating unconscious in the water. Or shot dead.

Branches shook overhead; leaves rustled at the skit-
tering of a squirrel or raccoon. She held her lantern
higher, searching the dense shadows. She and Jared
were still at the beginning edge of the woods and
Elise turned, glancing behind her.

Several yards away a shadow detached itself from
the black silhouette of trees and moved toward her.
She stopped, then stepped out of the woods, angling
her lantern to the east. Amber light spread over the
grass, eating away the shadows, finally revealing her
brother.

Head bowed, he limped out of the trees, leaning heavily on his crude walking stick. He moved slowly, unevenly, as if each step was a painful labor.

"Logan!" she cried out, tears of relief burning her throat. "Jared, there he is!"

She snatched up her skirts and hurried toward him.

Logan's head snapped up and his eyes narrowed, feral and sharp like a cornered animal's. He backed away, though the look in his eyes changed to recognition. "Stay back," he snarled.

Elise skidded to a stop a few feet in front of him. As the lantern light peeled away the darkness around him, she was startled at the savage gleam in his eyes, the harshness of his handsome features.

"Elise." Jared's voice came quietly behind her. "Go easy."

Go easy? Forevermore! All she could think was that DeWitt hadn't hurt her brother. She rushed forward, throwing her arms around him and sobbing. "Oh, I was so worried. I thought you'd been hurt."

He stiffened against her, both hands gripping his stick.

She drew back to look at him, overwhelmed with relief. She touched his face and he recoiled, pushing away her hand.

"Logan?"

With clenched fists, he hobbled back a step. "Don't sneak up on me."

Startled and hurt, she blinked at him. "I didn't mean to."

His lip curled and he stood rigidly braced, as though he was protecting himself from her.

Jared walked up behind her and touched her shoulder. "Give him a minute."

Elise frowned over her shoulder at Jared. Did he understand what was happening? If so, she wished he would tell her.

"Logan?" Jared said in a low voice. "You all right?"

He stared blankly at Jared for a moment, then a guilty look knifed across his features. "Yeah."

Elise looked from him to Jared and back again. She didn't understand what was going on, but Logan seemed to relax. The band across her chest eased. "I was so worried when I couldn't find you. Where have you been? What are you doing out here?"

"Walking," he said flatly, shifting another step away.

Walking?

"I do that a lot."

"You scared your sister to death," Jared put in, moving up beside Elise.

Logan rubbed his neck and stared up at the sky. "Were you checking up on me?"

"Of course not!" she exclaimed.

"Well, don't."

"I . . . wasn't." She looked to Jared in confusion.

He squeezed her elbow, speaking to Logan. "Ready to go back or need some more time?"

Logan's eyes narrowed, then he shrugged. "I'm fine," he said shortly.

He stepped around both of them and headed for the house. His uneven steps were quick, choppy, and Elise feared he would tumble over the rough ground.

She hurried after him, staying close but sensing that

he didn't want her touch again. She tamped down the hurt she felt at his actions. Why did Jared seem to understand so much?

"Remember how plentiful our corn crop was?" Logan's features still carried that hard, worn look as he gazed over the empty field.

"We can plant again."

He shrugged, staring out over the stray sprigs of moonlit grass that pushed up through the rutted ground.

Jared kept an easy pace behind them, and his lantern light merged with hers to clearly illuminate the way.

"Look at this!" Logan exploded, throwing his arm out in an expansive gesture. "Wasteland, all of it. They left us nothing. Nothing!"

She wiped her hands down the front of her worn blue calico and followed her brother's gaze, staring out over the fallow earth, the empty fields, naked of life, devoid of hope.

"We can barely find food enough to eat."

"We're fine, Logan. We have more than many people do." Her heart ached at the dark change in her brother. "The garden isn't large, like Mother's, but it will suit us well."

"I know you're doing the best you can, Elise, but stop trying to paint such a rosy picture."

Stung, she looked away. They arrived at the house in silence and she reached out automatically to assist Logan up the porch steps, then refrained. He seemed to want nothing to do with her. How was she supposed to help him if he wouldn't let her?

He opened the front door and stepped inside, bidding her over his shoulder a brief "Good night."

"Good night." He acted as if he were dismissing her from her own house. What was wrong with him? "I'm glad you're all right."

He nodded curtly and turned.

"It wouldn't pain you to tell Elise the next time you go out," Jared asserted in a low, commanding tone.

Logan froze, and for an instant Elise thought he would explode. He turned, his voice chilling. "She's not my keeper, Kensington. And you aren't hers."

Elise gasped, stunned at Logan's cutting tone.

A muscle flexed in Jared's jaw and he pinched the bridge of his nose, as if he was seeking patience.

Her brother limped inside and Elise watched as he made his way painfully up the staircase. "I don't understand. Why is he acting this way?"

"I've seen it happen to a lot of men, Elise. Sometimes when they're treated so brutally, they change forever."

Sadness stabbed at her and she turned to Jared. "You mean, he might never be the Logan we've always known?"

"There's no way to tell." His voice softened. "I'm sorry."

"There's got to be something we can do."

"Just give him some room. He has a strong mind and a strong heart. He'll come around."

"Do you really think so?" She wished she were as certain as he sounded, and suddenly she was very glad he was with her.

Compassion and fondness lit his eyes. "Of course."

It was the gentlest smile she'd ever seen on him and her heart turned over. She'd gone to him tonight knowing instinctively that he would help her. And he had, without hesitation.

"Thank you for helping me. I guess I overreacted, but when I couldn't find him—"

"It was no bother. I'm glad he's all right." He caught her gaze with his. "Are *you*?"

"Yes." She gave a nervous laugh, suddenly very aware of standing so close to him. "I do feel a little silly for dragging you out so late."

"No sense in that," he said lightly. "I'm just glad everything turned out for the best."

Gratitude warmed her. Smiling broadly, she rolled up on tiptoe and laid one hand on his shoulder, intending to kiss his cheek.

What was she thinking? She started to draw away, but his hand, big and warm, covered hers, staying her. Trapping her. She glanced up sheepishly, then caught her breath.

His eyes blazed with fierce hunger, mirroring the desire that throbbed through her body. He lowered his head, giving her ample opportunity to pull away.

She should.

She would.

But instead, she waited for him. She wanted to feel his lips on hers again, wanted to feel that wild kick of her pulse, the hard strength of his chest against hers.

Their gazes locked and he tasted her, tugging tenderly on her bottom lip with his teeth. Her heartbeat wheeled and she arched toward him. His lips covered hers, gently yet confidently, and his tongue dipped inside her mouth.

A shudder ripped through her and she gripped his shoulder. His hand tightened over hers. He touched her nowhere else, yet she felt him in every cell of her body, pulsing with light and fire as if he'd branded her. Her breasts grew heavy; her nipples puckered and she wanted to feel him next to her, his bare skin next to hers.

This was lunacy.

It was dangerous.

She loved it.

She wanted him to touch her everywhere, with his hands, his mouth, but restraint vibrated in his big body, rippled in his arms. He drew away, his eyes dark and sultry green.

She could barely breathe. Her mind was completely blank.

"Good night," he said softly.

She nodded, dazed and floating.

The door clicked softly shut behind him and she groped behind her for the banister, sinking down on the bottom step.

That had been a mistake.

Hadn't it?

She gulped in a deep breath. Yes. It had.

He suspected her of being connected to Onash. As much as she longed to explore things between them, she couldn't become involved with Jared. Since their conversation tonight on the verandah, a steady wariness had grown in her.

He had helped her with Logan, but she couldn't

become further involved with him. She couldn't lean on him or go to him about her problem with DeWitt. *DeWitt*.

In her panic about Logan, she'd pushed aside the chilling visit from DeWitt, but now it flooded back with razor sharpness.

A surprising rage took hold. She was tired of his threats, tired of his games, tired of being at his mercy. He had something to lord over her; she needed something to use against *him*. She froze.

Of course. A man like that had to have secrets he didn't want discovered, but how could she go about finding them?

Her first impulse was to ask her brother, but Logan was in no shape to share this burden. Tonight had definitely proven that. She would have to handle it alone. She would figure out a way.

Elise came downstairs the next morning, her lips still tingling from the touch of Jared's. She hadn't dreamed of him, hadn't even stayed awake, but the memory was there, imprinted on her skin as certainly as the flesh over her bones. The gentle kiss had weakened her knees and made her realize her feelings for him were more than physical.

He reached a place deep inside her, a place she had guarded since the beginning of the war, afraid to give her heart to anyone, friend or otherwise, for fear they wouldn't return.

Though she knew Jared wanted her—she wasn't so naive she didn't recognize that—she could read nothing more than desire in his kiss, his burning stares.

Just thinking about him heated her blood and sent a shiver under her skin. She forced her thoughts away from Jared, replacing them with the more unpleasant ones of Tullar DeWitt.

She had no idea how to go about finding information on DeWitt, but she had to try. The whole idea made her feel sneaky and sordid, but she was tired of being under his thumb.

And she couldn't live with herself if he followed through on his threat against Logan. Again sadness welled up as she thought of her brother. He was simply not himself. Jared had come closer to reaching Logan last night than Elise had, but even that connection had been tentative.

Sighing, she shook off her gray thoughts and focused on her plan. She wore a faded red-and-white-striped morning dress, modestly cut with three-quarter sleeves. Next to the turquoise silk, it was in the best shape. Her mother's lone glove nestled in her skirt pocket.

Unwilling to wake Logan, she had slipped a note under his door. Rest and time were the only things that would erase the tortured shadows in his eyes, bring back the sun-browned color to his face. She herself had slept better than she had in a long while, exhausted from all that had happened last night, first with Jared, then with DeWitt, and then her fear that something had happened to Logan.

She pulled on her riding gloves, intent on the front door, when she heard a noise in the dining room. Moving into the doorway, she saw Logan running his

hands over Mother's mahogany table. Compassion
tightened her chest and she went inside.

He spun, a startled, cornered look sharpening his
features. "I told you not to sneak up on me."

"I'll make more noise next time." She refused to
give in to the hurt that jabbed at her.

He closed his eyes, regret chasing across his craggy,
sallow features. "I'm sorry."

She took another step closer, smiling yet approach-
ing him cautiously. "I'm going into town."

He gave a barely perceptible nod, his gaze riveted
on the dark, gleaming wood of the table. He limped a
couple of steps down its length, his palm sliding over
the piece possessively.

The gesture was reverent and yet heartbreakingly
lonely. As though he saw in the waxy reflection all the
things that had been and would never be again. A
shared pain rose up in her, but she curbed the urge to
go to him.

He stumped unevenly around the table, his gaze
focused blankly on the dark wood. His limp seemed
more pronounced today.

"Did you sleep all right?"

He gazed at her blankly for a moment. "I suppose."

She laced her fingers together, nervous and uncertain. "We can switch beds if you'd like. Mine is a little
more comfortable."

"It's not the bed, Elise."

She nodded, her throat burning. Her brother bore
dark moods like battle scars and a restless violence
that boiled just beneath the surface. Yes, she had
made the right decision not to tell him about DeWitt.

How could she burden him when he was so obviously tormented?

She wished fervently that she could help him. "I know it was hard on you, Logan."

"It wasn't like a day spent plowing the fields, Elise," he said impatiently. "It was hell."

"I know that." She wanted to go to him, hold him, but he held himself rigidly apart from her. "We've got each other. We can help each other."

Pressing his fingers to his temple, he squeezed his eyes shut, pain drawing white lines around his mouth. "There's nothing you can do."

"Not if you won't let me!" Agony slashed at her.

He opened his eyes and they glittered, bleak and bitter. "Leave it, little one."

"I can't. I love you. I want you to be all right."

"Well, I'm not all right." His shoulders sagged and he made his way over to the settee, easing down gingerly. "I don't know if anything will ever be all right again."

"It will, Logan." She stepped toward him, willing him to believe her. "You'll see."

Grimacing in pain, he arranged his leg at a comfortable angle in front of him.

"Won't you at least let me take you to see Dru?"

"Who?" he snapped. "Oh, the doctor. No."

"Logan—"

"No, Elise," he yelled, his rage barely contained. "Leave off."

"All right."

He exhaled loudly and slumped into the corner of the settee, staring into the empty fireplace.

She wanted to shake him, tell him he was lucky to be alive and to have a home, but she reined in her rapidly mounting irritation. "May I get you something while I'm in town?"

He glanced back at the whiskey bottle Jared had brought last night, now empty on the table. The fierce hunger on his face alarmed her.

"No," she said firmly, desperately. "No."

"I don't need anything." He looked away, shutting himself off from her.

He might as well have said *I don't need you.*

Her heart ached, and yet anger unfurled deep within her. Where was her brother? She wanted the Logan who teased her out of her nightmares, who joked way too much, who used to follow her beaux around with a scowl and muttered threats.

She wanted him the way he used to be. But they had all changed, hadn't they? Guilt shot through her. He was home. That was what mattered.

She hoped in time he would find some peace, that they all would. "I won't be long."

He didn't answer and pain twinged as she walked out of the room. *I still need you, Logan.* But she didn't say the words aloud. They wouldn't be welcome.

The leaves had started a slow turn from green to yellow to orange, but Elise was barely aware of the gentle approach of fall as she rode to town. Caught between thoughts of Jared's kiss and her brother's pigheadedness, she chafed the whole way.

She had become accustomed to riding astride and at the moment rode sidesaddle, though she knew that wasn't the reason for her restless frustration. Determinedly putting aside thoughts of Jared, she concentrated on her brother. She wanted to help Logan, but short of being obnoxious and pushy, she was at a loss.

Perhaps Dr. Hawthorne could help. Elise gave Majesty a kick, impatient now to reach Moss Springs. She wasn't exactly sure how to go about finding information on Tullar DeWitt, but at least she could do something about Logan.

Moss Springs moved in a lazy rhythm today, steady but not frantic. There were still too many Yankee blue uniforms for Elise's peace of mind, but she supposed Gramps' advice was taking hold. The entire nation needed to rebuild, put the past behind it. If she wanted her brother to be able to do that, she must do it as well.

She realized that part of her frantic worry about Logan was because she feared what would become of him should her part in the Onash murders be discovered.

She reined up at the livery and left Majesty with Coralee Bronson, realizing that if the woman who owned the livery had been able to tell Jared something about Claude Onash, she might be able to tell Elise something about Tullar DeWitt.

All Coralee knew was that DeWitt lived at the New American Hotel while his new home, Delavant Hall, was being refurbished. It wasn't much, but it was a place to start.

The task of learning something incriminating about the man suddenly seemed daunting, and Elise fought

off the feeling that she was completely out of her ele-
ment. She had to do *something*. She stood outside the
livery, studying several women who moved across the
street between Bailey's Dry Goods and the millinery.

Hammers clanged, ringing testimony to the new
businesses, the growing presence of Northerners.
Though the mood had shifted from destruction to
construction, Elise couldn't stifle a surge of resentment.

Her entire world was upended, just as Logan's was.
Her gaze swept the dark street crowded with wagons
and horses and small children darting about. Elise
picked up her skirts, hurrying over to the doctor's
clinic.

She stepped inside and closed the door.

Dru sat at a small desk in the back corner, writing in
a thick book. She glanced up, then laid down her
quill. Rising, she came forward, her gray eyes sparkling. "Good day, Elise. How are you?"

"I'm well. Thank you." Elise pulled off her riding
gloves, clutching them tightly in one hand. "I'm hoping you can help me."

"Is it about Thomas?"

"No." Elise smiled. "I'm here about my brother."

"Ah, yes, I heard he had returned. I'm so glad."
Dru smiled warmly. "Is he all right?"

"He's in one piece, but he's so different."

"How do you mean?"

"Harder, cruel almost." She searched for the right
words. "I don't know how to describe it. He doesn't
seem to care about Fairbrooke or what I do with it.

Last night, I couldn't find him and I was beside my-self. He was walking in the woods! In the middle of the night! Then he was angry because I was upset."

"He's listless? Easily agitated?"

"Yes." Relief swept over her. She'd known Dru could help.

The doctor nodded sympathetically. "I'm afraid many soldiers experience the same reactions upon re-turning home."

"I hate it desperately. You should see his eyes, so empty, so bitter." Elise shuddered. "You didn't know him before. He was so charming and funny and or-nery. Always protecting me, which I didn't necessarily appreciate," Elise added dryly, "but now I wouldn't mind it. It's as if I've become the protector and he's a stranger in the house."

"He'll have to come to terms with what's hap-pened, with his part in the war. And with the fact that it's finally, really over. It would be a mistake to think he can easily forget the surrender or any of the rest of it."

"He was also held prisoner." Elise's heart ached at the thought of his twisted leg.

Dru's eyes glimmered with compassion, and she squeezed Elise's hand. "How awful! I'm so sorry."

"I don't know everything that happened to him—he won't tell me. But they beat him, broke his leg . . ." Her voice rose in anger and she pressed shaking fingers to her lips. "I'm sorry. I imagine our prisons were every bit as horrible. His leg—it's never healed quite right."

Dru nodded. "I'd be happy to do whatever I can."

"I can't bear to see him this way, but I guess I should simply leave him alone, at least for now . . ."

"You shouldn't allow him to wallow in the memories. I've observed a number of war veterans and have found it's best to give them something to do."

"He has no interest in *anything*. Except whiskey."

"No! Don't let him indulge that."

"I won't. Don't you think he just needs some time? To get over what happened to him?"

"He does, yes, but he also needs to know that he's needed, that you depend on him."

"I do."

"Sometimes the best way to show people that is to force them into action or feeling."

Elise grimaced. "I don't know . . ."

"Trust me. He's locked in a deep place and needs help getting out. He needs to know there's light. You're that light."

"Really?"

Dru nodded.

"What do you think about his leg? Do you think it can ever be repaired?"

"I'd have to look at it."

"He won't come to town. I've already tried that, but maybe—" Elise shot a hopeful look at the doctor.

"What?"

"You could come to Fairbrooke. That is, if you don't mind." Elise moved in front of the doctor, willing to beg if necessary. After what she'd told Dru about Logan's moods, she might never want to examine him. "I can pay you, not a lot, but some. It would mean so much if you would come."

"It might be too soon. Are you sure this is a good idea?"

"You said not to give in to his moods."

"So I did." Dru tapped her chin thoughtfully. "All right. I'll do it."

"He'll hate it." Suddenly anticipating the look on his face, she grinned. "There's no telling what he'll do."

Dru's brows drew together. "You seem to be enjoying the prospect an awful lot."

This would help. It had to. "Yes, I definitely think you should come."

"Unarmed?" Dru asked wryly.

Elise chuckled. "It would probably be wise to bring a weapon."

"I was joking." The doctor arched her dark blond brows. *"Aren't you?"*

"I don't think so." With a half-smile, Elise pulled on her gloves. "Don't worry. I'll be there if he gets out of control."

"He can't be that bad!"

Elise shot her a look. "Believe me, these days he's no prize. And as unpredictable as a wild animal."

Hesitation clouded the doctor's strong features and she eyed Elise speculatively.

"Please?" She feared her teasing had gone too far. "Please."

After a brief pause, Dru nodded. "Oh, how bad can he be? I'll come out today, probably late afternoon."

"I can't thank you enough. I really appreciate it."

CHAPTER TEN

What was the little chit doing? Tullar stood in his
small upstairs office at the bank, watching as Elise
Worthen emerged from the doctor's office, stared up at
the bank, then hurried across to Bailey's Dry Goods.

After a few minutes, she stepped outside. He
squinted against the shimmering sunlight, seeing her
stare again at the bank. She studied it for several minutes then crossed the street once more, making her
way down the new boardwalk that connected the
bank, the millinery, and the hotel. She disappeared
from his vision and he had the sudden uncanny sense
that she had just walked into his bank.

He slipped out of the office and walked to the small
back stairway. Stepping noiselessly down the narrow
passageway, he halted at the bottom, surveying the
lobby. This stairway had been built specifically so he
could watch the goings-on at any time and have clear
view of the vault.

Sure enough, she was here. She stood at the teller
window closest to the door, several hundred feet from

him so that he couldn't hear what was said. Mr. Burns, Tullar's head teller, listened intently to her then nodded. Stretching out a bony, ink-stained hand, he pointed toward Tullar's downstairs office.

She nodded at Mr. Burns, her attention riveted on Tullar's imposing desk and leather chair. Curiosity and amusement niggled at him. *What was the gal up to?*

Wondering if she had finally decided to give him the money, he started to step out of the stairway, but she pivoted and walked out the door. Tullar frowned, then hurried back upstairs to the small office and a better vantage point.

She had never been in the bank before, and her coming in now made him not only curious but suspicious. He skirted the small desk and halltree, reaching the window in time to get a glimpse of her red-and-white-striped skirts as she disappeared under the awning of the New American Hotel. The hotel where he lived.

Tullar didn't know what she wanted, but if it was about the money, she would've asked to see him. Suspicion shifted into foreboding. He grabbed his new felt bowler, slammed it on his head, and hurried after her.

Expectancy hummed through Jared, sizzled in the air just as it had in the moments before Mosby disbanded the Rangers rather than surrender to the Federals. He watched Elise, as he had since she'd left Fairbrooke this morning.

He didn't know what he hoped to find, but since

her troubled visit to him last night, he'd had the un-settling feeling that something was about to give.

All morning, certain thoughts had woven through the suspicions in his mind. Mixed with hard questions of what she knew about Onash were memories of her mouth opening under his in willing surrender, images of his hands parting her thighs and wrapping them around his hips.

Jared cursed, thumbing back his hat and shifting to a more comfortable position against the wall of the church. Trick stood behind him, the stallion's breath hot on his back, burning with the sun through his white cotton shirt. Elise stepped into the bank, and Jared's curiosity sharpened.

What was she doing? He'd watched from the saloon while she visited Dr. Hawthorne. When she'd gone into Bailey's, Jared had moved to the north end of town and taken up a post at the corner of the church. Of all the activity in town, none issued from this small, steepled building, which sat stoically silent. He wondered absently where the Reverend Lyle might be today.

Jared just couldn't figure her. Her steps were pur-poseful, her visits not overly long except for the one to the doctor.

She stepped out of Bailey's, and in admiration he watched the gentle sway of her striped skirts as she crossed the street and walked into the bank. That damnable want he felt every time he saw her, stirred. Images floated back, soft as gossamer, binding as steel. Since last night he hadn't stopped thinking about her. He wanted to touch her bare flesh, explore

the heat between her legs, thumb her nipples to aching awareness.

Frustration and restless impatience sheared through
him. He couldn't have her, but he was a fraction away
from shucking convention, honor, and common sense
and taking her, relieving this ache inside him that
daily bored deeper, hollowing out his gut.

He'd even considered visiting a whorehouse in
Rocky Mount, but he wanted Elise and no one else.

Which confused the hell out of him. She had lied to
him about Onash and who knew about what else. Her
admission that she knew Onash wasn't the only thing
that nagged at Jared. Last night she had been terrified, nearly hysterical with the fear that something
had happened to her brother. And when they'd found
Logan, she had nearly cried with relief.

Something was going on, but what? His instincts
had nagged at him so, he had stayed at Fairbrooke all
night and kept Elise in his sights all morning.

She hurried out of the bank and up the boardwalk
to the hotel, her steps determined. He straightened.
Now what?

When she disappeared inside, he waited a few seconds, then slipped out from behind the corner of the
small stone church. Hurrying across the street, he angled down to the hotel, still amazed at the blatant
change in the town.

Moss Springs bore the scars of war, obvious in the
gouged earth, the charred remains of houses and businesses on the outer fringe of town. But there was also
the brazen addition of virgin-pine buildings, gleaming
wood, the taunting clang of hammers, and the smell of

pine resin in the air, boasting that there would be a new South, come hell or high water.

To Jared, the New American Hotel seemed more ostentatious than necessary, though it wasn't gaudy or, he supposed, even decorated in poor taste. He simply resented its being here at all. He stepped up on the new boardwalk and paused just outside a set of wide double doors. One stood open in welcome, a stray wedge of sunlight glinting off the lead glass inset of the door's upper half.

Pretty fancy for Moss Springs, he noted absently. He stayed well out of sight, but peered around the door and saw Elise standing in front of an imposing oak counter.

Four wooden pillars, each slightly larger around than Jared himself, marched in a well-spaced line between him and the counter where Elise stood. A sallow-faced man behind it shook his head solemnly in response to something she said.

The floor, also wood, gleamed with polish. Beside each pillar were two leafy potted plants and a brass spittoon. The ceiling was high and vaulted; plaster moldings gleamed with new white paint. The scents of new wood and lacquer teased Jared's nose as he stepped inside and slipped behind a pillar where he had a clear view of Elise and the desk.

To the right of the desk was a sturdy staircase, the wood shiny with wax, the steps bare of runners. His gaze moved back to Elise, and surprise flared through him.

A tall, slender man with snow-white hair walked up

behind her. Dressed in a finely tailored frock coat and trousers, he took her elbow and pulled her around.

Jared stiffened at the familiar way the man touched her. Elise visibly jumped and when she tried to pull away, the man tugged her to one side of the imposing desk and spoke in a low voice.

Instinctively Jared started forward, then halted. He couldn't reveal himself, not even to satisfy his overwhelming urge to tear the other man limb from limb. He'd never felt such bloodlust, not even in the midst of battle. Certainly not over a woman.

Fighting the urge to rip that hand from Elise's arm, Jared studied the man's smooth, handsome profile. He didn't look any older than Jared's own thirty years, except for that snow-white hair.

Elise and the man had their heads close together. Jared couldn't see her face, but she was no longer pulling away from him. Irritation scraped through him.

Had she come here to meet a man? To a *hotel*? Did she care nothing for her reputation?

He cautioned himself to remain detached. If she had come for a rendezvous, it was none of Jared's concern.

The hell it wasn't! How could she kiss him the way she had last night, then meet another man today?

That same irritation jabbed into his gut with the steady punch of a doubled fist. It felt strangely like jealousy.

He drew up short. Jealous? Him? Impossible.

He was simply concerned about Elise, and the protective instinct he'd been trying to escape since Logan's return now flared back in full force. Subduing the persistent impulse to haul her out of the hotel, he melted back behind the pillar.

"I asked what you were doing."

DeWitt's voice flowed smooth as silk, but Elise felt the bite of his words. He had caught her unaware as she was asking the desk clerk if DeWitt indeed lived in the hotel. Frustration rolled through her at her inability to get into his room as she rushed to think of something to tell DeWitt.

His grip bruised her arm. "Miss Worthen, are you looking for me?"

"No." She tried to tug away from him, but his glove-clad hands tightened on her upper arm.

"Do you have something for me?"

He thought she had the money. "No. I told you I didn't come to see you."

"Then what are you doing here?"

"You're not the only person in this hotel."

"It appears I'm the only person who cares that you're here."

The words rolled savagely off his tongue, and Elise wondered wildly if they were somehow a veiled threat. "My brother knows I'm here so if something happens . . ."

He laughed, a soft cruel sound that raked over her. "Ah, yes. How is your brother?"

"You vile, despicable man!" she hissed, tugging to free her arm.

He held her with a grip like steel. "You're safe enough for now. I've yet to get my money."

She glared at him, wondering if she had taken leave

of her senses. He could easily put suspicions about her
in Sheriff Restin's mind, and she should be wary of
antagonizing him. And it would do no good to protest
that she still knew nothing about his money. He cared
only that she found it.

He eyed her with amusement. "If it's not my company you seek, I can only wonder what you're doing
here. I heard you asking the hotel clerk about me."

She remained mutinously silent, her thoughts
whirling. Did it matter what she said? He would believe nothing. Panic nudged at her, but she steadfastly
kept it at bay.

He leaned closer to her, speaking in a conspiratorial
whisper. "I've seen you today, Miss Worthen. Going
about town as if you've some type of purpose. I saw
you in my bank, asking about my office."

Surprised, she stilled. Where had he been? How
had he known?

"Oh, yes. I had quite a fetching view of you, my
dear."

His breath whispered over her cheek and she shuddered in revulsion, struggling not to panic.

His fingers bit into her arm and he tilted his head
closer to hers. "If there's nothing you want from me,
you'd best stick to your own business. The sheriff will
be interested to hear about Claude's little trip to your
home. Do I make myself clear?"

She nodded, her throat so tight she could barely
squeeze out a breath.

"*Do I?*"

"Yes," she bit out, straining against his hold. His
gaze tracked over her, repulsively cold and flat.

He propelled her out the door, nearly lifting her feet from the floor. She went quietly because she could hardly cause a scene in public, not with his threats hanging over her head.

Frustration and fear clashed. She bit back a scream of pure anger.

He practically dragged her down the front steps and tipped his hat to her. "Remember what I said. Don't get any more ideas in that pretty head of yours. I will tell you what to do and when to do it."

She wanted to slap his face and clenched her fists against the sweeping urge. He released her, her arm throbbing from the bone-biting pressure.

As he walked away she stared after him, massaging the aching flesh of her upper arm. Anger burned to an icy rage inside her. She would find a way to best him. She would.

Jared frowned as he watched Elise rub her arm. Had the man hurt her? She was staring after him, but she didn't appear to be smitten with him. In fact, from what Jared could see, she looked quite upset. What the hell was going on?

She picked up her skirts and stalked across the street, anger vibrating in every slender curve. Jared was well and truly confused. Who was that man and what was he to Elise?

Satisfied that the man was no longer a threat to her, Jared tore his gaze from her and walked to the counter. The same reed-thin man behind the counter who had spoken to Elise turned with an ingratiating smile.

"May I help you, sir? A room?"

"I need some information."

"Our rates are—"

"No. The man who was just in here, the well-dressed one with the woman?"

"Mr. DeWitt?"

Jared touched his hair. "The man with white hair, not much older than me?"

"Yes, sir. Mr. Tullar DeWitt."

Tullar DeWitt. Why was that name familiar? Of course! "Thank you."

"Do you want to leave a message, sir?"

"No." Jared made his way outside, his gaze shifting to the bank. Tullar DeWitt was the new owner of the bank. The man who'd called in the Worthen loan on Jared's first day home. Why had Elise met with him? For another loan on Fairbrooke?

If that were so, then why hadn't she made an appointment with him at the bank? That damn jealousy sawed through Jared, but this time it was coupled with suspicion. Had she struck some sort of bargain with the man in an effort to get a loan? It wouldn't be inconceivable for her to follow in her daddy's footsteps and do so, but Jared couldn't imagine her doing it.

She had looked intensely upset, not as though she were considering a business proposition. Unless the man had made another type of proposition?

That unfamiliar fierceness surged through Jared again. He had a few questions to ask around town about Elise's new friend.

An hour later, Jared headed out to Fairbrooke. He'd

learned nothing positive about Tullar DeWitt. Most people were leery of the man, if not downright hostile toward him. He had ruthlessly confiscated property for the bank within weeks of giving loans on those same properties.

He had bought several lots in town with the plan to build more businesses. DeWitt owned the bank and Delavant Hall, and according to Mr. Bailey, had offered three times for the store, each time becoming more agitated when Bailey refused to sell.

Three things in particular nagged at Jared. Tullar DeWitt had come to Moss Springs at the same time as Claude Onash.

Tullar DeWitt, a native of South Carolina, had an abundance of money after the war. Federal money.

And though he couldn't swear to it, Mr. Bailey believed that at one time or another, DeWitt and Onash had been partners in a few ventures, Delavant Hall being one of them.

Was Elise aware of DeWitt's connection to Onash? Was she somehow connected to both men? Concern wound through Jared. She could be in danger if she wasn't careful. The man's eyes were too cold, his features too cruelly handsome to evoke trust.

Admittedly, Jared hadn't liked the easy way in which DeWitt had touched Elise, but there was more churning inside him than jealousy. There was also apprehension, which mushroomed as he headed for Fairbrooke.

He kneed Trick into a flat-out gallop. Elise was a fool for getting involved with such a man, and Jared intended to warn her about further dealings with Tullar DeWitt. He hoped she would listen to reason.

Elise fumed the whole way home. She'd gotten nowhere in her plan to learn anything about DeWitt, and now she half feared Restin would be waiting for her when she arrived home.

Elise's arm still throbbed from DeWitt's vicious grip and her anger throbbed right along with it. There had to be a way she could escape his blackmail, but short of confessing to the murders, she didn't know of one.

She rode down the drive toward the house, relieved to see no horses or wagons, no sign of the sheriff. She reined up in the barn, the problem still worrying her like a stray splinter. She would think of something. She had to.

After unsaddling and rubbing down Majesty, Elise went to the house. Slipping off her gloves, she stepped into the dining room, surprised to see Logan asleep on the settee. Fondness welled up in her. In sleep, he looked more like the brother she had known.

Gone were the brutal shadows in his eyes, the bitter lines around his mouth and eyes. He shifted, moving his bad leg, and a faint frown drew between his brows.

Thank goodness Dru had agreed to come. As upset as she'd gotten over seeing DeWitt, Elise had nearly forgotten about the promise she'd wrung from the doctor. She hoped Dru's visit wouldn't go as badly as Elise's visit to town.

She laid her riding gloves on the edge of the dining

table and started upstairs for the money she'd promised Dru. She halted on the bottom step, wondering if she should risk using any more of the money she'd taken from Claude Onash.

Jared was too suspicious, and if he hadn't already, he would soon be asking more questions in town about her. Perhaps Dru would take payment in food. If not, then Elise would use some of the money.

That decided, she walked through the foyer to the back of the house. Taking a floppy straw hat from a peg beside the back door, she went out to the garden to get carrots, greens, and potatoes.

The warmth of the sun on her back calmed her churning emotions, and she worked off her frustration by stabbing the trowel into the dirt repeatedly. She loosened vegetables, moving her fingers through the dirt, soothed by the scent of grass and growing vegetation.

Sweat trickled between her breasts, down her temple, and her hair worked itself free from the tight braid she wore. Focused on the rage that sifted through her, Elise dug and pulled and uprooted, wishing she could uproot DeWitt as easily. Tendrils of hair straggled in her eyes and she pushed them away with the back of her hand, now dusted with dirt.

Despite her protests, DeWitt had known exactly what she was doing. Perdition! She was ill-suited to skulking about and gathering information for blackmail.

There had to be something else she could do. She stabbed the dirt with the trowel, wishing it were De-

Witt. Staring down at her hands she saw again the Onashes' blood, and guilt seared her.

Yes, she'd done murder, but she'd had no other choice. She'd done what was necessary in order to survive. And, despite being forced to go along with DeWitt's white-trash tactics, she would do what was necessary now. She would think of a way to even the odds between her and DeWitt. With or without Logan.

Several minutes later she gathered her basket of vegetables, walking back inside the cool interior of the house. She washed her hands in a basin next to the pantry door and dried them on a small towel.

"Who are you?"

Elise perked up at her brother's blunt words and she hurried into the foyer.

Dru said pleasantly, "I don't believe we've been introduced—"

"Are you lost? Do you have business here?"

"Yes, I—"

"Dru, I didn't hear you drive up!" Elise walked into the foyer, noticing that Logan stood stiffly in the dining-room doorway, his gaze hard and unblinking. "Have you met my brother?"

"Well, not formally." Dru switched her medical bag to her left hand and extended her right, gloved in soft butter kid. "How do you do, Mr. Worthen."

Logan shot a glance at Elise, but he took Dru's hand and bent low over it. "You have me at a disadvantage."

"Logan, this is Dru Hawthorne." Elise moved up

beside him, removing her straw hat and fanning herself.

"Hawthorne?" He frowned. "As in the doctor?"

"Yes." Dru smiled, her gray eyes lighting warmly.

Logan scowled and dropped her hand as if it were poxed. "You've wasted a trip, Doctor. I don't know what my sister told you, but I don't require the services of a physician." His gaze raked over her. "Or a woman."

Elise's eyes widened at Logan's rudeness. A quick glance at Dru showed the other woman was also surprised, but she didn't seem overly offended.

"Your sister asked me to take a look at you and I agreed," Dru said pleasantly, firmly.

"Well, this is all the look you'll get." He turned on his heel and limped into the dining room.

Elise cast an apologetic glance at Dru and cautioned her to wait a minute. She hurried after Logan. "What is the matter with you? She drove all the way out here. You can at least let her look at your leg."

"I told you I didn't want to see her."

"Logan, she won't do anything you don't want."

"She already is, by being here."

Anger fluttered. "You're being ridiculous. Where are your manners? She is a guest in our home, whether *you* invited her or not."

"Mr. Worthen, if I may have a moment?" Dru spoke from the doorway, startling both brother and sister.

Elise turned, wondering if she had made a mistake by asking Dru to come.

Logan stared past Elise, his features locked in an

impenetrable mask. She suddenly realized that if she hadn't known her brother, she would be quite intimidated by him. Dru, however, didn't appear to be.

"If you'll let me explain what I intend to do, I think you'll find it's nothing to make you uncomfortable."

"Lady, you make me uncomfortable just standing there with that damn black bag."

Elise's jaw dropped. She had never seen her brother behave in such a way, not even to people he disliked.

The other woman walked into the room, her chin angled stubbornly. "Mr. Worthen, let me assure you I've had proper training and I worked with patients throughout the war. I have extensive experience—"

"I just bet you do," he sneered.

Dru's lips tightened and a flush spread up her neck. "Couldn't you at least let me check you over since I promised your sister?"

Logan turned and walked slowly over to the settee, easing himself down. "You'll pardon me if I don't stand. As a cripple, I have trouble doing that for long."

Elise bit her lip. This was a bad idea, the worst.

Dru followed him over to the settee and knelt in front of him. Opening her bag, she set it on the floor. "It will be easier if you're sitting."

Logan leaned right into her face. "You can just get your Yankee self out of here 'cuz you're not touching me."

"Logan!" Elise rushed over to the settee. She was mighty close to losing her temper, guest or no guest.

"It's all right." The doctor's gaze never wavered from Logan's, and her voice remained even and reasonable. "Now, what could it hurt for me to simply look at your leg, Mr. Worthen?"

"Well, I'll tell you what." He leaned back into the settee, his voice lowering suggestively. "I'll show you mine if you'll show me yours."

Elise thought she would suffer apoplexy on the spot. "Logan, what has gotten into you?"

Dru blushed a deep rose, but her chin came up and she spoke in the same silky-steel tone that Logan had used. "I'm sure you can insult me beautifully, Mr. Worthen, but that's not going to help your leg. Now, are you going to be a big boy and let me have a look or are you really that afraid of little ol' me?"

Surprised laughter bubbled out of Elise and she clamped a hand over her mouth, watching Logan with some misgiving.

Her brother glared at Dru, then struggled to his feet. "Your esteemed Northern boys did this to me, lady. I wouldn't let a Yankee butcher touch my leg if you were the last breathin' person on God's earth."

He turned on Elise, struggling for balance and catching himself on the corner of the settee. "I told you to leave me alone, to quit pestering me."

"Lower your voice," she hissed, her anger and desperation merging. "I was only trying to help you."

"I wish I'd never come back. I wish I'd never seen the outside of that prison!"

Elise blanched and nausea kicked in her gut. "You don't mean that."

Dru moved until she stood nose to nose with Logan, and her voice trembled. "I'd like to break your leg myself for that selfish cruelty, Mr. Worthen. Your sister loves you and I'm starting to think her a saint for it."

"Nobody asked your opinion, Yank," he sneered, lowering his face threateningly to hers.

Elise wanted to jerk Dru away from him, but the doctor stood her ground, anger vibrating through her body. "When you decide to stop blaming everyone for your problem, you know where my office is."

"It'll be a cold day in hell before I come crawling to a damn Yankee butcher."

Dru snatched her bag from the floor and snapped it shut, walking to the door. "Good day, Elise."

"Oh, Dru, I'm so sorry." Elise followed her. "I had no idea he would go this far."

"I certainly don't blame you." Dru opened the front door and halted abruptly.

Elise barely caught herself from slamming into the doctor.

"Excuse me," Dru said.

"Pardon me." Jared's deep voice resonated through the foyer, and Elise peered around Dru.

His gaze went speculatively from her to the doctor, and he removed his hat. "Is everything all right?"

"Yes." Elise gestured to Dru. "Jared, this is Dr. Hawthorne. Dru, this is Thomas's grandson, Jared Kensington."

"How nice to meet you, Mr. Kensington." Dru's northern accent was clipped due to anger, but she smiled winningly and extended her hand.

He bowed over it. "A pleasure. I'd like to thank you for taking such good care of Gramps. Elise told me his recovery is all due to you."

"*That* was my pleasure. Your grandfather is a charmer."

"Yes, you'd best watch yourself," Jared warned teasingly.

Why was he teasing Dru? He'd only just met her. Piqued, Elise glanced pointedly at his hand still holding Dru's. Amusement glinting in his eyes, he released the doctor.

Truly annoyed now, Elise waved him inside. "Logan's in the dining room. You can see yourself in, if you'll pardon me."

"Certainly." He turned to the other woman. "It was nice to meet you, Dr. Hawthorne."

"Oh, Dru, please." The doctor smiled easily at him.

"Dru, then." He smiled, his features softening in a way Elise had never seen.

She stepped between them, taking Dru's elbow and guiding her around Jared. "Thank you so much for coming, Dru. And I apologize for Logan. I had no idea he would act so awful. I mean, I thought he'd be angry, but nothing like this."

"I admit I let my temper get the better of me, but I think this is a good sign."

"You do! After those things he said to you? I was mortified!" Elise was aware that Jared still stood on the porch, watching the two of them. She moved down the steps, pleased when the doctor followed. "He would never have behaved in that way before."

"It's all right. I've heard worse. I don't know why I allowed him to goad me, but perhaps something will come of it."

"I don't see how." Elise shook her head, amazed that Dru wasn't insulted beyond belief.

"You never know. Now, you'll come to me if you need anything further?"

"Yes. If you're willing."

"Don't give it another thought." Dru laughed, climbing into the buggy and glancing at Jared, who still stood on the porch. She placed her bag under the seat, lowering her voice. "He's a friend of your brother's?"

Elise looked over her shoulder, her skin tightening at the intense green gaze Jared focused on her. "Yes, they've been friends forever."

"Hmmm. He seems more interested in you."

Elise's gaze shot to Dru and she flushed. "Me?"

Dru smiled knowingly.

Elise glanced at him, dread curling through her. She was coming to know that determined look in his eyes and it didn't bode well for her. It was no kiss he was thinking of, but more questions. Was that why he still waited on the porch?

Just then he turned and went into the house, and the tension Elise always felt around him eased. Dru might think Jared was interested in Elise, but she knew it was more because of his curiosity and the suspicion he seemed to wear like a second skin.

Resentment overtook her. She was frustratingly, constantly aware of him, and Jared maintained a polite distance. Though Elise knew she should do the same, she was suddenly tired of it. And lonelier than she'd been in years.

She remained outdoors until the doctor had disappeared, doubts niggling at her. Had she done the right thing by enlisting Dru's aid? The doctor's visit with Logan had gone poorly, as poorly as Elise's trip to town.

Moving into the house, she halted as Jared and Logan walked out of the dining room.

"I'll wait for you down here," Jared said as Logan walked past him toward the stairs.

Her brother glared at Elise and passed in front of her, dragging his bad leg. Doubt surged back, stronger than before.

Jared walked over next to her, his arm brushing hers. His gaze followed Logan as well. "I've never seen him that angry. He hasn't stopped talking about 'that brazen woman' since I walked in."

"Maybe I shouldn't have asked her to come." She chewed at her bottom lip, wishing Jared wouldn't stand so close. The musky heat of him scattered her thoughts, eroded her determination to keep a distance. She forced herself to remember the way he'd relentlessly demanded answers from her last night. "Dru thinks his anger is a good sign."

"I think she's probably right."

"You do?" She glanced up at him, then wished she hadn't. Single-minded intense purpose, directed at her, shone in his green eyes.

His gaze roamed her features for a moment. "It was probably the smartest thing you could've done."

"Really?"

Jared nodded. "Logan needs something to get his mind off himself. You're a good woman, Elise."

His smile was tender, encouraging, and Elise's

knees wobbled. Awareness thickened the air between
them. Elise knew she should move away, look away,
something to break the hold his gaze seemed to have
on her.

"I saw you in town today."

She froze. "Oh?"

"With a man."

"A man?" she echoed, panic shifting through her.

"You should choose your beaux more carefully."
Jared's voice was low and seductive, his gaze moving
to her lips.

Her beaux? Surprised and confused by his words,
she stared at him. "I beg your pardon?"

"Mr. DeWitt, the man you met with this morning?"
His words were deliberate, his gaze piercing. "Isn't he
your beau?"

CHAPTER ELEVEN

"*M*y beau?" He'd seen her with DeWitt! How much had he seen? Where had he been? Had he been spying on her?

Jared glanced back toward the stairs, checking for Logan she presumed, before he continued in a low seductive rasp, "He's quite wealthy, your Mr. DeWitt. But the word about town is not good."

Her Mr. DeWitt? Revulsion and panic crowded in on her and she could barely get a breath. "You asked questions about him?"

"Of course."

His offhand manner sparked her anger. "What business is it of yours, Jared Kensington?" she demanded in a harsh whisper.

His voice slid over her like midnight velvet. "Your brother wasn't there to watch over you, so I did."

He expected her to believe he'd snooped about De-Witt because he was concerned about protecting her? "I don't need either one of you looking after me."

"DeWitt seems a shady character, Elise. From what I learned . . ."

"It's none of your affair." She struggled to keep her voice down, not wanting Logan to overhear. She tried to step around Jared, but he planted himself squarely in front of her, his broad chest nudging hers.

His gaze traced slowly over her face, then down to her breasts. "He had his hands all over you."

"He did not!" Her skin tingled and her breasts grew heavy, throbbing as if he were touching her. "We were . . . talking. That's all. He—he owns the bank."

"I know he owns the bank," he hissed. "I was here the day he sent Anthony and Restin to collect on that lien, remember?"

Of course, why hadn't she thought of it before? Paying off that lien had spawned Jared's suspicions in the first place.

"That was no business meeting I saw. He seemed to touch you as if he had a right." A savage light flared in his eyes and he inched closer, backing her against the wall, his chest and thighs tempered steel against the softness of hers. "Does he?" .

Her heartbeat kicked up. She stared in rapt fascination at the muscle flexing in his jaw, the raw hunger in his green eyes. He was acting like a betrayed suitor. At the realization, twin emotions of pleasure and irritation wound through her, but she grasped at the excuse he'd offered. "It *was* a business meeting."

"Why did you see him?"

Because he's blackmailing me, she longed to throw at

him. But of course she couldn't. "That's really none of your—"

"I don't think Logan would approve of you seeing him. For any reason." Jared angled his body into hers, the scent of sun-warmed male and leather and horse-flesh surrounding her. "DeWitt has a reputation for being a coldhearted bastard. You shouldn't be carrying on with him at all."

"I'm not *carrying on* with him." She squeezed her elbows between them and pushed against his chest. "I *was* trying to get a loan."

She couldn't budge him. He shifted and flattened one palm on the wall behind her, imprisoning her completely. "That little scene I witnessed this morning might have been about business, but it wasn't loan business."

Apprehension and anticipation inched up her spine. Jared's breath mingled with hers, sending a tingle across her skin. She wanted to lean into him, feel his lips on hers. She knew she was a fool.

Though he might think less of her, it was better that he believe she'd seen DeWitt for a loan. "Please don't tell Logan. I don't want to burden him with this and Mr. DeWitt may not approve it anyway."

She was going to hell for lying. She knew it as surely as she knew her next breath. But she had no choice. If DeWitt learned Jared had seen their meeting and was suspicious of their motives, she *knew* he would make good on his threat to contact the sheriff.

Jared sighed and pinched the bridge of his nose. "Why will you never answer my questions?"

"Why do you ask so many?"

His gaze bored into hers, probing, edged with anger. Elise swallowed, wondering if she'd pushed him too far.

A noise sounded at the top of the stairs, causing both of them to jerk. She took advantage of the moment to duck under Jared's arm and step several feet away from him.

Logan moved into sight and boomed, "Kensington, may I borrow a horse tomorrow?"

Elise stared up at her brother, trying to calm the sense of panic that nipped at her.

Jared shrugged, obviously surprised. "Sure."

"Somebody needs to take a look around Fairbrooke," Logan grumbled, turning on his heel and disappearing around the corner at the top of the stairs. "Take it in hand."

Elise's gaze shifted to Jared's and her eyes widened.

He grinned, causing her stomach to knot as he called after her brother, "Care for some company?"

"Fine."

Logan's tone was flat, but Elise heard the grudging pleasure beneath the words. She smiled up at Jared, hope bursting through her chest. "Maybe that visit from Dru *did* help."

"Maybe." His gaze narrowed on her again. "About that business with DeWitt?"

"Please don't say anything to Logan."

He folded his arms across his chest and studied her as if trying to decipher a riddle. "If I don't believe you about the loan, neither will he."

"Please?" Desperation tightened her throat. "Jared—"

"I won't say anything about your visit with De-Witt."

"Oh, thank you—"

"*If* you'll promise to stay away from him."

Elise exhaled in exasperation, wondering how much ground to give. "I might need to see him again."

"I told you I don't believe it's about money."

That was the one thing she had told the truth about.

"I mean it, Elise. You'd better watch your step with that character. I don't know how you're mixed up with him, but I don't like it."

It wasn't jealousy in his eyes now, but deep concern. Fighting the impulse to tell him to mind his own business, she said quietly, "I'll be careful. I know what he is."

"I hope you do." Jared slammed his hat on his head and opened the door, grumbling, "I thought you had better sense than to see someone like that."

"Well, I would never—"

He silenced her with a look and stepped onto the porch.

She marched after him. "He's not my beau!"

Jared's glittering green gaze impaled her. "Then tell him to keep his damn hands to himself. Or I will."

Stunned shock held her silent for a moment. As he mounted his horse Elise moved onto the porch, prepared to tell him he had no right to interfere with her life, but a tiny spiral of pleasure worked its way through her.

He cared what happened to her. *To her.* Not to Logan's little sister, not to someone he'd sworn to look after. Her.

But her pleasure was shadowed with dread. He didn't believe her story about seeing DeWitt for a loan. And he was right about Logan. If her brother ever shook off his melancholy long enough to notice what was happening around him, he wouldn't believe it either.

She had to find DeWitt's money—or a way to get him to leave her alone—before Jared discovered the truth.

Why had Elise met with DeWitt? Jared didn't buy for one minute her story about getting a loan. If that were true, she would've met the man at the bank. He also knew the man wasn't her beau. He'd only said that to try to startle something out of her.

As he rode the next morning with Logan, unease steadily settled over Jared like building fog, growing deeper, denser, obscuring the clear path of duty he knew he should take. His mind was a mass of jumbled confusion.

He wanted to shake answers out of her and at the same time, he wanted to kiss her, run his hands over her lithe body. It was beyond him how this cursed hunger could grow, when he *knew* she was involved in something suspicious. *He knew it.*

He and Logan rode along the west borderline of Fairbrooke, the side closest to Jared's home. Neither of them said much, but Jared sensed that his friend's tension eased as they rode around the property.

They wove in and out of the woods bordering the Worthen land, edging their way around the plantation, taking stock of the fallow torched fields that were spotted with blackened patches of ground and bare places worn slick by passing horses and soldiers. Jared wished some of Logan's newly gained peace would work its way over him. He didn't know where to go next.

Questioning Elise was like trying to hold a trout with buttered fingers. Especially when he found himself less and less willing to pursue his suspicions. And more and more hungry to satisfy this lust steepling inside him.

Even now he could smell her sweet scent on his skin and wanted to touch her. He wanted to hear her pant his name in ragged passion, wanted to feel her tongue on his, feel her small, delicate hands stroking him, urging him into her—

"Jared! You there?"

He jerked toward Logan, struggling to separate Elise's voice in his mind from her brother's. He shook his head. "Sorry. Just admiring the view."

They reined up at a clear bubbling creek to water their horses. Morning sunlight glared off the water, shooting diamonds of light onto the grassy bank. As youngsters, they'd come here often to swim or fish.

"My leg hurts like hell." Logan dismounted, slowly and carefully, but with more ease than Jared had seen since his return. Unhooking a canteen from the pommel, he limped to the water's edge and knelt to fill the canteen. "So, are you going to tell me what's on your mind?"

Jared dismounted, stifling a chuckle. Logan would
hardly appreciate learning the specifics of Jared's
thoughts about Elise.

He should've known Logan would pick up on his
preoccupation, but he was uncertain about how much
to tell his friend. Jared wanted to tell all of it, but
since Logan's return he'd been ill-prepared for any
such news.

Jared wondered if now was the right time. He
wouldn't confide his suspicions concerning Elise;
he couldn't bring himself to be that forthcoming.
Besides, what did he have to show against her? Nothing. But he did want his friend to know what he was
doing.

"Well?" Logan rose and turned to face him, wiping
his mouth with the back of his hand.

Jared reached in his trousers pocket, removing
Cam's letter and handing it to Logan. He walked past
Logan and dipped his hand in the clear water, rubbing
it across the back of his neck. The scent of crushed
grass and moist earth drifted in the air.

Logan glanced at the Seal of the United States
Treasury Department and Campbell McMillan's name
at the bottom. "You're working for Cam? For the
Treasury? Hell, I can't believe that!"

"Neither can I," Jared said dryly.

Logan slanted a glance at him. "Are they blackmailing you?"

Jared chuckled. "No. It's partly to repay a debt and
partly to get a start on rebuilding Briar Rose."

Logan frowned. "What debt?"

"Cam. He's the one who found out where you

were. I'd been looking everywhere, asking everyone, but couldn't learn a thing. Cam was in a mess with Secretary McCulloch because some money was stolen by one of his agents and—"

"And he wanted you to find it. He's no fool. He knows what trust Mosby placed in you." Logan handed back the paper with a faint smile. "So you traded favors?"

"Something like that." Jared returned the paper to his pocket, studying a grandaddy sweet gum that guarded the gurgling water. "If that stolen money isn't recovered, he stands to lose his job and possibly be brought up on charges."

"He had nothing to do with it!"

"It was on his watch."

"No matter that Cam wouldn't steal so much as a breath of air if he thought it belonged to another man. Even though he is a Yank." Logan exhaled sharply. "That's only one of the things I hate about the army." He pushed back his hat and eyed Jared speculatively. "They're giving you adequate compensation?"

"More than." Jared scratched his neck, plucking a thin twig from the branch above him. "Three thousand dollars."

"Three thousand dollars?" Logan's jaw dropped. "They must want that money bad."

"Just before Appomattox, a shipment of cotton was seized in Richmond."

"By an authorized Treasury agent," Logan surmised dryly.

"Who else? Though the agents were entitled to twenty-five percent from the seizure, one of them decided he wanted it all. We know who he was, and I've established that he had a partner. The two of them killed the other agent and took off with the money."

"Currency?"

"Yes."

"Why not a draft?"

Jared shrugged. "The buyer wouldn't deal with a draft and the Treasury intended the money to be used to handle the currency-for-gold exchange, so they agreed to hand over cash."

"And you think there's a clue in Moss Springs?"

"The man lived here, but no one's seen him in a while."

"Hmmm. Maybe he moved on."

"Considered that, too, but I've been asking some questions." Jared stripped the pliable bark from the twig he held. "Looks like he might have met with foul play."

"Killed?" Logan's eyebrows shot up.

Jared shrugged. "That's what I'm thinking."

"And no sign of the money?"

"Not really." He tossed the twig into the water. There was the disturbing fact that Elise had paid off her father's lien with Federal money, but Jared wasn't willing to share that information with Logan. Not yet anyway.

Besides, it was possible Elise had already confided in Logan and Jared wanted nothing he said to raise his friend's suspicions.

All during the return ride to Fairbrooke, a sense of dark expectancy hung over him, a swelling energy in the air that hinted at some unforeseen, unanticipated consequence.

They rode onto the grounds from the northeast, coming up on the back of the house. Trick and the mare Jared had loaned Logan needed no urging toward the barn; they swung past the garden and up between the house and the barn.

Jared and Logan dismounted, leaving the horses to graze beside the pump. As they came around the corner of the house, Logan stopped abruptly.

"Who the hell is that?"

Jared followed his friend's gaze to the porch. He could see Elise clearly, but could only make out the bell-shaped profile of a man speaking to her.

Logan leaned heavily on his walking stick, forcing his steps faster.

Jared lengthened his strides and came around the corner, getting a clear view of Elise's visitor. He could also see the paleness of Elise's face, the concern that tightened her features. "It's the sheriff."

"The sheriff?" Logan limped faster. "What the hell does he want?"

That was exactly what Jared wanted to know.

"You want to ask me about Claude Onash?" Panic clawed through her. DeWitt had set Restin on to her in retribution for her snooping. She knew it.

From the corner of her eye she saw Jared and Logan coming around the front of the house. Her legs wobbled, but she forced herself to stay on the porch and not bolt into the house.

"Sheriff, to what do we owe the pleasure?" Logan

moved awkwardly past Toby Restin and up the porch steps to stop beside Elise.

She glanced at him, surprised and relieved at his protective stance. This was more like the Logan she had known.

She chanced a look at Jared, who looked as fierce as Logan, though wary speculation burned in his eyes as he moved to her other side.

Restin's fleshy lips curved into a semblance of a smile and the dank smell of snuff drifted to her. "I just came out to ask your sister a couple of questions."

"Concerning?" Logan drew to his full height, gripping the walking stick tightly.

Restin's gaze moved to the crude cane for a moment, then back to Elise. "There's a couple of men been missing for a while. Claude Onash and his son."

"Why would my sister know anything about that?"

" 'Cuz she was here while you wuz at war." Restin smiled, glancing pointedly at Logan's twisted leg.

Elise felt her brother stiffen and laid a hand on his arm. "I believe I already told you I didn't know them."

"Well, ma'am, I believe what you told me was that Claude didn't talk to you about no lien." Restin grinned, showing brown-stained teeth. The odor of cheap whiskey mingled with the sourness of tobacco. "But I got some information says that he and his son came out here to see your daddy, about seven or eight weeks ago, concerning this property."

"I already said I'd never seen him."

"Ah, yeah. So you did." The sheriff hooked his thumbs under the straps of his grungy suspenders.

"But I've learned from an interested party that Claude and his son were squatting on your daddy's property. There, up in the northeast quarter. A little cabin there."

"What?" Her shock was real. *How had he learned about that?* No one, except she and her parents, had known.

She noted the sharp, startled look her brother gave her.

"What 'interested' party?" Jared demanded, tension ripping the air around him.

"Cain't be tellin' that." Restin puffed up like a windblown petticoat, his black eyes turning pebble hard. "I heard he had a run-in with your pa. Reckon it could'a been about that lien at the bank. Or it could'a been about him squatting on your daddy's property. Now, missy, you got anything you want to tell me?"

Fear and dread reached for her, but Elise fought them off. "I already told you I didn't know anything about that lien."

"Lien? What lien?" Logan looked from Elise to Restin.

"I'll tell you later." Her heart threatened to pump right out of her chest as she met the sheriff's gaze. "There was no run-in."

"Hmmm, is that so? That ain't how I heard it."

"I never saw anyone there." That, at least, was true, but Elise wasn't even sure how she managed to speak. Her throat was too tight to squeeze past a breath. She felt Jared's intense regard, and sweat prickled her palms.

"Well, you know I'll have to investigate."

"Perhaps you'll do that when you have something solid to go on?" Jared stepped forward, towering over the squatty sheriff.

Logan moved up, too, both of them flanking Elise like immovable columns. "My sister has answered your questions. Perhaps you'd best go."

"Be right happy to." The sheriff touched his limp dirty hat and edged down the porch stairs. "But I'll be back."

Panic hammered like a giant fist in her temple, and she felt light-headed. She stood quietly with Jared and Logan, resisting the urge to grab hold of them both and steady herself.

No one spoke until Restin disappeared down the drive, then Logan turned to her. "Why the hell didn't you tell me Papa had taken out a lien?"

The combined pressure of Restin's questions and Jared's quiet suspicion abraded her nerves. "Up until today, you haven't exactly cared what was going on here!"

"Well, I do now!" Logan sputtered, anger flushing his features.

"Whoa." Jared shifted closer to Elise, his heat reassuring her. "Take it easy, Logan."

Logan eyed Jared for a moment, then held up a hand. "All right. Elise, I'm sorry. I was just shocked to hear about a lien."

"Well, so was I." She rubbed her forehead, decisions and questions and information pressing in on her. What was she going to do?

Logan gentled his voice. "I guess you need to catch

me up. I'm . . . sorry for the way I've behaved since I returned, but I can help you now. At least, I'll try."

Elise nodded, but her attention was focused on Jared. He was too quiet and she couldn't stop the panic that rolled through her.

Restin had brought to light another connection between her and Onash. All she needed was for Jared to become curious about that sharecropper's cabin, but she could read nothing in his eyes.

He studied Logan for a moment, then moved down the steps. "I'll leave you two to talk."

"You're going?" Dismay sharpened her voice.

Logan nodded at his friend. "Thanks for riding with me today."

Elise saw the determination that tightened Jared's jaw, the glint of purpose in his green eyes, and dread skated over her. What was he planning? She took an involuntary step forward.

"Keep the horse, as long as you need her," he offered to Logan.

"Thanks." Logan turned to Elise, frowning slightly. "Are you all right?"

She couldn't take her gaze from Jared, watching until his broad shoulders disappeared around the corner of the house. "Yes, why?"

"You look like you've seen a ghost."

"Don't be silly." She managed a wan smile, her breath knotting in her throat as Jared thundered past, a hand raised in farewell.

She lifted a hand, unable to stanch a frantic burst of urgency. Something told her that wherever Jared was going meant trouble for her.

She became aware then of Logan's measured gaze
on her. Pulling her eyes from the dust churned up by
Jared's horse, she met her brother's speculative look.

"Anything else you want to tell me?"

Dread and suspicion and downright resentment
boiled through him. The Onashes had been squatting
on Fairbrooke. *And Elise had known.*

Jared had read it in the paleness of her face, the
dark fear in her eyes, the tightness around her soft
lips.

Misery knotted his gut. Every crashing blow of
Trick's hooves echoed the agony slamming through
his body. He didn't want Elise to be involved. He
didn't want to find out for certain that she'd lied about
Onash. He didn't want to find anything at that sharecropper's cabin.

He knew the answers were there, and he had to go.
Yet he resented the hell out of the duty that forced
him to swing Trick back to the north, take cover in the
woods that bordered Fairbrooke, and ride for the little
cabin he hadn't visited in years.

Each strike of Trick's hooves ripped at Jared's
nerves. Agony and anger fused inside him and he
rode. Because he had no other choice.

CHAPTER TWELVE

"*N*o one's lived here for at least five years." Gramps looked around the small cabin that squatted in the middle of the clearing. "I don't know what you think you're going to find."

"I hope I don't find *anything*." Apprehension skittered across Jared's shoulders as he plunged the shovel into the dirt.

He hadn't intended to bring his grandfather, but he had run into him hauling rotten fence posts to Fairbrooke to share as firewood. Gramps had insisted on accompanying Jared and he'd allowed it. When Gramps set his mind on something, he was harder to shake than a flea.

The small cabin was just over the rise from where Jared and Logan had been only an hour ago. Already Jared had searched inside the house, finding nothing. Outside, he'd scanned the trees and bushes, finally detecting a slight mound in the dirt beneath the thorn bush where he now dug. The spindly sprawling bush was shaded by trees, carpeted by cool moss, and prickly enough to be an ideal hiding place.

Something was here, something in the earth that would give him a clue to Onash. And Elise's connection to the man. Jared felt it in the humming of his blood, the dread that slipped around his neck like a noose.

Elise had stated to the sheriff that she'd never seen the Onashes here, but she'd *implied* they had never been here. If Restin's information was correct and the Onashes had lived here, then Elise had lied. Again.

It was becoming disquietingly obvious to Jared that there was no reason for her to lie unless she had the money. Or a hand in Claude's disappearance. He tossed a spadeful of dirt to the side, glancing up.

The unrelenting glare of the midday sun framed the rawness of the sagging cabin and its rough wood, underscoring the emptiness that emanated from the house. The cool fall air seethed with secrets, a sense of mystery.

Whatever Jared uncovered today would be revealed in stark, uncompromising detail, and the thought spurred a sweep of misgiving.

Gramps stood quietly to Jared's right, surveying the property. "What makes you think anyone's been here?"

"I learned today that Claude and Pervis Onash lived here."

"Did Curtis know that?" Gramps' eyebrows snapped together.

"I think he found out." Jared wondered again how

the Worthens' deaths were linked to the Onashes' disappearance.

With each shovel of dirt, anxiety cinched his chest so tight, he couldn't breathe. Though he'd been hesitant and uncertain about allowing Gramps to join him, Jared was suddenly grateful that he wasn't alone.

He didn't want to think about what it would mean if he found a clear sign that the Onashes had been here, what it would mean if he tied Elise to them. It would not only imply her guilt but would mean she'd *manipulated* him. He who'd vowed never to be led around by a woman the way his father had been.

Gramps ceased his pacing and stilled, as though he sensed the agony and dread cresting inside Jared. As he dug, growing more certain of what he'd find, his movements grew slower, more reluctant. Three feet into the ground, he jabbed something solid.

Jared turned another shovelful of dirt and the thick, dank odor of death burst from the ground. With shaking hands, he pushed aside the loose earth, revealing a body. It was decaying but still identifiable as a man.

"Hell." Jared bowed his head.

"Saints preserve us!" Gramps muttered behind him.

Bile rose in Jared's throat, along with denial. He turned over the body and saw the face of a young man, thin-featured and streaked with blood. His eyes were matted shut and a bullet hole gaped in his chest. Pervis?

"Oh, dear." Worry lowered Gramps' voice.

No, Elise couldn't be involved in this. Not murder. Jared looked away, trying to gulp in air that seemed to have evaporated. Rolling the body out of the way, he found another body beneath. This one was heavier, older.

He sucked in a deep breath, dread coiling through his gut like sharp wire. Jared couldn't recognize the man's features, but the corpse was missing two middle fingers on the left hand. It was Claude Onash.

Anguish drilled into him. It all made sense— Onash's disappearance, Elise's ability to pay the lien. She had the money, but had she *killed* them? If not, then why deny knowing them? Why hide the bodies? Of course, he couldn't prove that she had anything to do with these bodies. Yes, she had Federal money in her possession, but maybe Curtis had indeed had some money put aside.

Claude was heavyset, but his chest and once ample belly were a mangled hollow cavity. From the wounds on his back, it looked as if he'd been shot at least four times.

"Lord have mercy," Gramps breathed.

Jared blinked, his vision blurring. He told himself that Elise had had no part in these murders. Someone else could've killed them and buried them here. But her links to them were too coincidental.

His soul burned. "Why, Elise? Why?"

"You can't think *Elise* had anything to do with this!"

At Gramps' exclamation Jared realized he'd spoken aloud. He wished he could cover up these bodies and ride out. Misery lashed him as he looked up at his grandfather. "Yes. I think she did."

"That's absurd! Why? Why would she do such a thing?"

Jared glanced at Claude's motionless body. "I'd say thirty thousand dollars is enough of a reason."

"Elise would never kill anyone, let alone for money!"

"I don't want to think she killed them, but she evidently has some Federal money, when no other honest Southerner does." Jared willed away the choking pressure in his chest, but it grew sharper. "How else do you explain the way she paid off the lien on Fairbrooke?"

"Not by killing these men." Gramps defended Elise, his face flushed.

Jared didn't want to believe it either, but he could not ignore all the suspicions that had led him here. Hauling in a deep breath, he turned back to the bodies. He carefully lifted Claude onto the shoulder of the pit and as he did, a piece of clothing fell loose, draping over the dirt.

"That girl had nothing to do with this." Gramps paced the short length of the grave. "I know her."

"I'm sorry, Gramps." Jared reached for the material, thinking it was part of the man's shirt. But the fabric was bunched and wrapped around Claude's middle, like a bandage. He frowned. "I know she's involved somehow. I just can't prove how yet."

"She didn't take that money. And if she killed these men, she had a good reason."

Jared tugged until the complete piece of fabric came free in his hand. It wasn't the man's shirt as he'd first assumed.

No. He held the garment at arm's length and dread slashed him.

It was a woman's dress.

He closed his eyes, regret and denial surging through him. Gramps spoke beside him, but Jared wasn't listening. His head spun and he wished he'd never agreed to take this job.

Why would a woman's dress be buried with Claude Onash? To hide the corpse? Stanch the gunshot wounds? The worn, thin fabric was matted and stiff. The bodice, which buttoned up the front, was ripped to the waist and the right sleeve was torn. Stained with blood and black dirt, it was difficult to tell the color, though he could see the garment wasn't large. It could easily fit Elise.

Denial surged through him. *She couldn't be involved, not to this extent.* His heart reached for an escape, anything to allow him to deny what his instincts screamed. He had no proof she was involved, but he felt it with gut-searing certainty.

Misery pulled at him. Stumbling to his feet, he dragged in another breath, wanting it to cleanse him of suspicion, of duty. He clutched the dress in his hand, wishing he could make it disappear, wishing he'd never found it.

"That dress doesn't prove anything," Gramps said stubbornly beside him.

Hating himself for what he had to do, Jared turned to his grandfather. His voice rasped with pain. "Do you recognize it?"

Disbelief paled the older man's face, and his gaze narrowed on Jared.

"I have to ask." He knew how much store his grandfather set by Elise, but Jared had a job to do. Gramps had spent more time with her than anyone else. If the dress belonged to her, Gramps would probably know. "Have you seen it on Elise?"

Anguish pinched Thomas Kensington's leathery features and resistance stiffened his body.

"Please, Gramps?" Jared's voice was hoarse and tortured. "I don't like this any better than you do, but I have no choice."

"I'm telling you, boy." Gramps' eyes blazed. "Elise has nothing to do with this."

"Please answer me, Gramps."

The other man held Jared's gaze, challenging.

Jared's throat ached; his heartbeat slammed against his ribs with unerring, punishing precision. He wanted to be wrong. He wanted Gramps to say, unequivocally, that the dress didn't belong to Elise. That he had seen someone else wearing it.

Gramps lowered a reluctant gaze to the dress and stared for a long moment. He took it, turning it front to back. "Hard to tell anything with all this dirt on it. I don't recollect."

"Gramps—"

"That's the God's honest truth, boy. If she ever wore this dress, I don't recollect." Gramps pushed the dress back at him. "I can't even tell what color it is. Can you?"

"Guess I'll have to ask around."

"But I didn't say it was hers!"

"You couldn't say it wasn't." Sadness tugged at him

and he reached out a tentative hand to his grandfather. "I know you didn't want to do that."

Gramps eyed him for a moment, compassion tightening his eyes. He shook Jared's hand then grabbed him in a brief hug. Releasing Jared, he said, "Maybe she really *isn't* involved."

Jared stared down at the dress in his hand, a sense of foreboding crashing over him. "I'd sure as hell like to suspect anybody but her."

Gramps squeezed his shoulder in silent comfort and he turned back to the shallow grave. Moments later he and Gramps had the bodies loaded in the wagon with the fence posts and covered with an old blanket.

They angled east through the woods toward Moss Springs, and as they came to the road leading to town, Gramps wheeled Trick to the west and Briar Rose.

"You can take care of this on your own. I won't be a party to it."

"I'll be home as soon as I can," Jared said.

Gramps nodded somberly. Though his eyes were shaded by the brim of his hat, Jared could feel objection in his grandfather's stare. He turned the wagon toward town, resentment boiling inside him.

He didn't want to ask questions about Elise, didn't want to know the truth. He realized painfully that the truth would affect more than his job. It would destroy every tender feeling Elise had for him. Despite telling himself not to care, he did. Very much.

Jared walked into Restin's office and blinked at the dingy interior. Dark brown walls, tobacco-stained floor, and oatmeal-colored curtains combined to make the place cramped and suffocating. Toby Restin sprawled in a creaking chair, feet resting on his desk and snoring like a hibernating bear.

Jared tugged off his gloves and thumbed back his hat. "Sheriff," he said loudly.

The sheriff blew out a snort that sounded like a bleat, but didn't move.

"Sheriff!" Jared pushed at the man's boots, causing the chair to wobble.

"What!" Sheriff Restin's eyes flew open and he toppled, clutching at the edge of the desk for balance. Steadying himself, he glared at Jared. "Whadda ya want?"

"Got two bodies outside." Jared jerked his thumb toward the door. "I know one is Claude Onash. Would you care to take a look at the other one?"

Restin frowned, pushing his way out of the squeaking chair. "What are you talkin' about? What are you doin'?"

"Aren't you looking for Onash?" Jared inquired coolly.

"Why, you know I am." Restin edged his bulk from behind the desk and walked to the window, peering out. "What are you doing with 'em?"

"I found them."

"But why?" The sheriff turned back to Jared, running a hand down the front of his wrinkled stained shirt.

"It's my job." Barely keeping a civil tongue, he flashed his papers from Cam. "I'm an agent with the United States Treasury."

"Huh?" Restin's eyes bulged and he glanced out

the window again. "Where did you say you found 'em?"

"That's confidential." Jared strode outside and stepped down next to the wagon, shooting an impatient look at the sheriff.

Restin followed, whining as if Jared had stolen a marble from him. "But I'm the law around here."

"I'll handle the investigation from here on."

"Murder ain't a federal offense." Restin peered curiously at him. "Why are you so interested?"

"So you do know *something* about the law." Jared jerked a thumb toward the bodies in the wagon. "Well? Do you recognize them?"

Restin peered over the edge, then drew back sharply, his features scrunched in distaste. "Yep, that's Claude."

"And the other one?"

Restin spared another quick look then nodded. "It's his boy, Pervis. See that heel lift in his left boot? He has—*had*—one leg shorter than the other."

"Very good." Jared slapped one glove against his palm. "Now, the only thing you need concern yourself with is removing those men from my wagon."

"You cain't tell me to butt out! This is my town!"

"You'll be interfering in a federal investigation." Each word was pronounced with deadly precision. "If you have a problem following my orders, I suggest you contact the Secretary of the Treasury."

"Well, mebbe I just will."

"Fine. In the meantime, if you interfere, I will have you relieved of duty. That means don't ask questions.

Don't talk to anyone about this. Am I making myself clear?"

"Yes." Restin's fleshy lips flattened and his black eyes crackled with anger.

Jared pulled on his gloves. "Good. I'll be back in a while. You can get those bodies and bury them."

"Where am I supposed to do that?" Restin smoothed down the front of his shirt, his lips pursing rebelliously.

Jared's patience was at an end. "Since the man visited his wife every Sunday at her grave, I assume he'd like to be laid to rest next to her. Wouldn't you?"

Restin nodded and Jared turned on his heel, walking across the street. He sucked in a deep breath, trying to shore up his strength for the task ahead. He didn't want to ask anyone about Elise and that dress, but he had no choice. The sooner he began, the sooner he finished it.

No! It couldn't be. Horror curled through her. Elise squeezed her eyes shut, unable to process the scene before her. *It couldn't be.*

She slowly opened her eyes, praying everything at the sharecropper's cabin would look just as she had left it. But one thing was glaringly different.

The shallow pit beneath the thorn bush, where she'd buried the Onashes, gaped like an open wound. Empty. Completely empty.

It was devastatingly obvious from the turned earth, the clear boot prints in the soft dirt, that someone had taken the bodies. Nausea roiled through her and she shivered, despite the pulsing heat of the day, the gentle breeze, the rounded call of a bobwhite.

Dread knotted her insides, her breath coming in short gasps as though she were being pounded with a frozen fist. Someone had discovered the bodies. Who? *What would she do?*

She knew Restin's earlier visit had been a deliberate message from DeWitt that he controlled this sadistic game between them. Her poking around yesterday had obviously angered him. But had he also sent Restin to the sharecropper's cabin?

Afraid that the sheriff might indeed have gone to the cabin, Elise waited until Logan took his borrowed horse and rode out. Then she had ridden here as fast as she could.

She moved out from behind the trees, panic and fear choking her. *The Onashes were gone. How could they be gone?*

She edged to the right of the grave, helplessness closing over her like suffocating darkness. Where were they? What had happened?

Foreboding drummed through her with the heavy, sinking rhythm of a funeral dirge. There was no sign of the bodies, no money, no—

Her dress! Oh, stars! Her dress had been wrapped around Claude. A shudder ripped through her and she trembled.

Who had been here? Who had found them?

Restin?

Or Jared?

Either way, she would be discovered. What was she going to do?

In a burst of frenzied panic Elise snatched up her skirts and ran. She had to leave Fairbrooke. That was the only way she'd be safe. The only way she would escape Jared or the sheriff.

Her heart wrenched at the thought of running from her home, from Jared, but she didn't allow herself to contemplate it. She had to go. And quickly.

If he was the one who had uncovered the bodies, she knew he would come straight for her. Somehow. Somewhere. Sometime.

Unless she left.

Fear numbed her mind and Elise moved mechanically, finding herself in the saddle and barreling through trees and dense undergrowth toward home. Toward escape.

Resentment and reluctance crowded through him. Jared strode toward the saloon, and with every step he wished he could ride out of town. Wished he didn't have to ask anyone about this dress.

He had brushed off as much of the dirt as he could, but the garment was badly soiled. As Gramps had pointed out, even Jared couldn't discern the true color of the fabric, though he could tell it was a small floral print.

The dress could belong to anyone. Jared told himself that over and over, as if by repeating it he could make it true. The one thing that kept him moving across the bustling street was the hope that someone would positively identify the dress as belonging to someone other than Elise.

But the dread ticking through his veins dimmed the

hope. He knew she was involved and he hated like hell to find out how much.

Slim's answer was the same as Gramps' had been. He didn't recognize the dress and Elise's name was never mentioned.

Jared strode down the street to the livery, questioning Coralee Bronson. Neither did she recognize the dress.

He threaded his way between horses and wagons and walked inside Bailey's Dry Goods. Mr. Bailey was regretful, but couldn't identify the dress.

Jared's reluctance shifted to frustration. He couldn't prove Elise's involvement. And he couldn't prove she wasn't involved.

He walked outside, admitting what he'd skirted since he'd found the bodies. He was going to have to confront Elise.

From the corner of his eye he detected a movement, and glanced over to see Sheriff Restin carefully closing the door to the jail and moving down beside the wagon.

Instead of tending to the men Jared had brought in, the sheriff scurried across the street and disappeared into the bank. Jared frowned. What was Restin up to?

Maybe he should make certain his instructions were followed, but at the moment Jared was more concerned with Elise. There was one more person he could ask.

He strode to the doctor's office and stepped inside, the smell of antiseptic and lye soap tickling his nostrils.

A woman's voice, soothing and low, resonated

through the clinic. Dr. Hawthorne peeked around the curtain in the back. "I'll be right with you."

Jared nodded, removing his hat as he looked around. The floors were spotless; the glass gleamed like a mirror. Sunlight poured into the small clinic, gilding the old furniture, the cabinet next to the far wall that housed medicines and the shorter one next to it that bore heavy leather-bound volumes.

Dr. Hawthorne and a young woman, very much with child, walked out from behind the screen. Jared smiled and opened the door, stepping back so the two women could pass in front of him.

Dr. Hawthorne smiled her thanks and patted the woman's shoulder. "Now, Tilly, everything's just fine. Your time is drawing near. That's why you're having these false labor pains."

"Thank you, Doctor. I admit I was worried, but Tim was more so." The young woman smiled, curving a protective arm around her belly.

Dr. Hawthorne smiled. "The first baby is always a little nerve-racking. Your husband was wise to insist that you come see me."

"Thank you." Tilly smiled shyly at Jared and walked out the door.

The door closed and Dru walked around him to a ceramic basin, washing her hands. "Mr. Kensington, how nice to see you! I hope your grandfather's all right?"

"Yes, he's fine. Sends his regards."

She smiled, drying her hands on a clean towel next to the basin. "What can I do for you?"

"I wonder if I could ask you a question."

"Certainly."

Jared pulled the dress out of the brown sack he'd gotten from Slim. "Do you recognize this dress?"

The doctor's brow puckered as she took the dress and spread the bodice over her palms, considering the garment. "No, I don't think so."

"Are you sure? You've never seen it before?"

"No." Dru studied him for a moment, then gave a brief smile. "I'm not lying, Mr. Kensington. I have no reason to."

"I apologize, ma'am." Frustration churned inside him. "I didn't mean to imply—"

"Your grandfather's been good to me. If it weren't for him, I would've been run out of town on my first day."

"Really? Why's that?"

She gave him an odd look. "Well, considering I'm from the North. And a woman doctor."

"Ah, yes. What did bring you here?"

"It's as good a place as any," she said lightly, turning away from him.

He sensed myriad answers. Since the war, everyone he knew was moving to the West or the North or to Texas.

She smiled. "How's Mr. Worthen doing?"

"He's taking more of an interest in things." Jared was relieved to be able to report some progress on Logan. "Although he's no closer to coming to you for his leg."

"I didn't expect so," she said with a laugh. "But the other is good."

Jared considered her for a moment longer. "I thank you for your cooperation."

"It was no problem. I'm sorry I wasn't more help."

Jared nodded, turning for the door. He still knew nothing about Elise. Damn, he was going to have to show her the dress and hope she had answers he could live with. A sudden impulse flared and he glanced over his shoulder. "Doctor, I wonder if you could tell me anything about Claude Onash? Maybe you saw him for some reason?"

"No," she said shortly, striding around an examining table and walking toward her desk.

Jared's eyes narrowed and he turned, watching her carefully. "I just brought in his body and that of his son. They're dead."

Her head jerked toward him, and after a pause she said, "Well, I can't say I'm sorry about that."

"Is that right?" Jared's senses pricked up. "Why not?"

"It's no secret that I think the man was despicable."

Despicable enough to kill him? "Did he do something to you?"

"I'm thankful I never met him, but I did treat his wife several times." She paused, angry color flushing her cheeks. Her voice hardened. "For broken bones, cuts and bruises, that kind of thing."

Jared frowned at the doctor's obvious contempt for a man she'd never met. "Several times? An accident or—"

"He beat her, Mr. Kensington." Dru's voice hardened with bitter sarcasm. "Of course, it was his right and the sheriff wouldn't do anything about it. Nor would anyone else."

"*He beat his wife?* He visited her grave every Sunday!"

"Not anymore, thank goodness." Dru exhaled a deep breath, gripping the edge of her desk.

Jared posed the question more to himself, but spoke aloud anyway. "Why would a man visit his wife's grave every week if he treated her with such disrespect?"

Dru shrugged, looking suddenly tired. "I'm sure I don't know."

"Hmmm."

The doctor slanted a sharp look at him, questions clouding her eyes.

Jared touched the tip of his hat. "Good day, Doctor."

"Good day."

She followed him to the door, staring out at him as he strode back toward the sheriff's office. Jared was aware of her curious gaze, but his thoughts circled in on Elise.

He had the bodies. He had the dress. But where was the money?

Did Elise hold all the answers?

The time had come to find out.

CHAPTER THIRTEEN

*P*anic choked her. Her heart thundered in her ears and cold sweat slicked her palms and between her breasts.

Elise grabbed her mother's worn valise from the bottom of her wardrobe and yanked open her bureau drawers. Tossing ragged petticoats and chemises and pantaloons inside, Elise forced herself to take a breath. Then another.

Her chest ached as if she hadn't breathed since she'd left the cabin. She snatched her turquoise silk from the wardrobe, questions charging at her. Where would she go? Where was Logan? Was leaving her only choice?

Minutes ticked by and no one appeared on her doorstep demanding to know why she'd killed the Onashes. Desperation overwhelmed the panic. Logan would know what to do, but he was nowhere around. She'd called for him upon returning home, but there had been no sign. Nor was his horse in the barn. Where was he?

She turned in a helpless circle. Should she go now? Should she stay and talk to her brother? Where would she go? She had no family except her uncle's widow in Richmond, and they had heard nothing of Aunt Eleanor since before the war. Her aunt had likely evacuated the capital along with everyone else.

Elise knew running would only point to her guilt. But if she stayed, would anyone believe in her innocence?

Her hands and feet were icy with apprehension. She trembled as if she'd just stepped from the frigid winter waters of the brook behind the house. What was she going to do?

As her breathing slowed, reason returned. Whoever had discovered the bodies had also discovered her dress, but they couldn't prove it was *her* dress. Could they?

She canted her head, listening for the rumble of horses coming for her. But she heard only the normal sounds of day—the squawking of birds headed south, the occasional grating of a branch against the downstairs window, the sporadic whistle of the wind through the trees and around the house.

She stared blindly at her wavy reflection in the window. No one could prove that dress belonged to her. Surely it was stained with blood and dirt beyond recognition . . . Anxiety gnawed at her and she systematically, rhythmically wiped her hands down the front of her skirts.

If Jared had found the dress, wouldn't he have already come here? He was too smart, those eyes too penetrating. But what authority did he have? Her head came up and she grasped at the realization. Despite his suspicions, he had no authority!

He wasn't the law. She didn't have to convince *him*. She had to convince Sheriff Restin, if it came to that.

Only confession would rid her hands of the sticky feel of blood, but confession would result in prison. Elise wasn't going to prison. She sank down on the bed, her hand trembling on a petticoat she'd been ready to shove into the valise.

As she had a thousand times before in her dreams, she recalled the bitter odor of gunpowder, the deafening shots she'd fired. She remembered lying pinned beneath Claude's heavy bulk, fighting for her life as her parents and Rithy already lay dead.

No one could prove anything. She clung to the thought even though fear nicked at her confidence. She needed Logan. He would know what to do.

She stilled. Had that been the snort of a horse she'd heard? The jingle of harness? Apprehension snaked up her spine. Was she imagining things or was someone—

"Elise?" Logan's voice boomed up the stairs, followed by the closing of the front door.

She dropped the petticoat, rushing out of her room to the top of the stairs. "Oh, Logan, where have you been?"

"Fishing." He looked tired, but more animated than she'd seen since his return.

She gripped the wall, fighting to maintain some semblance of calm. "I need your help."

He gazed up the stairs at her, wiping a hand across his sun-flushed face. "What is it?"

"I need to tell you something—"

The thunder of hooves interrupted her and she glanced worriedly at the front door.

Logan frowned, turning. "Who is that?"

He limped toward the door just as the brass knocker clanged against the wood. Once, twice, three times.

"I'm coming!" Logan threw open the door. "Kensington, what is this?"

Desperation razored through her, and she pressed a hand to her heart knocking painfully against her ribs.

"Logan." Jared's quiet voice carried upstairs. "I need to see Elise. Is she home?"

She closed her eyes, uttering a silent prayer. *Send him away, Logan. Send him away.*

"What's wrong?" Logan stood back to let his friend inside.

Sweat prickled her neck and she took a step forward, able now to see Jared at the foot of the stairs.

"Get her please—" He broke off, his gaze meeting hers.

Logan frowned, looking up at Elise in puzzlement.

Hands clammy with dread, she gripped the wall, searching for balance.

Regret glinted in Jared's eyes.

"What's happened?" She hoped he couldn't hear the chattering of her teeth. "Is something wrong?"

"Yes." Logan stepped in front of Jared. "What's this about?"

Jared's steely gaze fastened on Elise. "I found two bodies tonight. On your land, at the sharecropper's cabin."

"What!" Elise and Logan cried out in unison.

"One of them is Claude Onash. The other was identified as his son." Jared moved up the stairs toward her, with Logan hobbling behind. "I don't suppose you know anything about that."

"No." She clamped her jaw so tightly she thought her teeth would snap.

"Onash? Are these the men the sheriff was looking for?" Logan edged around Jared, pushing a hand through his hair. "Again, Kensington, I ask you . . ."

Fury crested on Jared's features, drawing them into a taut unfamiliar mask. He pulled his arm from behind his back and thrust something at her. "I suppose you don't know anything about this either."

Her breath jammed in her chest. She didn't have to look. She knew it was her dress, covered in blood and dirt, taken from the body of Claude Onash. Barely able to take a breath, she forced herself to look down as if she'd never seen the dress, as if she'd never wrapped it around that murdering bastard's body.

"N-no, I don't." She met his gaze then, hers challenging, his dark with fury and pain. "What is it?"

He shook it out, his movements sharp and savage. "It's a damn dress. It was wrapped around one of the bodies."

Her eyes widened, but she couldn't speak.

"Is it yours?"

"No." She was going to hell. She knew it.

He leaned into her face. "You're lying."

"Now, see here," Logan erupted, moving protectively in front of Elise. "That dress could belong to anybody. Why would you think it belongs to Elise?"

She swallowed, her heart slamming painfully against her ribs. He couldn't prove it was hers. He couldn't.

"Just a hunch I have."

"A hunch? Is this the case you're working on? You think Elise is somehow involved in that?"

"Case?" Alarmed, her gaze shifted from Jared to Logan then back. "What case? What are you talking about?"

Logan glanced at Jared, speaking tentatively, "Jared's working for the Treasury Department. Some money was stolen from the government just before the end of the war and he's been sent to find it."

As Logan talked, Jared never took his gaze from Elise. She was unable to look away from him, riveted in morbid fascination. Horror mushroomed inside her, spreading like vile poison. He was working for the government? For the Treasury Department?

Just like Onash.

"The Treasury!" she spat. "How can you work for the most corrupt department in the government? Every one of their agents is a lying, thieving no-account."

"Not all," Jared corrected roughly, a muscle flexing in his jaw.

"If you work for the likes of them, that speaks volumes about your character. Or lack thereof."

He grabbed her arm. "Whatever you think of me is immaterial. Those dead men are wanted for federal robbery. Whoever killed them took the money. Now, I have a job to do and if you want to keep your pretty little fanny out of prison, you'd best 'fess up."

She didn't know if it was the insulting way he referred to her person—*pretty little fanny indeed*—or the accusation that she had stolen money. She wrenched away from him. "I have nothing to confess."

Logan folded his arms over his chest and stared balefully at Jared. "You have nothing here that points at Elise, yet you're so certain she's involved. Why is that?"

"Some things she's told me don't add up."

"What things?" Logan demanded.

"Ask her yourself." Jared's eyes flickered with some unidentifiable emotion. She thought it might be betrayal, but what reason did he have to feel betrayed?

Elise swallowed, her legs weak and watery. She'd thought he had no authority and it turned out that he was working for the government! He might not be able to prove her involvemet yet, but if he ever did, he had the means to make her pay.

Jared leveled a flat stare on her. "No one's seen the Onashes since the day they came out here to discuss something with your father."

She longed to tell him that Claude Onash's discussion consisted of using a knife and the butt end of a gun, but she kept her mouth stubbornly shut.

"So what?" Logan snorted. "That doesn't mean she killed them."

"But you did, didn't you, Elise? You killed them and you took that money."

They tried to rape me! She wanted to scream out the truth, but he'd used that silky, seductive tone on her when trying to get answers before.

He leaned closer, until his breath whispered against her face. "You've told lie after lie. Now I'm calling you on them."

Anger boiled inside her. Jared had been working for the government this whole time. Had he been coming around her, hoping to get evidence? Had he suspected her all along?

And she'd thought he had feelings for him! "And what about the lies you told?"

He drew back, plainly confused. "I've told no lies."

"No. You just conveniently omitted that you were working for the government. While you were pretending to honor a promise to my brother, you were instead spying on me."

"That's not how it was." Hurt and shock flared in his eyes. "I'm losing my patience with you."

"I've already told you *and* the sheriff all I intend to. These questions are becoming quite tiresome and I have no intention—ouch!"

He gripped her arm, hauling her up to him, thrusting the dress into her face. "I know this is yours and I know you have that money. How else could you pay off that lien of your father's?"

"She told you how." Logan tried to wrestle his way between them. "Papa had some money set aside."

"Then why would he need a loan in the first place?" Jared's gaze, bitter and sharp, speared into her.

She struggled against his hold, biting back the words she wanted to scream in her defense. She would tell him nothing. *Nothing!*

"You can't prove anything. Especially not about

that dress!" Logan tried to pry Jared's hands from Elise. "Hell, even I can't tell what it looks like! How can you tell who it belongs to?"

Elise met his gaze, her jaw tight, her eyes stinging with angry tears. "You're calling me a liar, when you've lied all along. Coming around to take care of me, when the whole time you were just looking for answers."

"I think you're in trouble, but I can't help you unless you tell me the truth."

She pressed her lips together to stop their trembling. How could she trust him, especially now, knowing he was officially bound to bring her to justice? "I'm in no trouble."

He pushed her away, looking suddenly tired and haggard. "Don't force my hand on this, Elise."

"I'm not forcing you to do anything." She rubbed her arm where his touch still burned her flesh, and struggled to keep a hold on her emotions. She wanted to scream out a confession, erase that frigid distrust from his eyes, but she was no fool. Jared would arrest her before she even got the words out of her mouth. At least right now he could prove nothing.

Logan pushed his way between Jared and Elise, anger vibrating in his body. "Don't handle my sister that way. You have no authority for any of this."

"You know I do." He ran a hand over his face and shook his head, looking over Logan's shoulder to her. "I can't arrest you for their murder, Elise, but I can arrest you for interfering with an investigation."

"How can that be?" Logan demanded.

"She knows something about Onash and he's the

one who stole the money. If she doesn't cooperate by telling me the truth, she goes to jail."

"The hell she does!"

"How could I interfere when I didn't even know there was an investigation?" she said hotly, stepping out from behind her brother. "You can't arrest me for anything."

Regret merged with the fury in his eyes. He studied her sadly. "You're interfering right now by not telling me what you know."

"She already told you she doesn't know anything!"

Jared kept his gaze on Elise. "Well?"

She fought the urge to squirm under his intent, expectant regard. He knew about the Onashes. Yes, he certainly did. But he could prove nothing. On the other hand, he didn't know anything about Tullar De-Witt. And if Elise breathed one word about him, something terrible would happen to Logan. "I have nothing to tell you."

He nodded, not one hint of surprise on his face. "So you're saying that the money you used to pay off your father's mortgage didn't come from Claude Onash?"

The trap closed a little tighter. "I didn't say anything about money or Claude Onash. You did."

"Yes." Rage flushed his features and muscles corded in his neck. "I say you killed those men and stole that money. You have anything to say to that?"

"Does this place look to you as if I have *any* money?"

"That's not what I asked you," he said between clenched teeth. "I don't expect you to be waving it in front of my face like a damn flag. I do expect you to tell me where it is."

"*I don't have your stupid money.*" She *hadn't* stolen the money. Exactly.

"Elise, I found this dress at the sharecropper's cabin."

"Well, I'm not the only woman around here!"

"You're the only one I take notice of," he growled, jamming a hand through his hair. He exhaled loudly. "Why would you be so vexed if you didn't have something to hide?"

"I don't like your attitude," she shot at him. "And I don't like feeling I've been manipulated."

"I think all the manipulatin' around here was done by you. You're involved and I'll prove it."

"You'll be wasting your time."

His gaze rested on her face. For an instant she saw regret darken his eyes, then it was gone. He turned and jogged down the stairs, that damning dress dangling from his fingers. "I'll be back."

"Don't bother," she yelled, wishing she could relieve this pressing darkness inside her chest.

He didn't even turn around, just strode across the foyer and out the front door.

Unease and dread scraped her raw nerves and she leaned against the wall, feeling suddenly exhausted. "Oh . . . my."

Logan squeezed her shoulder. "It'll be all right, little one. I don't know what's going on, but I'll find out."

She glanced down, lacing her fingers together, then

looked at him. "Aren't you going to ask if I . . . killed them?"

Surprise stole across his face. "I know you *didn't*." He kissed her cheek and hugged her again. "Are you all right?"

She nodded glumly. She had to tell him the truth. Not only because she couldn't bear it alone any longer, but because she needed help.

"We'll get this sorted out tomorrow." He limped across to his room. "Try to get a good night's rest. I'll see you in the morning."

She squeezed her eyes shut, bracing herself for the disappointment and shame she would soon see in his eyes. "Logan?"

"Hmmm?" He turned in the doorway.

"I think you should. Ask me, I mean."

Apprehension tightened his features and he took a tentative step toward her, groaning. "Oh, hell."

Tullar stepped into the sheriff's office, grimacing in disgust at the stale odor of sweat and old food. He hated coming to the jail, and to combat the musty odors he left the door open. "Mr. Anthony said you were looking for me earlier today."

"Claude and Pervis turned up."

DeWitt slammed the door shut. "What!"

"Yep." Restin nodded, his jowls quivering. "Jared Kensington brought 'em in."

"Kensington?" Tullar's mind quickly sorted through the implications. "How did he get involved?"

"He's working for the Treasury Department."

Tullar stared, completely taken aback. Alarm thudded at him. "What do the Onashes have to do with the Treasury?"

"He didn't say." Restin hooked his thumbs in his vest and shook his head.

Kensington was tracking the stolen money. Tullar knew it as sure as he knew his own name.

"All he said was 'it's a federal investigation' and told me to keep my nose out of it." Restin sniffed. "I been watching him. He was all over town today asking questions."

Tullar turned to the window, staring out at the streets that had emptied as the afternoon grew late. It wouldn't be long before Kensington's investigation led him to Elise Worthen. And she could send him straight to Tullar.

"He told me to stay out of it, but I thought you'd want to know. Since he brought in Claude and Pervis's bodies."

"Yes, very good." Urgency wound through Tullar. Now that Kensington had found those bodies, it was likely he'd soon suspect, as Tullar did, that Miss Worthen had some part in the Onashes' deaths. While Tullar didn't give two hoots about that, he did care that Jared was closing in on the money.

A Treasury agent? Damn! This necessitated a change of plans. No more toying with the delectable Miss Worthen. Tullar had to get that money and leave—fast.

He stared out at the late-afternoon rays of the sun bathing the town in a red-gold glow. Resentment surged. He'd thought to settle down in Moss Springs,

buy the respectability he'd never had in South Carolina, but this news changed everything.

Now he had to find that money and leave, maybe
go to Texas or California or Canada. He'd be safe
there. But he owed Miss Worthen one final visit. He
knew she had that money. Where else could it be?

She was the one person who could connect him to
Onash and the money. Once he got it, she would have
to die.

He had been patient this long. He could wait until
dark to see her. Until he had a plan. One that would
take care of Elise Worthen and her brother for good.

"Whatcha want me to do, boss?" Restin edged up
beside him, worry flushing his jowly features.

"You just sit tight."

"I can help."

"What I need is for you to keep me apprised of
anything you hear about Claude. *Anything.* Can you do
that?"

"Yeah."

"Good. I'll be in touch." Tullar spun and slammed
out the door, plans whirling in his head.

He walked first to the bank, intent on drawing up
papers to facilitate his sudden exodus. Frustration
clawed through him and unleashed a suffocating sense
of urgency. He had to have that money. Now.

He would come up with something very special for
Miss Elise Worthen.

CHAPTER FOURTEEN

Jared rode for home, feeling as if he'd been plunged into hell everlastin'. Rage, regret, and betrayal ravaged his insides. He had to get away from her.

Midnight clasped the air in a tight fist, making it impossible to breathe. The wagon bucked through ruts in the road, careened around corners, and Jared slapped the reins harder against the bay's rump. Trees blurred into sky, grass into mountains.

She was lying about the dress. Just as she'd lied about knowing Onash and the money she'd used to pay the lien. But how did he prove it?

He kept seeing her lying blue eyes, those soft lying lips. Hurt and anger merged until he couldn't tell the difference. Until he wasn't sure there *was* a difference.

Jared swore and closed his fists tight around the reins. She'd gotten to him and he'd allowed it. He, who'd sworn never to be vulnerable to a woman, who'd sworn never to forsake duty for emotion, *ever*.

Elise had slid under his skin like a needle, painless until he felt the sting to his soul. When had she burrowed so deeply into his heart? Did it matter? She had. And now they both had to pay the consequences.

Because he knew Logan so well, he thought he'd known Elise, too. But he didn't know her at all. Had she really believed she wouldn't be found out? *With all that money?*

The wagon shot through the gate leading to Briar Rose and Jared started with surprise. He eased back on the reins, slowing Brownie to a walk. The last time Jared had been this angry, he'd slammed his fist into a tree and broken two fingers. He'd been six at the time, right after his mother left. He wouldn't do that now, though he longed to hit something, someone.

Seeing the house steadied the churning crush of emotion inside him. Peace sifted through the anger, soothing his ragged nerves, the sting of betrayal, for the first time since he'd pulled that dress from Claude Onash's grave.

Home. Here he could decide what to do. It was possible Elise *wasn't* connected, that everything leading to her was strictly a coincidence. He wanted to believe that, even though doubt rushed through him.

After unhitching and rubbing down the bay, he headed for the house, anger still scoring his insides like a hot iron. He strode inside and to the small sitting room, dropping the paper bag that held the dress on a small, scarred table. Yanking off his gloves, he tossed them on the table as well. He hated that dress—the gritty feel, the rancid dirt odor, its very existence.

Without a pause he headed straight for the tall walnut cabinet that had been Gran's pride. Pulling open the middle door, he reached inside for a bottle of whiskey.

"Damn." He'd given the last of it to Logan.

Slamming the door shut, he knelt and opened the door in the belly of the cabinet. Light gleamed off the two remaining bottles of his grandfather's best private stock of bourbon. Jared grabbed one, sighing in desperate relief. He wanted to get stinking dead drunk.

He hadn't had a drink since the night Logan had been taken, but this was a special occasion, wasn't it? *Hell, yes,* he told himself bitterly. He'd just learned that the woman he— *He what?* Loved? No.

Liked? Yes. Befriended.

He'd just learned that the woman he'd come to care about, a woman he'd come to consider a friend, a woman he'd thought different from other women, had been lying through her teeth since he'd returned home. Hell, yes, this was a special occasion.

Throwing back one hot gulp of liquor, he savored the burn all the way down his throat and into his belly. Sliding a chair over to the window that looked out over the stream, he sat down.

Pouring another shot of bourbon, he tossed it back, welcoming the fire that matched his rage. Sunlight streamed over the grove of fruit and walnut trees outside the window, fingering through the branches to dapple the leaf-scattered ground in muted patterns. Birds chirped and called. A squirrel nibbled frantically at a seed, then scurried across the porch railing.

Life rolled on as normal, as though the darkness of hell hadn't just burned through Jared's soul. He wished he could disappear, forget.

Yes, he wanted to forget. Not only the horror of dragging that dress out of the ground, but the tantalizing softness of Elise, the feel of her melting into him. And the desperate panic and fear in her blue eyes only moments ago.

She had been frightened, her eyes dark with near hysteria. *She should be afraid*, he thought savagely, raising his glass again. She should be afraid of *him*.

Because he was going to get to the truth. He was going to get that money, no matter what he had to do to get it. Reluctance and determination merged.

"Jared, that you?" Gramps spoke from the door.

"Yes." Jared sipped at the bourbon, welcoming the heat that took the edge off his rage. He wanted enough liquor to dim this slicing sense of betrayal, of manipulation. He didn't want to feel anything for her, the little liar.

"Did you speak to Elise?" His grandfather stepped toward him. "Are you *drinking*?"

The surprise in the other man's voice tweaked Jared's pain. "Yes, Gramps."

Thomas Kensington laid a hand on Jared's shoulder and moved in front of him. "What happened?"

"I showed her the dress. She denied everything."

"Maybe she's telling the truth."

"No one in town could identify it either." The words grated like ashes in his throat. He wanted to be finished with this.

Pleasure flared in Gramps's eyes. "That has to be good for Elise."

He surged out of the chair, his fingers squeezing

around the glass. "It doesn't prove her innocence, Gramps."

"I think you're wrong about her, boy."

"I wish I was." He recalled the warmth and desire in her eyes. *Before tonight.* Suddenly struck by an alarming thought, he looked at his grandfather. "Gramps, did you tell Elise I was working for the government?"

"No." Thomas walked to the table and stared at the dress. "You asked me not to tell anyone."

"You're sure?"

"Well, I guess I can remember something like that!" Gramps flared indignantly.

Jared nodded. "Sorry."

He was relieved about that at least. If she really hadn't known he was working for the government, then she had only been protecting herself, not trying to dodge the law. A tiny part of him wanted to believe she had been justified in whatever she'd done.

He swore and slammed the bottle on the table. What was wrong with him? Why was he looking to excuse her? *She'd lied.* Willingly. Knowingly. *To him.*

Gramps folded his arms across his chest and considered Jared. "What did Logan say?"

"What do you think he said?" Jared gave a short bark of laughter, opening the bag and pulling out the dress, his fingers tightening on the stiff fabric. "He didn't believe it either. I hope he can talk some sense into her."

Gramps put his hand on Jared's shoulder and squeezed, offering silent comfort and strength.

Jared covered his grandfather's hand, wishing for a

brief instant that Gramps could make everything better with a promise, as he'd been able to when Jared was a boy.

"It'll work out, son."

Gramps' deep reassurance almost made him believe it, but he didn't see how things could be resolved without hurting him and Elise, Elise most of all.

Gramps started out of the room. "I'll get us something to eat."

"All right." Jared folded the dress, pausing when something caught on his callused fingertips. He unrolled the dress, surprised to see a dainty corner of lace protruding from the pocket.

Foreboding sawed through him. He pulled the piece free and his breath jammed. Distantly he was aware that Gramps had returned with a tray and was saying something about thinking twice.

But Jared's attention riveted on the piece in his hand and recognition slammed into him. Glancing at Gramps, he rasped, "I've got to go."

Gramps frowned. "Are you going to tell me what you're doing?"

"No." His fist closed over the delicate fabric, squeezing until his knuckles ached, as if he could crumple the damning piece into tatters. "I don't want you caught in the middle of this."

Gramps eyed Jared sternly. "Be careful, boy. Be very careful. You could ruin that girl's life."

"I know." As he turned for the door, his shoulders sagged with fatigue and dread. "I know."

Once outside, he paused on the bottom step and slowly uncurled his fist. Pain and denial hammered at him; he could barely force himself to look, but neither could he ignore what lay in his palm. A dainty lace glove—dirty, discolored, but the exact match to the one Logan had given him months ago.

Betrayal and helpless anger poured through him. He could no longer dismiss what his instincts had been screaming at him. Elise was well and truly involved. And Jared now had the evidence to prove it.

Stuffing the glove deep into his trouser pocket, he quickly saddled Trick and rode out, urging the stallion into a flat-out gallop across the field. They neared the split-log fence surrounding Briar Rose, and Trick's muscles bunched as he gathered speed to take the fence.

Jared let the stallion have his head, thinking for a split second that if fate were merciful, the horse would stumble and Jared would break his neck. But the black stallion cleared the fence with the ease of familiarity and practice.

Jared had given Elise the chance to tell the truth. Now he must lie in wait for her to move for the money, and he knew it would be tonight. He rode for Fairbrooke, agony spearing through him.

"I killed them. I'm a murderer, plain and simple." Frustration and helplessness coiled through her. She could still feel Claude's body pressing her into the stone of the porch, smell the rancid odor of blood as it soaked her dress, the dress Jared had shoved at her only moments ago.

She and Logan now stood in the dining room. Elise

rubbed her palms down her skirts, tormented by the remembered feel of blood on her hands.

Logan gripped her shoulders. "What happened?"

In a flat, toneless voice she told him how Papa had discovered Claude and Pervis at the sharecropper's cabin. He'd come storming into the house and grabbed his Enfield rifle. By the time he stepped onto the porch, the Onashes were waiting for him.

At the first shot Mama had gone running onto the porch. They'd stabbed her in the doorway. Elise had heard the shots from upstairs and, clumsy with fear, had finally managed to load Papa's Colt. But Rithy had arrived before her, and by the time she raced downstairs, they were all dead.

"Pervis came after me . . ." She sucked in a deep breath, her heart pounding, words tangling in her throat. Panic choked her and she put a hand to her chest in remembered fear.

"He tried to rape you?"

She nodded, rocking herself, trying to banish the frigid chill that crept through her. "He ripped my dress and . . . touched me. I shot him. Then Claude attacked me, pushed me to the porch, and I . . . killed him."

Logan cursed violently. Though his arm about her shoulder was comforting, she felt his body vibrate with rage. "They got what they deserved."

"I agree." Weary frustration wound through her. "But do you think the Yankee troops will agree? We're under martial law, Logan. They won't spare an ounce of sympathy over a Virginian killing a Treasury agent.

Not if this new government would sanction someone like Claude Onash."

He sighed deeply and ran a grimy hand over his face. "I can see why you kept it a secret."

"I considered going to the sheriff, but I couldn't."

"After meeting him, I think that was wise, as well." Logan walked over and took a nearly empty bottle of whiskey out of the silverware cabinet. "But Jared—"

"No." She rose, moving to the dining room table and gripping its edge. "Jared works for the government too. He won't turn his back on that."

"True, but he could help you." Logan pushed the glass of liquor at her. "Here, drink this."

"I'm not going to prison." She took a small sip, coughing at the sharp burn down her throat. "Not after what they did to Mama and Papa. And Rithy." She shook her head, clenching her fists. Though relieved that someone finally knew her secret, she was terrified about the prospect of Jared's finding out. "I'm not going."

"Little one, Jared already thinks he can tie you to the missing money. If you know where it is—"

"I don't . . . exactly."

His gaze sliced to her. "What does that mean?"

"I took some from Claude Onash, but—"

"You took some?" Logan spun toward her, hitting his leg on the settee. His face crumpled in pain as he grabbed the corner for balance. After a few seconds he said, "Damn! How much? Where is it?"

"No, it's not what Jared suspects. When I moved Claude's body into the wagon, I saw the money sticking out of his pocket. I had no idea it was stolen!"

"But you took it?" His voice was incredulous.

Elise stiffened. "I didn't plan to, but there it was. I thought it was the least he owed for what they did."

Logan grimaced. "I don't know if Jared will see it that way."

"You can't tell him, Logan." She rushed over to him, horrified. "He'll send me to prison! He's honor-bound to do it and you know how he is about honor."

"I'm so ashamed, Elise." He hung his head. "You've been going through this alone."

"Now you know. That's what matters."

"Well, I haven't been much help, but that's going to change."

"What are we going to do?"

"I don't know." He huffed out a breath, easing down onto the settee. "You're taking more of a risk by not telling Jared. He was angry when he left, but he's fair-minded—"

"No!"

"You're better off trusting him than forcing his hand."

"Absolutely not. You heard him. He thinks I killed Onash for that blasted money." At the memory of his accusations, pain shunted through her. She'd been a fool to believe their friendship had developed into something deeper. Sighing, she turned to her brother. "There's a man named DeWitt—"

"The banker?" Logan stepped toward her.

She nodded, tightening her grip on the glass of whiskey. "He thinks I have the money, too."

Wariness clouded Logan's eyes. "What does *he* have to do with this?"

"He knows Onash was here before he disappeared. I'm pretty sure it was DeWitt who sent Sheriff Restin out to question me."

Her brother grimaced. "Is anyone else involved?"

"No."

"Thank goodness."

"He's been blackmailing me. He told me if I didn't get the money for him, he would go to the sheriff and tell him that I'd done away with Claude."

"Which you did." Logan groaned, closing his eyes.

"I never admitted it to him. And now Jared's found the bodies. Don't you think he'll go straight to the sheriff?"

"Kensington doesn't have to clear anything with Restin. He's an authority unto himself."

"The precise reason why I don't want to tell him." She set the glass down, her fingers clumsy with apprehension. "Anyway, DeWitt has threatened to tell the sheriff everything, including that we learned about Claude and Pervis living on our property."

"Which explains why Restin was out here earlier today saying just that." Her brother folded his arms, a thoughtful look coming over his features.

Elise laced her fingers together. "Logan, I'm really frightened of DeWitt. He follows me everywhere. He's been in the barn. He was at Dru's the other day when I took Gramps to town. He threatened to hurt you if I didn't do what he wanted."

"No wonder you were beside yourself the other night when you thought I was missing," he murmured sympathetically. "I've been a selfish bastard, wallowing in my own anger and self-pity. I'm so sorry."

"Logan." She laid a consoling hand on his arm. "That's behind us now. I'm just glad you're all right."

He clasped her shoulders, looking intently into her face. "Something else is going on between you and Jared."

"What do you mean?" She stilled, her voice sharp.

"He was furious when he left here and I don't think it was because he couldn't get information. I think it was because *you* wouldn't tell him anything."

Elise looked away from her brother's penetrating stare, but she couldn't ignore what she'd come to realize over the last few weeks. Amid all the lies and deceit, she had come to care for Jared Kensington. But he didn't care for her. If he did, he never would've accused her of killing someone for money. How could he think so little of her?

Tears stung her throat and she turned away from her brother's steady gaze, wiping surreptitiously at her eyes. "No, there's nothing between us. Not like that."

"I wouldn't be so sure."

"He already suspects me of lying, murder . . . theft." She gave a painful laugh. "And I guess I've done all those things. When he learns the truth, I doubt he'll be forgiving."

Logan limped over and hugged her again. "Sorry, Sis."

"You're here now." She wrapped one arm around his waist and laid her head on his shoulder. "You can help me find that money."

Logan shook his head, his jaw tightening stubbornly. "With DeWitt involved, surely you can see we're better off telling Jared?"

"No! DeWitt's already made threats against you, Logan. If he finds out that you know or that we've told Jared, there's no telling what he'll do. It will be something awful. I know it!" She clutched at him, desperate to convince him. "Please, Logan. Don't say anything to Jared."

"I don't like it." Frustration sharpened his words.

"We don't need Jared's help. I want to prove to him that I didn't take that money. At least not the way he thinks I did."

"Your damn pride could get us both killed." He arched a brow. "I hope Jared appreciates the difference between your killing Onash for the money and taking it after he tried to kill you."

"I don't care if he does or not," she snapped, her temper boiling again.

Her brother planted his hands on the table, leaning in close. "You'd better care. He's in a position to help you."

"You're not suggesting Mr. Duty-Before-Anything-Else would stick out his neck for me?"

Reluctant amusement glinted in his eyes and he shook his head, grinning fondly. "I've seen the way he looks at you, Elise. I haven't been *completely* oblivious since I returned."

For an instant, hope welled up inside her that perhaps Jared would forgive her, but then she remembered his anger, the betrayal on his face. "Logan, I told you—"

"Don't worry, little one. I won't go talking out of turn, but you'd be better off to take a chance and tell him. I would trust you with Jared. I wouldn't trust my worst enemy to DeWitt. Or Restin."

She shook her head, her jaw clamping tightly.

"Even if you turn over the money, there's still the matter of the Onashes."

"I know," she said bleakly. "What do you think Jared will do about that?"

Logan shrugged, dread sketching his features. "He probably has to report what he suspects."

"Well, we'll just have to find that money and hope for leniency."

"For now, I'll help you, but if we don't find something soon, we tell Jared."

She shook her head. "He won't believe me. He thinks I'm capable of terrible things."

Logan sighed. "Can we at least discuss it again later?"

She hesitated, swayed by the concern in her brother's eyes. "We can talk about it, but only talk."

"This is one big mess, Sis." Logan eased down onto the settee. "Are you sure you're all right?"

"Yes." She sank down beside him, sadness tugging at her. "I wish I'd never killed them, but I had to."

"If you hadn't, you'd be dead." Logan's voice was hoarse. "That's not a price I'm willing to pay. I'm glad you weren't either."

"Oh, Logan!" She wrapped her arms around his neck and hugged him tight. "I'm so glad you're home."

"I won't make you regret it again, Elise."

"I know." At last her brother was home, really home. And he was going to help her.

She could see it now, Jared's rising curiosity, the frequent trips to check up on her, always asking her about town or Onash. She'd been fool enough to believe that he might actually be coming to care for her as she had for him.

Logan patted her back. "We'll get through this, Elise. I swear."

"Thank you." She buried her face in her brother's neck, grateful she had him back, yet unable to stem the wish that Jared was the one holding her. Even knowing what he thought of her.

Twilight glittered over the land like silver satin. In the woods bordering Fairbrooke, Tullar gathered up an armful of leaves and brush, carefully covering the bulky object he'd bought in Rocky Mount.

He had gone to the neighboring town to get what he needed and had paid a young boy to purchase the object from the blacksmith.

Walking in a wide circle, he surveyed his handiwork and a broad smile stretched across his face. Logan Worthen would never suspect a thing. Until it was too late.

And no one would connect Tullar to the Worthens' misfortune.

Now all he had to do was wait for darkness.

CHAPTER FIFTEEN

Anger, reluctance, and confusion still burned through him, just like the liquor. Jared hid Trick in the trees down by the Worthens' cemetery and slipped behind trees and bushes until he reached the house.

The early fall chill of the night did nothing to cool the heat of his blood. Walking past the barn, he stood beneath Elise's window and looked up, agony and want carving through him. How could he ignore the glove he'd found?

Light flared in her room and he inched back into the shadows. The curtains fluttered as she moved to the window. The candlelight shone behind her, haloing her hair in soft gold, emphasizing the proud thrust of her breasts, the trim tuck of her waist.

Desire shunted through him and he clenched his fists against it. For a moment he allowed himself to imagine her velvet skin, ivory against the copper of his, her breasts full and quivering in his hands, her nipples hard and ripe from his mouth. Want lashed him and his erection throbbed.

She bowed her head against the glass and he wished he could see her face. Was she planning to run? To get the money?

Tortured raw emotion shot through him. There was a reason she'd lied. There had to be. Was he grasping for an excuse because he couldn't forget how she'd opened his heart, couldn't forget how she'd surrendered when he kissed her?

He swore viciously. Past experience urged him to believe his instincts only, to believe that Elise had lied to hide the fact that she'd murdered two men for money. But Jared couldn't make himself believe it. He'd come to know her fierce loyalty, her strength, her *honesty*.

But did he really know her, a little voice taunted. How could he ignore that glove?

He considered resigning from the job, but he couldn't do it. He'd given his word.

If only she'd told him the truth tonight, he might have been able to help her, but now he must do his utmost to catch her in the lie. No matter what it cost him. No matter how he hurt Elise.

Agony ripped through him and he squeezed his eyes shut. He had no choice.

And what of Logan? Did he know the truth? Had he known since his return? Jared wondered if he could convince Logan to talk to Elise, get her to confess. There was only so much help Jared could give her and by her refusal to admit what she knew, she had tied his hands but good.

A noise in front of the house startled him and he pulled his gaze from her window, listening intently to

the soft night sounds around him. He'd been im-
mersed in thoughts of Elise and anyone could've
walked up. Alert now, he moved silently to the side of
the house, edging up to the corner of the porch.

Light rippled onto the porch, then the front door
clicked shut. Someone was leaving the house or going
inside. Logan?

Jared cursed his preoccupation with Elise and
scanned the yard and length of the porch, but he saw
no one. There were no horses or buggies to indicate
anyone other than Logan and Elise was here. Only
one set of uneven footprints—Logan's—in the gathering night frost.

With one last look at her window, Jared slipped into
the nearest abandoned cabin, where he had a clear
view of the entire front of the house and the west
side. He could see everything. And hoped he would
see nothing.

Despite the cool night, sweat sheened her body and
she shivered. Apprehension plucked at her raw nerves
and she exhaled a ragged breath. For long moments
after she and Logan parted at their doors, Elise stared
out the window.

Jared worked for the government and he sought a
truth that could destroy her. She was willing to give
this man her heart, her body, but not the truth.

How long before Jared could prove she had killed
the Onashes? Moonlight slanted into the room, washing everything a pure silver. She rested her head
against the window. She would never be pure again.

Perhaps Logan was right and they should tell Jared,

but every part of her rebelled against it. He believed the worst of her and she wanted to prove him wrong. Besides, she couldn't dismiss DeWitt.

When he learned that the Onashes had been discovered and that someone else was after the same money he was . . . Elise shuddered to think what he might do. To any of them.

She pushed her sweat-dampened hair out of her face and sucked in a long draft of air, struggling to control her frantic heartbeat, the fear sliding through her like a blade.

The silence of the house echoed around her. On the bedside table a candle flame hissed into wax. She could hear only the rushing of her heart and the occasional push of the wind. Doubts swarmed through her and she slid out of her wrapper, climbing onto her bed.

Plastering her back to the heavy wooden headboard, she drew up her knees and huddled into herself. Unbidden came the image of Jared holding her the day he'd told her about Logan, his tender concern, his fervent attempt to convince her that Logan was fine. Of course, he hadn't suspected her of anything then.

Even so, in the last weeks she'd learned he was strong, compassionate, decisive, *single-minded*. If she confessed, would he help her? Or would he follow his duty? Should she take a chance and tell him? Or finish it on her own?

She didn't want to remember the gentleness in his eyes, the unquestioning loyalty that had brought him here in the first place. His words still cut her and she resolved to prove him wrong.

Jared waited inside the open door of the small, boxy cabin. Air circulated through the sturdily made one-room house only if the opposite door was also open, but he didn't want to risk alerting anyone to his presence. So he waited as close to the open doorway as he dared.

The air was tight and sparse, cold. He rubbed his hands together, flexing his fingers inside his gloves. A sharp pewter moon spilled bright light across the yard, the house, the trees, painting everything in ghostly brilliance. Soft night sounds surrounded him. Soothing in another time perhaps, but nothing soothed him tonight.

He glanced up at Elise's room, still lit, and rolled his shoulders against the tension in his muscles. He wanted to get stinking drunk, but he couldn't allow anything to cloud his judgment. Not tonight when he expected Elise to make a move for the money. Hell, he wanted a drink! He cradled his head in his hands for a moment, closing his eyes against a piercing agony.

Unbidden came the memory of their last kiss. She had surrendered so sweetly to him. He recalled the warmth and desire in her eyes. *Before he'd shown her that dress.*

His eyes snapped open in an effort to dispel the wispy images. The front door of the house opened and he straightened, watching Logan hobble down the steps and slowly, unevenly make his way across the yard toward the woods.

Jared's instincts quickened. Logan was going for his nightly walk. So far, Elise hadn't made an appearance, but perhaps she was waiting for her brother to leave.

Fatigue curled around his insides, deep and wasting. He was so damn tired of this case, the lies, the paths leading to places he had no desire to go. A familiar emptiness spread through him, the same hollow feeling he'd experienced after Logan's capture.

And regret. He regretted what he'd said to Elise. Anger had gotten the better of him. He'd been so certain she'd manipulated him. But how could she, if she knew nothing of his job?

He wanted to hold on to his anger, wanted to absorb its brutal assault and never again be taken in by her lying blue eyes. But a rational corner of his mind whispered that she was innocent—at least of murdering Onash for the money.

He wanted to believe there was a good reason for her involvement. Yet she *had* paid that lien easy as you please. His gaze shifted to her window, and he noted absently that the candle still burned. Did she have the money or not? The only thing he knew for certain was that his heart ached as though torn in two.

If Elise really didn't have the money, then where was it? The most obvious answer was that Onash's partner had the money, but who was Onash's partner?

The closest thing Jared had to a suspect was Tullar DeWitt. DeWitt had been linked to Onash in several ways—arriving in town at the same time, their partnership—but so far Jared had nothing concrete on the man. Elise was his only lead.

So he waited in the suffocating cabin, aching with regret and resentment that he had to watch her as if she were a criminal, when what he really wanted was to stride up to the house, beg her forgiveness, and claim her.

He cursed. After tonight, could she ever consider him as anything other than the enemy?

Jared shifted, careful of the creaking board where he sat. A sudden burst of wind cooled him for a moment and he let his gaze roam the grounds. Perhaps if he gave Elise a little time to cool off, he could talk to her again, convince her—

He stilled, peering into the shadows that stretched in front of the house. Had he seen something? Someone?

Shadows dovetailed on each other, creating a writhing ribbon of darkness around the trees leading to the house, the circular drive.

Yes, there it was again. A shadow shifted, then separated itself from the darkness and moved toward the house. Jared could tell it was a man and knew from the smooth gait that it wasn't Logan.

He rose, senses alert and prickling, careful to balance his weight so that he didn't make any noise. The man moved quickly yet purposefully across the yard, angling toward the house from the east.

Jared eased out of the cabin, slipping alongside the wall and keeping the house in full view. The man vaulted onto the porch from the side and made his way to the door. Moonlight slanted between the slender columns and Jared silently urged the man to step into the light.

He was dressed in dark clothes and wore a dark hat. Frustration rose up inside Jared. *Who was it?* The man reached the door.

Jared stepped away from the cabin, his hand on his revolver as he edged closer to the porch. The other man opened the front door noiselessly and, framed in a wedge of moonlight, he slipped inside.

In that moment Jared saw the man's profile and a tuft of hair. Pure white hair.

Tullar DeWitt! What was he doing here? Suspicion bit at Jared. If DeWitt and Elise were both connected to Onash, were they in this together?

Jared pushed away the thought, but the suspicion lingered. If Elise *wasn't* involved with DeWitt, then she could be in danger. Dread notched his insides and he sprinted for the house. The door was still ajar and he eased inside.

Darkness shrouded the downstairs rooms, but a pale gold light glowed from upstairs. Elise's room. The door was open and he could hear voices, low and intense, but he couldn't discern words.

Plastering himself to the far wall, he moved stealthily up the staircase, barely allowing himself to breathe. Holding his gun at the ready, he reached the top stair.

Elise's voice was breathy, nervous. "What are you doing here?"

"The Onashes were turned in to Sheriff Restin today."

"Yes, I—I heard."

"Your friend Kensington told the sheriff he's working for the Treasury."

"I didn't know until today. I swear." Elise sounded choked, her voice high-pitched and nervous. "He's been here, too. I didn't tell him anything."

Jared stiffened, suspicion nipping at him.

"You know what I want." DeWitt's voice was low, but clear.

"Y-yes. I have it."

"All of it?"

"I didn't count it, but it looks like a lot."

They could only be talking about the money.

Betrayal razored through Jared, weakening his knees and forcing him to grip the wall for support. She had played him for a royal fool. She was involved up to her gorgeous eyes with Tullar DeWitt!

Elise said the only thing that she knew would stall DeWitt. He was going to kill her. She knew that, too. The scent of sandalwood choked her and cold sweat slicked her palms. Her teeth chattered with fear, but she struggled to keep her reason.

She'd been scared witless when he pushed open her door, but somehow she hadn't been surprised. She'd known he would come sometime.

She had to escape. DeWitt's gaze slid over her, making her belly knot in revulsion. She wore only her thin nightdress and wanted to reach for her wrapper, but escape was more important right now.

She backed away from him, angling toward the door and edging alongside her heavy bureau. Savage determination glittered in DeWitt's eyes, making them cruel and febrile. Elise's breath locked in her chest.

She realized now that it didn't matter if she told him where the money was. He would kill her anyway. But if she could convince him that she had it, she might buy enough time to escape.

She was close to the bureau now, only steps from the door. She trembled and sweat slicked her palms, but she forced herself to think. Where was Logan? Even Jared would be a welcome sight.

DeWitt moved with her, blocking her escape, but now in a position where she might be able to shove past him. "Come now, my dear. Give me the money."

"I don't have it here, of course." She tried to keep the raw fear from her voice, the raspy desperation. "It's outside."

"Outside?"

"In the barn."

He studied her, suspicion narrowing his eyes. "You're lying."

"No! No, I'm not."

He advanced on her, removing his soft leather gloves and tucking them in the waistband of his trousers. His voice slid over her like groping fingers. "I wanted to think Restin's little visit lit a fire under you, but I guess not."

"I told you, it's in the barn."

"You won't need to worry about going to prison for killing Claude and Pervis, my dear."

"Wh-what are you talking about?" Fear choked her. She backed up a step, her thigh bumping into the bureau.

"You won't be going to prison at all." DeWitt closed in on her, so close that the scent of sandalwood overwhelmed her. "We have all the time in the world. I saw your brother leave on his nightly walk, so he won't interrupt us."

"He'll be right back—"

DeWitt grasped her around the throat and pulled her to him. His fingers bit brutally into her flesh, and black spots danced before her eyes. "I know his schedule. Don't forget I've been watching you for some time."

She clawed at his hand, struggling to breathe past the crushing pressure against her throat. He was right, of course. Logan would be gone for hours, as he always was.

"We can do this the easy way or the hard way."

Dizzy from lack of oxygen, she nodded, stumbling when he pushed her back from him.

"I'm sure if you think about this, you'll want to tell me where Claude's money is."

"But I—"

"I didn't want to do things this way." He gave a sigh that sounded almost like regret as he pulled something from his coat. He stroked a thin leather strap, holding it out for her inspection. "Look closely, my dear. This could do severe damage to your pretty face. I'm sure you'll agree."

Elise's eyes widened in horror. Tiny bits of glass were embedded in the leather. Just the thought of what the brutal strap could do to her nearly buckled her knees, and she gripped the edge of the bureau.

"Claude and Pervis were living in our sharecropper's cabin." Words tumbled out of her mouth, fueled by desperation. "Maybe the money is there."

"No good. Too obvious." He slid the leather lightly across his palm, eyeing her avidly.

She swallowed back a scream and scooted closer to the bureau. "What about his house in town?"

"No."

"I don't know," she cried out desperately. "I swear I don't. I've been telling you that all along."

"Well, that's a pity because you'll have to die anyway."

"No! I've told no one about you. No one knows."

"Can't take the chance that you'll change your mind." He smiled, a cold slash of lips against a bloodless face. Then he grabbed her by the hair.

Elise screamed, lashing out at him with her fists. He yanked hard on her hair, burning her scalp and drew back his arm to strike her with the leather strap.

"Let her go, DeWitt!"

Jared! Elise nearly swooned with relief.

DeWitt hauled her to him and turned in one smooth motion, holding her in front of him like a shield. "Move out of the way, Kensington, or she dies."

Jared squeezed the trigger.

Elise flinched and felt DeWitt sag behind her. His arms fell away from her, but before she could move he shoved her into Jared.

They slammed into the door. Uncoiling like a snake, Jared put her away from him and rose, aiming again at DeWitt.

The strap lashed out, catching Jared on one cheek.

Elise bit back a scream, terror crashing through her. Moving instinctively, she searched for a weapon and her gaze lit on the wash basin and pitcher. Her hand closed over the pitcher's handle.

DeWitt lunged at Jared again, flicking the strap at his eyes. Jared blocked the blow with one arm, firing with his other hand.

Elise rushed toward the men, and when DeWitt lunged for the door, she drew back with all her might and slammed the pitcher against his head.

But DeWitt never even slowed. He bolted out the door and crashed down the stairs, his laughter echoing behind him.

Jared gripped the door frame, staring blankly at Elise.

"Oh, no!" Horror raked through her and her legs went weak. "No!"

He staggered against the door, then slid to the floor and sat there motionless.

She had hit Jared! No, this couldn't be. Elise squeezed her eyes shut. This was a horrible nightmare. She hadn't really hit Jared with the pitcher. She couldn't have! But when she opened her eyes, he still sat there, dazed, blood trickling from a small cut at his hairline.

"Oh, my stars! Oh, no!" She knelt, afraid to touch him. "Jared, talk to me! Please!" *She had knocked him silly.* Distress clawed through her.

She lifted her hands to his face, then dropped them. Peering at him, she saw his eyes were glazed, unfocused. Close to panic, she dabbed at the trickle of blood on his forehead. "Look at me, Jared. Please."

• • •

Jared's world slammed to a stop and his legs turned to water. A high-pitched whistle sounded in his ear. Where was he? What had happened? He was half sitting, half leaning against something hard, and his skull ached as if it had been split in two.

Someone—Elise?—hovered over him. He reached for her, but touched only air. Pain speared through him and he squeezed his eyes shut. When he opened them again, there was Elise. And another Elise.

How could there be two of her? His head throbbed, fragmented memories floating through his mind, but he could make no sense of them.

What was Elise doing here? Why were there two of her?

He felt feather-light caresses over his face, his eyes. Soothing, calming, easing the pain. He wanted to close his eyes, sink into the darkness that beckoned, but pieces of memory, feeling . . . *something* nagged at him.

He moved his head, groaning at the pain that riveted through his skull. Elise bent toward him, her lips moving. He couldn't make out a word. "Pretty," he said, the effort costing him a spike of pain in his temple.

She stared down at him, concern darkening her eyes. Her mouth moved, but he couldn't understand what she said. Frustration grew along with the pain.

"What?" he said. "What?"

She leaned closer, pressing kisses to his cheeks, his jaw, his forehead. Her lips were smooth as rose petals across his skin. He liked it.

"More," he croaked, lifting a hand to her waist.

She drew back, her smooth brow puckered in a frown. "Jared, tell me you're all right. I thought I'd killed you. I couldn't bear it."

"I'm . . . fine." The blazing pain in his head ebbed and wispy thoughts formed into a concrete moment. His cheek throbbed. "DeWitt?"

"He's long gone."

Jared shifted, trying to lift himself, but agony drove through his temple. He touched his head, then scowled at the blood that came away on his fingers. "Why the hell did you hit me?"

"I didn't mean to."

Trying to get his legs under him, he eyed her accusingly.

"I didn't!" She rose, gripping his arm and helping pull him to his feet. "If I'd done it on purpose, why would I still be here, worrying myself sick about you?"

He didn't have an answer for that. The fog was clearing from his brain and he leaned heavily against the door. More memories gelled. "What the hell is going on with you? How did you get tangled up with DeWitt?"

"Well, I guess this means you're all right," she said dryly, tugging him toward the bed. She pushed him down and gingerly examined the knot on his head.

"Ouch!"

"Sorry," she snapped, probing harder.

He pulled away. "That hurts like hell."

"Sorry," she said more gently. "Let me look at it."

He sat quietly, his eyes closed, pain drumming

through him. The edge eased as he took in the soft
warm scent of her. Her hair brushed against his face,
soothing yet arousing at the same time. The warmth
of her body pulsed against him and he could feel the
swell of her breasts close to his mouth.

His throat ached and the pain in his head ebbed to
a dull throb. Still befuddled by the blow to his head,
he reveled in the gentle brush of her fingers, the soft,
teasing mist of her breath against his temple. Despite
his headache, another ache started down low.

"It looks like only a small cut," she said quietly,
dropping her hands and stepping back.

Opening his eyes, he gripped her wrist. "Are you all
right? I didn't even ask—dear Lord!"

His gaze locked on her throat and he gingerly
touched the angry red marks that marred her pale
flesh. Rage shook him. "He tried to choke you."

She closed her eyes, lifting her hand to cover his,
pressing it lightly to her throat. "I'm all right. Now."

Her pulse tapped faintly against his fingers, and beneath the heel of his palm he could feel the thump of
her heart. Her hair, smelling of lilac and sunshine,
draped sinuously over his wrist, between his fingers.
He grazed the barest of kisses on her throat and her
eyes widened, astonishment lighting the blue depths.

Their gazes locked and he read invitation, desperate need. A slow burn unfurled in his belly; want hammered through him and he cursed himself. He should
be comforting her, but instead he could focus only on
the swell of her breasts below his hand.

All the care and longing and desire he'd tried to

suppress surged to the surface. He forgot the questions that begged to be answered.

She framed his face in her delicate hands, pressing kisses to the corners of his lips, his chin, his jaw. "I was so afraid I'd killed you. You were so still. The blood—"

"Shhh." His hands rose to her waist as he steadied himself. "Are you sure you're all right?"

"Yes." Her breath teased his lips.

The want wrenched tighter in his belly, and a raging flood of desire, anger, and relief overtook him. She was all right. She was here, with him.

Driven by the need to reassure himself of that fact, he nudged her lips apart, careful to keep the kiss gentle, undemanding. But she whimpered and leaned full into him, her arms locking around his neck. Her mouth opened on his hungrily and when her tongue touched his, begging for deeper contact, his blood surged, savage and hot.

For a moment the throbbing in his head was outweighed by the soft feel of her, the heady triumph that she had come willingly to him. And the thought that slammed through him, over and over.

She could've been killed. She could've been killed.

Touching her, tasting her, was the only thing that mattered. Fevered, driven, he pulled her onto his lap. Despite her lies, despite her involvement with De-Witt, Jared couldn't turn away from her, didn't want to. He wouldn't.

CHAPTER SIXTEEN

*H*e kissed her, his lips hard and ruthless, demanding total surrender. Relief rocked through her and she met him, her mouth parting for his tongue. Still kissing her, he rose from the bed, sliding her body down his until her feet touched the floor. She gripped his arms, focused on the raw need raging through her body.

Distantly she acknowledged this might be a mistake, but she needed him. She wanted Jared to erase the ugliness of the night, the terror, and knew he was the only one who could.

Through her thin gown she felt his heat, his strength, his power. She wanted him to infuse her with that strength and warmth. To erase the fear circling her like a snapping wolf. His mouth took hers again and again, straining some invisible bond of control.

Fast and hard and dark, a primal urge to join with him rose in her. It was alarmingly intense, but Elise refused to slow. She couldn't. Some greater unknown force tugged at her. His urgency fed the restlessness gathering inside her, the elusive sense of completeness.

He sank down onto the edge of the mattress and pulled her between his thighs, his gaze roaming her face. The rough fabric of his trousers abraded the thin cotton of her gown. Broad, square-tipped fingers stroked her hair away from her face. Naked want sharpened the green of his eyes and drew taut across the blunt cheekbones and stubborn jaw.

She could feel restraint vibrate from him, sensed a part of him she couldn't breach, but she could also sense the need that echoed her own, the savage desire shimmering just below the surface of control.

He kissed her again, hungry and hard as if he couldn't get enough of her, releasing a wildness in her. His lips coaxed, tempted, seduced. He thrust his fingers into her hair, groaning.

She bent to him, her hands stroking his back, pressing him to her closer, closer. Her tongue played with his, and the glide of satin-rough flesh twisted a knot of desire low in her belly. She tugged at his shirt, pulling it up his torso.

He dragged his lips from hers and yanked the shirt over his head. His broad hands streamed through her hair, curved over her shoulders and the length of her spine to cup her bottom. She reached for his mouth, desperate for closer connection to him.

Kneading her soft flesh, his fingers teased her inner thighs and liquid fire streamed through her, weakening her legs. She ran her hands up his arms, loving the feel of supple muscle beneath her fingers.

His breathing harsh and ragged, he drew away and bowed his head between her breasts.

"Jared?" Anticipation, frustration, pulsed in a blinding wave through her.

He looked at her, his eyes glittering with savage need, but when he reached for her, his kiss was different. Slower. More deliberate.

An ache pulsed between her legs and she melted against him, shifting impatiently. She wanted to savor the harder texture of him, every different taste, but urgency flooded her like a churning river. Still she tried to follow his lead, to trust in his experience, sensing that something wonderful waited beyond this swelling anticipation.

His hands stroked over her shoulders, caressed her nape. She flexed her fingers in the dark hair of his chest. He shifted restlessly, pulling his lips from hers. She nearly screamed in frustration.

His gaze traced slowly over her face and down her neck to rest on her breasts. They grew heavy and her nipples tightened. Anticipation licked at her. But when he touched her, it was to move his hand gently, so gently, over her bruised neck.

Like the whisper of a feather, his hands stroked her, soothing, arousing, drawing that knot of need into a pulsing frenzy. Then he touched her breast, cupping her tenderly through the thin fabric of her nightdress. She moaned, arching fully into his hand.

He shuddered and his arousal pulsed against her hip. He pulled her head down to his slowly, giving her a chance to absorb what was happening. She met him, her tongue sliding against his as she pressed against his palm.

His tongue ravaged her, slowly unraveling every last shred of rational thought. Elise was aware only that his dark, musky scent merged with hers, that his supple skin was warm beneath her fingers, that his tongue torched fires in secret places she'd never known.

Wet heat gathered between her legs and she fitted herself more closely to him. He dragged his lips from hers and she struggled for air, some sense of reason. Fierce need crested his features, pounded in her belly.

He tilted her head away from him, his lips skimming lightly over her collarbone, the sensitive skin beneath her chin. When he mouthed hot, unintelligible words in her ear, she thought she would die from the pleasure of it.

Suddenly he grasped the hem of her nightdress. "Let's get this out of the way."

His voice was grainy with desire, sparking an urgency in her. A breath shuddered out of her as he dragged the gown over her thighs, her buttocks, her back, his fingers trailing softly in the wake of the fabric.

She held her breath, focused on the sensual glide of his rough fingers against the softness of her skin as he pulled the gown over her head and tossed it aside.

Sudden doubt stabbed at her and she raised her arms to cover her breasts. What if he found her lacking? What if he—

"No." He rose from the bed, his gaze blazing into

hers. "Don't hide yourself from me. You are . . . Lord, Elise."

The tortured desire in his shaking voice reassured her, though it didn't erase all her shyness. Her gaze flitted away from his, but flew back in surprise when he took her hand and gently guided her to the edge of the bed so that the backs of her knees hit the mattress. Her legs wobbly, she sank down and gasped in surprise when he knelt in front of her.

"Jared?"

"You honor me with something highly precious, Elise. Please don't be ashamed of it." Strong, hot hands splayed loosely at her waist and he gazed up at her earnestly.

Emotion tightened her throat. When she spoke, it was a whisper. "I'm not. I want . . . to please you."

"You do. More than I deserve." His gaze urged her to believe it, to believe in the heat shimmering between them, the unspoken fullness of her heart.

She knew then that she had fallen in love with him. Totally. Irrevocably. She leaned down to him, touched at the gentle reverence of his kiss. As he'd done to her before, she slipped her tongue inside his mouth. His muscles hardened against her and leashed power vibrated from him. She ran her hands down his biceps and up to his shoulders, savoring the feel of heat and supple muscle beneath her palms.

He pulled away, his eyes dark with promise. Trailing his lips across her sensitive skin, he nipped at the swell of her breast, then his lips closed over her. She arched her back, offering herself to him. Heat streaked between her thighs.

Her nipples hardened for him and she ached down low. She wanted him to touch her everywhere. She wanted to touch him. His other hand stroked her breast, then cupped its fullness, thumbing her nipple to aching awareness.

Liquid heat coiled between her legs. His lips trailed a path of fire and moist heat down her belly, across the sensitive cleft where her hip joined her thigh. She threw back her head, squeezing her eyes shut to take in the swirling circle of heat and light pulsing through her body.

Her breathing grew more shallow, more ragged. Her thoughts scattered and she felt herself slipping to a place where only feeling mattered.

His hands skimmed over her hips, then covered her buttocks, kneading, caressing. They moved to her thighs, spreading them slightly, his breath misting the curls at their juncture. Her belly clenched and she stiffened.

"Easy, darlin'. I won't hurt you."

She knew that. What frightened her was this powerful, overwhelming urge to completely lose herself in him. She fought against it, uncertain and apprehensive. But she couldn't fight the demands of her body.

He stroked the insides of her thighs, sending tendrils of heat spiraling through her. His tongue touched the sensitive skin, moving toward her center.

Instinctively she clamped her legs tight, her gaze flying uncertainly to his.

Passion flushed his face and his eyes burned like heated emeralds. "Darlin', let me. You'll see."

She knew she could trust him, knew he would

never hurt her, but it seemed her legs were locked. She squeezed her eyes shut, frustration sharp in her voice. "I want to, but I can't."

"It's all right. Easy." His voice, though strained, was soft. His fingers stroked gently over her upper thigh, soothing, coaxing.

Her legs relaxed, though her belly tightened with need. "Don't stop, Jared. Don't stop."

He bowed his head, the struggle for control plain on his features. Then he gazed earnestly at her, pain mixing with the fierce desire in his eyes. "I can give you pleasure, Elise. Without taking your maidenhead."

"No!" She gripped his shoulders, her gaze locking on his. "I'm not afraid of you. I trust you."

"It's all right if you want to change your mind. But you've got to tell me now." He squeezed his eyes shut, savage want creasing his features. "If you wait, I may not be able to stop."

"I don't want you to stop." She framed his face with her hands. "I know what to expect and I want that with you. I'm not changing my mind. I'm not."

"I only want you to be sure. I would never dishonor—"

"I want you. All of you." She pressed a long kiss on his lips. "Don't mistake my inexperience for doubt."

He nodded, a ragged breath shuddering out of him.

"I trust you. I'll do what you say."

He laughed hoarsely. "That's a dangerous thing to tell a man."

She smiled, some of her tension easing, and though she felt a blush heating her skin, she whispered urgently, "Don't stop. I like it when you touch me."

His eyes darkened with violent passion and his hand flexed on her waist. She kissed him again, longer, meeting his tongue with her own.

The languorous heat swept through her again, rendering her a slave to the commands of his touch, a willing prisoner to his body. This time when he nudged her thighs apart with his hands, she opened freely.

And when one long finger slid inside her tight hot wetness, she gasped. "Oh!"

She watched him, focused on the intense caring in his face as she was carried away on a crest of sensation. His finger moved inside her, drawing an edge to the languorous sensation of the moment before.

Heat coiled deep within her, startling yet intoxicating in its newness. She wanted to follow where it led, wanted to learn the secrets between a man and a woman. As long as Jared was with her.

He rose from his knees, kissing her deeply and pulling her against him. She wrapped her arms around his neck, astonished by the burning feel of his hair-roughened skin against hers, the scent of her on his hands, the sensitivity of her breasts against his chest.

Sweeping aside the rumpled covers, he laid her gently on the bed and stretched out beside her. Still kissing, she tugged him over her, wanting to feel his weight.

He lifted his head, questions in his eyes. In answer, she pulled him to her, stroking his face. *I love you.* But the words remained locked in her heart. On some distant level, she was aware that reality would interfere too soon with this idyllic break in time.

He pulsed, hot and demanding against her thigh. She reached down and gently stroked him. At her touch, he bucked.

She drew her hand away. "No?"

"Yes," he rasped, taking her hand and placing it on that very blunt, different part of him. "If you want."

She flexed her fingers experimentally, drawing a groan from him. She loved the way his eyes darkened. "Very much."

Her hand closed around him. He was like sheathed velvety steel, hot and pulsing in her hand. Moist heat exploded between her legs and she closed her eyes, surging on a sudden burst of power. His hand settled over hers, deepening the pressure.

She opened her eyes, aching to watch him. He smiled at her, dark and blatantly male, and her heartbeat stuttered. She ran one finger across his bottom lip, lifting herself for another kiss. He pulsed heavy and hot in her hand, the muscles in his neck and arms corded with restraint. She wanted him to lose control as she had.

With firm yet gentle strokes she measured his throbbing length until his breathing was as ragged as hers, his color high, the muscles in his arms straining. His eyes darkened and his fingers moved inside her, stroking, coaxing the heat that coiled low in her belly.

The knot of fire splintered, radiating out through her body, and a gasp jerked out of her. She reached for his shoulders.

"Let go, Elise." His voice sounded distant yet urgent.

"I want you . . . with me." She could barely

speak as sensation hammered at her from the inside.
"Jared! Jared!"

Heat built to fever pitch, ignited her body. Her hips
rose against his hand even as she pulled his head
down and met his tongue, hot and wet.

She arched up from the mattress, tugging at him.
"Now, Jared. Now."

He withdrew his fingers and rose above her, his features tight with need. "I'll be gentle, Elise, but there
will be some pain."

She nodded, caring only that he follow her into the
searing heat.

He lifted her hips and held her steady. A tiny fear
of the unknown surfaced, but the need was greater.
She reached for him, urging him on.

In one long, powerful thrust he surged into her.
Pain stung, then mushroomed into a searing ache. She
cried out, recoiling instinctively.

He held her close, gentling her, whispering soft
words. She didn't want to leave him, but wasn't sure
she wanted to finish it either.

He moved slightly, withdrawing a bit, and she felt a
void open up inside her. "No, stay. Please stay."

A labored chuckle rumbled out of him. "I . . .
couldn't go . . . if I wanted to."

He bowed his head as though struggling for control.
His fullness throbbed inside her, and she understood
by the strain on his face, the quivering muscles in his
arms and legs and back, that he was in physical pain
by trying to ensure that she wasn't.

She stroked his shoulders, his face. "Please, Jared.
Finish it. Give me release."

His gaze locked with hers. "Are you sure? I want you to be sure."

"Yes." She shifted to fit herself better to him, and felt her tightness close around him, felt his pulse beating inside her.

He eased out and back in again. On a gasp of sensation, she met him.

White-hot desire jagged through her. Her hands moved over his back, down to the taut muscles of his buttocks. She gripped him, holding on against the current that rocked her out of control. Muscle and sinew flexed beneath her hands.

He began to move faster and she matched him. There was no pain now, just a peak somehow out of reach. She existed on sensation alone. His chest hair rasped against her breasts. The hard muscles of his belly nudged her softer ones.

She tightened her legs around his hips, her breath coming in shallow gasps. Jared's gaze fastened on hers, his features sharp yet gentle in the flickering light. The hunger inside her wound tighter, burned brighter until it was a brittle flame. Finally it splintered through her with blinding speed.

Tiny spasms rippled through her body and she closed her eyes, recognizing her voice as a cry spilled out of her. Jared gave a powerful thrust and rasped her name.

She caught him to her, holding to the steady width of his shoulders. Her heart pounded in her eyes, her blood thundered.

He lifted himself on his powerful arms. "I don't want to crush you."

"You're not. Don't move yet." She caressed his back as he kissed her long and deep.

After a time her breathing slowed, as did his. A warm languorous feeling enveloped her. Jared rolled to his side and pulled her into him. "Are you all right?"

"Mmmm." Delicious sensations rippled through her, making her feel drowsy and replete and completely safe.

His hand stroked up and down her back. The heat from his body cradled her.

"Is it always like that?" she asked drowsily.

"It's never been that way for me," he said in a low voice.

"Me either."

They both laughed.

"Good," Jared said.

Reality tugged at her, the ugliness of what had happened with DeWitt, of what Jared must have overheard. The time had come for confession, and her heart clenched in pain.

She loved Jared and thought he felt something for her, but in the wake of the Onash murders, would that matter?

She should tell him the truth, all of it, right now.

He never should've stayed. They never should've made love.

Regret charged through him. He knew he would have to ask her about the glove, about DeWitt and the money. Jared knew he should wake her, finish it, but he couldn't bring himself to do it. They'd both been overwhelmed tonight, not only by DeWitt but by what had just happened between them.

Keeping at bay the ugly truth of what he must do, he pulled her into him, cupping her breast in his hand. He waited for dawn, torn between pleasure and pain at the feel of her naked body spooned against his.

She sighed and snuggled against him, as trusting in sleep as she'd been when they'd come together. Self-loathing twisted through him. Conflicting emotions pulled at him. He was bound by honor to complete his investigation. And he was bound to Elise by his heart.

The pounding in his head, which had completely disappeared, now stabbed back with a vengeance. He had to ask her questions he didn't want to ask, and she would have to tell him truths he didn't want to hear.

As pale gray light filtered into the room, he moved quietly out of the bed, searching for his clothes. He pulled on his drawers, then his pants. Scooping up his shirt from where Elise had tossed it, he also picked up her nightdress. He sank down onto the edge of the bed, staring at the thin material in his hand.

He could easily have rent the flimsy garment with his impatience, his frustration. He didn't want to do that to Elise. She was delicate, yet strong like this fabric. Stronger than he'd ever imagined. He didn't want to break her spirit by bullying the truth out of her, but he had to know.

He turned, his heart swelling at the sight of her beautiful face, free of worry and flushed with the soft blush of a woman who'd been fulfilled.

She opened her eyes and smiled. Then realization

stole across her features. Her gaze dropped to the sheet and she hitched it higher over her naked breasts, covering herself against him.

His grip tightened on her nightdress as though he could keep some part of them, of what had happened between them. Then he held the gown out to her. "You'd better get dressed."

She took the gown, her fingers brushing his, and anxiety darkened her eyes. She glanced away, pulling back as she sat up, carefully shielding herself from him. Loneliness stabbed him and he rose from the bed, affording her some privacy.

He could hear the rustle of cloth, the creak of the bed frame as she slid to the floor. He could put it off no longer. "DeWitt wanted the money from you."

"Yes," she whispered.

Jared bowed his head against the agony stretching across his chest. "The money I'm looking for?"

"Yes."

Pain sawed through him, nearly doubling him over, but he forced himself to look at her. "You've had it all along."

"No!" Anger ripped through her. He really believed she'd killed Onash for the money. "Not what you think."

"I heard you tell DeWitt—"

"I know what you must've heard, but I was trying to save my life." She clenched her fists, barely holding on to calm. She refused to cry, refused to fall apart, though she felt as if she could shatter at any moment. "I don't have it, I tell you."

"Elise . . ."

She stalked to the wardrobe and yanked open the doors, pulling out a petticoat. Reaching inside, she whirled back to him, thrusting a fistful of money in his face. "Here's what I have. Fifty-five miserable dollars."

Shock panned across his features and his gaze, dark with denial and checked anger, moved from her hand to her eyes.

"Take it!" She shoved it in his hand. "Take it!"

His fist closed around it and she spun away, wrapping her arms around herself. A chill burrowed into her soul, erasing every soft moment they'd shared, rendering their joining small and insignificant.

"Where's the rest—"

"I don't know." With effort, she kept her voice even. Anger and sadness and fear tangled inside her, scraping against her nerves. Her throat tightened, and before she started to cry she rushed on, "There was only four hundred and seventy-five to start with."

"No." His voice was coarse with hurt. "There should be at least ten or fifteen thousand, depending on—"

"Ten or fifteen thousand! I don't know anything about that kind of money."

"Elise—"

"I don't, Jared. I had only four hundred and seventy-five. I swear."

He sighed heavily, his voice cracking through the room. "Do you think this is easy for me?"

She closed her eyes against the sadness pressing her chest like a vise. "That's all I have. All I . . . took."

"Did you kill them?" His question was barely more than a whisper.

"Yes."

Regret creased his features. "Then if not for the money, why?"

She didn't have to close her eyes to relive the bleak, unforgiving details—her mother's beautiful blue eyes closed forever, her father's good hand stretched toward his wife, Rithy slumped lifelessly against the wall. "They killed Mama and Papa. Rithy, too, before I could even get downstairs with the gun."

"So you took revenge?" His words were a mixture of relief and apprehension as he stepped toward her.

"They tried to rape me." The words echoed in the room, stark and bare and ugly. She turned away, aware of his shocked silence.

"No!" The word was torn from him, full of rage and helplessness and raw pain. He moved behind her and his hand grazed her shoulder. "Elise."

She nearly lost her composure. If she turned to him, she would break down and bawl. And it would change nothing. She moved away, feeling the loss of his hand as if it were her last steady support.

"I'm so sorry." Frustration rimmed his voice. "I don't know what to say."

"Just . . . let me tell you." She could barely get the words out. She didn't want to remember how she'd been too late to help her parents, didn't want to remember the blood, the horror, the fear that had swallowed her.

With choppy words, she told him how she'd found Mama stabbed repeatedly, blood soaking the bodice of her butter-yellow poplin. Papa lay behind her, barely recognizable from the knife and gun the Onashes had used. And Rithy's coffee-colored features were swollen and bloody from the vicious beating he'd taken.

Elise was barely aware of what she said, her words coming faster and faster in an effort to purge the memories. She focused on the pale morning light creeping through the window.

And when she finally faced Jared, feeling shaken and weary and guarded, his face was flushed with fury, yet his eyes were ravaged by pain. Her pain, she realized with a start.

"They ripped my dress . . ." She glanced down, her skin shrinking at the memory.

Jared cursed violently and started toward her, but she stepped away. She couldn't forget why she was telling him the truth, why he had to know and what he would have to do when she finished.

"I took only what was in his pocket. It was four hundred and seventy-five dollars. Nothing else. I don't know where the rest of it is. I didn't know there was any more."

"And DeWitt?"

"He knew something had happened to Claude and Pervis. He knew they were out here." Fatigue washed over her and she pushed her hair out of her face. "*He* thought I'd killed them for the money, too."

Jared winced at the comparison.

"He threatened to turn me over to the sheriff if I didn't give him the money."

"He's been blackmailing you?" Disbelief vibrated

in his voice and he rubbed a hand over his stubbled jaw.

"You think I'm lying." Betrayal clawed through her.

"You killed them in self-defense."

"Yes." She swallowed back her bitter anger.

"So if you didn't take the money, why hide them? Why not report what they did?"

"To Sheriff Restin?" she cried, her voice cracking. "I would have no chance then. What Yankee would believe I'd killed a Treasury agent in self-defense? Who would care?"

"But Elise—"

"I'm not going to prison." She faced him then, her chest aching with dread. "They murdered my family. I shouldn't have to pay for protecting myself."

Jared shoved a hand through his hair, looking helpless and frustrated.

Anxiety swept through her and she tangled her fingers in her gown. "You believe me, don't you?"

Doubt and raw agony darkened his eyes. "It doesn't matter what I believe."

"You don't believe me." Her legs wobbled and Elise thought she would sink to the floor.

"It's not that simple!" he yelled. "The government may not—"

"I'm not asking about the government," she said tightly, trying to salvage her fraying control. "I don't care about them."

"Well, you'd better," he bit out.

"I care what you think." She stared straight at him.

Torment ravaged his eyes. "I don't make the laws."

"You only enforce them," she said bitterly. "If I

had that money, why would I still be here? Or why wouldn't I give it to DeWitt so he would leave me be? I'm not lying, Jared. I can . . . I can help you find it."

He hesitated, his tortured gaze boring into hers. "Who's to say you didn't know all along where it was?"

She recoiled as if he'd slapped her. "You don't believe that."

"No. Hell, I don't know." He pinched the bridge of his nose, looking torn. "You lied to me about everything else."

"You weren't honest with me either!"

"I never dreamed— Damn!" His rough voice rattled the window. "You should've answered my questions."

"I didn't want to tell anyone! Yes, I killed them, but I'm not proud of it."

"Hell." He ground the heels of his palms into his eyes. "I can't keep quiet about this, Elise."

"What?" Fear snatched her breath and she froze.

"I have to tell the Treasury Department. I have to turn in a report."

"You can't arrest me! You won't!" Horror sliced through her and she rushed to him, ready to beg if she had to. "You wouldn't turn me over to Restin!"

"No, I wouldn't." Uncertainty mixed with the anger in his eyes, and his voice hardened. "I don't give a damn about Onash's death. As far as I'm concerned, he deserved it. But there's still the money. I've got to find it. If you don't have it and DeWitt doesn't have it, then who does?"

"You know I don't have it. Your opinion should count for something with the government."

"With all the new people, who knows?"

"Are you saying you won't help me?"

"I'm saying I don't know if I can."

She stepped away from him, feeling abandoned and betrayed and utterly hopeless. "I think you should go."

"Elise—"

"Go."

"I can't." He exhaled loudly, a mixture of regret and frustration.

She was too numb to even summon anger. "I want you out of here."

"I know, but I really can't go."

She frowned, then painful disbelief chased through her. "You're putting me under arrest!"

He winced. "Not exactly."

"You are!"

"It's more like protective custody," he said through clenched teeth. "DeWitt is still out there."

"Go." Her voice broke and she turned away, closing her eyes at the sight of rumpled sheets on the bed they'd shared.

He didn't move.

Agony stung her nerve endings and Elise thought she would shatter from the pain. "Can't you give me some privacy at least?"

"I'm sorry. I never meant—"

"Just go." The words ripped out of her. She wrapped her arms tight around her waist.

Finally, blessedly, he opened the door. "I'm truly sorry."

"So am I."

He hesitated. She could feel his steady gaze on her and thought she would scream. She bowed her head, tears burning her cheeks.

"I never meant to dishonor you. I—I wouldn't do that."

The door clicked shut and Elise stared at the bed where only a short while ago she'd surrendered her heart, feeling as if her soul had been stripped clean. "I know."

CHAPTER SEVENTEEN

*E*lise stared blindly at the bed, listening as the sound of Jared's footsteps faded down the stairs. She knew he wasn't leaving, but she was grateful for this small distance.

I have to tell the Treasury Department. Who's to say you haven't known all along where the money was?

His words circled through her mind, carving deeply into her heart. She had surrendered everything to him. After what they'd shared, how could he believe she had the money? Couldn't he see why she'd kept the truth from him?

Why couldn't he trust that she had told him the whole truth? Her innate honesty forced her to admit that his hesitation was understandable. After all, she had lied for a long time.

But her hurt at his lack of trust was pushed aside by a building anger. She would find that money and prove him wrong. Determination fueled her steps to the wardrobe, where she pulled out her red-and-white-striped cotton dress.

Yanking off her night rail, she pulled on her chemise. She wanted to focus on the harsh, unrelenting set of his jaw, his unyielding tone, the doubt in his eyes, but instead she saw the tenderness during their lovemaking, relived the powerful push of his body inside hers, and felt again that aching sense of completion.

That brief instant of passion and safety and love had been snuffed out by the truth. In spite of what she and Jared had just shared, he couldn't, or wouldn't, shield her from the investigation into Onash's murder. She hadn't expected him to compromise himself or his job, but she had expected his support.

Foolish of her. Urgency needled and she stepped into her dress, fastening up the bodice. She had to find the money quickly, before he did. And before DeWitt learned she had revealed his part in this.

Grabbing her scuffed shoes, she worked them on, fuming. How could she have fallen in love with someone who didn't believe in her? How could she have thought he'd come to care for her?

But his concern, his passion, had been real, she argued. She knew he hadn't used her callously. They'd both needed each other, and Elise knew that deep down Jared felt something for her. But he hadn't forsaken his duty in favor of her. Neither would she sit idly by while he filed his report.

She paused and picked up Mama's glove, sliding it into her pocket. Working the top two buttons on her bodice, she strode out of the room and across the hall to her brother.

They had no time to lose, and she hoped the activity would dull the bone-deep ache of her soul. Sunlight filtered from her room into the cool hall. Trying to dodge memories of Jared's hands on her skin, his lips teasing her breasts, she knocked lightly on Logan's door, tapping her foot impatiently. "Logan?"

There was no answer.

"Logan? Wake up!" She pressed her ear to the door but could hear nothing. "I hope you're decent, because I'm coming in."

She opened the door and peeked around the frame toward the bed on the opposite wall. He'd removed the heavy draperies his first night home and gathering sunlight flowed into the room, eating away the shadows of the large area, slanting across the bed. *The empty bed.*

Suddenly alarmed, Elise rushed inside, her gaze taking in the crisply tucked linens, the pillow plumped and resting against the ornate wooden headboard. He hadn't slept here at all!

Your brother won't be interrupting us tonight.

DeWitt! Had he done something to Logan? Foreboding sliced through her, and she spun around, her heart pounding. She rushed down the stairs, considering and discarding endless possibilities, hoping that she would step outside and run smack into him. Perhaps he was up early. Perhaps he was already outside.

But when she wrenched open the front door, she found not Logan but Jared, tugging his shirt over his head.

She looked away from the flex of muscle in his powerful arms, the broad chest that had cradled her only an hour ago. "Have you seen him? Where is he?"

"Seen who?" He angled toward her, pulling the shirt down over his taut abdomen. "What is it?"

"I thought you were gone," she said coldly, heading down the steps. She tried to ignore the softening of her heart, the longing that he would look at her with the same need she'd seen on his face when they were joined. She didn't want to ask him for help, especially not now.

"What's happened?"

She walked around the side of the house. "Logan! Logan!"

Jared followed, his long strides closing the distance between them. "He's not in the house?"

"Will you need to report this, too?"

He slanted her a sideways glance and a muscle flexed in his jaw. "Logan," he called.

She regretted the words the minute she said them. Not only because they were petty but also because she was wasting valuable time when she should be looking for her brother.

They circled the house and returned to the front. At the bottom of the porch, she shaded her eyes and scanned the trees down the drive, the edge of the woods. "His bed hasn't been slept in."

"I don't remember hearing him come in," Jared said thoughtfully. "But we were—"

She clenched her teeth and gave him a flat stare.

He cleared his throat, a faint flush coloring his tanned skin. "Maybe he lost track of time. He could've fallen asleep out here."

"Something happened. I know it." She rubbed her temple, reluctant to tell him about DeWitt's comment, then reminded herself wryly that Jared was already involved. Fear shifted through her and she turned to him.

"Last night, when DeWitt came to my room, he said he didn't have to worry about Logan interrupting him. I thought he meant because he'd seen Logan leave, but now . . ." Apprehension skipped up her spine. "Do you think something's happened?"

"We'll go look for him."

Jared reached for her, but she sidestepped him and headed across the field. "Should you be involved? I mean—"

"He's my friend, Elise," Jared said, his clipped, precise tones evidence that he was trying to hold on to his anger. "That has no bearing on the case, if that's what you're asking."

She hadn't meant the question to be flip, but she and Jared were already at cross purposes. No sense delving into it again.

He easily caught up to her. "He's out here, in the woods somewhere."

"He's got to be all right." She wanted to trust the certainty in Jared's voice, wanted him to vanquish the dread pressing against her ribs.

They made a thorough search of the woods with never more than three feet separating them. They skirted thick bushes and clusters of light blue chicory, unheeding of the low beds of purple violets. Tension swelled and they didn't speak again.

Elise couldn't bear to give voice to the fear that

clawed through her. What if Logan was hurt? What if he was—

No. She wouldn't allow herself to dwell on the worst. Pushing through a thick growth of bush, she nearly stumbled over her brother.

He lay on his back, motionless, eyes shut, his face pale and waxy. Alarm thundered through her and she knelt beside him, shaking his shoulders. "Logan? Logan, talk to me!"

"Careful, Elise. Don't try to move him."

At the quiet warning in Jared's voice, she looked over her shoulder at him.

Wariness and concern etched his features and he stared at Logan's feet. She shifted her gaze and horror cut her breath.

A bear trap! Logan's leg was caught between the jaws of a steel monster. Its teeth had sheared through his woolen trousers, and even in the dense light of the woods she could make out the bleached gleam of bone.

Nausea rolled through her and sweat trickled down her spine. "How are we going to get him free? What do we do?"

"I can get him free, if you help me." Jared glanced around at the surrounding trees, then disappeared around the trunk of a thick oak. "I'll be right back."

Elise turned to Logan, tamping down the hysteria that fluttered at her. Even unconscious, Logan's face was creased in pain, and she smoothed her hand over his forehead. What had he endured before he'd lost consciousness?

DeWitt had done this, damn him!

Nearby she heard the crackle of Jared's steps, the quick chatter of a squirrel. A lush bed of violets cushioned her brother, but the scent of loamy earth and moist darkness rose up, nearly choking her. "Hang on, Logan. Jared's coming."

Jared returned with a sturdy tree branch as thick as his wrist, and moved down to the trap. "I'll open the trap with this and you pull his leg free."

She nodded, feeling suddenly weak and dizzy.

"Elise?" he said sharply. "Can you do it?"

"Yes." She couldn't lose Logan, too. She looked up at Jared, gathering her strength. "I'm ready."

He nodded, planting his bootheel against the bottom ridge of the trap. Logan still lay unconscious, thank goodness. Leaning on the branch, Jared used the leverage of his weight to work the wood between the metal jaws.

He gritted his teeth, pushing against the building tension of the trap. His arms quivered with the effort and muscles corded in his neck. Even in the dim light of the woods, Elise could see sweat sheen his face. The trap yawned open with a grating moan.

"Now, Elise! Now!"

She lifted Logan's leg, but his trousers snagged on the trap's teeth. She tugged, panic rolling through her.

"Hurry, Elise," Jared rasped, his voice labored.

She knew his strength had to be waning. She pulled hard on Logan's leg, praying that he stay unconscious. Resistance met her, then pressure gave and his leg came free.

"I've got him!"

"Look away," Jared commanded harshly, just before he jumped away from the trap.

The steel monster snapped shut and the branch Jared had used splintered; chips and ragged slivers rained over the three of them.

Elise kept her head down, covering Logan with her body as best she could, all the while crooning soft words to him.

Jared knelt across from her, breathing hard.

She looked up, dread winding through her. "It's bad, isn't it?"

Jared glanced at his friend's shredded trousers, the mangled flesh and nodded.

"It was DeWitt," Elise said, her voice a whisper of hate as she took in the dark stain of blood on the ground.

"Probably." Jared's voice was rusty with fatigue as he rose. "I'll get the wagon."

In his eyes she read concern and regret for what had passed between them earlier. "We'll be fine," she assured him.

"I won't be long."

She nodded, looking down at Logan, and her heart turned over. "Don't you leave me, Brother."

Jared stood there for another moment, then hurried off.

He moved through trees and brush, his footsteps muffled by the grassy carpet. Elise concentrated on holding on to her brother. She couldn't lose Logan, too. Not after what had just happened with Jared. Not after everything else.

Jared's return was heralded by the rattle of wagon wheels and the jingle of harness. He reappeared, lifting Logan carefully over his shoulder and carrying him to the wagon.

Beneath Jared's wrinkled white cotton shirt she could see the powerful flex of muscle in his back and arms. Solid, strong. Helping her again.

Elise moved around him, slipping into the wagon and helping ease Logan onto the weathered floor.

Just then her brother regained consciousness briefly and focused his gaze with difficulty on Jared. "Damn . . . that hurts."

Hope flared in Elise's heart, but he promptly passed out again. Jared vaulted into the wagon and grabbed the reins, clucking to Majesty.

Elise made Logan as comfortable as she could, cursing every bump in the road that jostled his injured leg, wincing every time she looked at the gaping wound just below his knee. She only prayed they had found him in time and that Dru could do something.

During the whole trip one thought circled beneath the surface of her concern. The man who was helping to save her brother's life, the same man she'd fallen in love with, was also the man who could destroy her.

Several hundred feet north of where he'd set the trap, Tullar waited in the trees, nestled in the deep shadows of a thick walnut and a bushy honeysuckle. His left arm, where Kensington had shot him, had finally stopped bleeding, thanks to the strip of shirt that he'd ripped off and applied as a tourniquet.

Hours ago, when he'd escaped with only this

wound, he'd sworn not to leave Fairbrooke until he'd made a thorough search of it. It seemed he'd waited here endlessly, but he was weak and needed the rest.

Finally Elise Worthen had realized her brother was missing and now, as Tullar watched her pull away in the wagon with Kensington, hate spilled through him. Kensington had stayed in the house all night and Tullar suspected the gal had told the Treasury agent everything.

Tullar's horse, borrowed from the town livery, was still tethered on the back side of the woods, completely out of sight. As he waited for the rattle of wagon wheels to fade, he sucked in a deep breath against the fire in his arm. He'd never been wounded, not even in the war, and the sight of his own blood had nearly caused him to pass out.

Quiet settled around him, and after a few moments he levered himself to a standing position and headed deeper into the woods, intent on reaching the drive and the thick line of trees there. He meant to make damn sure Elise Worthen hadn't hidden his money somewhere. Then he would kill her.

He kept his rage in check, reaching the edge of the drive and slipping through the shadows of the tall oak trees as he moved toward the house.

Fifteen minutes later he stood in the middle of her bedroom, breathing hard and cursing violently. He clutched his arm, which had begun bleeding again.

He'd found only fifty-five Federal dollars crumpled on top of the bureau. Fifty-five dollars. If Elise Worthen had the rest of it, it wasn't in this room. Rage climbed through him, threatening to swallow him in a black haze.

He had to find that money.

You will make it, Logan. You will.

Elise stood in Dr. Hawthorne's office and watched Dru run her hands experimentally over Logan's leg. The doctor looked at Elise, concern darkening her gray eyes.

Doubt shot through Elise and her hand tightened on Logan's. Strangely, it was Jared's comforting presence that kept her from panic. "Well?"

"It's bad, but I think I can help him."

"Oh, thank you," Elise breathed. "Thank you!"

Logan's eyes fluttered open. "Where . . ."

"You're with Dr. Hawthorne, Logan." Elise leaned down, speaking calmly, though her heart thundered so loudly she was sure he could hear. "She's going to look at your leg."

Dru fished a pair of scissors from a small cabinet beside the examining table and bent over Logan's pants. She cut away the trousers, exposing the mangled, bloodied part of his leg.

Elise closed her eyes, unable to bear the sight of her brother's twisted and torn flesh.

Dru moved to Logan's head. "Mr. Worthen, can you hear me?"

He nodded, his eyes still closed.

"I need to remove your pants."

"Brazen . . . woman."

Hope flared and Elise gave a nervous smile.

Dru grinned. "Your sister can do it, if you'd rather."

"No!" Logan struggled to open his eyes, groping for Dru's hand.

Elise started in surprise, glancing up to find Jared looking stunned as well.

Sweat beaded on Logan's waxy skin. "Please make . . . her go."

Dru's gaze slid to Elise, questioning.

Desperate to stay with him, Elise shook her head. "He doesn't know what he's saying. He's delirious."

Jared shifted at the other end of the table. "Elise—"

"Go," Logan croaked. "She . . . goes . . ."

Dru's eyes darkened with compassion as she looked at Elise again. "It will be better for him if he's not overwrought. We can move him behind the curtain, give him more privacy." Gesturing behind her, she indicated a small enclosed area at the back of the clinic.

Elise didn't understand Logan's insistence, but she nodded, willing to do whatever he wanted. "Just help him."

Dru and Jared carefully lifted Logan and carried him to the rear of the clinic. Elise followed, standing at the open end of the curtain, watching nervously as Dru settled Logan on the exam table.

The doctor smiled. "You may come in after I'm finished."

Jared walked to Elise. "I'll wait with you."

Elise chafed at being separated from her brother, but she knew Dru would do her best. She nodded and walked around the curtain with Jared.

Moving to the window, she stared out at the bright

daylight, the bustle of people just starting their normal routines. She wanted to turn her face into Jared's chest and feel his strength. Instead, she reached inside her pocket and stroked the familiar lace of her mother's glove.

Turning back toward the curtain that shielded her brother, Elise studied the silhouettes outlined on the thin fabric. She could see Dru working over him, removing his belt then his trousers. Elise remembered with a sad smile the day Dru had come to the house. Logan had been awful to her, yet she helped him now as if she had no memory of it.

Logan moaned and Elise bit her lip, starting forward. Jared touched her elbow and she stopped, sighing.

For the next few minutes all was silent. Elise wrapped her arms around her waist, comforted by Jared's nearness, yet pained at the same time.

He stood only inches away, his musky heat reassuring. Though he offered silent support, he didn't reach for her.

Dru stepped out from behind the curtain. "I've given him some laudanum. While he's sleeping, I'll need some help, Jared."

He nodded and moved toward her.

"What are you going to do?" Elise hated the fear in her voice, but she couldn't lose Logan, not when she'd finally gotten him home.

Dru wiped her hands on a clean cloth, leaving smears of blood on the stark fabric. "I'm going to reset his leg." At Elise's frown, she explained, "The trap snapped his bone cleanly. If I reset, it will help his limp."

"You mean you can fix his leg?"

"Well, not fix, but definitely make it less painful for him and he'll be able to get around easier."

"Oh, Dru! Thank you!"

"Don't thank me yet." The doctor gave a wry smile. "I have a feeling when he wakes up, he'll be none too happy that I got my hands on that leg after all."

"If he wakes up, I don't care if he's mad enough to yell down the walls," Elise said happily, feeling a burst of hope.

Dru gave her a tired smile and motioned for Jared to follow her inside. Elise hesitated. Perhaps Logan wouldn't want her to see this either.

Dru glanced over her shoulder. "You may come if you want. I've covered his leg."

"I don't understand."

"He has scars, Elise." The other woman smiled gently. "He didn't want you to see them."

Tears burned Elise's throat as she strode behind the curtain. What horrors had her brother endured? "I want to be with him. How can I help?"

Dru positioned Jared at Logan's head, instructing him to hold Logan under the arms and provide a brace with his body. Dru asked Elise to hold Logan's leg steady, in a manner she quickly demonstrated.

The doctor had covered his leg with a pristine sheet and now she folded back one corner, exposing the twisted, mangled limb. Elise spoke softly to him one minute, urged him on with determined words the next.

Her gaze rose to Jared's and locked. The color drained from his face and his eyes darkened with agony. He swallowed hard, bracing Logan's upper body as Dru had shown him. He kept his gaze on Elise's, as if he drew the same strength from her that she did from him.

Dru positioned herself at Logan's foot, gripped his leg and twisted sharply, pushing up at the same time. A low pop sounded and bone crunched.

Elise winced, fearing for a moment that she might retch. It was over in less than a minute, but the sound grated in her ears.

"Good," Dru breathed.

As she quickly stitched the gashes in Logan's leg, Elise moved to his head. Dru wrapped the limb tightly in bandages, then took two thin strips of wood and positioned them on either side of his calf, directing Jared to hold them while she wrapped a bandage around to keep them in place.

She knotted the last bandage down at his ankle. "He'll sleep for a while."

"Will he be all right?" Elise stroked a wayward lock of hair from Logan's forehead, relieved to see that he slept peacefully.

"We'll have to wait and see. I'm not sure how much blood he lost. Right now, we need to watch for infection. I cleaned everything well and it looks good, but we won't know for at least twelve hours."

"I want to wait with him."

"Elise, maybe you should go home and get some sleep. You didn't get much last night."

Though Jared's voice was gentle, his reminder pricked her like a dagger. She kept a check on her temper. "I'll stay. You may go, if you like."

"No." He ran a hand across his eyes.

She didn't want to notice how tired his eyes looked, the tight lines of fatigue that etched his rugged features.

Dru glanced curiously at both of them, but said nothing. Instead she moved beside Elise and placed a palm on Logan's forehead. "No fever yet. That's a good sign."

"Is it all right if I stay?"

"As long as you want," Dru reassured her. "I've got some things to do, but I'll be back to check on him."

"Thank you." Elise released Logan's hand long enough to hug the woman who'd become such a good friend.

"If you notice any changes, send for me. I'll be at the restaurant, then at Coralee's to check on her boy."

Elise nodded and Jared murmured his assent, his gaze resting thoughtfully on his friend.

Dru looked once again at Logan's leg, then drew the sheet fully over his limbs. With an encouraging smile, she disappeared around the curtain.

Dru's footsteps faded as she made her way upstairs to change. Jared's gaze shifted to her and Elise resisted the urge to squirm. His eyes were tender with compassion—and memories of last night—and she didn't want to acknowledge either one.

He stepped toward her and she recoiled, her nerves

raw and exposed. Hurt flared in his eyes, then hardened to anger.

He reached behind her and pulled a chair forward,
plunking it down sharply. "I thought you might be
more comfortable sitting down."

Embarrassed that she'd misread his gesture, she
swallowed hard. "Thank you."

He nodded and moved away. Sadness and regret for
the distance between them pulled at her. "I don't
know what I would've done if you hadn't helped me
with Logan."

"You're pretty resourceful, Elise. I somehow think
you would've managed."

Despite the anger in his eyes, his words were ear-
nest. If he could be civil, so could she. "You don't
have to stay," she offered. "If you'd rather not."

Jared shook his head. "I don't want to go far until I
know how he is, but if you're going to sit with him for
a while, there are a couple of things I need to check
on."

In her concern for Logan, the urgency to find the
money had faded. Now it returned. "About DeWitt?"

Jared's eyes hardened to cold, unforgiving jade.
"I'm going to find him. He tried to kill you last
night."

"What about the money?"

"I'm going to find that, too."

They stared at each other, remembering the words
that had passed between them. Elise didn't offer to
help again and Jared didn't ask.

Perhaps he hoped to find the money while she
played nursemaid. No matter. Once her brother was

declared fit, she would find that money, regardless of what Jared said.

He eyed her speculatively and opened his mouth as if to speak. Then resignation crossed his features and he turned away. "I'll be back soon."

"All right." She hesitated, then added, "Good luck."

At the foot of the examining table, he turned to look at her, hunger and tenderness burning in his eyes.

Her chest tightened and she caught her breath. "What is it?"

"Nothing." But his gaze roved over her slowly, as if memorizing her. "Nothing."

With that he was gone. She sank down into the chair, overwhelmed with fatigue and reaction and a pressing loneliness.

She bowed her head, squeezing Logan's hand tightly, telling herself that her tears were for her brother, not for what she and Jared had lost.

CHAPTER EIGHTEEN

*B*eing so close to Elise frayed the edges of his control, and the walls of the clinic seemed to press in on him. Jared walked out, barely tempering his frustration and desperation.

Overrun with love, relief, and anger, he stepped into the alley between Dr. Hawthorne's clinic and the telegraph office and backed against the wall of the clinic.

Propping one booted foot behind him, he closed his eyes and hauled in a deep breath. What a damn mess!

If he didn't put some distance between him and Elise, he would do something stupid like order her never to set foot anywhere without him, and he could well imagine how that would go over.

She was safe, for now. And the doctor was hopeful that Logan would be all right. Now all Jared had to do was find DeWitt.

Relief, frustration, and vicious rage meshed together, causing his head to throb, but for the first time since he and Elise had made love, Jared let himself feel.

Beginning with her confession about the Onashes, he had become increasingly numb: at the forced distance from her, then at the shock of finding Logan, but mainly at hearing that Claude and Pervis Onash had tried to rape her.

Jared tunneled a hand through his hair and realized he was shaking. He wished he had known before they'd made love. What if he'd frightened her? He knew he couldn't have stopped—he needed too badly to sink himself into her—but he could've gone slower. Something.

He'd fallen in love with her.

He'd known it for a long time, but had ignored, dismissed, denied. He could no longer do that. He faced the admission as if it were a capture he'd been eluding—with his eyes wide open and his heart laid bare.

There was peace in finally saying it to himself, and a humbling sense of awe. And beneath it all, frustration. Yes, he loved her, but unless he could think of a way to help her without breaking his word, he would lose her.

He purposely hadn't told her about finding the glove. He hadn't the stomach, not as her entire story unfolded.

Anger churned inside him. Elise shouldn't have to go to prison for protecting her home, her person—for doing what all of them had done during the war. But she would have to be accountable for killing an agent of the government, even if the bastard had deserved

everything he'd gotten. It would work in her favor
that Onash had stolen the money and deserted the
job.

Jared pulled the glove from his trouser pocket and
stroked it pensively. Reluctant to wire Cam with his
latest discovery, Jared knew he had to nonetheless.
But—

He straightened, hope flaring. There was *something*
he could do for Elise. He didn't have to tell Cam
everything. Not yet. Tucking the glove safely away, he
hurried to the telegraph office and sent a short wire
informing his friend that he had found Onash dead
and he had a suspect in the case, but not the money
itself.

Jared didn't give Elise's name, knowing if necessary
he could plead discretion to Cam. While he waited for
Cam's return message, Jared could look for DeWitt
and that money.

Standing outside the telegraph office, he scanned
the main street of Moss Springs. Where was the bastard? That forceful, unfamiliar blackness he'd felt
upon hearing Elise's story reached into his soul. De-
Witt had taunted and frightened and threatened Elise.
When Jared found the man, he would pay, not only for
his own outrages but for what the Onashes had done
to her as well.

His steps fueled by determination, Jared strode to
the New American Hotel. The desk clerk said he
hadn't seen DeWitt since the man left for work yesterday morning. Jared asked to see DeWitt's room and
the clerk balked, until Jared showed his papers from
the government. He found nothing in the room to

indicate that DeWitt had left town or that he had the money.

Jared then tried the bank, only to hear that DeWitt hadn't been seen since the close of business yesterday.

He refused to go to the sheriff. A visit from him might tip off DeWitt, and if it didn't, Jared knew Restin would soon inform the man. Jared stopped at the hotel restaurant and ordered two of the day's specials. After eating his, he took the chicken and mashed potatoes back to Elise.

She sat beside Logan, still holding his hand. She agreed to eat but only picked at her food, her gaze staying locked hopefully on her brother's face.

Jared was relieved to see Logan's color had improved, but his friend hadn't stirred. Jared was concerned about Elise, too. Dark circles rimmed her blue eyes, and fatigue stole the color from her face. He wanted to put her to bed, to stand over her like a sentry until she slept, but he kept that thought, and his hands, to himself and went out again in search of Tullar DeWitt.

He learned from Coralee Bronson that DeWitt had leased a horse yesterday and still hadn't returned it. A visit to Mr. Bailey and then another to the hotel yielded nothing. It was late afternoon when Jared started back to the clinic.

As he stepped onto the porch a boy from the telegraph office ran up with a message from Cam. Jared read it quickly, urgency unfolding within him. Cam and General Schofield, a Union commander who had been unofficially put in charge of Virginia after the

war, were en route from Washington and would arrive
tonight. That didn't leave Jared much time.

He returned to Dr. Hawthorne's clinic, and this
time he found Logan groggy but awake. And lecturing
his sister.

"Talk some sense into her, would you?" Logan en-
treated weakly.

"Good afternoon to you, too," Jared drawled,
pleased to see his friend lucid and strong enough to
express concern for Elise.

Pain puckered Logan's features. "Elise refuses to
go home and get some sleep. I don't see how she—"
He sucked in a deep breath and grimaced, squeezing
his eyes shut.

Elise rose to her feet, still holding his hand. "I'll get
Dru to give you something."

"No," Logan said hoarsely. "I can't live on damn
laudanum."

"But—"

"Take her home," he said desperately to Jared.
"She's driving me crazy."

Jared chuckled, looking at Elise. "You've got to
consider that irascible charm a good sign."

She wrinkled her nose at him, looking back to her
brother. "I told you I won't leave until you do."

"Elise, you heard the doctor. I could be here for
days. It won't hurt anything for you to get some sleep.
Trust me, I'm not going to run away," he said dryly.
"And I'd feel much better knowing you weren't wasting away from lack of sleep or food."

Dru walked around the curtain in time to hear Logan's last words. "He's right, Elise. He won't be doing much moving about until tomorrow at least."

"I might surprise you," he grunted, looking affronted.

"Hmmm. We'll see."

The doctor was unimpressed and Jared bit back a grin. If anything would get his friend up and about, it was the belief that he couldn't do something. Dru Hawthorne evidently read people very well.

Elise sighed. "All right. I can't argue with all of you. But I'll be back bright and early."

"I expect you to," Logan said gruffly.

She bent and kissed his cheek, and Jared saw him squeeze her hand.

Logan's gaze moved to Jared, pain still sharp in his eyes. "Take care of her."

He saw Elise stiffen, but she said nothing. Jared gave a two-finger salute. "Whatever you say. I'll bring her back good as new."

"I'm not a gun you're loaning out, Logan." Her dry quip wrung a weak chuckle out of her brother and a smile from Dru.

Jared smiled too.

"No. A gun I could control," Logan said weakly, gaining a smile from Elise. His gaze sought Jared's. "Find DeWitt."

Jared nodded somberly.

Elise glanced sharply at him, but allowed him to hold open the curtain as she walked through.

"He'll be fine," Dru called behind them.

"Thank you," Elise said again. As Jared opened the

door she paused, and canted her head toward the curtain.

His gaze followed hers to the squared-off area where her brother lay. At first Jared wondered at Elise's intense concentration, but then he made out Logan's gravelly voice.

"I'd like to echo my sister's thanks. If it weren't for you . . ."

"Mr. Worthen, you're not about to get sentimental on me?"

"Could you just let me say what I have to?" His words were weak but impatient.

"Go ahead." Dru's shadow rippled across the curtain as she bent over Logan's leg.

"You didn't have to help me at all, after the way I treated you at Fairbrooke."

"I don't withhold medical treatment, even from surly men," she said smartly.

Elise's gaze shot to Jared's, and wonder spread through her eyes. He grinned at her amazement and whispered, "Looks like Logan and Dr. Hawthorne might hit it off after all."

Elise smiled, a dazzling smile of pure joy, and it kicked his gut like raw whiskey. He barely caught Logan's next words.

"You would certainly have been well warranted to refuse me after—"

"After you said you wouldn't come crawling to me if I were the last doctor on God's earth? Yes, I suppose I would have. Now, really, Mr. Worthen, you must rest."

"Logan," he said gruffly.

"What?"

Jared's eyebrows rose at the astonishment in Dru's tone.

"You can call me Logan. I'd like it if you did."

A long pause filled the room and Elise pressed closer to Jared, smiling widely. For the first time in hours, he felt warmth flare between them again.

"Well," Dru said, as though exhaling a shocked breath. "Well."

"After I got stuck in that damn trap, I couldn't even move, let alone *crawl*, to a doctor, *any* doctor. Don't you find that even a little ironic?"

"It wouldn't be polite to point out such a thing," Dru said primly.

Jared laughed and grabbed the door. Clapping a hand over her mouth, Elise walked quickly outside before they could be caught eavesdropping.

Jared could tell the exchange between her brother and the doctor had lightened Elise's spirits, and he hoped she would concentrate on that rather than on asking him what he'd discovered about DeWitt. He might as well have wished to hold the moon.

They were no sooner in the wagon than she turned to him. "Did you find out anything?"

"Not really." He recounted his fruitless search for DeWitt and also informed her about the unreturned horse from the livery.

He knew if he didn't tell her, she herself would question everyone about DeWitt, and Jared had no intention of allowing that. Not while DeWitt was still roaming about.

As he spoke she nodded in all the right places, but

kept quiet. She drew into herself, aloof and cool, and he cursed the distance between them.

Their silence lengthened as they drove to Fairbrooke. He studied her profile, forlorn and distant. The one time she looked at him, he glimpsed bleak uncertainty in her eyes and knew he had put it there.

He wanted to erase the shadows in her eyes, apologize for his lack of faith in her. "Elise, I'm—"

"Thank you for helping me with Logan," she said primly, keeping her gaze averted, her hands twined together in her lap. "I appreciate it."

He didn't want her damn gratitude. "You're welcome. Listen, about the money—"

"I know." She froze him with a flat stare. "*You'll* find it."

"What I was going to say—"

"I think we've both said enough." She looked out over the rolling hills, the fog ringing the crest of the Blue Ridge Mountains.

"Dammit, Elise! I'm trying to apologize."

"Leave it be, Jared."

She wouldn't even look at him. She was shutting him out, absolutely, undeniably. Regret charged through him, and he clenched his teeth as he reined up in front of Fairbrooke. "If you'd let me speak—"

"You've kept your promise to Logan." She gathered her skirts and climbed out of the wagon. "You've no more obligation here."

She headed into the house and he scrambled down from the wagon, seething with frustration. "Would you just listen to me for a minute?"

She was already inside and headed up the stairs. He

pinched the bridge of his nose, fighting the urge to go after her and kiss her senseless. Hurrying up the stairs behind her, he considered locking them together in her bedroom. At least that way she would have to listen to him.

He slammed to a stop just before he ran into Elise, who'd halted in the doorway. The sight of her bedroom hit him like a blow to the gut, and all thought of talking vanished.

Bureau drawers were yanked out, spilling undergarments and stockings. One wardrobe door swung open, creaking with slight movement. The mattress had been shoved half off the bed frame and her draperies ripped from the window.

The mattress was slashed from head to foot and on the sides. Feathers gaped from the ticked cover and the bed frame ropes lay exposed like a naked lover.

Jared took it all in with a glance, reaching automatically for his Colt. He checked behind the door and under the bed, looking for the intruder, but the room was empty.

"It's gone!" Elise cried.

Jared spun toward her, slipping the gun back into his waistband. "What is?"

"The money." She slapped the corner of the bureau. "Remember? You put it here."

"DeWitt," Jared raged. "Now I know why I couldn't find him in town."

Elise scooped up a torn chemise from the floor, pale-faced and glancing uneasily toward the door. "Do you think he's still here?"

Jared shook his head, a decision made. He had to do

something to help Elise, duty be damned. "Get what you need and let's go."

"Where?" Wariness crept across her features.

Jared scanned the disarray of her room, wondering where DeWitt was now. "Home. To Briar Rose."

"No!" She looked surprised at the force behind her words, but she shook her head stubbornly. "No."

Jared stared at her, anger and hurt drilling into him. She would rather stay here alone than come with him? He bit out, "You needn't worry that I'll ravish you. Gramps will be there."

She flushed angrily. "I'm *not* worried."

Regret pinched at him. After everything that had happened, she had a right to be wary of everyone, including him. But he couldn't leave her alone again until he'd found DeWitt.

He tried to gentle his words, but they brooked no doubt. "It's not a choice, Elise. You're coming with me."

"Don't use that high-handed tone with me," she snapped, her face pale and drawn. Immediately regret clouded her features. With a look that somehow managed to combine defiance and fear, she snatched up her nightdress, tucked it under her arm, and grabbed her wrapper. "Very well then."

Jared knew without a doubt it was going to be the longest night of his life.

As they rode to Briar Rose, Elise pressed close to her side of the wagon. She felt raw, exposed, completely vulnerable, because of Jared. Her nerves jangled with a stinging restlessness and she wanted distance from him. But common sense echoed that he was right. She shouldn't be alone until DeWitt was apprehended.

Just for tonight, she told herself. She need only stay with him for tonight.

Fatigue washed through her and she wished she could sleep. It seemed only seconds later that Jared shook her shoulder.

"Elise, we're home."

She opened her eyes, her thoughts sluggish as she slowly came to herself, recalling where she was. And why. She pulled away from him.

The front door opened and soft gold light spun onto the porch. Gramps stepped outside. "Jared, that you?"

"Yes." Jared set the brake and stepped down from the wagon. "Elise is with me."

"Elise?" The older man hurried down the porch steps to the wagon. "Is everything all right?"

Elise clutched her few belongings and allowed Gramps to help her down, trying to ignore the concern in Jared's face as he stood to the side. She didn't want to soften toward him, didn't want to turn into that broad chest and let him soothe her. Until that money was found, nothing would be all right.

As they walked inside, Jared quickly related the latest happenings to his grandfather, including Logan's injury and the recent break-in at Fairbrooke.

Gramps hugged Elise tightly, his green eyes warm and determined. "If Dru says Logan will make it, then he will. That woman is one fine doctor."

Elise nodded her agreement, stifling a yawn. The last day had sapped her strength and being this close to Jared blurred her anger at him. The hollow emptiness she'd felt since confessing to Jared seemed to burrow deeper.

"Elise, you look done in." Gramps peered at her. "Can I get you something to eat? Some coffee? Or buttermilk?"

She smiled and squeezed his hand. "I think I'd just like to rest."

As exhausted as she was, she couldn't imagine sleeping, but neither could she stay down here with Jared.

"Of course." Gramps guided her toward the short staircase. "You can have Jared's room. It's the second door upstairs."

Her gaze shifted uncertainly to Jared, and her heartbeat stuttered at the raw need she saw in his eyes. She wasn't sure she could bear even the small closeness of being in his room. A protest rose to her lips, but she stymied it, refusing to let him see that it might affect her.

She started up the stairs, then paused, realizing Jared hadn't removed his hat. Turning, she searched his eyes, recognizing the single-minded purpose that glinted there.

She frowned. "You're going out again."

He glanced away, a muscle working in his jaw. "I'll only be gone a short while."

She moved back down the stairs. "I think I should go too."

"I don't want you involved," he said shortly.

She stared flatly at him.

"Let me do this, Elise. Don't make it more difficult by insinuating yourself—"

"Where I'm not wanted," she finished harshly.

"I didn't say that." His gaze bored into her, steely with determination.

She was tired of fighting him, fighting herself, worrying about Logan. And in a rush, her own defiance drained out. She had every intention of finding that money once she'd had some rest. Jared could do as he pleased. She started back up the stairs. "Good night."

"Elise, you needn't be afraid." His voice stopped her halfway up. "You'll be safe here. I give you my word."

His word. Pain ripped through her and she closed her eyes briefly. She nodded and continued up the stairs. Awash with doubt, she stepped inside his room and closed the door. It wasn't his word she wanted, but his *heart*.

Pushing away the admission, she dropped her nightclothes into a chair beside the bed and began unbuttoning her bodice. She slipped out of her dress and stood in her shift, trying to ignore the dark, musky scent of Jared.

The white cotton shirt draped carelessly across the back of the chair where her clothes lay, the waxy coal smell of boot black. Spinning away, she crawled into the bed. But when she laid her head on his pillow, the scent of male and leather and smoke rose around her. Loneliness welled up and tears burned her throat.

He was only downstairs, but it felt so very far away. It was nearly impossible to believe that last night they'd been in the same bed, loving each other . . .

She rolled over on her back, hoping to escape the haunting muskiness of him, the awareness tingling through her body. Shoving away thoughts of Jared, she focused on Logan.

She replayed the conversation she'd overheard between him and Dru, and she smiled. Though she hated leaving Logan alone, she knew he was in Dru's more than capable hands.

Elise tried to close her eyes, only to be ambushed by images of Jared. Unbidden came the memory of the fierce possession in his eyes when their bodies had joined, the torment she'd glimpsed a moment ago. Her heart ached at the distance between them, but she wouldn't close it.

He didn't believe her. She understood that he had to follow through on his investigation. Why couldn't he see that she had no reason to lie about the money?

When she'd confessed everything, Jared's eyes had gleamed with understanding and vengeance, not condemnation. Still, he couldn't turn his back on the investigation. Her head understood, though her heart broke at the reality.

Whatever feelings had been between them had to be ignored. He was duty-bound to finish the job and that included exposing her part in the Onashes' deaths. She had never felt so alone, so abandoned. She stared at the ceiling, studying the ripple of moonlight merging with shadow, waiting for dawn.

"Go to her." Gramps turned to Jared as soon as Elise closed Jared's bedroom door.

"She wants nothing to do with me." Jared stalked into the sitting room, yanking off his gloves.

Gramps followed him. "Talk to her, son."

"I tried earlier. She's not interested." He braced himself against the fireplace, bowing his head, torn between wanting to force her to listen to him and leaving her be.

DeWitt was still out there. Jared urged himself to go in search of the man, but he couldn't tear himself away from Briar Rose. Not yet.

Gramps moved to stand behind him. "Try again, Jared. Tell her how you feel."

"It doesn't matter how I feel." He pushed away from the mantel and paced in front of the fireplace. "I have a job to do."

"It *always* matters," his grandfather said quietly.

Jared wanted to believe that, but it hadn't mattered with his mother.

Gramps touched his shoulder, waiting until Jared looked at him. "You've allowed Elise to get past the barrier."

"I'm not a damn fort." He sensed where this conversation was heading and he wasn't interested.

"I'm talking about Cecily."

Anger surged through him and Jared clenched his jaw. "We won't speak of her."

"We will." Gramps' voice was unrelenting but gentle. "She left you, true. But she was a bad woman, Jared. Shallow and selfish. Elise isn't like your mother and you know it."

"Yes, I do know it. That's not the problem." Want curled through him, shifted to need. An ache deeper than physical ground into him—it was the need to set things right with her, *things between them*, damn the consequences to his job or the case.

"Do you love her?"

"Gramps—"

"Do you?"

Jared closed his eyes, uncertainty and reluctance pushing through him. "Yes."

"Then tell her."

He fought his pride and his heart. His heart urged him to make amends, give her promises he'd never given another woman. Just the thought that she was upstairs, *in his bed*, battered at his resolve to stay away. "I believed she had the money. She'll never forgive me."

"Give her the chance."

"But—"

"You trust her. You love her. Go, Jared. You've never felt this way about a woman. You never will again."

Still duty pulled at him. "Even if I could prove she had nothing to do with the money, why would she want me?"

"Do you believe she doesn't have the money?"

"Yes."

"Then damn this so-called proof! Tell her. Before it's too late, boy. Before you lose your chance. *Before tomorrow*."

He knew Gramps was right and he started for the stairs, quaking as if leading his first night-raid. Seeking reassurance, he touched the glove in his trouser pocket. If she wouldn't forgive him, he had one last thing to offer her.

Knocking softly on her door, he glanced over his shoulder to see Gramps staring up at him, smiling in encouragement. Jared nodded, his nerves jangling as he forced himself to wait.

Soon he heard the shuffle of bare feet, then she opened the door, belting her wrapper. Upon seeing him, wariness clouded her eyes. "Jared."

"I need to talk to you."

Quick tears sprang to her eyes. "Not tonight. Please."

Moonlight silvered the thick curls that hung down her back and over her shoulder, spilling like vibrant silk, making her slender neck appear elegantly pale. She was so beautiful, so strong, so loyal. Desire and love tightened Jared's chest. "Just hear me out, Elise."

Sadness pulled at her delicate features and she started to close the door.

Desperation leapt through him. He couldn't let her face Cam and the general without knowing how he felt.

He jammed his boot between the door and the frame. "Please, Elise."

CHAPTER NINETEEN

*H*e stepped inside, and for a long moment neither of them moved. He stood stiffly by the door as if lashed to the spot. Uncertainty and hesitation vibrated from him. The soft whisper of their breathing filled the air between them, aching, uncertain. Jared's strong features were carved from shadow and moonlight. She saw the hope in his eyes, the earnestness, and her heart tilted.

The crest of his left cheekbone bore the raw cut from DeWitt's leather strap. Elise stared at the mark, overcome with the realization of how much Jared cared for her brother. And how much he cared for her.

"I want to apologize." He jammed a hand through his hair and shifted uncomfortably. "I should've told you last night that I believed you."

She canted her head. "Did you believe me last night?"

He hesitated.

Hurt lanced her and she gave a tight smile. "I'd prefer that you didn't lie."

"I'm not lying now." Agony ravaged his strong features. "I'm truly sorry for hurting you."

She stared at him for a long moment, reading doubt and regret in his beautiful eyes. She believed him, but what did it matter? "I accept."

"I want . . . another chance, Elise. For us." He shifted a step closer, his gaze burning fervently. "I've never felt for a woman what I feel for you."

For an instant she was speechless. And humbled. She knew what it had cost Jared to admit that, especially after she'd lied. "There's too much bad between us, Jared. We can't go back. I lied to you. You can't trust me. Can that be forgiven?"

"I wouldn't have thought so before, but I do now. I *hope* so. I'm willing to try." His gaze moved over her, softly desperate, and he jammed his hands in his trouser pockets. "I didn't want to trust you, but I did somehow, even when I knew you weren't telling the whole truth. Before, I thought all that mattered was not getting hurt the way my mother hurt me. I wouldn't allow myself to be blinded by a woman, like my father was, but . . ." His voice lowered, vibrating with need. His eyes glimmered. "The chance of losing you hurts me more than anything else could."

Elise's heart tilted and she wanted to reach out to him, but how could they ignore his sworn duty? "Jared—"

"If you tell me you don't feel anything for me, then I'll . . ." He paused, looking nonplussed. "Well, I won't believe you."

He gave a crooked smile and she nearly smiled in

return. His mixture of confidence and uncertainty charmed her, but reality was too close.

"What about the investigation?" she asked quietly, lacing her fingers painfully so she wouldn't touch him as she longed to do.

Indecision and bleak realization sharpened his features.

Her heart ached, but she continued. "You still don't have the money. I still have no proof that I didn't take it. You can't fix that, can you?"

"No." Fierce determination crossed his features, then resignation. "No, I can't. But I can do this." He reached in his pocket and held something out to her. "It's the only way I know to convince you of my true feelings. Maybe this will help you to understand."

She frowned, puzzled over what he held. Hesitantly she took it from him, and disbelief slammed into her. "My glove?" She lifted her gaze to his. "What are you doing?"

"Take it and go," he urged. "This is the only thing that can really link you to Onash."

She blinked dazedly at the stained lace, her thumb stroking it. "Where did you get this—" She broke off, realization stabbing through her. He had found it in Claude's grave, in her skirt pocket. And he was giving it to her. She was stunned at the faith he placed in her, and tears crowded her throat. "You know I don't have the money."

"Yes." His gaze, deep with confidence, locked with hers and he took her hand. "But I can't prove it. Take the glove and go, darlin'. Cam is coming in late tonight with a general. I know you killed those men in self-defense, Elise, but I don't know this General Schofield. I don't know what he'll do. If he finds you guilty of murder and wants to put you in prison—I can't let that happen."

He hadn't said he loved her; he didn't need to. She could read it in the desperation tightening his body, the fervent concern in his voice. He would risk his own job, his own reward, his own integrity for her. Emotion swelled in her throat, and she knew then that she could face whatever she had to, as long as Jared was beside her.

She shook her head, her thumb stroking the glove. "I won't go. I can't leave Logan. Or you. I'm tired of running, tired of the lies. Yes, I killed those men, but I was in the right of it. I want to try to prove it. And I want you to help me."

Protest flared in his eyes, but there was also admiration. "You've got to go."

She turned and placed the glove gently in her skirt pocket before moving back to him. "What happens to you if I leave?"

"Don't worry about that."

"Tell me."

He looked decidedly uncomfortable. "I'll take care of it."

"I can't let you do that." She touched his stubbled jaw, awed that he would risk his good name for her. "You're noble and honest. I love those things about you. How could I ask you to forsake them for me? I won't."

"Elise, I can resign." He covered her hand with his, pressing her palm to his face. "Lord knows I didn't want to become a permanent agent of the United States Treasury. I don't have to tell Cam anything."

"How would you live with yourself? I could never ask you to do something like that."

"Not even to save your life?" he asked harshly.

Whether she escaped with Jared's help or went to prison, she would have no life without him. Whatever the future held for her, she couldn't compromise his integrity.

His hand moved to her arm, cupping her elbow. "We have time. I haven't given Cam a suspect yet. I wanted more evidence, wanted—"

She kissed him, full on the mouth.

He stared, astonishment stealing across his rugged features. A smile lifted one corner of his mouth. "Elise?"

She kissed him again, soft and coaxing and deep. "You believe me," she said against his lips.

"Hell, if you kiss me like that again, you could tell me you are Mary Todd Lincoln and I'd believe you." He pulled her closer.

"Why?" She pressed a kiss on his jaw, the underside of his chin.

He nuzzled her temple, his breath warm, sending shivers of sensation down her neck and arms. "Why what?"

"Why do you believe me? If there's no new evidence—" She stopped, pulling back to eye him accusingly. "You're not saying this because of your sense of responsibility to Logan?"

He grinned. "No. I can quite honestly say Logan isn't even on my mind right now."

"Then why?"

He drew back to look into her eyes. "Because I trust you."

Her heart constricted. "You do?"

"And I love you."

Elise drew in her breath, afraid she'd imagined the words.

He framed her face in his hands. "I love you, Elise. Do you . . . Can you . . ."

She gripped his wrists, a tremulous smile breaking free. "I love you, too, Jared Kensington."

Disbelief flared in his eyes. "After everything I said, what I almost did? All the accusations?"

"I made them, too." She traced his lips with her fingers. "Tonight I don't want to dwell on the past. Only right now."

Tenderness shone in his eyes, mingled with a growing wonder. "I love you."

Her heart gave a funny flip and she smiled. "You don't have to make any promises."

"I'm not."

"You just did. You promised to belong to me and only me."

His gaze, dark and seductive, locked on hers. "Then hold me to it."

Wonder and disbelief soared through her. Was this really happening? "Are you sure?"

In answer, he lowered his head to hers, covering her lips in a hot, leashed kiss of power and commitment and freedom, hinting at abandon and a future she couldn't bear to contemplate for fear she might lose it all in a few hours.

He raised his head, naked hunger glittering in his eyes, and Elise felt an answering tug low in her belly.

Tonight might be all they had of a future and she didn't want to waste another minute of it.

Rolling up on tiptoe, she curled her hand around his neck and brought his lips to hers again. Curve to hardened muscle, soft contours to tempered ones, breast to chest, thigh to thigh, she lost herself in the warmth seeping through her, the feel of Jared's chest cushioning her breasts, the coaxing power of his kiss.

"I want—"

"Me too," he said roughly, raining gentle kisses on her eyelids, her nose, her temple. Abruptly he pulled back. "Last time, I went too fast. Did I hurt you?"

"You were perfect." She smiled up at him.

Doubt clouded his eyes. "I don't want to frighten you. Tell me . . . Show me, Elise."

Her gaze fastened on his, excitement stirring at the prospect of being the one to control their joining this time. A sense of freedom unfurled inside her and she drew the tip of his finger into her mouth. Reaction jerked through his body, his eyes blazed like heated emeralds, and she smiled.

Slowly she dragged his finger from her mouth, scraping her teeth lightly along his flesh, tasting salt and the dark essence of him. She planted a kiss on his palm and flicked the sensitive center with her tongue. He lifted a hand to her hair and dragged his fingers slowly through its length.

Flattening her hands on his chest, she leaned forward, misting his throat with her breath. His hand slid down her back to the curve of her bottom, not moving, just resting in tantalizing agony, setting off a flurry of nervous sparks inside her.

She caught his gaze and smiled at the intense desire smoking in the green depths. She unbuttoned his shirt, pressing a warm, moist kiss to his hair-dusted chest. Undoing all three buttons, she tugged the hem from his waistband and lifted it over his head.

The shirt fell somewhere behind him, and Elise turned her attention to the sculpted muscles of his chest, the buckled muscles of his abdomen, already taut in reaction to her. She ran her hands slowly down his chest and belly, then back up again.

He stood unmoving, his only reaction a sharp clenching of his jaw. He seemed to sense that she needed to control the moment and he allowed it. Allowed her to slip the buttons on his trousers and tease his belly with her fingertips. Allowed her to move behind him and flick her tongue on the smooth skin between his shoulder blades, run her hands over the brawny power of his arms.

She pressed against him, savoring the weight of her thinly clad breasts against his back. A muscle corded in his neck. Moonlight shadowed one side of his body, but her touch told her it matched to perfection the unyielding strength of his arm, the supple flex of muscle in his shoulder, the thick power in his lean legs.

She kissed his back again, nipping and laving, tasting his flesh, stoking the gathering restlessness inside her. Swept with a sudden wanton urge to taste every part of him, she moved in front of him again.

He grabbed her to him for a kiss, a teasing duel of

tongues before he let her go. Impatience vibrated in his body, but he let her continue.

She ran her fingers inside the waistband of his trousers and watched in fascination as the muscles of his belly contracted beneath her fingers. He hauled in a breath. Liquid fire feathered between her legs, urging her on, but she denied the clamorings of her body.

His arousal, bold and impatient, nudged her hip and she wanted to see him, to touch him. Suddenly nervous, she couldn't meet his gaze as she pushed the trousers from his hips.

Her attention was centered on his thick arousal, pulsing and pale and strong in the shadowed light. She touched him gently, stroking the length of him with trembling fingers.

His hand clamped on her wrist. "Do you plan to torture me for long?"

"*Is* it torture?" She stayed her hand, afraid suddenly that she might have hurt him, that his pleasure might have shifted to pain.

A breath shuddered out of him and a crooked smile flashed. "It's a torture I will gladly endure, but I can't keep my legs under me."

She smiled shyly and guided him to the wide leather chair at his desk. Knowing she could affect him so powerfully played havoc with her willpower. On the one hand, she wanted to go slowly, learn every inch of him, make tonight last forever. On the other, she wanted to merge their bodies, satisfy her own body's craving for him.

Uncertain about what to do, she pushed him down in the chair and knelt between his legs. Her hair streamed over his thighs and he wrapped one long strand around his finger. The sound of their ragged breathing peppered the air.

She ran her hands up from his strong calves over the curve of his knee and up his thighs, enjoying the feel of crisp hair against her smooth palm. When she leaned forward to kiss his belly, her breasts brushed his arousal. She could feel the tap of his pulse against her pulse, and heated wetness bloomed between her legs.

She kissed his belly, the curve where his hip joined his thigh, working her way toward that so different part of him. Desire spiraled higher, burning to white-hot fury. She wanted it to last, wanted to feel this uninhibited indulgence forever.

Her hands slid down his hot, hair-roughened thighs, stroking and caressing. He quivered beneath her, his breath coming in strained gasps. His muscles drew taut as a bowstring beneath her questing hands, and he shifted restlessly in the chair, gripping the arms until his knuckles blanched white.

She caressed his throbbing length and his hands buried themselves in her hair, holding her steady, anchoring him. His hot velvet length, like satin and steel, throbbed in her hand, mirroring the frantic beating of her heart and somehow symbolizing the joy, the freedom, she might be forced to give up come tomorrow.

She stroked him, tested the weight of the downy sacs at the base of his arousal. Like the lash of a velvet whip, restlessness urged her on.

"Elise," he groaned. "Lord—"

She barely heard him, so swept away was she by the power that strained at the edges of his control, the abandon she sensed in him. A drop of heated silk spilled out of him, and she stared in wonder that she had caused him to come so close to losing control.

Completely enthralled, webbed in the seductive warmth of their bodies, she touched her tongue to him. He bucked violently, his hands clamping tighter on the chair arms.

She looked up to find his head thrown back, neck corded, his eyes narrowed to slits. She tasted him, taking in salt and the deep darkness of male.

He pulsed warm and smooth beneath her lips. She could feel his strength, his power, flow into her. Frenzy rushed through her blood. She wanted him, all of him. Her hands tightened on his thighs. She pulled her lips from him, pressing hot openmouthed kisses on his thighs, his belly.

He cursed hoarsely, viciously, and pulled her up by the arm, his entire body quivering. "Have . . . mercy," he panted. "It will . . . be over . . . too soon."

She rose, untying her wrapper and slipping it to the floor. When she reached for the hem of her nightdress, his hand clamped over hers, pulling her atop him. She settled on his lap and in one smooth motion, he slid the nightdress up her thighs, his arousal teasing the warm, wet core of her.

She gasped, her thighs opening for him as she sought to merge her most sensitive flesh with his. He held her steady, hovering above the promise of paradise, his eyes narrowed with hunger and fierce love.

His hands slid under her nightdress and callused palms cupped her breasts. She moaned, swept up by a frenzy that begged release. His thumbs stroked her nipples into aching peaks. Impatience and desire spilled through her. She leaned into him, kissing him hotly and recklessly, demanding.

She moaned into his mouth and his hands tightened on her breasts. She was on fire, felt as if she would splinter apart and fly to the stars. She wanted to feel him inside her *now*. Stroking the deepest core of her, joined with her in a way that would bind them forever.

His hands moved to her waist as he kissed her, gently then fiercely by turns. Sensation skimmed along her nerves, obliterating reason, thought, time. Jared became her soul, her spirit.

His hands flexed on her waist and he lifted her, settling her over the hot pulsing part of him that strained toward her. Sleek and huge, he slid inside easily, guided by slick heat. She gasped, her eyes flying open, her gaze locking with his as she sank down, fully accepting him.

Sensation spurred through her, snatching her breath, and for a moment the only steady thing in her world was his green gaze locked on hers.

"Jared," she breathed.

"I know," he rasped, his features sharp with restraint and desire.

She wanted to move, *quickly*, *now*, but his hands locked her in place. Her body stretched to accommodate his fullness, the searing heat, the pricking tingles of her skin.

He kissed her once, gently. Restraint vibrated in the corded muscles of his neck, his arms, the tightly tender hold on her waist, the quiver of his taut abdomen beneath her.

She flattened her hands grasping his shoulders, struggling to hold on to some measure of reason. He reached between them and touched the little nub at her entrance, causing a moan to rip out of her.

Restless energy shot through her and she shifted. His eyes darkened with savage desire, a possession she'd never seen, and he began to move, slowly, torturously slow, drawing out each long stroke of his body inside hers until she thought she would scream.

She caught his rhythm, completely unsure if she could discipline herself to follow this slow pace, but the confidence in his eyes urged her on.

"Take me, Elise," he rasped. "All of me."

She gripped his biceps, following the long glide of his near withdrawal with the sinuous deliberate push of her body down his. A breath shuddered out of him. His nostrils flared; his eyes narrowed with pained rapture.

She knew the fine balance between torture and pleasure, felt it cut through her as he stroked out again, then back inside, filling her more completely every time.

Her gaze locked on his, she lost herself in the rhythm. Sweat slicked her hands, his chest. A moan slipped out of her as her body unraveled one slow skein at a time, only to be fused again with the stroke of his body back into hers.

She felt the surrender of his heart, saw the complete vulnerability in his eyes, and knew if this was the only future they would have, she could survive. The brittle core of heat building inside her knotted higher, blazing, burning her from the inside out.

She kept her gaze locked on his as her inner muscles clenched around him. She cried out, her body taking over, moving faster, searching for the ultimate fullness just out of reach. When the core of need shattered inside her, she cried out his name.

Light splintered through her, scattering sensation to her fingers, her toes, pooling in an ache in her heart. His hands braced her back as she arched toward him and cried out. He climaxed with her, rasping her name, and Elise collapsed against him.

For long moments she simply lay there. She had no sense of time, drifting on a cloud of sensation. As her body cooled, the sound of ragged breathing filled the room. Heat rose around them, permeated the sweet scent of sex. Darkness and heated male surrounded her.

She buried her face in his neck. "Oh . . . my."

He chuckled, still pulsing inside her, his breath rattling in his chest. She curled her hands weakly around his tempered biceps. He dropped his head against hers, one hand lazily stroking the length of her back.

"I love you, Elise."

Her heart clenched and tears stung her eyes. She lifted her face to his. "I love you too."

The words implied a future they might not have, but Elise didn't care. She would carry no regrets from this night.

His arms tightened around her, and for a moment

they sat in silence, wrapped in an invisible bond that would never be broken. Regardless of what the future held.

Too soon, reality intruded with a cruel slap. Jared gently lifted her from his body and rose to get her wrapper. He turned toward the washbasin and brought a wet cloth to her. He knelt and tenderly cleaned her and when he had finished, she returned the favor, her heart breaking.

Gripping the damp cloth, she rose in front of him. "You're leaving."

"Only to meet Cam and the general." He reached for her hand. "Then we'll figure out what to do."

A chill scuttled through her and she squeezed his hand, releasing him and turning away before he could see the sudden tears in her eyes.

Behind her she could hear the rustle of clothes as he pulled on his drawers, then his trousers. The faint scent of man and leather misted her skin. Uncertainty coursed through her, but there was a new sense of peace. She knew what she had to do. Turning to him, she touched his arm. "I trust you more than anyone I know."

He frowned. His shirt dangled from his hand and his trousers were still unfastened. "Elise?"

"I trust you with my life." She moved in front of him, soaking in his heat, exhilarated and frightened by what she was about to do. "I know if I'm with you, things will be handled as fairly as possible."

"With me?" he echoed, alarm flashing through his eyes. "What are you saying?"

"I'm turning myself in. To you. When the time comes, I want you to take me in."

"No!" Near panic darkened his eyes, and his shirt fell unheeded to the floor as he gripped her shoulders. "I can't do that! It's bad enough that Cam and General Schofield are coming, that I was the one who brought them. I can't turn you over to them!"

"And I can't bear to go with anyone but you." Her voice was soft as she fought the sobs crowding in her chest. "I know you won't let anything happen to me."

He shook his head, completely stunned. "I have no influence with this general, Elise."

"If you're with me, I can handle whatever he decrees."

Agony sharpened his eyes and he groaned, "Elise . . ."

"Please, Jared." She gripped his arms, willing him to understand that this was the only way she could survive what was to come. "I can't do it without you."

"This is no kind of choice!" he exploded, pulling her close and pressing her head to his chest. "Damn this job."

"Will you do it? Please? For me?"

"You can still leave!"

She shook her head. "No more running. Please?"

His arms tightened around her, and for a long moment there was only the thunder of his heart against her ear, the warmth of his body seeping into hers. Then his shoulders sagged. "Yes."

She pulled back, looking at him with tears blurring her vision. "Thank you."

He shook his head, frustration edging his words. "I hate this."

"I know." She touched his face, gathering strength from the knowledge that they would be together. "We still have a little time to find DeWitt and the money."

He stroked her cheek with one knuckle. "Yes."

She slipped out of his arms and picked up her nightdress, exchanging it for her chemise, which she pulled on over her head. "What if he's already found it? And left?"

"Then I'll find *him*." Jared's voice was hard, his eyes narrowed to slits in the pale light.

Elise shivered at the unforgiving glitter in his eyes, the rigid angle of his body.

He shrugged into his shirt and buttoned it. "We'd better hope he hasn't found it yet."

Pulling her dress over her head, she lifted her hair out of the way. "It makes no sense to me."

"What's that?" Jared sat down in the chair where they'd just made love and pulled on one boot.

Buttoning her bodice, she glanced at him. "I can't understand why a man so devoted to his wife would do the things he did. Murder my parents and try to rape me."

Jared leaned forward, resting his elbows on his knees and steepling his hands beneath his chin. Concentration furrowed his brow. "I don't know how devoted he really was."

"What do you mean?"

"Dru said she treated Onash's wife for cuts and bruises. Several times."

"You mean . . . he beat her?" she asked in a horrified whisper, her hand going to her throat.

"That's what Dru thinks and she probably knows."

Nausea roiled through her stomach. "How could he do that?"

Jared shook his head. "I've never understood men like that."

"It's as if he were two people." She reached behind her for her stockings, straightening suddenly. "If Claude beat his wife, then why would he go to her grave every Sunday?"

"Why indeed?" Suspicion narrowed Jared's eyes and he pushed himself out of the chair.

"What are you thinking?"

"It's just a hunch. I don't even see how it could be possible."

"What?" An idea took shape in her mind and refused to disappear. "Would he go to her grave every week out of guilt?"

"Maybe, but that doesn't fit with the image I have of the man," Jared said dryly.

"There has to be some reason, like atonement, or maybe he was just putting on an act," she suggested, the idea nagging stubbornly. But it was too fantastic to consider.

"That's more like it. Unless . . ."

"Unless what?" Elise could no longer ignore the thought that kept badgering her.

"Unless there's something there he wants." He reached for his gun. "Or needs."

"Like the *money*." There, she'd said it aloud. But how could it be?

"I don't know if it's even possible, but maybe—"

"*Maybe* that money is somehow hidden at her grave?" Elise finished for him.

"It's crazy," they both said in unison.

She surged up from the floor. "How could he get to it without everyone seeing him?"

"I'm going to have a look. DeWitt might have already thought of this too."

"I'm coming with you."

"Elise, no. DeWitt is still out there and—"

"I'm not staying here," she said firmly. "You said we could look for the money together."

"Darlin'—"

"My name is at stake here. Why should I stand by and do nothing? You're fighting with everything you have. I'm asking for the same chance."

A pained expression crossed his face. "Logan will have my hide."

"He's in no shape to do anything," Elise said smartly, allowing herself to feel the hope that her brother *would* be fine. "By then, we could have the money *and* DeWitt."

"Elise," Jared warned, though she wasn't sure if it was directed at himself or her.

She snatched up her dress and pulled it over her head. "You'll need someone to cover your back. I'm good with a gun and I'm your only option."

"Gramps can go . . ."

"Then I'd be here alone," she pointed out, bending over to fish her shoes out from under the bed.

Jared clenched his teeth. "If I say no, you'll just follow me, won't you?"

She sat down on the floor again and yanked on her shoes.

"Hell."

"Does that mean yes?" she said sweetly, adjusting her skirts and holding a hand out to him. "Now help me up."

Less than twenty minutes later, they rode for town. Jared made sure Elise was flanked on either side by a Kensington. She and Gramps rode in the wagon, pulled by Brownie.

Jared rode beside them on Trick, filling in his grandfather on their hunch about the money's whereabouts. Gramps thought their idea made sense, but he didn't have any further suggestions as to how Onash might have hidden the money at his wife's grave.

Hope edged around the uncertainty and doubt that hovered in the air.

As they reached the edge of town, Elise said, "I want to stop first and check on Logan."

"He needs to know what's going on anyway," Jared agreed quietly.

A light burned in the back of Dr. Hawthorne's clinic, and for a moment Jared experienced a pang of panic. Was Logan all right? Had there been further complications?

Through the window they could see Dru at her bookcase, hair unbound, but still dressed, and she soon answered the door. All three of them filed inside.

"He's doing well," Dru whispered with a glance back toward the curtain. "No fever, no sign of infection, and he's even eaten a little this evening."

As Elise hurried to her brother's side, Dru frowned questioningly at Jared. "Is everything all right?"

In the midst of explaining what had happened earlier, Elise's voice cut him short.

"Logan, you can't!"

Jared, Gramps, and Dru walked around the edge of the curtain to find Logan with his shirt open and unbuttoned, struggling into his pants.

"Logan," Elise said. "I didn't come here for this. I only wanted you to know what was going on."

"I can help. I don't plan to sit idly by while you and Jared go after DeWitt."

"And what kind of help do you think you'll be?" Dru demanded, hands on her hips. "You can't even walk."

"Just watch me." He eased out of bed, pulling his trousers up and belting them with one hand. Pain distorted his handsome features.

Trying to gauge his friend's condition, Jared shook his head. "You should probably listen to Dru. I don't want your death on my conscience."

"I'm not a corpse yet and I don't intend to lie around like one, with Elise's future at stake. There's got to be something I can do."

"Yes, you can climb right back into that bed," Dru ordered.

"I can wait for Cam." Logan's gaze met Jared's, imploring.

Jared understood the helpless frustration in his friend's eyes. Neither could he sit idly by if their roles were reversed.

Gramps cleared his throat. "I could go with Logan, if it would ease your mind, Dru."

"I don't know—"

"It's settled," Logan said, easing awkwardly onto the edge of the bed and grabbing a boot. "Gramps and I will wait for Cam and the general. Stall them if we need to."

Jared tried again to dissuade Elise, though he knew he was wasting his breath. "Elise, wait here with Dru. I'll come back straightaway—"

"No." Her voice wasn't strident, simply firm with conviction and plain refusal.

He sighed and shared a sympathetic look with Logan, who was struggling to pull on his other boot. "Elise and I will meet you after we've checked out Myra's grave."

"Very well then," Dru said in exasperation as she knelt in front of Logan. "Let me help you before you fall flat on your face and are no good to anyone."

"Careful, Doctor," Logan growled. "You keep talkin' that way and you'll turn my head with your charm."

Gramps chuckled and Elise smiled, pressing a kiss to her brother's head as she moved past him to leave.

He grabbed her hand. "Sis, be careful. I . . . I . . ."

"I know, Logan." She squeezed his hand. "I love you too."

He flushed, but nodded. She kissed Gramps on the cheek and hugged Dru, then followed Jared out the door.

She slipped her hand into his as they stepped into the dark street.

He glanced over, his heart tightening at her dainty profile, the curve of her lashes. His fingers curled around hers. "Ready?"

She looked up at him and nodded, love and courage shining in her eyes. Jared hoped like hell they would find something at Onash's grave.

CHAPTER TWENTY

Alarm kicked at Jared. He stood with Elise in front of Myra Onash's headstone, both of them staring at a small hole already dug out of the earth.

"DeWitt's been here." Nerves prickling with awareness, Jared turned in a slow circle and surveyed the thick clumps of trees that shaded deceased loved ones by day, provided deep cover by night. A low-lying fog seeped down from the mountains, wisping over the ground, veiling the night in ghostly light.

Footprints comparable to those of a man of DeWitt's size were visible in the night dew of the grass, leading away from the headstone and toward a cluster of azalea bushes. Jared drew his Colt and approached stealthily. Elise waited behind him, and he was relieved to hear the click of her gun, too. But his search yielded nothing.

He returned to the headstone and knelt, staring at the granite washed to silver by the moonlight, the slender twin arms that supported its base. Hoping they had interrupted DeWitt before he found the money, Jared sifted through the loose dirt in front of the stone.

"Onash wouldn't *bury* the money," Elise said quietly. "It would be too difficult to retrieve."

"I agree, but where else do we look?"

She stared for a long moment at the headstone, then walked around it. He followed her example, racking his brain for a hiding place.

He turned, scanning the trees behind them. "Maybe it's hidden in a tree or a bush, one nearby."

She nodded and together they searched for a knot-hole or a hollowed-out place in a trunk, but found nothing of that sort.

"It's got to be here somewhere," he said.

"But where?" Still strangely quiet, she walked over to the headstone and stared down at it. "Maybe it's not a hollow place in a tree, but—" She stopped, tilting her head as if she'd had an idea. Then she shook her head. "No, it couldn't be."

"In the headstone?" Jared hurried over to her, doubtful but willing to consider any possibility. "But how? Where?"

They peered down at the arms that extended on either side of the stone, then looked at each other.

"I don't know," Elise gritted out in frustration.

"Let's take a look."

Together they sank to their knees. Jared ran his hands along the front lip of the stone, feeling for an opening or a crack or a space that would indicate the stone might have slipped out of place.

Elise ran her fingers along the back side, then lifted astonished eyes to Jared. "Oh, my!" she breathed.

"What is it?"

She pushed against the corner of the arm, and the stone moved aside with a muffled grating sound to reveal a hollow space. They stared at each other in shock and disbelief.

"Go ahead," Jared urged, tension coiling tight around his middle. If the money was inside, Elise had every right to find it, after what she'd suffered at Onash's hands.

She reached inside and her mouth dropped open. Her gaze shot to his, fringed with wonder. "Jared!"

She withdrew her hand and he stared in disbelief at the bills she held, neatly banded together in slim stacks.

"Damnation!" he breathed, sitting down hard. "It was in plain sight the whole time!"

"No wonder he came here every week!" Elise sagged down beside him, staring in shock at the money in her hand.

"How much is there?"

"I don't know." She peered down at the money. "There are twenties and fifties and hundreds. I think there's even more inside."

Jared dipped his hand inside the open space of the headstone and pulled up another handful. "I've never seen so much money in my life!"

"Neither have I," Elise exclaimed excitedly.

The click of a gun cracked the silence behind them. "Enjoy it, because that money is the last thing either of you will ever see."

• • •

DeWitt! Fear jammed Elise's breath and she slanted a desperate look at Jared.

DeWitt stepped out of the shadows and leveled a revolver at the base of Jared's neck. He jiggled the weapon, punctuating his words. "Hand it over, my dear."

Elise shuddered at the familiar silky tone. "Don't hurt him."

DeWitt's teeth flashed ivory in the darkness, and she could imagine the hard glitter in his eyes. Jared stiffened, rising to his knees, and DeWitt drilled the gun into his head.

"Not another inch." DeWitt's voice cracked like flint on stone. "Drop your gun."

Jared hesitated, his gaze darting to Elise. She still had her gun in her pocket and the silent urging in his eyes told her to use it.

As Jared pulled his gun from his waistband, DeWitt snatched it from him and stuffed it inside his own. "Put your hands behind your head."

Jared did as ordered, and Elise took the opportunity to slide her right hand into her pocket. Her fingers tightened on the butt of her father's Colt.

DeWitt's gaze moved to Elise. "And Miss Worthen, drop your gun, too."

"But I don't—"

"I know you're never without it." His eyes glittered like ice in the pallid light. "Now do it or Mr. Kensington will have a nice hole in his head."

Jared's eyes urged her to defy DeWitt, but she couldn't risk Jared's life. She didn't care if DeWitt did take the money; if only he would leave them both alive.

"*Now*, Miss Worthen," DeWitt's voice lashed at her.

With a silent apology to Jared, she removed the gun and dropped it on the ground.

"Now," DeWitt said with satisfaction. "Bring me that money."

"Let her go." Jared's voice was clipped with anger. "She's involved in this, too. She can't afford for anyone to find out. Your secret will be safe with her."

Elise protested silently. She couldn't leave Jared, no matter what.

"How touching!" DeWitt's eyes gleamed at Elise. "Seems you have a champion."

"How's that gunshot wound?" Jared taunted DeWitt, though his gaze never left Elise.

She pressed her lips together to keep from crying out. DeWitt was going to kill both of them, and if he didn't, she was going to prison for killing Onash while DeWitt went free. She chafed against her forced helplessness, her mind racing for an escape.

"I won't tell you again, my dear. Get that money and bring it over. Now!" he ordered, drilling the gun into Jared's temple.

She scrambled to her feet and bent to gather the remainder of the money tucked inside the headstone. She glanced at Jared, hoping to read his eyes. They were filled with love and pain and regret.

There had to be a way they could escape DeWitt. After what they'd shared tonight, she refused to believe it could all be over so quickly.

Jared's eyes were urgent, expectant, and seemed to

be trying to convey something to her, but she couldn't tell what. She could read only the love in his eyes, the determination in his squared jaw, and the clenching of his hands.

"Hurry up!" DeWitt barked.

She moved in front of Jared, cupping the money in her outstretched hands. Tension stretched across her shoulders and her breath rasped in her ears. Greed lit DeWitt's eyes, but he didn't reach for the money.

As Elise passed in front of Jared, he dipped one shoulder and shoved into her thigh. She stumbled and fell, dropping the money. Recognizing Jared's attempt to buy them a chance, she rolled away, already searching for her gun or Jared's.

Before DeWitt could squeeze the trigger, Jared swung around and butted him in the stomach with his head. DeWitt's breath *ooomphed* out and the gun went off.

Elise screamed and scrambled back toward the headstone, her fingers dragging through damp cold grass, searching for her gun.

Jared punched DeWitt, the sound of fist on jaw cracking like a whip in the night.

With a powerful lash of his leg, DeWitt kicked Jared under the chin, causing Jared's head to snap back as he fell to the ground.

Where was it? Her hands slid through cool grass, moist earth. Jared must've kicked her gun when he and DeWitt started fighting.

"Stop, Miss Worthen!" DeWitt's voice cracked like brittle glass. "Don't move another inch."

She froze on her knees and looked up, horror

clutching at her insides. Slowly she straightened, sitting back on her heels.

Jared lay pinned to the ground, DeWitt's foot planted squarely on his chest. DeWitt's gun barrel drilled right between Jared's eyes.

"You're going to watch me blow out his brains, then I'll finish with you."

"No, please!" Her fingers inched through the grass. She thought she felt something hard by her heel and reached back a tentative hand to grope for it. The smooth barrel of her gun greeted her tentative touch, but there was no time for relief. Only action.

She had just seconds. DeWitt cocked his gun a second time.

"Take the money and go," she begged, gripping the barrel and sliding her hand to a more firm hold. "Just go. Please don't kill him."

"Shut up." DeWitt glanced around. A few lights flared on the edge of town and he licked his lips nervously.

"Pull the trigger, you bastard," Jared snarled. "The law will be all over you in minutes."

"Jared, no!" Elise pulled the gun firmly into her hand. Keeping it behind her back, she slowly rose to her feet. "Please, Mr. DeWitt. Tullar—"

"I would've liked to spare you, my dear, in return for your getting rid of Claude. And, of course, for finding my money. But you know too much."

"Don't kill him. Please don't. He's right. I can't afford to tell anyone what I know. I just want to be left alone, forget any of this ever happened."

"You'll change your mind as soon as I ride off." He

drilled the gun harder into Jared's forehead. "How does that feel, Kensington? How does it feel to know you're going to die in one minute? You'll never have a woman again. Never have a smoke or play cards. Never say good-bye to your mama. I want you to sweat. I want you to feel the fear."

"Go to hell," Jared said succinctly.

The next few seconds were a blur seared on Elise's memory.

DeWitt thumbed back the hammer. "Say good-bye, my dear."

"No!" Elise screamed, pulling the gun from behind her back. She aimed and fired, never giving herself a chance to hesitate.

Surprise etched DeWitt's features. He stared down at the dime-size spot of blood growing larger on the front of his pristine white shirt, right at his heart. His features went slack and he toppled to the ground.

Jared rolled to his knees, staring in wonder at Elise. She dropped the gun, smoke burning her nostrils, shock wending through her. "Oh, my. I've done it again."

"Elise? Are you all right?" Jared suddenly stood in front of her.

She looked up at him through blinding tears, his features blurry, and realization unfolded. "You're all right. You're all right."

"Thanks to you."

The noise of gathering voices drifted to them and he glanced over his shoulder. "Go, Elise! There's still time. Go, while you have the chance."

"Go?" She shook her head in confusion, vaguely

aware of the silhouettes moving toward them. Some-one from town was coming. "I can't leave you. Not now."

"If you don't go now, darlin', you won't get another chance."

"I can't—"

"You saved my life. Let me do something for you."

"You already have, Jared. You've given me hope."

"You've got to go now." He kissed her quickly, pushing her toward the trees. "You can hide some-where until it's safe to get out of town."

"What about your job?" She turned back to him. "What about Cam?"

"I'll handle it."

"But Jared—"

"I love you." He gave her a little shake. "I can't bear to turn you over to him."

"I'm not leaving."

"Elise—"

"Here comes Logan and Gramps. With Dru and—"

"Cam and General Schofield," Jared finished ur-gently. "Go, darlin'. Go!"

"It's too late."

The four men and Dru strode toward them, close enough now that she could see the concern on Logan and Gramps' face, their barely controlled anger.

Dread hammered at her and she edged closer to Jared. His arm tightened around her as the men stopped in front of them.

Greetings were short and brusque. General Scho-field was a thin man with sooty hair and bony features. A thick mustache slashed across his upper lip. Jared's friend Campbell McMillan was a handsome, broadly built man, shorter than Jared and Logan by nearly a head, but wiry and tough-looking. His speculative gaze moved from Jared to rest on Elise.

After Jared exchanged a brief salute with the general, he briefly explained about finding the money and being ambushed by DeWitt. "Elise Worthen saved my life, sir."

"Very brave of you, miss." The general inclined his head, impatience crackling in his dark eyes. "Lieutenant Kensington, perhaps you could meet with me and Captain McMillan? Brief us on what you've discovered. Your telegram stated you had no suspect. Perhaps together we can get to the bottom of this."

"Sir—"

Elise interrupted Jared. "I'm the one you're looking for, sir."

"Oh, Elise." Logan closed his eyes, looking pained.

Dru gasped.

Jared's grip tightened on her arm and the general's black gaze shifted to her, piercing.

"This young lady is suspected of murdering Agent Onash?" His soft voice didn't match the sharp, bony angles of his face or the stern, unforgiving hardness of his eyes.

Apprehension feathered up her spine, but Elise lifted her chin, focusing on the love surrounding her in Jared, Logan, and Gramps.

"Yes, sir." Jared stiffened beside her and he gestured toward DeWitt's lifeless body. "DeWitt tried to kill me, but Elise killed him instead. She could've left me here to die, but she didn't. I think you should take that into account."

Her head whipped toward him. She would never have left Jared with DeWitt. He squeezed her waist in warning and she kept silent.

The general's eyes narrowed speculatively on them, then moved to DeWitt's lifeless body. "Self-defense, Lieutenant?"

"Yes, sir."

General Schofield knelt, lifting DeWitt's eyelids, then pressing two fingers to the side of his neck. The general rose, rawboned fingers stroking his mustache. Onyx eyes drilled into Elise. "I guess we'll continue this tomorrow, Miss Worthen. In a formal hearing."

"General Schofield, sir?" Campbell McMillan stepped forward, his voice low and gravelly. "Why don't we just get on with it? This is why we came. All interested parties are present and accounted for. There's no reason for delay."

"A hearing in the middle of the night?" Schofield frowned.

Cam nodded. "There's nothing against it in the handbook, sir."

Logan slid at glance at Cam, his lips twitching.

General Schofield gave Elise another weighty stare. "Hmmm. Sounds fine to me. Lieutenant Kensington?"

Jared glanced at Elise and she nodded. The sooner it was over, the better.

"We agree, General."

Again the general eyed Jared and Elise speculatively, but when he spoke it was to Cam. "Well, Mc-Millan, where do you suggest we convene?"

"Perhaps the sheriff's office," Logan suggested dryly. "I'm sure he won't mind."

"That'd be fine." Toby Restin stepped forward, bobbing his bald head. "Just fine."

For the first time, Elise noticed Toby Restin. He'd been completely silent during the proceedings, standing well back in the shadows behind the general. As he moved into the light, she blinked. There was something different about him. . . . The sheriff had combed his hair, donned a clean shirt, and forgone his snuff.

"Very well. Let's proceed." The general turned sharply and made his way through the trees back toward town, fully expecting everyone to follow him.

Logan and Gramps and Dru smiled, whispering encouragement as they gathered around her.

Jared squeezed Elise and said in her ear, "Cam's fair. He'll do what he can."

She nodded, apprehension snaking through her. Was she about to lose her future with Jared, when they'd just found each other? It didn't bear thinking about.

Logan fell in behind them, with Dru walking slowly beside him, occasionally reaching up to steady him with an arm around his waist. Gramps and Sheriff Restin made up the rear of the small train, carrying DeWitt's lifeless body between them.

The walk to the sheriff's office seemed interminable to Elise. Dread scraped across her nerves, lashed her insides into a quivering knot. She silently prayed

for the courage to accept whatever the general de-
creed, and begged in her heart for mercy. If asked, she
would have to admit that she would kill Claude Onash
all over again for what he'd done.

Behind her, she heard Logan speak to Sheriff
Restin in a low aside.

"If I were you, Sheriff, I'd find a new job. In a new
town." Logan's voice hardened and Elise shivered at
the retribution she knew was in his eyes. "When word
gets out of your association with DeWitt, you won't be
welcome here."

The sheriff sputtered a reply and Elise turned her
attention to the building in front of them. The jail.
Where she could spend the rest of her days. Or be set
free.

Trying to keep the desperation out of his voice,
Jared outlined his tracking of Onash and the money,
relayed his information about DeWitt, and finished up
with the events in the cemetery.

General Schofield heard it all with an inscrutable
expression in his eyes. Jared wanted to beg for leniency on Elise's behalf, but wasn't altogether certain
his plea would be well received.

The general's black gaze shifted from Jared to
Elise, then back again. He gave a curt nod. "You're
dismissed, Lieutenant."

"But sir—"

"Lieutenant." The other man cut him off. "If your
services are further needed, Captain McMillan will
fetch you."

"But—"

"That will be all."

Jared struggled with his conscience. He hated leaving Elise alone, but by staying he risked incurring the general's anger. She nodded, summoning a brave smile. With one last encouraging look, he squeezed her hand and walked out, closing the door behind him.

"Well?" Logan and Gramps, waiting outside on the jail's porch with Dru, hurried toward him.

"Well, she's in there alone." Jared walked to the edge of the planked porch, staring out into the black velvet night. Silence weighted the air, heavy, dense, seething.

Frustration churned through him and he shoved a hand through his hair, glancing back at the door. "Damn. I *think* the general's fair, but who knows if he'll see things the way we do. I only hope Cam has some influence. He knew Onash was trash."

"He was a conniving son of a bitch and I hope he rots in hell for what he did to our girl," Gramps exploded.

Jared nodded in agreement and anxiety gnarled his insides. What was happening in there? Was Elise all right? Would the general grant her a pardon? Minutes scraped by, eroding his patience, his restraint, fueling the desperation inside him.

The quiet was deafening, flicking his nerves like a blade. He leaned against a post, feeling the starch seep right out of his legs.

Logan eased down on the porch, wincing as he adjusted his injured leg. Dru helped him, then moved to stand quietly beside Gramps.

Logan looked at Jared. "Is there something you need to tell me? About you and Elise?"

He glanced at his friend, relieved to see patient understanding rather than disapproval in Logan's eyes. "I love her."

"I figured," Logan said quietly.

Jared pushed away from the post. Why was it so quiet? He couldn't hear Elise or the general, nothing. He paced in front of Logan. "It started out as a promise to you, then turned to suspicion, then . . . I don't know how it happened." Desperation edged his words. "If she goes to prison, I don't know what I'll do."

"We'll find a way to get her out." It was a savage promise.

Jared nodded, fighting the impatience that steepled inside him. Clouds scudded across the moon, dousing the brilliant light and rendering the town a vague shadow.

Jared stared out into the bleak darkness, his heart clenching. Without Elise, his future would be this dark, this blank, this empty. He was tired of death and weakness and annihilation. With Elise, he had the chance to build something bright and new and strong.

She had brought warmth and meaning to his hollow soul, opened a place inside him he'd locked up long ago, and spawned a trust he'd thought never to give again.

Their future together could be ending even as Jared sat helplessly out here. Even now General Schofield could be sentencing her to prison. Anger crested inside him and he tried to fight it, telling himself that

Cam would use what influence he had on Elise's behalf. But Jared couldn't sit still any longer.

Pivoting, he burst into the sheriff's office, dimly
aware that Gramps and Dru had cried out in surprise
behind him.

The general's eyebrows shot up, Cam grinned, and
Elise whirled, startled.

"You can't take her, General." Jared walked straight
to Elise, noticing the fresh tears on her cheeks. Fear
clutched at him. Had her fate been determined, then?
"You can't take her. She killed those men in self-
defense. She was only doing what the rest of us did
during the war—protecting her home, her life. She
shouldn't be penalized for it."

"Jared . . ." Elise began.

He squeezed her hand, urging her silently to let
him finish. "She killed only when she had no choice,
no other means of escape. I can't lose her. I love her."

"Jared," Elise breathed, her hand tightening in his.

"Lieutenant Kensington," General Schofield said,
narrowing his eyes. "Perhaps you'd like to—"

"Will you marry us? Now?" Jared couldn't dodge
the desperation any longer.

Elise's eyes widened and she shook her head. "No,
Jared, it's not what you—"

"Say you'll marry me, Elise." He faced her, his
heart thundering in his ears, sweat slicking his palms.
"General Schofield can perform the ceremony."

"You'd marry me, thinking I had to go to prison?"

"I'd marry you no matter what."

Tears welled in her eyes. "You'd wait for me?"

"Forever." He pulled her close, his hands flexing

on her waist. "Say you will, Elise. Say you'll marry me."

She smiled. "I will . . ."

"Can't you do this, General? Before you pronounce sentence?" Jared held her close, his heart feeling as if it were being ripped from his body.

General Schofield scowled, but his eyes glinted mischievously. "Miss Worthen, would you prefer to tell your eager fiancé the news?"

Jared frowned, his gaze shifting from the general to Elise.

She smiled tremulously. "I'm free, Jared. I've been pardoned."

"You're free?" Shock rolled through him, taking a few seconds to penetrate the determination and desperation that had driven him to interrupt the general. "You're free!"

He whooped and scooped Elise up in his arms, twirling her around. Joy tightened in his chest until it threatened to burst. Tears burned his eyes as he captured her lips with his. "I love you, Elise."

"I love you."

Laughter erupted from Logan and Gramps and Dru, who stood in the door behind them. Schofield banged a fist on the desk and everyone quieted.

His solemn gaze met Elise's and his eyes suddenly softened. "Miss Worthen, for any distress caused you by the new government of these United States, I beg your forgiveness."

Elise's eyes widened.

"How about marrying us, General?" Jared grinned

at Elise, lowering his voice for her ears only. "What about it, Elise? Will you marry me now?"

"What!" Gramps and Logan spoke in unison.

"A wedding at midnight," Dru said dreamily.

The general laughed and a broad grin split Cam's ruddy features.

Logan limped forward. "Kensington, you'd better do this right. My sister deserves—"

"Hush, Logan," Elise said quietly, her gaze fastened on Jared's. She flattened her palms against his chest, love shining in her blue eyes. "Yes, I'll marry you now."

Triumph and awe curled through him and his hand tightened on her waist. "Right here?"

"Yes. Anywhere."

Behind them, Cam spoke with awed wonder. "Well, I'll be damned."

The general rose and extended his hand to Jared. "That's one duty I'd be happy to perform."

With Gramps, Logan and Dru as witnesses, Jared and Elise were married in the sheriff's office.

After a hearty round of congratulations, he pulled her close for a soft kiss, then lifted her in his arms.

"Jared!" she protested, though she wrapped her arms around his neck.

He shouldered his way between Logan and Gramps. "Not to be rude, but you can all talk to us tomorrow." He gazed down at Elise, hardly able to believe she was his wife, *his* forever. "Or maybe the day after."

Elise laughed softly, pressing a kiss to his lips. "You should put me down."

"I don't ever want to let go of you again." He kissed her deeply, not caring that they stood in the jail, surrounded by people.

She drew away, flushed and breathing raggedly, her eyes smoky with desire. Answering need flared inside him and Jared moved to the door.

Gramps stayed Jared with a hand on his arm and embraced them both. "Go with my blessings. Now you're my real granddaughter."

"My blessings, too," Logan said gruffly, kissing his sister's cheek, then shaking Jared's hand.

Dru dabbed at her eyes with a dainty handkerchief. "I know you'll be very happy."

"We should have a toast over at Slim's," Logan suggested.

"Mr. Worthen, you're in no shape to be toasting," the doctor said indignantly. "Or walking, for that matter."

"Woman, it's not every day my sister marries my best friend."

"You've had quite enough excitement for the day," Dru insisted.

"That's the problem with women doctors. Think they know everything. It's possible you don't—"

Jared had been blessed with wonderful family and friends, but right now he wanted to get away from everyone. Stepping outside the jail, he cradled Elise close. He wanted to tell her how she'd healed his heart, opened his eyes in ways he'd never imagined possible, but mostly how she had restored his faith in love.

She laughed softly, tracing his lips. "You're doing this backwards, you know."

"What's that?" He smiled down at her, his heart full.

"You're supposed to carry me across the threshold *into* a place, not out of one."

"Not supposed to get married in a jail either." He grinned, moving to the side of the building and sliding her to the ground. Shielded by shadow, Jared leaned against the wall and pulled her into him, nuzzling her lips. "Where should I take you? Your house or mine?"

"Ours."

"And where would that be?"

"Right here." She placed her hand over his heart and stared up at him.

His hand covered her smaller one and his gaze burned into hers. "Tonight, you saved my life and made it yours."

"You would've given your life for me, too. You put your job on the line. Your honor." The clouds parted and moonlight spilled over them with soft brilliance, revealing the total vulnerability shining in her eyes. "I love you, Jared."

"I love you." He pressed a tender kiss to her lips. She was his, forever. "All along I've been torn between duty and my feelings for you, until I realized my heart knew the only truth. My heart will always belong to you."

"Then I'm home." she said, fitting her mouth to his.

"For always," he murmured.